DISORDER

DISORDER

book one

KATIE LOWRIE

AUTHOR'S NOTE

This is the part where cool authors add a playlist to let you know what they listened to when writing, or you know, what songs fit the mood of the book you're about to read.

I listened to the Hamilton Soundtrack on repeat or had episodes of Liv & Maddie running in the background.

So... Sorry for that.

I am not worthy

P.S. A quick heads up; the vocabulary, grammar, and spelling of *Disorder* is written in British English.

To Papa,
Thank you for pushing me to pursue my dream.
Thank you for always having my best interests.
Thank you for being you.

DISORDER

NOUN
a lack of order; disarray; confusion
a deviation from the normal system or order

VERB
to upset the order of; disarrange; muddle
to disturb the health or mind of

Prologue

I knew that things had taken a turn for the worse when I
looked into His eyes and could see the true depth of His
hate.

His eyes, normally a startling bright blue, were now a dark
indigo filled with anger and loathing. I could see the exact
moment that the mist descended.

I shivered.

I wasn't sure what else to do, and I didn't know where I
could run to; a place where He wouldn't find me.

Trapped.

The worst part was the fact that I'd been blind to my situation and had walked willingly to my fate. I was the reason I
was here; there was nobody else to blame. For this I hated
myself, maybe even more than I hated Him in that moment.

I couldn't help but ask, 'W-why are you doing this?'

I had to know. I was certain something must have
happened in the last few hours to have caused this change. No

part of me could accept that this had been coming for longer ... the alternative was just too much to think about.

'You don't belong here, Sky.' He smirked at me. 'You never did.'

I crumbled. I could feel the tears pricking my eyes, and I was trying my hardest to stop them from falling. The second I let a tear fall, I knew that this would all become real. That He really was looking at me like I was worthless. A look I hadn't seen on His face in the last six months.

I should have known better. I should never have fallen for the Beast, and I most definitely should never have thought of myself as the Beauty.

Chapter One

Even the birds outside knew that today was different to any other. They'd been outside my bedroom window incessantly chirping for the last three hours and, fuck me, I wanted to hurt them.

Today was my first day at Hawthorn Academy, and if being completely honest with myself, I was absolutely bricking it.

Being a loner, I'd always been, well, alone. I found friends overrated. Already, in my sixteen short years of living, I'd found out that in this life all I could rely upon was myself. God, even my family were a total waste of space—not that they were even going to notice me gone. Hell, they would probably just assume I was at a friend's house for the next six plus months.

'Skylar! Skylar! Get down here at once!' Mum shouted up from the kitchen and I knew that if I didn't make an appearance downstairs within the next few minutes, she'd send up

Andy to get me—which was something I definitely did not want to happen. Andy was my mum's new, totally useless husband. He had no job, no money, and absolutely no manners. Since I first met him he'd given me an icky feeling and I didn't think that would ever stop. He'd never outright been inappropriate with me, but some of his lewd comments, and the way he looked at me, made me super uncomfortable sometimes.

'I'll be down in a minute Mum, just let me finish getting dressed,' I hollered back, hoping she'd hear me and give me a moment. I wouldn't put it past Andy to disrespect my privacy and just barge into my bedroom without invitation if given the chance. Okay, maybe a bit melodramatic. He hadn't done it before, after all, but sometimes I could sense his presence outside my closed door while I changed; a shadow lingering underneath the door frame.

I rushed around my room and threw on a vest top and joggers at lightning speed and hot-footed it down the stairs as fast as I could. As I turned the corner into the kitchen, I nearly walked straight into Andy's chest. He looked down on me, smiling, and winked. Goosebumps covered my entire body in seconds, and yet, I couldn't look away from his searing gaze.

'You should watch where you're going Sky, never know who could be around the next corner,' Andy said as he winked again. He turned around and walked further into the kitchen to sit by my mum, almost making me believe that I'd imagined the entire last minute.

'Oh, there you are, Skylar. Did you buy me what I asked for?' Mum asked the moment I entered the room. Her tone of voice made it obvious to me how frustrating she found me.

Cora, my mum, looked old and haggard. Her blonde hair

resembled straw, coarse and dry, and it looked to me like she'd taken her make-up tips from a local clown. Honestly, she'd been looking that way for years, and I tried to find it in myself to have love for her, but I struggled. It always made me feel super shitty though, as everybody should love their Mum, right?

'Course I did. I put it in the hallway last night when I got home,' I said, gesturing towards the hall to where the carrier bags still were.

I worked in the local supermarket during the summer holidays, so often Mum would send me a long list of items she needed me to get for her so I could use my staff discount to make it cheaper. Not that it mattered, seeing as she had never once paid me for anything I had brought for her, or Andy.

'Cheers, love. Remind me again why you can't do more this week?' she asked, her over-plucked eyebrow raising slowly.

'I've told you so many times, Mum. I'm starting at Hawthorn Academy today. You know, the big elite boarding school on the hill. We definitely spoke about it ...' I tapered off mid-sentence when I noticed that neither Mum nor Andy were even paying me any attention anymore. They were staring at her phone, probably at some crappy selling page post that was selling a used sofa for pennies, so cheap because really it belonged in the nearest skip.

'Yeah, yeah, Sky. Course, I remember,' she said, but her face said otherwise when she looked up from her phone. Honestly, the woman was constantly attached to that thing. Around a year ago she was adamant that she'd never trade in her trusty Nokia as she "couldn't handle technology like that". Then Andy came along and voilá—the woman had a brand new shiny toy that she loved more than she loved me.

'What did I even just say, Mum?' I sighed, knowing that I'd lost them both. Not that I really had them to begin with, but ya know, sometimes in my head I was important to her. I am her only child, after all.

'School on the hill, Sky. Honestly, I'm just trying to watch this video that Leslie sent me and all you keep doing is ruining it.'

So, yeah, there she is, ladies and gentlemen. The woman who birthed me.

Leslie's her best friend and just as boring and desperate as she is. The two of them were in constant contact, pretty sure they even told each other when they were going to the toilet—they were just that close.

'Alright well, guess I'll be going upstairs to check my packing.' I looked around the kitchen of the house I'd lived in for the entire sixteen years I'd been alive, and I knew that I wouldn't miss it. Just another place that I hated.

My mum wasn't abusive; she'd never laid a finger on me. But she didn't care about me. Not one bit. I'd always been at the bottom of her list of things to give a shit about—even our menagerie of pets had always come before me, including the time we had two ferrets named Bert and Ernie. I'd become used to it now.

As I got up from the table Andy regarded me, a thoughtful expression on his face, and I could tell that whatever he was thinking about hurt. I wish I knew the thoughts running through his mind—and why he seemed to be aiming them at me.

The fact the man was thinking that hard was a major red flag. My mind screamed *"DANGER!"* and I couldn't place why. Yeah, he'd always been a creep, but I'd never felt scared of him like I did in that moment.

The moment passed, and I was left wondering whether I'd imagined it entirely.

✦

BY LUNCHTIME I'D CHECKED, AND TRIPLE CHECKED, MY packing and the list of items the Academy required me to bring. Actually, I'd been checking every day for the last two weeks.

When I'd received the letter of acceptance, I had been a little startled at first. It had arrived at the beginning of the summer break, with no postmark. It was a strange letter, to put it mildly, and even though it had been a month since I'd received it, I still re-read it every now and again to make sure I wasn't reading it wrong.

Dear Miss Skylar Crescent,

It is my pleasure to inform you; you are the recipient of Hawthorn Academy's newly established annual scholarship fund. There were many worthy candidates, but after looking through your application thoroughly, we believe you are a perfect fit for our fine establishment.

Enclosed is a list of items you will need to bring, and a list of those the Academy will provide.

We look forward to seeing you on the first day of

term, September 4th, and hope you are pleased about
this news.

Yours sincerely,

— *Ms Hawthorn, Headmistress*

The list of the items I had to provide contained the obvious items you'd expect to find on a boarding school list, such as toiletries. Then there were some more unusual ones. For example, I had to bring new lingerie with tags still on in one of the school colours. Seeing as the main school colour was a dark bottle green, this had been pretty hard to do. Especially as the money I made working wasn't enough to buy expensive shit. It was barely enough to buy non-expensive shit. Before this, my underwear collection came from the local supermarket. I wasn't sure I wanted to know why my lingerie was of importance to the Academy. I had tried to do some research into the scholarship, and the school itself, but my online searches hadn't yielded many results. It was like the school was one big secret. All I could find was your generic bullshit about the school, its benefactors and famous alumni.

The whole scenario was strange as fuck because I didn't recall even applying for a scholarship at Hawthorn Academy. When I'd emailed Ms Hawthorn to ensure that I was the correct recipient, I received a very curt email response that made it clear how irritating and stupid she found my enquiry to be. According to her, the name and address being correct on the invitation was confirmation enough it had gone to the correct person. Which made sense to a degree; the scholarship was "newly established", after all. Guess that explained why I couldn't find much information online about it. Plus, I was so desperate to leave this place that I didn't question it more; even if I should've.

The list of what the school was providing contained items I'd expected to see and ones I would never have believed. They were providing the school uniform itself, which was fair, uniforms could be pricey; same for the textbooks I would need. The school was also providing me with a laptop for studying and a mobile phone—not sure why, but I wouldn't complain.

There were some pretty unusual items on the list; the school would provide health check ups and any protection deemed necessary. What the fuck did that even mean? I wasn't sure what I was getting myself into, but surely it had to be better than the life I was already living?

Reading the list once more in my room, I paused when a large thud sounded outside in the hallway. I tried to ignore it and continued to read, but dread slowly rose in my stomach. I turned around to look just as my bedroom door pushed open, revealing Andy standing at the threshold, smirking at me.

'Off to your fancy school today, ain't ya?' he asked, his words slurred. The smell of stale beer instantly surrounded me.

'Yeah ...' I started to say, but tailed off as he took a step closer to me, entering my personal bubble. I took a step back, feeling the backs of my legs hitting the side of my bed, while trying to smile as if nothing was wrong.

'Guess I won't be eyeing up your body for much longer. Pity. You really are quite stunning when you try, Skylar,' he said, as I tried to hold back a gag. Knowing Andy, he probably thought of his words as a compliment of sorts.

He took another step towards me, a larger one this time;

close enough for me to see the broken capillaries on his nose. He stumbled and fell. Or at least at first I thought that was what had happened, but when he grabbed me and pulled me tight against him, I knew he had stumbled on purpose.

I could feel his body pressed against mine, the hardness in his joggers making vomit rise in my mouth, and I knew that this was what he had intended to do when he entered my room. A last-ditch attempt to grab me before I left. His closeness suffocated me, my heart started to beat faster.

'M-my mum will wonder where you are,' I said, my stutter showing how surprised I really felt. I didn't even attempt to pull the *"I'll tell Mum"* card as I knew she wouldn't listen anyway—or care.

'Oh, but Sky, that's where you're wrong. I told your mum I was coming up here to talk to ya. You're going to meet a load of fancy wankers at this fancy school, so I told her I'd warn you about them. She doesn't suspect a thing,' he said, once again slurring most of his words, making his cockney accent even thicker than usual.

I shivered, knowing he was telling the truth, I could see it in his small, evil, brown eyes. He'd obviously seen his opportunity and pounced on it, knowing that I would leave later today and wouldn't tell anyone.

He was so close the smell of stale alcohol on his breath invaded my senses. Revolting, rotting, and putrid—just like him. In that moment his face loomed closer to mine, his eyes making his intentions clear. I tried to turn my face, to look away or shout out, but his hands clamped to my cheeks, keeping my face in place. He kissed me, shoving his tongue deep in my mouth and moving it around violently with no mercy. His tongue felt slimy against mine, and I could taste the beer he'd been consuming all morning. Without thinking, I raised my knee into his crotch, causing him to stumble backward, losing his balance.

Andy seemed to come to his senses, grimacing through the pain I'd caused him. He shook his head at me in disappointment.

'You'll pay for that Skylar, just you wait,' he spat out ominously and stormed out of my room.

All I could do was stand still in shock, thinking of all the ways I could rake my tongue to get him off of me.

✦

THE LONG, SLEEK, *EXPENSIVE* BLACK CAR ARRIVED AT noon.

The driver, a tall dark-haired man with dark sunglasses on, even though it wasn't sunny, handed me a Non-Disclosure Agreement the moment I'd opened the front door. No greeting, just a piece of paper thrust into my hands. Confused, I wanted to know more, but when I asked him to elaborate, he clammed up. All he *would* say was that he couldn't say more until I had signed the document. *Insert eye roll here.*

I read the agreement as thoroughly as I could in the short time I had and was pretty sure I hadn't just signed over my firstborn. Well, fifty percent sure at least.

'The car is ready for you, Miss. I'm able to answer questions you may have on the journey, but I must insist that we leave right this instant,' he said in a low, tense voice, with a tone that brooked no argument. I beamed at him, hoping he'd soften, but I barely got a lip twitch back. *Tough crowd.*

'Do I have time to say goodbye to my family?' I asked him,

knowing that I *should* go say goodbye to Mum and Andy; not that it mattered to them.

'Be quick please, Miss. We're on a tight schedule and must be at the Academy for the welcome briefing from Ms Hawthorn at two.'

I dashed to the kitchen and found my mum and Andy once again looking at something on her phone. Andy acted like what happened upstairs hadn't taken place; and trust me, I wouldn't be the one to remind him.

'The cars here,' I said, but before the sentence had fully left my mouth, I knew that they weren't listening to me. 'I won't be home until after the New Year.'

'That's lovely, sweetheart. Have fun,' Mum said, looking at me. Her hand moved quickly, in something that sort of resembled a wave, then looked back down again. You wouldn't have known that her only child was leaving, would you?

Oh fuck it, why bother?

I stormed back to the front door where I noticed my luggage gone—the driver must have already put it in the car. I filled my lungs with air, taking in a deep breath, and made my way towards the fancy car idling on the street. Towards my new life.

Once inside, I hoped that the driver would start talking to me, but that didn't happen. He handed me an information pack and mumbled something about how I should take a quick glance at it on the drive to the school. At first, it looked like a map of the school and my class schedule; you know, normal introductory school things. But as I kept flicking through, the last few pages made me pause. It was a social calendar of sorts, with galas and parties listed.

How wonderful.

I'd never been one to socialise often; attending galas sounded intimidating to me. For years I'd suffered from terrible anxiety, and recently it had only got worse. I struggled to make phone calls to takeaways.

The car finally moved away from the only home I'd ever known. The thought of attending these events and galas playing heavily on my mind. I had to remind myself to breathe —in through the nose, out through the mouth. Or wait, was it the other way around? Oh well, not like I'd attend a party today.

Anxiety would be the death of me, I swear.

Chapter Two

The Hawthorn Academy loomed at the top of the hill. The car ascended at a snail's speed; so slow that I started to hyperventilate—well, maybe that was a bit dramatic. My breathing got faster at least. The more I worried, the more my anxiety grew as we got closer to the top.

As the car slowly travelled up, I spotted block shaped buildings on the right-hand side of the road and when I looked out of the other window, large sports fields were directly in front of me, and in the background, a line of trees as far as the eye could see. They moved with the wind, swaying to and fro in a unified frenzy. Red berries covered them, creating an eerie view. Pretty, too, but mostly eerie.

My mind ran on a loop of constant questions the entire trip up the hill. Questions that I couldn't exactly ask the driver. Things like: What if I made no friends? Or what if I couldn't keep up academically? Some of the kids I'd be sharing classes with were rich, and I had no doubt that they had the best private tutors. For all I knew, they could be fluent in frigging Latin!

Talking of Latin, the school had a motto; I knew this because they had printed it on all the letters they had sent me, and on the school website I'd found when searching for more information. The motto looms above the car on a sign upon entering the Academy grounds.

Large and sinister, welcoming me—or maybe warning me.

AUDENTES FORTUNA IUVAT. DULCE PERICULUM.

It literally translated to English as:

FORTUNE FAVOURS THE BOLD. DANGER IS SWEET.

So yep, there's that.

✦

AFTER THE CAR HAD—FINALLY—PULLED UP TO THE FRONT of the main building, I realised just how big this school really was. Even what I'd seen from the car didn't fully convey the sheer size of this place.

I had always known it was large, but it turned out that what you could see from the bottom of the hill was only the tip of the iceberg. The hill had hidden so much. It made me wonder just what else was being hidden in plain sight here.

On the front of the main building, a stone gargoyle sat above each corner of the large dark wooden double doors. The couple's beady eyes looking down on all who entered; their presence menacing and foreboding. A chill crept up my spine, the cold seeping into my bones.

Ha. Listen to me. I sounded like a badly written gothic

novel. Nothing worse than sounding like *Wuthering Heights*—
trust me; it happened to be my least favourite classic.

'We're here, Miss,' the driver said, stating the obvious. He
looked me in the eye and I got the feeling there was so much
that he wished he could say to me but wouldn't dare to.

'Thank you. Do I need to grab my bags or ...?' I trailed off,
uncertain of myself. It was one of the things I hated most about
myself. My inner voice could be strong and feisty; my actual
voice, not so much.

'I'll take them and somebody will deliver them to your
room after inspection,' he said and smiled, gesturing for me to
leave the car. I clutched the handle tight, my knuckles turning
white, and pressed down. The fresh, brisk September air
outside hit me and I nearly stumbled at the sheer force of it.
Being on top of the hill meant the wind would be stronger
here, something I needed to remember.

Moving towards the building in front of me, I spotted a
group of blonde girls nearby in my peripheral, clustered
together in a pack.

All talking at once, looking at me, pointing and laughing.
Self-doubt hit me, and I could feel shame rising in my cheeks,
colouring them. Their actions instantly pissed me off. All of
them were of a similar height and build—you know the type,
slim and petite.

The four of them were around my age, too.

How wonderful.

I reached the stone stairs that lead to the building; I mean,
of course there were stairs. Every Academy story I'd read had a
grand staircase leading into the school where, usually, the
female main character would glance up and see a group of
scary, hot guys giving her an ominous look from the top.

When I looked up though, all I could see was a stern-looking woman impatiently waiting for somebody. Pretty sure that *somebody* was me. So I made my way towards her, trying to keep calm and act as if I wasn't about to shit myself any moment.

'Hello, I'm Skylar Crescent,' I said as I held out my hand for the woman to shake. I knew instantly that she wouldn't take it though. Her look of impatience mingled with disgust, twisting her features, creating a fairy tale hag appearance of sorts.

'Yes, hello there, Miss Crescent. I'm Ms Hawthorn, the Headteacher here at Hawthorn Academy.'

Everything about this woman was grey. Her eyes, her hair —even the colour of her skin. It didn't seem as if she got out much.

'I'm here to welcome you to our fine institution. As I stated in my letter to you, you are the only recipient of the scholarship fund this year. There is one other recipient, in the year above, who will be along shortly to give you the tour,' she said, her tone one of irritation, making it obvious she thought little of me.

I smiled at her, hoping that she'd notice and not think I was some uncouth heathen. The look she gave me told me that my smile wasn't helping matters; if anything, it was probably making it worse.

'Here she comes now,' Ms Hawthorn said and looked over to my left. 'I'm sure you and Miss Luck will get along just fine.'

Then she turned around and just walked away without so much as a "Goodbye". Leaving me stood there, alone, as I awaited the arrival of somebody called Miss Luck. What were the odds that she lived up to her name and was a lucky person?

As the girl got closer, she wriggled her fingers, and I warmed towards her in an instant. The first thing I noticed about her was her long, dark auburn hair as it swished back and forth in the wind as she walked. At five foot five, I'd always been the same height as most other girls my age, but I could already tell that with her, I'd feel like a giant. An inviting enough smile with straight shiny teeth—too perfect, almost. Little laugh lines lived on either side of her mouth. She was curvy in all the right places and it suited her; I bet she got a lot of attention from the boys here.

'Hey! You must be Skylar, right?' she asked. The girl looked closely at my face, taking it all in. I nodded in response, too nervous to talk just yet. She smiled and said, 'I'm Clover. Yes, I am aware of just how wank my name is. My parents apparently decided from birth that I deserved to be ridiculed.' She rolled her eyes, and I wasn't sure how to respond. Do I laugh and agree? Do I nod my head, hoping that was the correct response? After I finished thinking of these questions, it hit me that Clover had continued talking and I had *not* been taking any of it in.

'... what do you think?' she asked and looked at me expectantly, yet I had no clue how that question started. I stared blankly back. I must have looked like such a brain-dead zombie to her at that moment. *Great first impression, Sky.*

'I am so s-sorry. I sort of spaced out back there. W-what do I think about what?' I asked, nerves jumbling around in my stomach. I thought I might vomit on the spot. My stutter had started already and I could feel the blush rising into my cheeks. I knew how much I judged people on first impressions, and I felt like I'd messed this one up for myself completely.

'No problem,' Clover laughed—with me or at me, who fucking knew. 'I was asking if you wanted to see your room first or the rest of the school?'

'I'd love the tour, thank you,' I said, quietly. We both made eye contact and smiled at one another. Now, I didn't want to be one of those girls who automatically believed they'd found a new best friend due to a shared look and circumstance, but I thought that maybe I could become friends with this girl— sometime in the future at least.

✦

'That's the pool building, but I'd avoid going there unless totally necessary,' Clover told me, pointing at a large red building on our left.

So far, I'd seen the buildings that held the classrooms and had been inside the large main building where the cafeteria (if you could call it that) and admin offices were. I hadn't antici- pated that the school would be this big, and, even armed with my map, I knew that I was going to get terribly lost. I'd always had such an awful sense of direction.

'Why should I avoid the pool?' I asked her, not sure if I actually wanted to hear the answer or not.

'Oh, well, that's where ...' Clover stopped herself mid- sentence. She scoffed. 'Talk of the devils.'

I turned my head, and I spotted three guys exiting the pool building together. Each of them had wet hair, and I reckoned I may have started drooling. The three of them were beyond gorgeous; tall, tanned and as rugged as a teenage boy could be.

'W-w-who are they?' I asked, my stutter rearing its ugly head.

'The one with blonde hair and blue eyes is Leo Hawthorn, the oldest of the three and trust me, he likes to wield the fact that he's a Hawthorn like a weapon. He's in my year,' she sighed, rolling her eyes, and I thought that maybe there was more to it.

I nodded my head as she continued, 'The one with red hair and a cheeky grin is Griffin, but everybody calls him Griff. He's in your year. I'd be careful of that one if I were you.'

I nodded again. Obviously, now I'd be wondering why I should be careful of Griff, but then he caught my eye and focused his cheeky grin in my direction. I had to stop my mouth from opening of its own accord. He winked, and I averted my gaze fast.

'Last but not least is Oliver Brandon—only call him Ollie if he tells you to. He's in your year too and is one of the most sought-after bachelors at this school. Be careful. All of the girls here would fight for even a speck of his attention.' Clover's eyes locked with mine and somehow managed to convey every emotion at once. It felt overwhelming.

Oliver was by far the hottest guy of the three. I swore that my ovaries were screaming just looking at him. He had that whole chiselled jaw thing going on; you know, imagine the character of Charles Brandon in the early seasons of *The Tudors*. That was who Oliver reminded me of, but he also had something that was uniquely his own. He noticed Griff looking over in our direction and turned his head to see what the fuss was about.

Our gaze collided. I gasped at the sheer intensity of it. Like Leo, he had blue eyes, but his hair was the colour of hazelnut.

That light brown that looked good enough to eat. My heart pumped so fast; it felt as if it was trying to leave the confines of my body.

Jesus Sky, get a grip.

'Is that a bad thing then?' I asked. Clover looked at me perplexed and I added, 'The fact that the other girls want him?' I felt so naïve. At my previous school, I minded my business and didn't have any friends, really. I had never needed to know the inner workings of a group of girls before, or how they operated.

'Oh, honey. It's a very, very bad thing.' Clover looked at me with sympathetic eyes. I noticed that they were the same shade of green as our uniform, but I didn't want to compliment her on how unique they were in case she thought I was making a dig. She'd been nice to me for the few hours I'd known her, and I *definitely* did not want to screw up what could become my first ever friendship.

At that moment, I could have sworn that the air around us began to change, and no, it wasn't because the wind had picked up. Well, the wind *had* picked up, but that wasn't why.

No.

The boys were heading towards us.

Shit.

Clover stood next to me, staring at them, then rolled her eyes, her irritation at their existence clear.

I froze. I didn't know what to do. Should I introduce myself? Should I stay silent? Would I end up stammering and making an absolute fool of myself? There were too many variables running through my head and I could feel a panic attack building. Wires were short circuiting up there, frazzling. My anxiety always got worse around new people and new situations, and often I couldn't handle it. My vision faded; black slowly creeping in around the edges. My breathing was so fast, yet I wasn't taking any air into my lungs. The tightness hurt.

Suddenly, the three of them stood in front of me. Tall, imposing and dramatic.

Griff glanced at me, his gaze amused, yet assessing. Leo looked bored by the whole situation. But it was Oliver who I focused on. Well, as much as I could focus on anything whilst simultaneously hoping that I didn't pass out. He looked at me with pity shining in his blue eyes, his lips curved up at the edges in a sympathetic smile.

'Everything okay here?' Oliver asked, looking at Clover, but we all knew he was talking about me.

'Sure is. This is the new girl, Skylar. Sky, I told you who these three are. If you know what's good for you, you'll take whatever they say with a pinch of salt.'

'No need to be like that, Clo. We're all friends here. I'm sure Sky can make up her own mind, can't you?' Griff asked, looking at me. He smiled again, and I realised that the grin must be his trademark look. He definitely had to know how endearing it was.

'H-hi. Yeah, I g-guess,' I said. *Oh, great—I stuttered.* My breathing still sounded like I'd been in a boxing ring for all twelve rounds, too. Now I was definitely making a fool of myself.

'Oh cute, did you hear that, Ollie? She stutters,' Leo said, looking around himself as if he would rather be anywhere else. His tone filled with derision; I knew he was over this entire situation and wanted it to be finished as soon as possible. He kept looking away, ensuring that he wouldn't make eye contact with either me or Clover.

'So she does. Sky, was it? Nice to meet you. Welcome to Hawthorn Academy. Clover here will make the school rules clear for you, I'm sure. Wouldn't want you to forget any now, would we?' Oliver smirked, his tone teasing. After he'd finished his sentence, the three of them walked away. No more words said.

I looked at Clover, and her face had gone as red as her hair, showing her anger.

'Those boys will be the death of me, I swear it. Every time I'm near them, I just get so blood-boiling mad! Don't listen to them, seriously. The three of them think they rule this school because their families are rich.'

I laughed. Clover was quite funny, seemed genuine, and I hoped that I hadn't blown it by having my moment when the boys had come over. Making a friend here was vital. I'd never been around this many rich kids before, and I hadn't grown up with money. I assumed that if Clover was here on scholarship too, then she would understand how I was feeling—overwhelmed. It had only been half a day, and already I needed to process a lot.

'What did they mean by rules?' I asked. Although Oliver had sounded like he was teasing, maybe he had been serious after all.

'Oh, didn't you read through your welcome pack? Duh,' she hit her head playfully, 'of course you didn't! Let's go to our room now and we can talk more there. I can show you the Hive too. To be honest, it's probably best we talk about all this in private anyway.' Clover's words, and tone, were light as a feather, but I could feel the heaviness of her statement living beneath the surface.

'Our room?' I asked. It was the part of her sentence that I'd homed in on, happy to hear that I wouldn't be living alone in this strange place.

'Yeah. As the only two scholarship students here, we have to share a room as our funds only cover the basic necessities, or some kind of crapola like that.'

'My letter said that the scholarship fund was new?' I asked. 'I guess it makes sense that we're sharing a room.'

'Mhm. I'm sure you'll be thankful for that in due course.'

Clover's cryptic answer did nothing for my anxiety, but I attempted a smile—pretty sure it came out as more of a grimace.

Chapter Three

Our room was larger than my one at home, that was for sure. Most likely one of the largest rooms I'd ever been in, to tell the truth. Two double beds were placed on each side, plus a little kitchenette and an en-suite bathroom were attached too. The light cream colour of the walls went perfectly with the black furnishings dotted around the room. I loved it. It resembled how I'd always wanted my bedroom at home to look. Happiness filled me that this was where I would be living for the next two years. Strangely, I hadn't really put much thought into where I would be living while attending the Academy. Whenever I'd thought of the Academy, it had taken on a mythical quality in my mind; dreamlike and hazy, almost.

Clover flopped down on (I assumed) her bed and sighed extra loud. I wanted to ask why she'd sighed so deep but I felt self-conscious. I didn't know the rules here, and I felt completely out of my comfort zone. Who knew whether I should ask how she was?

Luckily for me, Clover broke the silence first.

'You can call me Clo, by the way. I know it sounded super shitty and sarcastic coming from Griff, but that's the nickname I answer to. It's the only nickname I can get away with, really. Nobody wants Ver to be their nickname, I can tell you that. The bitches always shortened it to Over, which was highly original as you can imagine.'

I smiled at her. Her tone of voice and her open face really were comforting. A feeling started spreading through me and I felt welcome here; even if for the time being, I only felt it in our room away from everybody else.

'Back at your old school?' I asked.

'Er, right ...' Clover's eyes shifted around the room, no longer looking at me or trying to catch my eye. 'I need to fill you in on some things, Sky, here at Hawthorn I mean. The girls that go here can be actual twats nearly all the time. Leo and I were friendly when we were younger, and the girls here didn't like that one bit.' Clover looked out of the window, her tone softening when she spoke again. 'They call themselves *The Set*.'

She rolled her eyes so hard, I thought they were going to leave her face.

'*The Set*? Original.' I laughed, trying to ease the tension that had seeped into the room. I could taste it. This urgency that hadn't been there before. I knew Clover wanted to tell me more.

'Yeah. There's four of them and they are the biggest bitches I've ever met. I don't use that term lightly. Their names all begin with the same letter like some knock off *Heather's* shit.'

'So, who are they?'

'Well, two of them are in my year and then there are two in your year. Each year there's two new members from the lower school because of the oldest two graduating.'

'Right ...' I said, slightly confused. The scholarship was open to sixteen-year-olds for the final two years of schooling, but the Academy itself teaches pupils from the age of eleven. Pupils who had parents willing to spend thousands a year in order for them to attend.

'So, you have Olivia and Odette; they're in my year. Then there's Ophelia and Oralie, the new ones this year. Most of the time, they use their words to keep people in check. They have escalated to actual *pranks* in the past, though, and believe me when I say that there's nothing harmless about *those*.' Clover's eyes met mine from across the room. 'Read the rules, Sky. I know it sounded like Oliver was making fun when he mentioned the rules, but they really do exist.'

'Where is this rulebook?' I asked. I couldn't recall seeing it. 'Is it in the Welcome Pack?'

'Of sorts,' Clover replied, getting up a screen on her phone. 'This is Hive. An app that the school designed to keep students aware of news, etcetera. Now, it's controlled by *The Set* and the boys—'

I stopped her mid-sentence and asked, 'Do the boys have a group name?'

I'd been impulsive, and I could feel my face going red. It was a valid question in this alternative world I'd found myself in; in the bully academy books I read they always had a group name, but, fuck me, I felt stupid asking it.

'Oh yeah ...' Clover laughed, 'But let me make one thing clear. The boys will never refer to themselves that way, so probably best not to say it to their faces. It's more something the O's and the rest of the students say, okay?'

'O-okay,' I said. In my head, I fully expected her to tell me they were the *Kings*, or *Princes*. You know, the names that seemed to pop up the most in books, or so it seemed.

'They call them *The Sect*.' I could see that Clover was trying her hardest to keep her face semi-straight. 'Apparently those names have been in place ever since the school opened in 1850. This school has always had some kind of self-opposed royalty. So fucking sad.'

After this, Clover couldn't keep her laughter in any longer. Tears started streaking down her face, a level of hysteria plain to see. So obviously, I did what everybody else did when watching a laughter meltdown unfold. I started laughing too.

The hardest I'd laughed in a long time—maybe the hardest ever. That kind of infectious laughter that made no sense to anybody else, that when you tried to stop, you'd catch one another's eye and start up again.

It was in that moment, lungs burning in protest, that I felt a genuine connection to Clover. We were both here on somebody else's money trying to get by, and if the names I'd learned of other pupils were anything to go by, we were probably the only two with hippie names. Translation: names picked out by people who never believed their children would amount anything of themselves. We would see about that.

※

THE REST OF THE EVENING PASSED, AND AS IT PROGRESSED, I found myself falling for Clover. Not romantically, but in the way girls do when they want to be friends with somebody and want them to love them and befriend them in return. A major girl crush.

I had learned more about both *The Set* and *The Sect* too, which I saw as a major plus. Although they'd been around since the school's establishment, their role had changed over the years. Since the 1950s, they were a way to keep the younger students and any scholarship recipients in line—not that there have been many. We were the first in at least twenty years. It created order and stopped anybody from rising too high above their station in life. I had rolled my eyes at all of this, but I could also believe it. Rich people definitely had different priorities. I had often wondered how I would afford to keep food in the house or rent paid, and then there were these fuckers worried about some eleven to sixteen-year-old dating somebody in a different pay bracket. Madness.

'Want me to show you the rules on Hive?' Clover asked after talking me through the history of the groups. I had also attempted to read some of my Welcome Pack, but it was exactly as I had predicted. It barely had any actual information about the school. It was mostly verbatim of what I had found in my online searches; that the school produced well standing members of society who became CEOs and Prime Ministers.

I glanced at my class schedule, as most of the lessons were in subjects I had studied before. Then there were subjects I hadn't ever thought I'd be able to study, such as Philosophy and Ethics. Clover had explained that because I'd only joined in the twelfth year, luckily, the school didn't expect me to study Latin. I had laughed at that. *Of course, they all knew frigging Latin.* French was on my curriculum instead.

'Go for it,' I told her. 'Surely none of them are that hard to follow?'

'It's not that they're hard to follow per se. It's more of just what each rule means in actuality.'

I didn't like the sound of that. The school had provided me with a phone, a laptop and other necessary supplies like they had said they would. It was strange. I had never owned a phone or laptop this expensive. My mum may have had the newest iPhone, but I had been holding on to my trusty Blackberry for years, praying that it wouldn't die on me. It's not like I had needed a phone to talk with friends, anyway.

Clover and I had got up the Hive on my laptop and were looking at the page that contained the rules. It read:

Rules of Hawthorn Academy:
As decided by The Sect and The Set.
All students must adhere or face the dire consequences.

I looked at Clover and asked, 'What does it mean by "face the dire consequences"? Sounds like something that would happen in a bad made-for-TV movie.' I laughed.

She did not. If anything, her face got even more serious as she said, 'Seriously Sky, I don't want to be *that* person, but I mean this. You do not want to find out. Do not give them any reason to look at you. They all saw you today and the O's definitely know that the boys spoke to you. Do us both a favour and just stay away.'

'I promise Clo, I'll try.' Her seriousness had put a chill inside of me. We had been joking all day about the other kids that go here and about rich people. At no point had she sounded so sombre. I couldn't tell if her tone was sombre because she had experience of what happened personally or if she had just seen some messed up shit in her first year here.

Rule One: DO NOT approach *The Sect* or *The Set* without being summoned first.

Rule Two: DO NOT look at the above-mentioned groups unless deemed necessary.

Rule Three: DO NOT bring shame upon your family or this fine institution.

Rule Four: NEVER date someone above your class without asking for permission.

Rule Five: NEVER turn down the invitation of somebody from *The Sect* or *The Set*.

WE WILL PUNISH ANYBODY FAILING TO ADHERE
TO THE ABOVE AS WE SEE FIT.

I GOT COLDER AFTER READING EACH RULE. TECHNICALLY, I had already broken one of them without even meaning to. I had looked at the girls who had been laughing at me, and I had *definitely* looked at the boys before they had come over to us. I wondered what they meant by "deemed necessary". How could you know whether to look at them? Should I just ignore them unless they talked to me and looked at me first?

I am so confused.

'Clo, what is the punishment like for breaking these rules?' I wondered whether it could be as serious as it seemed. Surely not? The students here were aged between eleven and eighteen. How could the punishment really be that severe? The faculty must know about this if these groups have existed for as long as the school itself.

'Well, it totally depends on what rule you break and who you've pissed off. The boys play dirtier than the girls, remember that. Girls will be blatant and in your face; boys, they'll ruin your life without you even knowing they lifted a finger.'

'How comforting,' I said in a dry tone. I could feel in my bones, though, that she wasn't making any of it up. Clover really believed what she was saying. I wasn't saying that it wasn't true but, *c'mon*, maybe it was a slight exaggeration.

'I'm not exaggerating, Sky,' Clo said, her eyes cutting into mine.

Well, there went that theory.

Clo didn't notice my distracted look and continued talking, 'I've heard stories that would make you run far from here. A couple of years ago, somebody upset *The Sect*, and it was horrible. I'm not sure what they did, and I doubt they did anything to justify what happened to them, but they ended up in the hospital. They'd tried to take their own life. It was dark.'

I gulped.

The air became thick, and suddenly, I found it hard to breathe. I felt like I had earlier, when the boys had been approaching me. My vision started to fade, black around the edges once again. The last thing I remembered was staring hard at Clover and trying to communicate just how trapped I was feeling in my own body.

Chapter Four

I opened my eyes, expecting to see Clover's scared ones looking back at me.

That was not what I saw.

At all.

Bright blue piercing eyes were looking down at me. You know when you could tell something just by looking into somebody's eyes?

Well, I could tell that these eyes held secrets; lots of them.

'Hey there, are you okay?' The owner of the eyes asked. I blinked, trying to adjust to my new surroundings. The azure eyes belonged to Oliver, and I was staring into their light.

Wait, did this count as rule whatever?

I hoped it didn't. He had looked into my eyes first, not the other way around.

'I-I-I'm fine, I think.' *Man, I wished this stutter would just piss off.* 'Where am I?' I asked. I couldn't see around him to figure out where I was. I was hoping I was still in my bedroom, but surely that didn't explain his presence?

'You're in the school's Hospital Wing,' he answered, and all that was occupying my mind was that I really was in an Academy novel now. An entire wing dedicated to ill students didn't bode well, right?

'How? What happened?' I asked, having no recollection of the events, like, at all.

'You passed out. I was about to knock when Clover burst through the door saying something about how you were acting strange and blacked out,' he said, gazing at me, intently. 'So, I carried you here, to the Hospital Wing.'

I nodded. In theory, his story made sense. Clover had been looking at me strangely before I blacked out. I had no idea why he would be outside my room, though. Surely he hadn't been coming to seek *me* out ... but then again, I didn't know where his room was located, so I guess he'd passed by and went to knock.

'T-thanks. I appreciate it, you really didn't have to. Sometimes I get anxiety attacks and feel faint,' I told him, hoping that he'd leave now that I'd woke up. Then it hit me. 'Where's Clover? Did she not come with us?'

'Clover's outside the room. I said I'd let her in once you were awake,' he said, his eyes shining with humour. *What a beautiful boy*, I thought. I shook my head and laughed out loud.

'A beautiful boy?' he asked, chuckling.

Realising my error, I stopped laughing abruptly. Oliver's lips twitched, but he stopped himself from laughing anymore than he already had. My gut felt wrong, sick, and full of nerves. I could not believe I said that, that I had put those words out into the universe. I wondered what he thought of me now.

'I'm beautiful? Really? You don't think that I'm sexy?' Oliver said with an amused look on his face, but I could see a hint of something else lingering in his gaze. A kind of heat that made me feel a certain way. I imagined how dominant he'd be in private, and I could feel my cheeks going red. Being as pale as I am, my cheeks always showed my emotions, which had caused some awkward situations in the past.

'I—' I started talking, attempting to prevent him from looking so intently at my cheeks. He cut me off.

'I'm joking, Sky. I'm glad that you've noticed me,' he said, seeming genuinely perplexed, shaking his head, as if he couldn't quite believe that somebody like me would think so highly of his looks. Which, let's be honest, was the biggest load of bullshit acting that I'd seen in a while; maybe ever. I didn't say that to him, though.

'Everybody notices you, I'm sure. Ever considered that they're too scared to look at you. You know, because of all of those rules on Hive?' The moment the words left me, I wished I'd kept my mouth closed. Of all the things I could have said, I had to say something about the rules. About the fact that he and his friends thought that they were untouchable. Eurgh. What was wrong with me?

'Maybe you should remember that fear is good. Being scared can ensure you live. That you don't make life-threatening mistakes. Ever considered that, Little One?'

The second those words left his lips, Oliver left the room, taking the heat with him. His words—fuck, the entire conversation—had made me feel frozen inside. Was that a warning or a threat?

✦

Not long after Oliver walked out, Clover entered, obviously curious what had passed between the two of us, but I was staying tight lipped. I hadn't even had time to process what had happened myself. Not that much *had* happened.

I knew that Clover meant well. Ultimately, though, I had to remember that I had only met her today; I didn't know her, not really. Although I had felt a kinship with her and felt as if a strong friendship would form between us, I didn't want to give her all my trust and then have it thrown back in my face in the future. I had no idea who I could truly trust in this place, and I would not make that big of a decision on my first day.

The nurse was sour faced and miserable looking. You know when people's lips looked as if they'd been sucking on a sour gobstopper for hours? All pursed and puckered. Her eyes and hair were both grey and lifeless. Dull. I asked her if I could leave and go back to my room. I really didn't need to be there any longer, my vision had returned to normal and I no longer felt faint.

'You'll leave when I have permission from Master Hawthorn,' she replied. My mind instantly went to Leo, and I wondered why he had anything to do with me getting out of here. Clover just shrugged though, so I didn't think too much of it.

The main reason I wanted to leave was to get settled in my bed and prepare for the next morning. A huge assembly for the entire school would take place first thing, and attendance was mandatory. I was already nervous enough about starting the school year as it was, but now I knew there would be rumours flying around about the "New Girl" and the real reason she had ended up in the Hospital Wing with Oliver by her side, of all people.

After another hour or so, the sour nurse finally relented. She must have heard from Leo. Or realised that it was absolutely bloody ridiculous to keep me there on the whims of a seventeen-year-old boy. Either way, ten pm had long passed by this point and my eyes could barely stay open. The entire day had felt like a clusterfuck of emotions. So much had happened in such a short period, yet I'd only been on school grounds for eight hours.

Clover had stayed with me the whole time and had been keeping the conversation flowing. She kept it light and surface level, which I was extremely thankful for, even if I didn't respond.

✦

WE QUICKLY MADE OUR WAY BACK TO OUR ROOM AND AS we did, Clover tried to help me figure out just where on the property we were—the second floor walkway that led to the Admin building, apparently. I nodded along, but my mind was elsewhere.

'Be quiet a second,' Clover spat out, stopping on the spot, and I halted too. 'Can you hear that?' she whispered. My ears strained to hear the sound she could hear, but if I was being honest, I couldn't hear a thing.

'What is it?'

'I'm not sure. But it sounded like noises coming from down the hall,' Clover said, pointing further down the corridor.

My eyes followed her finger, and I saw *them*.

There were two figures up ahead, standing close to one

another, so close that they were almost one. I couldn't make out anything but body shapes.

I put my finger on my lips, the universal signal for "Shhh."

I gestured to Clo to follow me as I slowly started tiptoeing my way towards the couple, doing my best secret agent impression.

Like the saying goes, curiosity killed the cat; well, usually I acted like the cat. It was as if a compulsion took over me and I had to know what was happening. I knew I should have just continued on my way and gone to bed. *Obviously, I should have done that.*

Creeping closer, still on silent toes, I realised who we were seeing up ahead.

Leo Hawthorn standing beside one of the O girls I'd seen earlier in the day. The two of them definitely kissing—potentially more. Heavy breathing filled the air, and I knew they hadn't noticed us. I wasn't sure which one of *The Set* he was with as I only knew their names; I had seen them clustered together before Clover had told me of their existence, but I had absolutely no clue who was who.

A gasp came from behind me, but when I turned my head to glance back at Clover, I saw her back running away. She had left me there without an explanation. What the fuck?

Close enough to them now that the girl heard Clover's gasp and the two of them had stopped making out to stare at me. The dim lighting of the hallway made it hard to see much, but it was light enough for me to make out their facial expressions—the girl was pissed.

Great.

'What are you doing here, New Girl? Can't you see that we're busy?' she spat. The girl had long, ice blonde hair.

Perfectly straight and down to her waist. It swished with every word she spoke.

'I-I-I ...' I couldn't speak. My tongue had become heavy and felt glued to my mouth. My vision blurred around the edges and I could feel moisture slowly covering my body. I hated myself at that moment. I hated how weak I felt.

'I-I-I ...' she mocked, looking me dead in the eyes. 'Leo can you hear this shit?' Laughing at me, she turned back to Leo.

'Leave her alone, Odette,' Leo snapped. He looked at me, his eyes taking in the full length of my body. He didn't look interested, he didn't look disgusted either, he was just... looking.

'You're seriously going to take her side?' Odette seethed. 'Honestly Leo, she's a poor, ugly, nobody. Probably riddled with disease, too.'

'Get off me,' he growled. Leo shoved her from him with such force that she nearly fell over; luckily, she caught herself in time. 'Go back to your room, Odette. I don't want to see you again tonight.'

Without even questioning his words, Odette huffed and stormed away. Not before delivering her parting shot to me, though. 'You better watch your back, New Girl. Oh, the things we could do to you,' she said, her words reminding me of a Seuss poem. Odette continued to laugh like a villain in a second-rate horror film as she disappeared around the corner and out of our view.

Leo faced me completely now. He didn't smile or show that he wanted to exchange pleasantries. He stood looking at me with a blank expression covering his face.

'Ignore her. She's a bitch,' he said, nodding down the corridor in the direction Odette left in. The thing was, I wasn't really taking his words in. All I could focus on, the fact running through my mind, was that I had broken their stupid rules and I would have to face the consequences.

'O-oh, it's okay. I know you'll penalise me,' I said. Yeah, nice going, Sky. Remind him of punishment. *I wondered what other stupid shit would leave my mouth before I could escape.*

'... If you are, come and tell me. Or Oliver,' he said, smirking. 'He'll want you to inform him of what the girls are doing to you.'

'I don't have permission to come talk to you without being summoned first,' I joked, tongue in cheek, recalling the rules in my mind. Pretty sure that was rule number one.

'I'm giving you permission now, aren't I?' He cocked his head, no longer looking disinterested. 'Don't disappoint me, New Girl.'

'Thanks, I guess ...' I mumbled, my sentence trailing off at the end, no idea what else to do, or say. I found Leo intimidating. At over six feet tall, he seemed giant compared to my five foot five—although he made me feel even shorter than that. *Or maybe he just made me feel small?*

'No problem. I'll see you around,' he said, all of his teeth showing. Sinister, almost. A threat.

Leo's strides were filled with purpose as he walked away. He didn't look back at me once.

After he left, I walked back to my room thinking back over what the fuck had just happened. I would definitely be giving Clover a piece of my mind—well, in my head anyway. I didn't want our friendship on the rocks before it ever had the chance to take off. I would however gently ask her to explain this shit to me.

I struggled back to my room; my weakness from earlier

causing half of the struggle, the other half because I had no idea where I was within the Academy.

If I had known that shit was going to go the way it did, I would have been seriously questioning why I had wanted to attend Hawthorn Academy.

Chapter Five

The whole school assembly was being held in the main building in the large auditorium. The enormity of the room took my breath away. The ceiling was so high it reminded me of a cathedral, or some place similar. One window contained stained glass, the beauty of it shining even from where I stood, but I couldn't tell from my position what the picture depicted.

Nobody seemed to pay attention to me or Clover on the surface, but the surrounding whispers sounded like angry bees, buzzing away; the stares as sharp as daggers when we weren't looking. After the run in with Leo and Odette last night, I didn't want to draw any more negative attention to myself, sure the girls were already plotting something for me. Something sinister.

'So.' Clover halted once we had reached the seating area and said, 'I have to go sit with my year.' She rolled her eyes in my direction, making it clear how unimpressed she was about that. In the time we'd been talking, she hadn't mentioned having any other friends here. Slightly odd, now that I thought about it.

'Where do I sit?' I asked her, looking around, not seeing a sign stating where each year sat.

'The school dedicated the last two rows of the stands to my year, and the two rows before that are for year twelve. Sit in any seat but try to get a seat on the aisle. Means you can make a quick getaway when it's over,' she said as she gave me a slight shove towards the steps and I made my way towards the rows she had pointed out. I took a seat near the end of the row, leaving the last seat of the row empty. Don't you hate it when people don't move all the way down the row and expect others to climb over them? Me too, so I tried never to do that.

I was looking around the room at the art on the walls, and the stained glass window, trying to pass the time. Clover was sitting a few rows behind me, next to Leo of all people; the two of them looked like they were in some kind of word battle. *Wonder how that happened.*

After a few minutes, I sensed a body dropping into the seat next to me.

'I hope you don't mind me sitting here.'

I groaned inwardly. I recognised that voice. Oliver's voice. Looking at him only confirmed it.

'Sure,' I said with a sigh, knowing that there was nothing I could say or do to change it. A very small part of me didn't want to. 'Of course I d-don't.'

One day soon I hoped that I could come across as a normal teenage girl and not some tongue-tied loser. Alas, today was not that day.

'Thanks. I feel like we haven't formally introduced

ourselves. I'm Oliver Brandon,' he said and held out his hand for me to shake. I sat frozen, uncertain. Had he forgotten yesterday? Or had it been a part of my imagination? Pretty certain we introduced ourselves yesterday and had multiple run-ins. Right?

'I'm Skylar Crescent,' I said as he moved his hand and placed it in mine. What happened next startled me. I shit you not. An electrical current travelled up my arm, starting in my fingertips. Shocked, I darted my hand away. Oliver looked smug, the speed of my action amusing him.

'I know who you are,' he said, the condescending tone not lost on me. After a beat he said, 'Leo told me about last night.'

'He d-did?' I asked, puzzled as to what he meant.

'Leo mentioned that he'd told you to come to me if *The Set* bothers you. He said you were worried about punishment for not following the rules, so I wanted to clear it up with you.' His eyes glinted with excitement when speaking of punishment, but the glint disappeared as fast as it had happened.

'T-t-thank you. I really appreciate it.' I'd been doing so well to control my stammer, but this guy was so hot. Up close, I would have sworn his blue eyes had flecks of silver running through them. His lips were full, and I really wanted to take a bite out of them. I could feel my face heating. My thoughts were clear on my face for all to see, my pale complexion giving it away. And my thoughts had gone to a really dirty place. Having his hand hold mine even for the briefest moment had me imagining where else he could use his hands. *Get a grip.*

'You're really cute when you stammer, you know. Makes me wonder how much I could make you stammer with my dick deep inside you.' The casual way in which he said this made me choke on air. It was so left field, but now those images filled my imagination to the point I couldn't see anything else.

'Errr,' I said, at a loss for words. I raised my eyebrows, not sure what the correct response to his suggestion would be.

With Oliver still looking at me suggestively, Ms Hawthorn walked to the centre of the stage and announced herself.

'Silence everybody,' she said, her tone assertive. Her gaze covered the entire room and with her words, every single student went quiet. A pin could have dropped and everybody would hear. 'Welcome to a new year here at Hawthorn Academy. We have a new scholarship student joining us this year by the name of Skylar Crescent. I hope that everybody will make her feel at home.'

I shrunk in my seat, hunching my shoulders to try to make myself as small as possible. I hadn't expected her to name drop me like that. The way she said it made it sound like a threat, paranoia playing with the deep recesses of my brain.

Also, did this mean I was the *only* new student this year beside the eleven-year-olds?

Oliver nudged me with his elbow and smiled widely. I thought his smirk was sexy as fuck, but wow, his smile was even better than his smirk.

'So, New Girl Skylar, how can I make you feel at home here?' he asked, having come closer to me, entering my space. His words whispered over my ear and made me tingle from head to toe. Goosebumps covered my arms, and I tried to focus on whatever Ms Hawthorn was saying.

Not that I *could* focus. Even just sitting next to Oliver made me nervous, and I counted down the minutes hoping this torture would be over soon.

'Enjoy the first week, students,' Ms Hawthorn said, ending her speech—a speech that I'd heard none of.

People moved in their seats and stood to leave. *Thank fuck.* But before I could leave in silence, Oliver put a hand on my arm to hold me in place.

'How about you join me tonight for dinner at my table?' he asked, and on noticing my reluctance he added, 'Bring Clover, too.'

'O-okay,' I said, a rabbit in the headlights. No other words would come to mind. And with that one word, I'd sealed my fate.

※

OLIVER DIDN'T SAY ONE MORE WORD TO ME AFTER I'D agreed to sit with him for dinner tonight. Fuck if I knew what to expect. Clover and I had eaten our breakfast in our room this morning as we'd overslept, and last night I'd missed dinner while sitting in the Hospital Wing with Oliver.

We'd missed our alarms this morning because we didn't get back to our room until late, you know, after that whole Leo and Odette shabang.

Clover met me after the assembly had ended and when I asked her what she and Leo had been discussing, her face turned sour and all she would tell me was that, "Leo's the biggest prick I know."

While walking down the corridor to our first class of the day, I remembered what I had agreed to. Here goes nothing.

'Clo ...' I mumbled, taking in a big breath to prepare for my next words. 'Oliver's asked if I'll sit at his table tonight for dinner. He said you can join us if you want to. I may have said okay ...' I trailed off when I saw her face. Clover looked at me like she personally wanted to deliver my death.

She stopped in the middle of the corridor, some poor kid bumping into her back and running off when she glared at him.

'I'm sorry, but what?! I thought I just heard you say that you'd agreed to sit with *The Sect* for dinner? But that can't be possible because there is no way you're that fucking stupid. Right?'

I squirmed. I knew she wouldn't take it well, but to drop the f bomb this early in the day meant that she was even madder than I had expected.

'I-I must be?' I asked, looking everywhere; anywhere that wasn't Clover.

'Skylar Crescent, didn't I say yesterday to stay away from those boys? Did you not listen to anything I said?' She was shaking her head and giving me a pitying look. I felt embarrassed. I *had* listened to everything she had told me, but when Oliver was asking me to join them, I just couldn't stop myself.

'I promise I did, Clo. It is one of the rules though, and ...' I was still looking around and trailed off when I saw Griffin approaching us, waving exaggeratedly at me. So exaggerated that he hit a girl in the face. Even that couldn't stop Griff's cheeky grin, planted firm on his face and I couldn't help but smile back at him. I reckoned he'd been following us since we left the auditorium.

'Yo girls, what's happening?' he asked loudly, and pulled me into an awkward hug that I hadn't seen coming as he trapped my hands between us. He buried his nose into the nape of my neck. 'Damn New Girl, you smell like girlfriend material.'

He let me out of the hug and all I could do was gape at him. I mean, seriously, did that line ever work on anybody?

'Just ignore him, Sky. The boy doesn't know when to stop.' Clover's bemused face made me smile. Griff seemed to have that effect on people. I always wondered if people that came across as easy going were actually hiding something darker underneath the surface.

'A-and what does girlfriend m-material smell like?' I asked, stuttering my way through the sentence. My smile stayed firmly in place, though. I felt so much more at ease with him than I did with Oliver or Leo.

'You,' he whispered, his hand caressing my face. He seemed super proud of his comeback.

'Oh, ha, ha Griff. You are such a wind up. Leave my girl Sky here alone. She's already sitting at your table for dinner, after all.' She rolled her eyes, making it clear once again that she thought I'd made a poor decision.

'New Girl, you are in for a treat! Please sit next to me, pretty please,' he said as his eyes met mine and his pleading tone made my insides warm. I had no romantic attraction to him, but he really was a force. He even batted his eyelids at me.

'F-fine,' I laughed, rolling my eyes at him and his over-the-top theatrics.

The three of us walked together to my first class of the day, History. The moment I entered the classroom, I spotted a few empty desks. I chose one in the back row and took my school laptop from my bag.

A velvety voice entered my ear, 'Fancy seeing you here.' Of course it belonged to Oliver.

'Yes, f-fancy seeing me in class at the school we both

attend,' I snapped. I hadn't intended to have my words come out so snarky, but the boy really put me on edge. Sometimes, when my anxiety couldn't handle a situation, it turned me into the biggest brat known to man. This was one of those times.

'Woah,' he said, raising his hands, palms facing forward, 'it's okay. I meant it in jest. You know, after we'd sat together for assembly, I didn't realise I'd be seeing you in my first class. I would have walked you here had I known.'

'Yes, w-well, Griff walked me here, so no sweat,' I said.

Oliver visibly bristled at that, and I felt a little smug about it.

'*Griff* walked you here?' he asked. The emphasis he put on Griff's name wasn't lost on me. I couldn't decide if the sheer fact that Griff had done something nice for me pissed him off most.

'Yep. He wants me to sit next to him tonight at dinner, too. Seemed super chuffed to know I was joining you,' I told him. Internally, I laughed. On the outside, I remained calm as a cucumber. I just couldn't help myself; riling up the devil must be my idea of fun.

'You'll do no such thing,' he growled.

I glanced around, taking it all in . The room itself looked a little different to the classrooms I was used to. Obviously, the technology here surpassed what I'd known. At each desk, a student sat with their school issued laptop. Plus, a smart board linked up to a computer took up the majority of the far wall. Honestly, at my old school the teachers were still using dry erase boards as the school had somehow spent all of their funding on the science labs.

'Hang on, Oliver. I'm s-sure I read in the rules somewhere

that us mere p-peasants cannot turn down the invitation of somebody from *The Sect*.'

Okay, so I knew I was holding out on a technicality. It was Oliver who had asked me to dinner in the first place, so I knew I should sit with him. But I hated the attitude and bullshit of it all. Yeah, I'd accepted his invite—I'd never specified who I would sit with, and he'd never asked.

The moment I'd referred to them as *The Sect*, though, Oliver's face had soured. His lips formed a point, and his eyes darkened.

'Call me Ollie.'

The teacher arrived, and he said no more. I remembered what Clover had said; nobody called him Ollie unless he'd told them they could. The teacher started the lesson, and I ignored *Ollie's* words. There was no way I would call him that; not yet, at least. We weren't friends for starters.

The lesson was about the art of warfare. Seemed fitting.

THE REST OF THE DAY FLEW BY AND I HAD MADE IT TO THE last period without making a total fool of myself. In each class, I took a seat in the back row, hoping that I would go unnoticed by everybody. *So far, so good.*

At least one member of *The Set* or *The Sect* from my year was in each lesson. Oliver had been in my History class and pretty sure we both had the same free periods, but I avoided him and went back to my room for them. Griff had been in my Philosophy and Ethics class. The two O girls, Oralie and Ophelia, had been in English and now I was at my last class of the day, French.

I walked into the room and my eyes went to Oliver's instantly. He was sitting in the back row with Oralie and Ophelia on either side of him, smirking at me. The only seat left in the back was next to Oralie, and although I didn't want to sit next to her, I knew that they had thrown down the gauntlet. I slumped into the chair and as I did; I heard a high-pitched voice.

'Oh, Ollie. Don't you think you should tell *that* girl not to sit there? She doesn't deserve to sit alongside us,' Ophelia whined, whilst trying to run her hand up and down his arm.

'Yeah, Ollie. She's a nobody. Did you hear that she interrupted Ode while she was with Leo last night? Bet she's one of those freaks who enjoys watching others get it on.' Oralie joined in. I couldn't help but look up to see his reaction. *Ollie's* eyes lit up at that thought. Was he a voyeur?

I tried my hardest to not roll my eyes. I really did. *But some reactions are involuntary.*

'Lay off her, girls. She's joining us for dinner tonight,' he said, his tone harsh.

My heart thudded. Stupid me hadn't fully realised that eating dinner with the boys would also result in us eating dinner with the girls too. No wonder Clover had been ready to kill me for accepting the invitation. After what had happened last night and this morning, Clo had definitely been keeping things from me. Things that I intended to learn—even if she didn't want me to.

I tuned my ears back into the conversation to hear, 'But whyyyyy?' coming out of Ophelia's mouth. Her whine was worse than the whine of a four-year-old who was meeting Santa at a local mall and wanted all the toys, but left with none of them.

I scoffed at her. Unfortunately for me, she heard it.

'What are you scoffing at, you swine?' she spat. Literally. Her spit landed right in front of Oliver, drawing my eyes' focus.

I laughed. *Swine?* Is this girl for real?

'I said, leave her alone, Ophelia!' Oliver raised his voice so loud that the entire classroom stopped what it was doing and turned to face us. Slumping down in my chair, I tried to make myself as small and invisible as I could. 'Move now, Oralie. I'm not playing around.'

'I'm sorry about her,' he said. I was still slowly sinking in my chair as Oliver sat down into the one Oralie had sharply vacated. 'About both of them, actually.'

I nodded. I would stutter if I replied to him. My brave behaviour towards him this morning was now a thing of the past.

The teacher entered the classroom and instantly shouted, 'Master Brandon, what are you doing in here?'

'Thought I'd learn some French, Sir.' Oliver said, the smirk clear on his face. Sure of himself and filled with an almost egotistical swagger.

'Get out, or I must tell Ms Hawthorn,' Mr Page said, his round face turning a shade of red that reminded me of a dark wine. I genuinely worried that he would have an attack of some sort, being both very short and very large. Nobody else seemed worried about his health, though.

'Oh, that isn't exactly a threat, Sir,' Oliver said, but stood and left the classroom anyway, winking in my direction before disappearing from view.

I rolled my eyes and chuckled lightly, even though he could no longer see me.

The rest of the lesson passed in a blur. All I could think about was the fact that Oliver wasn't matching up to any of my preconceived ideas about him. Clover had told me to stay away. The rules I'd read on the Hive also made me believe that I should steer clear. Only the girls had been acting exactly how I'd expected them to.

But Oliver wasn't acting the same as them. This was our fourth or fifth encounter now, and each one led me to further question my judgement. He'd been a dick yesterday when we had first met, then there was the whole Hospital Wing fiasco—I still didn't know why he'd been about to knock on my door. This morning he was a flirt in assembly, and every time I recalled that whole stutter/dick line I flushed. Now he was sticking up for me against these girls he'd known for years. None of it added up.

When the last bell of the day rang, I still hadn't figured any of it out. I spotted Clover waiting for me outside in the hall and I rushed out of the door as quick as I could, grabbing her arm when I passed her, and ran towards our room with her dragging along behind.

'Sky, what the hell happened to you?! Why are we moving so fast?'

'I'll explain when we get back to our room, just hurry!' I pulled her the entire way back to our room, then, once inside, I slammed the door behind us and locked it. I didn't want anyone "accidentally" entering.

Clover sat down on her bed, and I sat on mine facing her. Trying to catch my breath, I put my hand out to halt any words Clover might speak; our sprint through the school had once again reminded me I was super unfit. Raking my hands through my hair, I sighed.

'Clo. I think I'm in trouble,' I said, urgency in my tone.

'What do you mean, in trouble?' she asked, confused.

'Well, you know how you basically implied that I should avoid the pool building and the boys who occupy it?'

'Yes ...' Her eyebrows raised, climbing up her forehead.

'And you know how I agreed to sit with them for dinner tonight?'

'Yes ...' I could hear her getting impatient with me.

'Well, I think I'm developing a major crush on Ollie.' I blurted it out super fast, hoping that would make it easier. Like ripping off a band-aid or a waxing strip.

Clover gasped when I used his nickname.

'He's been so nice to me today, standing up for me against the O girls. Plus, he may have made a comment this morning about wanting to hear if I stutter with his dick deep inside me.' By the end of the sentence, I was whispering and my face must have been redder than a fire engine. I covered my face with my hands, trying to hide it from her.

Clover's expression turned to one of pity. She made the sign of the cross.

'Oh, honey, no.' Shaking her head, she said, 'You can't feel like that about him. Trust me when I say that he's not a good guy. I know he was there last night and was nice to you today but I promise you Sky, he has an agenda. It may not be obvious right now, but he definitely has one. Those boys do nothing without some kind of endgame. Even Griff can be a prick when he feels like it.'

'I know, I know. I don't *want* to feel this way!'

'Maybe we should just eat dinner here, get something delivered to the school gates? I'm just going to put this out into the universe so that when shit comes back to bite you, I can say I told you so, okay?'

I nodded.

Clo looked at me imploringly and said, 'Sky, you know deep down that he's playing you. Or that he has some kind of motive.'

'No. I don't know that for definite. We're going to go eat dinner with them, Clo. I'm not having people talk shit about me on my first full day. Plus, I'm pretty sure the rules say you can't turn down an invitation from them, right?'

'Right,' she said, reluctantly agreeing with me.

Chapter Six

The cafeteria—if you could even call it that—resembled a fine dining restaurant rather than a school dining hall. The sheer size of it overwhelmed me. I half expected Oliver and the others to be sitting at some kind of large top table like royalty, but actually they were occupying the large circular table in the very centre of the room. Which then just reminded me of the Knight's of the Round Table, but whatever.

Clover and I made our way to the table and sat in the two empty seats; me beside Griff like he had requested with Oliver on my other side. Clover had to sit between Leo and Olivia—and trust—her face made it clear how pissed at me she was for having put her in this position. I could tell that this table usually only had the seven of them and that they'd squeezed to make room for us—we were all quite cramped. I couldn't help but wonder why they'd gone to such an effort.

Servers came and took the table's order once we sat down,

as apparently they had been waiting for the entire group to be present. I'd never felt so out of place. I glanced at the Menu in front of me, but many of the dishes inside were foreign to me. Pretty sure somebody on the table next to us had snails on their plate. I had to keep reminding myself that I was at school. Even though everything here clarified that this particular school was for the superwealthy.

The O girls were doing nothing to hide their feelings about the situation. They were livid. All four of them kept looking at me and then each other, then Clover, then the boys. This went on for a full five minutes and nobody said anything during that time. It was awkward as fuck.

'S-s-so how was everybody's day?' I asked, trying to break the tension that was seeping into the atmosphere and tainting the air. The moment the words left me, I hoped my chair would dissolve into the tiled floor.

'That stutter is honestly the cutest thing. Don't you agree, Ollie? Damn, Sky. I'm hard just hearing it,' said Griff, who had his signature grin on his face, his dimples pressed in.

Well, that broke the tension.

'Oh, shut up dickhead,' Clover said whilst trying to contain her laughter. 'Do you think before you speak or does it just come out like word vomit?'

'My sweet lucky Clover, has anybody told you look hot when you're acting all fierce? Don't you agree, Leo?' Griff asked, his eyebrows raised in Leo's direction, teasing.

'Hm.' Leo clearly made any noise just to shut Griff up as he wasn't paying the slightest bit of attention to the rest of the group. He was too busy looking at Odette while she stared back. I thought I saw her hand moving underneath the table in a suspicious rhythm and my face heated.

Rich people are weird.

'Don't mind him, he knows the truth,' said Griff, nodding as if he had all the answers and could see inside Leo's mind. 'My day was perfect. I got my dick sucked in the caretaker's cupboard earlier and I'm hoping I'll get a repeat later.'

I was so out of my league here.

It sounded like a cliché, but I was still a virgin. A rather non-experienced virgin at that. The kiss from Andy hadn't been my first—I wasn't that inexperienced—but it was one of a brief list. I'd never in my life been around people who talked like this; so open and honest with no regard to who could hear them.

'Nobody needs to hear about you getting your dick sucked, Griff. Don't worry, though. I'm sure Oralie will repeat the favour for you for her dessert,' Clover said, her smile dripping poison, giving Oralie a look of pure condescension.

'As if!' Oralie sputtered, doing her best *Clueless* impression. 'I wouldn't go near *that* even if you paid me.'

What a basic bitch. I rolled my eyes and when I looked up; I found myself staring directly into Oliver's blue ones. They had a glint of menace, but he covered it up pretty fast and then they just looked bland.

'Nobody would pay for your mouth. More like you'd have to pay them,' Clover smarted back at her.

'I could kiss you!' Griff looked in his element, rubbing his hands together with glee. He reminded me of a bad cartoon villain, and I couldn't help but laugh. He looked at me and raised his hand for a high five. I gave him one and felt like maybe he wasn't so bad. But then Clover's warning from yesterday came back to me, and I had to wonder just what Griff kept hidden.

Food arrived, and the mood around the table hadn't improved. Other than the odd spurts of banter between Griff and Clover, nobody else said much.

Leo and Odette were still touching one another intimately, and I reckoned Clover had considered stabbing him with her steak knife multiple times.

Griff grinned wide and acted like everything happening around the table amused him; which it probably did. Ophelia, Olivia and Oralie were all conversing together and excluding Clo and I. Whispering about something we weren't privy to. Although I did hear both mine and Clover's names come up multiple times.

Then there was Oliver, who had put his hand on my thigh during the main course and was yet to remove it. Both of us silent, caught up in the moment.. His fingers moved in a slow circle, drawing a swirling pattern on my skin. My skirt had risen, and his hand touched my bare leg.

I felt slightly confused to why Oliver had invited me to sit with him for dinner. Other than the leg touching, he hadn't spoken to me once. Or to anybody at the table, come to think of it. I didn't know what I'd expected, but I had at least expected him to converse with me. You know, acknowledge my presence with words and not just his hand that now wandered higher up my thigh than it had a moment ago.

'W-w-what are you doing?' I whispered as low as I could, not wanting the rest of the table to hear me.

He leaned into me, pressing his mouth flush to my ear. His breath warm as it skated across my skin, causing shivers to erupt all over.

'Don't try and tell me you aren't enjoying it. I can feel the goosebumps; feel the excitement. You like this just as much as I do.'

'Like what?'

'That we haven't said one word to each other, yet I'm touching you, anyway. Taking what I want.' I felt trapped as his hand went higher, touching the outer edge of my underwear, teasing me. I gasped. Clover raised her eyebrow at me, a silent question. I nodded at her, hoping I didn't look as flustered as I felt. And boy, did I feel flustered. Oliver spoke the truth. I was enjoying this. It felt so naughty. Naughty that he hadn't said a word but pushed my boundaries, regardless.

'You're beautiful, you know that right?' I felt his tongue briefly graze my ear before he leaned back in his seat. *Fuck.* I was a goner.

The spell between us broke when Griff started shouting while flailing his arms around.

'Yo! Did anybody even hear what I said?'

'Yes. The entire room heard you, Griff,' Clover deadpanned. I nodded along, as if that were an accurate statement. I didn't want anybody to realise that my mind had been elsewhere for some time. 'Even Ms Hawthorn in her office must have heard you.'

'What shit you chatting now, Wanker?' asked Leo as he turned to face the table, looking at everybody in turn. Come to think of it, I couldn't think of a time yet where Leo hadn't seemed bored. But then it hit me. He hadn't seemed bored last night when I'd bumped into him and Odette. He had been the complete opposite, in fact. His eyes were amused then, and his face had given him away for just a moment.

Oh shit. I knew that didn't bode well for me; I just couldn't put my finger on why.

✦

THE REST OF THE NIGHT PASSED QUICKLY.

After dinner had ended, the girls had stormed off as a pack. Griff had walked us back to our room and hugged us both good-night, winking as he left. I was softening towards him; he was charming, and he seemed so laid back compared to the other two. Leo had disappeared the second we left the hall, but I had no idea where he'd gone to. He had left without saying a word to anyone.

Oliver had whispered that he would see me tomorrow and then also vanished down the corridor in the direction of the pool building. I'd gathered from conversations around the school all day that *The Sect* were a part of the school swim team and were the reason the school had so many accolades. I felt surprised, though. Only Leo had a swimmer's body. I would have sworn that the other two played football or maybe even rugby; some kind of contact sport, at least.

'Sky. What the hell was happening during dinner?' Clover pounced on me the second the door was closed—and locked—behind us. 'Don't even think about saying nothing because I swear, I am not that dumb.'

'Nothing. Seriously,' I said, blushing. She looked annoyed though, and I knew my answer wouldn't cut it. 'Okay, fine! Oliver may or may not have been touching my leg.'

I caved. I didn't want my only friend pissed off at me. Not like I'd had other people fighting over me today trying to become my friend.

'I bet he was. Be careful, Sky. I don't know why the three of them are acting nice to you,' Clo said, a warning in her green eyes.

I looked at her questioningly.

'Okay, the two of them,' she said, amending her previous statement.

I nodded. We both knew that Leo wasn't acting anything towards me except disinterested.

'Talking of being careful, *Clo*. What exactly did Leo say to you this morning?'

'Nothing.' She averted her gaze, opened her laptop and started some homework. It was a load of bullshit though, because yeah, we did have homework, but the girl had had two classes today—cooking and art.

'I'm asking nicely.' I fluttered my eyelashes at her, hoping she'd take pity on me and spill her guts. I could sense that she wanted to talk about it, but was scared of something too. I hoped her need to get it out in the open would win out.

'I promise that one day I'll tell all Sky, but today is not that day.'

I sighed and focused on reading. It felt strange to be reading reverse harem bully books set in an Academy now that I was living in one—an Academy, not a RH bully book. I had decided on reading a classic instead; *Pride and Prejudice* always made me feel better. It was one of those stories that I never tired of. Ever since I first read it, I knew that one day I wanted my own Mr Darcy. Well, maybe not quite like him. *But you know what I mean.* That all consuming, all encapsulating kind of romance.

After I'd read a few chapters and was getting comfortable, I could sense fidgeting on the other side of the room.

'Sky ...' Clover said, she looked unsure. Words on the tip of her tongue.

'Yeah?' I asked and stopped what I was doing. Darcy could wait.

'Have you ever been in love?'

In the short time I'd known her, I hadn't seen Clover look this shy or self-conscious. She was a badass, and she knew it. But this was a completely new side to her.

'Nope. I've never even had a boyfriend.'

'Oh. Right.'

'Have you?'

'Have I what?'

'Ever been in love?' I asked, sensing that she needed to talk about something plaguing her mind. She wouldn't have asked if not.

'I thought I was once. But now I realise it was just how it looked in the light.'

I smiled at her; the reference wasn't lost on me. I'd never really been into new music and I listened to the early 2010s "emo" bands a lot, but it was rare I found other people who loved them too.

'Skylar. I think you and I are going to be friends for life. Something's just clicked, you know.'

'I feel the exact same way,' I replied, beaming at her.

I wasn't lying, either. Something in my heart knew that I'd found a soulmate in Clover. Ride or die. It felt good after so many years of being a loner to feel like I had somebody in my corner. One who wouldn't judge me for the stupid decisions I was no doubt about to make for Oliver.

Trust me, I knew I would eventually throw caution to the wind in order to find out just what he wanted.

There was something drawing me in. Pulling me to him. Like how magnets reacted once they'd found their mate.

Chapter Seven

With no assembly scheduled the next morning, we didn't have to be up anywhere near as early. We also didn't oversleep, a major plus if you asked me. My first lesson of the day was History, a class I knew I shared with Oliver; I was nervous but anxious too. I wanted him to sit with me and give me attention. I also knew that his attention could all be one big falsehood. A trick played on the New Girl by the kids who ruled the school. Some whispers I'd heard since being here had been dark. Students seemed scared of them—Leo and Oliver in particular.

Clover had woke me up and thrown a croissant at my head, I hadn't set my alarm with enough time to go to breakfast but Clover had, and she'd grabbed some items for us when she'd run to the hall a moment ago. It seemed like breakfast was more casual than the fine affair dinner had been last night.

'Remember, keep yourself to yourself today, Sky. I know

you didn't have a bad day yesterday, but trust me when I say that these bitches are probably just trying to lull you into a false sense of security.'

'By bitches do you mean the O girls?' I asked her, and yeah, I knew the answer, but I wanted to make sure. They hadn't been *too* bad at dinner after all.

'Of course I do, Skylar!' she said as her face flushed. I laughed and when she saw my face she realised that I had been joking. Clover's shoulders deflated as she relaxed a little. 'You got me for a moment there. I genuinely believed that you didn't know who I meant.'

'Oh, come off it, Clo. I'm not that dense.' I stopped, and quickly added, 'Right?'

'Well ...' Clo's smile was growing super wide after a few seconds, 'No, you're not.'

'Phew.'

✦

Once again, Oliver sat next to me in History class and I tried my hardest the entire time to pay attention to Miss Woodlock and not anything that he tried to whisper to me. And believe me, he was trying to whisper A LOT of things. *Dirty things.*

Okay, maybe they weren't that dirty—phrases like, *"I wish I could kiss you all over, see if you taste as good as you smell"* or there was, *"One day soon I'm going to bend you over this desk and fuck you from behind"*. I took back all I'd said. It was filthy as fuck and all I could do was think about the scenarios he painted in my mind. I had no idea what war the teacher was telling us about. The only war I knew was the one going on between my head and, well, not my heart, that was for sure.

By the time class ended I was the colour of a fire engine and I think I may have even foamed at the mouth a little; which really wasn't a good look. I think even Oliver had believed I'd turned into a mindless zombie. I just couldn't wrap my head around it, though. I used to think that I could see through bullshit; I'd always seen through my mum and Andy. But with Oliver, I just couldn't figure him out. Was he really genuinely interested in me? Or was I a target for some kind of game I didn't know I was playing? I sighed. I made a mental note to myself to talk to Clover and find out if that was a possibility.

'What're you thinking about?' Oliver asked as we left the classroom and I moved towards my English class. He walked faster beside me to keep up.

'W-what?' I hadn't fully heard him, too lost in my head. 'Oh ... things.'

Great answer, Sky.

'By any chance are those things anything to do with what I said in class?'

'N-n-no,' I sputtered. 'Of course not. You just caught me off guard, that's all.'

'Sure I did. I'm also sure the reason your face went red has nothing to do with me either.' He looked so smug, so sure of himself. I knew I had to knock his ego a little, but I wasn't experienced in this kind of psychological warfare. I found it hard enough to not get distracted by his eyes, or his chiselled jawline. Even just looking at him, I felt myself getting hot. Then the perfect insult hit me.

'Oh, believe me. I was imagining your words ...' Oliver's

face lit up as I said this, his eyes glinting with mischief, but then I delivered the blow. Putting emphasis on the first word I said, 'But I replaced the thought of you with Griff.'

Take that, I thought, feeling good about myself for the first time in an interaction with him. Every other time we had spoken I hadn't been thinking fully, totally flustered at the situation.

Oliver didn't seem to find my words as funny, though. Instantly his eyes darkened in anger to an indigo instead of their usual light sky blue colour. He grabbed my upper arm tight, stopping me from walking further.

'What did you just say to me?' he rasped. His eyes hard, with no trace of humour left in them—or on his face for that matter. I'd made him mad, and a small part of me was happy about it. Served him right.

'I was f-fantasising about Griff,' I said. So yeah, the stutter didn't help me there, but by the look on his face, Oliver had only registered the words and not my awkward, stutter filled delivery.

'Griff?' he questioned, his face growing darker somehow. The pressure from his hand got tighter with each word he spoke. 'You're going to regret saying that, New Girl,' he spat. A tiny fleck of it landed on my cheek, and I tried to stay calm. Letting go of my arm, he turned around and stormed off, leaving me alone in the corridor. I rubbed my arm, knowing that he had probably left a bruise.

I continued walking and slipped into my English class, hoping that somehow I had become invisible. There had been many whispers since dinner last night, and I really didn't need anybody approaching me and asking questions that I truly had no actual answers for. I quickly found a seat at the back and took it.

Oralie and Ophelia entered the classroom together, staring at me as they did so. Instantly they started whispering to one another. I rolled my eyes at their behaviour. Even though I knew I shouldn't, I knew I was playing with fire. I had a feeling that the girls definitely took the rules more seriously than the guys did, and I shouldn't be pushing my luck—especially on the second day of term.

'Eurgh, Lia, why on earth is the New Girl looking at us?' Oralie asked, raising her voice to ensure that I heard her.

'Honestly Lee, I have no idea but she better stop right now if she knows what's best.' Ophelia answered, looking too happy for somebody that was delivering a threat.

'Bitch, don't you remember the rules? I *do not* deem it necessary for you to be looking at us right now.' Oralie snapped at me. 'And trust me, little girl, I will punish you.'

I sunk further down into my chair. Inside, I told myself not to listen to her words. That there was nothing she could really do that would hurt me. But let's be honest—she could do a lot to hurt me. Teenagers are cruel, and I had seen a lot of bullying back in my old school. I was clocking that maybe rich girls played even dirtier than those I had grown up with.

I watched as Miss Morris, our English teacher, swept into the room and started playing *Wuthering Heights* by Kate Bush through the whiteboard speakers, and I swear I died inside even more. The song was undoubtedly a tune, but it could only mean one thing; we were about to read it, and I couldn't think of anything worse. The facade of the main building had already reminded me of it, I didn't need to be studying it too. Every teenage fiction book I'd read had some kind of sick fascination with the love story of Cathy and Heathcliff but honestly, they were both toxic as fuck to one another and she dies halfway through the book. Definitely not my idea of a love story.

The lesson pretty much continued the way I had expected it to. Miss announced our new topic for the term, gothic literature, and Oralie and Ophelia spent the rest of the entire double period talking about me and trying to encourage others to do the same. I could hear the words, "scum", "slut", and "bitch" to list a few. They were slowly building an audience. The girl at the desk next to me kept staring at me, whispering that I'd really fucked up by angering *The Set*.

At first, it didn't affect me. I mean, I knew they were just trying to make themselves feel better about the fact that Oliver seemed to have taken an interest in me. But after the first hour, it sunk in and as the dark cloud of their words hit other students, I could feel myself breathing slower. It was like that first night in my bedroom again. The world blurred at the edges and I didn't dare talk as I knew I would be a stuttering mess, making no sense whatsoever. The room spun, my vision faltering. In my mind, the chair underneath me melted. I knew one thing for certain. I couldn't black out here. The girls would never let me live it down and I had heard nobody talking about my visit to the Hospital Wing last night, so maybe Oliver and Leo had kept that tidbit quiet.

✦

An hour of solo reading passed.

Miss Morris had realised that maybe the class wasn't actually reading the book in their heads and were actually more focused on aiming nasty words (and spit wads) at me—how original.

'Ophelia, dear, could you read aloud from the beginning of chapter three?' Miss Morris asked, surveying the classroom as she did so.

'Of course Miss, it'd be my pleasure,' Ophelia said, her tone sickly sweet. Like butter wouldn't melt. Nausea rose in my stomach, and I made a slight huffing noise. Kiss ass.

Ophelia started to read out loud, and I followed along in my copy, but after a few pages or so, Ophelia abruptly stopped.

'Miss, I feel like we should let somebody else read now. I don't want to bore people with my voice,' she tittered, or at least that was the only word I could think of to describe the noise she'd made. 'How about we let Skylar read, now? She is new and I wouldn't want her to feel excluded.'

Well, fuck me. It was obvious to me that Ophelia knew exactly what she was doing, although I honestly wasn't sure whether the teacher knew that she was being a bitch to me, or whether she genuinely believed that Ophelia was trying to "help" me. What help would it really be to me to read out loud to a class of pupils I'd barely met?

'Oh, what a lovely, inclusive, idea dear. Skylar, please stand and read to us from page thirty-six,' she said, her gaze finding mine. Her smile was encouraging enough, her eyes looked kind, too.

I knew that there was no way out of this. The fact I had to stand made it even worse as I knew that all eyes were on me, even though I was at the back of the classroom, every pupil turned to face me. I just prayed that I wouldn't stutter my way through this. I wasn't ready just yet for that kind of humiliation. I definitely didn't want to draw even more attention to myself than what had already been thrust upon me by eating dinner with *The Sect* last night.

I stood. Raising my book to read but also trying to use it as a shield so I didn't have to see the entire class looking at me. You would think that they'd be looking at their own copies in order to follow along and make notes or some shit—but apparently watching the New Girl flounder was more exciting. Which, yeah, it would be compared to *Wuthering Heights*, after all.

"'If the little f-fiend had got in at the w-w-window, she p-probably would have s-strangled me!'" Aware of the slow pace I read at, I tried to read faster, but the faster I read the more mistakes I made.

Not like it mattered. The entire class erupted in laughter the second I stuttered over the first word and didn't stop from then onwards. I could hear them repeating my mistakes, emphasising every stutter and trip.

'Not the "w-w-window",' said Oralie, nudging Ophelia in the side.

I knew Miss could hear them, and could see them making rude gestures at me, but she never once told them to stop. She'd turned a blind eye to proceedings, sitting at her desk drinking her coffee with no cares.

Of course, Ophelia and Oralie were jeering the loudest. The whispers surrounded me, saying about how I should *"go hide in my room"* and even worse, whispers saying I should *"go slit my wrists"* because *"she's so ugly only a blind man would fuck her"*.

It took everything in me not to cry. I could feel the tears forming in my eyes but I continued to read; even if it was at a slow speed filled with me stumbling over every other word.

Finally, the class neared its end, and all I wanted to do was get out of here as quickly as I could and disappear deep into the library where nobody would think to look for me. Thankfully lunch came next, followed by a free period, and I was so ready to become invisible.

I looked up as Miss Morris wrapped up the lesson and I saw Oliver standing in the doorway, leaning against the doorframe in that way that popular, hot guys seem to do *really* well. I shrank even further into my seat. I had no idea how long he'd been standing there, but I reckoned he saw at least some of what Ophelia and Oralie had started. His facial expression gave nothing away though and for all I knew, he could be standing there waiting for the girls to go to lunch with him. We hadn't exactly left things on great terms earlier. My arm still smarted from the way he'd gripped it so tight.

The class filed out of the room and I stood slowly, wondering if he would walk away with Ophelia and Oralie when they passed him. He paid them no attention at all. I waited until every single student had left the room and Oliver still stood there. He was definitely waiting for me.

'H-h-how long were you standing there?' I asked.

I vowed one day I would talk to him with no stutter, but (once again) today was not that day.

'Long enough,' he said. His clipped answer and tone told me all I needed to know. He'd witnessed what the class had done to me—what they'd been saying to me. He knew how they had all been laughing at me.

'R-right. Well, I'll see you later,' I mumbled. I tried to rush around him, but he caught my arm before I could get away. I grimaced; it was the exact same part of my arm he'd grabbed in the corridor earlier. The dark, twisted look on his face told me he knew how much this hurt me.

He tightened his grip, even though I'd visibly winced.

'Where d'you think you're going?' he asked, or demanded really.

'To the l-l-library,' I answered.

'But it's lunch. What are you doing about food?'

'I was g-going to grab something on my way there.'

'I'll join you. I have a free period after lunch too,' he said, finally loosening his grip around my arm. Oliver's lips raised at the corners, a semi-smile of sorts. One filled with warning.

I nodded, resigned to my fate, and let him drag me along beside him.

It wasn't until a lot later; I realised that I'd never told him I had a free period after lunch.

Chapter Eight

Heading straight for the library, I tried to ignore the imposing figure next to me. I kept trying to walk faster but with every two strides I took he only needed one, so there was no way I was going to out-walk him—or outrun him, if I ever needed to. I filed that away for future reference.

I also couldn't help but notice how handsome he was. He really had that whole, *I'm a good-looking guy and I know it*, vibe going on. Oliver really was hot, and I could totally see why all the girls here were hoping to one day land him.

We headed across the school grounds because even though you'd expect the English classrooms to be near the library; they were actually the furthest away. I tried my hardest to ignore Oliver the entire time, but he kept entering my personal bubble.

While queuing for lunch, the two of us stayed silent. The tension in the air was palpable, and all I wanted to do was get away. Everybody stared at us, the whispers growing louder each second. Eventually, we got to the front of the line and grabbed some sandwiches and put them in a to-go bag.

Leaving the hall with our lunch, Oliver asked me, 'You going to tell me what happened back there?'

'Back w-where?' I asked, pretending I didn't understand the question.

'Pretend that you don't know what I'm talking about all you want, New Girl,' Oliver said, shrugging, 'not like I'm going to give up.'

'I-it was nothing,' I said, the words flying from my mouth at rapid speed. I hoped he'd leave it alone. It was only my second day, and I didn't want to have the wrath of *The Set* fall on me this soon. It had already started in English and I prayed I wouldn't have to endure that in every class I shared with them. I wasn't that strong.

'That wasn't nothing, Sky. You were shaking, and on the verge of tears.'

'S-seriously Oliver, it was nothing.' I stressed his name, hoping he would take me at my word as I didn't want to rehash any of what had happened to him, of all people. I tried to pick up my pace, but he matched me step for step.

'Thought I told you to call me Ollie?' he asked, his irritation at my refusal clear.

'Y-yes, you did. B-but I decided not to,' I told him, not completely certain where this badass-ness had come from. Well, as badass as I could be with my stutter.

'And why is that, New Girl?' he asked, his tone dark.

'B-because we're not friends,' I said. I wasn't sure how he would react to this, but ever since he'd told me to call him by his nickname, I just couldn't bring myself to. Even in my head.

I'd slipped when talking to Clo the other night, but since then I'd been careful.

Oliver didn't answer me—not sure if he was ignoring my words or pretending he hadn't heard them. After what felt like a lifetime, but was in actuality probably only a few minutes, we finally made it to the library.

For me, the library gave away the school's age. Large, old and daunting, it looked to be one of the oldest buildings here. Clover had briefly taken me here during her tour but we hadn't focused on it for too long; not like she knew how much I loved books.

But I did. I loved reading, and I loved seeing all these books together, just waiting for somebody to pick them up and find the wonder that lies inside their pages. I used to spend all of my time at the local library in town. It had been my respite when things had been hard at home. Books were always there, and within the pages of books I'd found many friends and worlds that I would have done anything to visit—I still would if given the chance.

Being older now, I read more romance books that you wouldn't find in a library—but I still visited all the same. It was one place I could truly find peace.

Sadly, being in this library with Oliver meant that I probably wouldn't get much peace. I knew he hadn't finished his line of questioning and he was just waiting until I calmed down. Then he would pounce, like a beast from the shadows.

I found a table at the very back of the library to sit at, dumping my lunch, and my bag filled with my school books and laptop, down with a thud.

Oliver placed his food and bag down gently and took a

seat, meaning I had no choice but to sit next to him. Well, that was what I told myself, anyway, and I was sticking to it.

Once we'd sat next to one another in silence for five minutes—a fucking long time to sit with anybody in uncomfortable silence, believe me. Part of me felt excited, but the majority of me felt irritated.

The uncomfortable silence had obviously affected Oliver too, as he turned to face me and asked once again, 'What happened in English, Sky?'

'I-I told you, nothing important.'

'I saw the end. It was clear the girls were picking on you. I thought Leo told you to come to me if you had any trouble with them?'

I stayed quiet. Yeah, Leo had said that to me, but I hadn't believed him. I thought he'd been lying or; I don't know, trying to make me feel better or something. I felt stupid saying this out loud, though. I felt stupid saying mostly everything out loud; especially when I stuttered like a little bitch.

Oliver's face darkened, his eyebrows furrowing, and his mouth as straight as I'd ever seen it. He resembled the Oliver I'd seen leaving the pool house back on the day I arrived. When Clover had warned me about them. Shit, that had only been two days ago! I must try to remember that the girl I'd formed a bond with here—make that the only person I'd connected with—made it very clear that I should stay away from *The Sect*. Obviously that included the present company. Rule number five could kiss my ass. If he invited me to dinner again, I would refuse. Or I at least believed in that moment I would.

'Sky, I won't repeat myself. Come to me or Leo or, fuck, even Griff if you need to okay? Don't ignore me.'

'O-okay, I'll t-try to remember.'

'Please tell me what happened,' he said. The sincerity in his tone and the pleading look in his eyes made me finally cave. Also, the fact that he had actually said please to me made my heart warm a little.

'I-it was nothing. Oralie and Ophelia thought it would be funny to have me read aloud.' I sighed, and said, 'And my stutter definitely makes reading in c-class hard.'

'They're just mean, rich girls Sky. I'll talk to them.'

'P-please don't,' I whispered. The last thing I needed Oliver to do was talk to them and make them want to hurt me even more than they already seemed to. I wanted to fly under the radar; not become a beacon.

'Fine. But I swear to God Skylar, if you do not tell me about them in the future, I will spank you so hard you won't forget again.'

I choked on my sandwich. He just slipped these dark, flirty sentences into conversation and expected me to take them, no questions asked. I blushed at him, which only seemed to make him more smug.

'Y-y-you wouldn't.' My words sounded a lot more confident than I felt and let's be honest, my words didn't exactly sound overly confident seeing as I constantly stumbled all over them.

'Oh, I think you'd be surprised at just what I would do to you, New Girl. Ever since I first saw you, I've wanted to get under that skin of yours and see the true you. Figure out exactly what makes you tick.'

His blue eyes stared into mine and it felt to me as if he wanted to see into my soul. Which was absurd, right? We'd only known each other for a few days. When I first saw him, the connection between us had sparked to life, but I definitely only felt attraction; not obsession. He seemed the type to obsess over small things. Guess I was one of those things, now.

'I d-don't know why. I'm not important,' I said. My voice quavered, and my true opinion of myself seemed to bleed through my words. I could feel them in the atmosphere; threatening to choke me with embarrassment. Man, I was pathetic and chances were at this rate anyway, that Oliver would notice pretty soon just how much of a loser I truly was.

'Don't say that,' he said. His harsh tone surprised me. Fucking shocked me, actually. I thought that maybe he'd just agree with me or something. Oh, wow. Even I was rolling my eyes at me in my head. 'You are important.'

We both fell silent after that.

We finished our lunch, and both started on our homework because, believe me, this school didn't subscribe to the whole no homework in the first week thing like my previous school did. Nope. From the very first lesson, we'd been given essays to write and books to read.

It was quite nice to work side by side in silence. Every now and again I found my gaze wandering in his direction. He really filled the uniform out nicely. His broad chest and wide shoulders looked so good in his white shirt, and even though he was wearing a bottle green blazer, he was really making it work for him. You know that saying, *"wear clothes and don't let the clothes wear you"*? That sprung to mind whenever I looked at Oliver.

But obviously, the silence couldn't last forever.

Oliver turned to face me, and the look on his face told me he really didn't want to say the words about to leave his mouth.

He sighed and whispered, 'Sky, why don't you think you're important?'

I closed my eyes and did that whole—I wish the ground would swallow me whole thing—but it didn't work. When I opened them, his face was even closer than it had been, and his eyes were staring into mine. Attempting, but failing, to unravel all of my secrets.

'I n-never have. I guess I never had many friends or family there to t-tell me otherwise. Believe it or not, Oliver, I've always been a bit of a loner.'

I hated focusing on my lack of friends and the fact that my family didn't give a shit about me. My mum may be the worst, but she kept a roof over my head to a certain extent and she never abandoned me. Even if sometimes I thought my life would have been better if she had.

My dad, on the other hand, was somebody I'd never met. He'd split from my mum when I was a few months old and nobody ever really talked about him much. I mean, I knew that he existed once upon a time and that he and my mum came from totally different upbringings and backgrounds but that was all I knew.

Not having friends was a whole other thing. When I was really young, it used to bother me that the other children would play at one another's houses, or would invite each other to birthday parties, and things like that. I never got invited and as we all grew up, birthday parties turned into sleepovers, and then house parties, and camping out in random fields.

Mostly, I had nothing in common with the girls I'd grown up around. They were interested in boys and makeup and having the newest clothes and all that kind of material rubbish. I just wanted to read and escape into the book world. I had no time for boys, and makeup and clothes were luxuries I couldn't afford. Before Andy came along, I was lucky if my mum even remembered to fill the fridge with edible items.

Oliver speaking brought me out of my thoughts.

'Believe it or not, New Girl, I can believe that.' He was laughing—at me or with me, I wasn't completely certain. I smiled at him though. Not like I should care what one it was. 'But now you don't have to be. You've made friends with Clover, right?'

I nodded and said, 'Yeah, she's g-great.'

'And you're now a part of the inner circle too, what with us inviting you to hang with us.'

At his words, I looked away, the bookshelves suddenly seeming more enticing to me. I could hear an underlying threat —or something like a threat—hidden underneath his kind words. Why did I get the impression that being a part of the inner circle was the last thing I should want?

'I g-guess.'

'Did you mean what you said earlier?' he asked.

He changed the topic so fast I almost got whiplash turning abruptly to face him once more.

'About w-what exactly?'

'What you said about Griff? Imagining him doing the things I whispered to you.' He leaned closer; his words whispered against my ear and I shivered at the slight touch of his lips.

'N-no.' I shook my head, both in response to him, but also as an attempt to clear the fog that my mind seemed to have clung to it. 'I j-just said those things to make you m-mad.'

'Would you believe me if I said it worked?'

'Y-you deserved it, Oliver.'

'Please, call me Ollie.' he said, almost pleading with me and I couldn't help myself; that factor made me smile with satisfaction. There wasn't much I could do to piss him off, yet calling him by his full name seemed to work. I highly doubted that many people ignored him when he gave a direct order; let alone when he asked politely.

'I'll think about it. But I still d-don't think we're friends.'

I pushed my chair out, stood up, and moved away from the table. I needed to create some distance between the two of us. I could still feel his whisper in my ear. His lips had grazed my cheek and the featherlight touch of it lingered.

I quickly found my way to the non-fiction section of the library—a secluded area at the very back, with a dead end made up of bookcases. No other students were around, and I sighed in relief. My shoulders raised and lowered again with the motion. It was a deep sigh. I needed to find a history book to complete the assignment Miss Woodlock had given us, and I did not want anyone stepping inside my personal bubble. One time, I'd had an anxiety attack in the store I worked in as somebody had come too close to me when I was stocking a shelf. They'd reached across me, innocently enough; my heart had stopped and my vision had wavered. How humiliating.

I heard footsteps coming up behind me and I was just about to turn around when a hard body pressed up against my back. An arm came up on either side of me, caging me in, stopping me from going anywhere.

'Running away, New Girl?'

His words whispered against my neck. I went to turn my head, but he moved his hand in order to hold my neck firmly in place.

The only thing I could hear in the silence was our breathing. I swore the people around could hear my breathing throughout the entire library.

Oliver started placing small kisses up and down my neck. I moaned in a mix of frustration and arousal. His hardness pressed into my back and all I could think about was how he must look naked.

He grabbed me by the waist, hard, and flipped me around so we were facing one another.

'God, you don't realise just how fucking sexy you are, Skylar.'

Then his lips touched mine, devouring them. The action was almost violent. The way he forced my mouth open—the way he used his tongue against mine.

The kiss was anything but sweet and I could feel his hard length pressing up against me, which only made me want it elsewhere. My hormones were racing through the roof and I tried to focus on what was happening, to stay in the moment.

One of Oliver's hands was in my hair, gripping it tightly; the other hand squeezed my nipple through my bra. The pain mixed with the pleasure and I moaned even louder. I was so turned on, I couldn't think straight. The way he was making me feel was unlike any way I'd ever felt before. I was riding high, enjoying his attention.

'Fuck,' he groaned.

He stopped the kiss abruptly.

He moved away from me, creating a gap between our bodies. His expression dark, his emotions shutting off in front of me.

I went to say something, but the tension between us had grown and I knew he was overthinking what had happened.

Without another word, Oliver turned and walked away from me. I say walked, but it was definitely at a faster pace.

My fingers involuntarily touched my lips in a daze. I looked around and luckily found myself alone.

I felt like I was living in my very own twisted tale; left in a library, the feared monster gone, my heart slightly thawing.

Chapter Nine

I had been looking forward to my new Philosophy and Ethics class the most, as it hadn't been offered at my previous school; yet another advantage the scholarship here could give me. I had to remember that. I couldn't forget that my end goal was to graduate from here with the best grades I could get in order to apply at the best Universities. There was no way I was going to waste this opportunity.

Griff strode into the classroom, looking like he had no care in the world, which when I thought about it was probably the case. Ever since meeting him, I'd never once seen him take anything seriously. He constantly cracked jokes and made everybody around him smile. Or groan.

He fell into the chair on my right, looking at me questioningly as he said, 'Well, well, well, New Girl. What have we here? You look a little ... flushed.'

I wanted to smack him, and hide from him, simultaneously. I decided not to respond to him, mostly because I had no idea what to say. I was still processing what had happened with me and Ollie in the library.

Shit.

I thought of him as Ollie.

It was official. *I was fucked.*

Griff couldn't fully see the turmoil going on in my mind though as he continued talking and said, 'So, Sky. Would you say the History section or the Science Fiction section is better for hookups? I'm asking for a friend.'

I rolled my eyes at him, trying my hardest not to smile but feeling my lips twitch, anyway. He sure was persistent though, got to give him that.

'New Girl, I'm messing with you. I definitely give zero shits about you hooking up amongst the library shelves. Actually, I'm sort of cheesed off that I hadn't thought to try it before.'

'C-cheesed off?' I giggled. Then quickly put my hand over my mouth.

The damage was already done.

'Was that a giggle I just heard, New Girl? Damn. I did *not* have you down as a giggler,' he teased, unleashing a bright smile in my direction and I swear to you, I was almost blinded by his teeth. 'Now you've made me wonder how your giggle would sound with me doing all sorts of naughty shit to you.'

'W-w-what is it with you guys and w-wondering how I'll sound when you're inside me?!' I asked, definitely raising my voice too loud, but I couldn't help it. First Ollie with my stutter and now Griff with my giggle.

'I'm just messing with you, Sky,' he said, his eyes matching the sincerity of his words. He had called me by my name, for starters. 'Ollie, I can't vouch for. He definitely wants to know how you'd sound around his dick,' Griff added as an afterthought.

I then made a noise that I couldn't even find the word for. It was like a mix between a guffaw and a chortle. I covered my mouth again because, seriously; I needed to try harder to keep a hold of myself.

'I'm sure he doesn't,' I sputtered, whilst trying to stop myself from laughing more. I just couldn't understand it. Even though Ollie *had* just kissed me in the library, I couldn't compute in my mind that he actually wanted me.

I was a game to him. Nothing more.

'I'm serious, that boy wants you bad. Even threatened me after what you said to him this morning about fantasising about me. Super handy for the ego, love. I knew you wanted a piece of the Griff-man.'

'Please never refer to yourself as the "Griff-man" ever again,' I said, rolling my eyes. I couldn't stop my laughter, now that it was coming full force. A tear escaped from my eye, trailing down my face until I could taste it on my lip.

'New Girl!' he said, surprised. 'Your stutters disappeared.'

'Oh,' I said as I shook my head in confusion. I hadn't even realised it. It must have gone at some point during our conversation. The only other person I'd been able to talk to here with no stutter was Clover—the only person I felt comfortable around, after all. But there was something about Griff that eased my anxiety. I think it had something to do with the fact that he didn't seem to take anything too seriously. He was full of jokes and had made me smile more than anybody else here. 'I guess your bullshit has made me realise there's no reason to be nervous around you.'

'Should I take that as an insult, New Girl? Cause I gotta say, that doesn't sound too flattering.'

'No. You should actually be super happy about it. Means I like you.'

'Well, then!' He slapped his hand to his knee, and I giggled again at his enthusiasm. He smiled, teeth on show, and said, 'You should've just said that.'

I smiled back as the teacher, Mr Somes, entered the classroom. He was a towering beanpole of a man, sort of reminded me of the tall one from *Fantastic Mr Fox* by Roald Dahl—one of my favourite stories growing up. Roald Dahl's stories had always fascinated me. For a child with no father and a shit mother, his stories had shown me that there were many children out there suffering at the hands of stupid adults.

In all honesty, I barely paid any attention to the Ethics lesson, even though I'd been so excited about it. My mind still stuck in the library—my time with Ollie replaying in my head on a constant loop. A sick perversion that wouldn't leave me, and every single time, the scene progressed further. Or I did something different, evolving the fantasy further.

I felt so frustrated and stupid. I knew that Oliver wasn't actually interested in me and that this was surely some big game to them all. The fact that Griff had known what happened when we'd got to class meant that *somebody* had already told him. My money was on Ollie, as nobody else had been there. Not that we'd seen. Not that I would have even noticed anyway, but that was neither here nor there.

Right?

*

AFTER CLASSES HAD ENDED, I MADE IT BACK TO OUR DORM room in record time.

I desperately needed to talk to Clover. I had to get her opinion on just what had happened today. It felt like so much had changed since I saw her this morning for breakfast. I was positive she'd roll her eyes and tell me that I was making a huge mistake. Regardless, I wanted to hear it, anyway. I needed talking down from the ledge I seemed to have found myself on.

Entering our room, I could see Clover sitting on her bed, engrossed in something on her laptop screen. She looked up at me and instantly said, 'Spill.'

'Spill what?' I asked, shaking my head in wonder at how she could tell I had gossip after only looking at me for a second.

'Spill whatever it is that you wanna tell me. You look fit to burst, plus, you made it across campus super fast.'

'I can walk fast when I want to.' I shrugged, trying to calm down the thoughts racing through my head. Even I could hear the defensiveness in my tone, though.

'Just tell me Sky, and we can talk whatever it is through.'

'So ...' I took a deep breath, and said, 'I may have kissed Ollie earlier.'

I threw myself onto my bed in a super dramatic fashion, the mattress screaming in protest. I covered my ears, knowing that a squeal was about to come out of Clover's mouth.

In 3 ... 2 ... 1 ...

'You WHAT?!' Clover asked, her voice shrill. So loud, I wondered if anybody lingering in the corridor could hear us.

'Well, actually. He kissed me. In the library.'

'With his tongue,' Clover said and started laughing, and I wasn't positive but I reckoned she was trying to make some kind of *Cluedo* reference. You know, the board game with Miss Scarlett and the rope.

'Yeah, with his tongue,' I joked back. Even just talking about it made me visualise it in my mind. I could still feel Ollie's lips on mine and feel his chest pressed up against me; chills covered my arms.

'Wait up a minute!' Clover gasped. 'You're fucking calling him Ollie now, too? Oh hell no, Sky, what on earth are you thinking?!'

'Pretty sure I wasn't really thinking.' I pondered for a moment, and said, 'Actually, I *was* thinking, but they weren't exactly PG thoughts.'

'You definitely weren't thinking, Skylar. This is going to blow up in your face, you know that right?' she asked, her face exasperated.

'It might not,' I said, petulant as a child. I looked away from Clo's evil eye—it seared me.

'Oh, baby girl, it definitely will,' Clover said and looked at me with pity.

'What makes you so sure?' I asked her, mostly because I wanted to believe that things could work out for me. The way Ollie kissed me was so different to what I'd had before. He kissed me with passion, with no restraint, and by God, the boy could do things with his tongue.

'I just know, Sky. I know these boys. I've known them forever and not once has Ollie ever taken an interest in any girl. Not being funny, but you're on scholarship here. Did you not read the rules?'

'Course I did. We read them together and scoffed over them, remember?' I asked, rhetorically.

'Right. So you'll have remembered rule four. The one that

says about dating above your class; and you can bet that you and Ollie dating is something they wouldn't be okay with.'

It surprised me that Clover knew the rules off by heart, number and all. 'But surely he doesn't have to ask for permission?'

'Sort of not the point, Sky. The point is, I find all of this highly suspish,' Clover said, her eyebrows knitted together.

'So, w-what, you don't think Ollie could actually fancy me?' I asked, my lip quivering slightly, a little upset by her statement. I didn't want to be that girl, but her words had hit me in my self-esteem.

'No sweetie, I don't mean that,' Clover said, throwing a compassionate look my way. My bed depressed as she sat down beside me and pulled me into a one-armed hug. 'I just mean that it seems funky to me, that's all. On tour day the boys definitely saw you as a new toy to play with, and now we're meant to just believe that Griff is your friend and that Ollie wants you? I'm sorry, but I don't—I can't.'

'No, I know. I get it. I do.' I hugged her back, so glad that I had her on my side. 'I just need to think about all of this logically. Not get caught up in what happened. Who knows, it may have meant nothing to him and I'm getting all worked up for no reason.'

'I mean this for your sake, I hope not. But yeah girl, keep your guard up just in case it is all bullshit.'

'You're right.'

We dropped the conversation, and Clover moved on to telling me about her day that was totally uneventful compared to mine.

I tuned her out, making encouraging conversation noises every now and again, and thought of the events of the day.

Fuck me. I'd known that I fancied Ollie. Who wouldn't, after all? But I also hadn't expected him to do that, and as much as I talked a good(ish) game with Clover, I was in way over my head. I didn't want to get my hopes up, but I knew I would, anyway; no matter how much I didn't want to.

'Wait, Sky. I heard something about what happened in English.'

'Oh ...' I turned back into her words, sighed and asked, 'What exactly did you hear?'

'That those absolute bitches picked on you, forced the teacher to pick you to read out loud, and took the piss out of your stutter.'

'Yep. That's basically what happened,' I mumbled as moisture filled my eyes. I'd been trying so hard all day to forget about what had happened. I knew that if I put too much energy into thinking about it, I would bawl my eyes out all night and not stop. Something I really did not want to do. I hated crying and was always more likely to cry when angry than when I felt sad. Yeah, I understood how messed up that sounded, but I'd been that way ever since I was a kid.

'I know this is going to sound so fucking stupid Sky, but you really need to ignore the O girls. Or at least try and rise above it all. I've been there, and it's shit.'

'Thanks, I think?'

Although Clo's words hadn't been the best, or the most uplifting, they were the truth—her truth. I could appreciate that she was trying to help me. I still didn't know the full story of Clover's past, and I could sense that now wasn't the time to ask her about it, but I was aware that shit had gone down in her past between her and *them*.

I knew now that all I could do was try and survive this

place. I mean, it had only been in one class and it hadn't been too bad. I just need to grow a thicker skin. Or something.

I planned to ignore *The Set* while I tried my best to put the kiss with Ollie behind me. Easier said than done for sure, but I had to try.

For my sanity.

Chapter Ten

The rest of the school week passed pretty uneventfully.

Well, actually, I was totally bullshitting.

It wasn't completely without drama at all. *The Set* had announced on the third day of school—the day after Ollie had kissed me in the library—both in the hallway and on the Hive, that I was persona non grata to them and that nobody should enjoy my company or make me feel welcome. What that meant exactly, fuck knows. All I knew was that the rest of the student body helped them in their tirade against me.

Clover declared it all to be bullshit the second Odette announced it and had made it obvious that she would stick by me, regardless. She'd said, *"They're just twats, Sky. Definitely not going to let them decide who I can and can't be friends with. I've got your back."*

There was one aspect of it all that I felt positive the O girls couldn't have predicted though, and that was the fact that both

Ollie and Griff ignored them now. They sat with me in every class that we shared, and the four of us had taken to sitting with each other at breakfast, lunch and dinner. I'd told them they didn't need to; especially as Leo had chosen not to leave the girls and still sat with them for meals. I didn't want either of them to feel as if they were choosing me over one of their longest friends—and over school tradition. From what they'd told me, the three of them had been friends since birth. Well, something like that anyway.

When I'd mentioned to them they didn't need to choose me, I got two similar—but also completely different—answers.

Griff had declared that, *"There's nothing those little bitches can do to make me side with them. Gosh, New Girl, what do you take me for? A total dickhead? I'm on your side, Sky."* I'd smiled and hugged him when he'd said that to me. He was slowly growing to be one of my favourite people. Although, let's be honest, there weren't many people fighting for that spot.

When asked, Ollie had said, *"I'm in the best place for me right now. I'm by your side, Sky."*

I did notice the "right now" in Ollie's response, but honestly, I couldn't really expect more than that from him. Not like we meant anything to one another. Yeah, we'd kissed in the library one time, but nothing had happened, or been said, since. He hadn't even brought it up or anything. Not the kiss and not the fact that he'd left me in the library, alone. Even the flirting and whispered dick lines had died down to nothing. Not going to lie, it for sure made me question myself and every interaction we'd had together. Had I made it all up in my mind? Did he not want to talk about it with me? Or was it meant to add an aura of mystery? *Fuck if I knew.*

I tuned into the conversation happening around me.

'So then I said, you telling me you don't want my d in your v? Apparently that was not the right thing to say *at all*. She went and got her brother and told him what I'd said. He was a big motherfucker too,' Griff said, in the middle of telling some story about this girl he'd tried to pull at a school party a few years back.

'Serves you right!' Clover laughed and I could tell she was enjoying the story, even if her expression showed disbelief. Griff had a way of telling a story that gripped you entirely, holding you by the balls until the very last sentence. Even when he wasn't coming across in the best light, you still wanted to give him a hug and keep him safe. Sometimes, he was too much of a cheeky dickhead for his own good.

'It doesn't serve me right at all. I didn't even say anything offensive to her.'

'Pretty sure she got offended when you offered to show her your dick mate,' Ollie said, joining in with the conversation. A smirk on his face, clearly amused at Griff's antics.

The four of us were sitting together in the restaurant-like dining hall, waiting for our food to arrive, and I could sense the eyes of *The Set* on us constantly. Leo, however, paid no attention to his surroundings. He looked so bored, and as if he believed he was completely above the hierarchy bullshit the girls were trying to drag the entire school down into. Whether he agreed with them or not, he still chose to sit with them over us.

None of it made sense to me. Leo was the one who had told me to come to him if the girls had picked on me. So, why he would now choose them and ignore me, confused me slightly. I tried not to think too much about it, though. Leo didn't owe me anything. We'd barely had any interactions with one another after all. Odd, though.

'Narh, that wasn't it at all,' said Griff as he shook his head at Ollie's words. 'I technically never offered to show her my dick. Just offered to put it inside her.'

'Bit of a technicality, mate,' Ollie joked at the same time as Clover spoke.

'Cause that's so much better,' she said, wiping tears from her eyes, the story too much for her. Recently, I'd realised that a lot of Griff's stories revolved around some kind of sexual situation; or something that he'd said or done to some girl or another.

'W-well, I'm sure she felt blessed for you to even offer,' I said, joining in with their banter.

'See, Skylar gets it,' Griff said, putting his arm around me, pulling me flush to him. He did this often, making me feel cared for and happy. 'She's my new favourite. The two of you can piss right off.'

We all reacted to his words at the same time. Clover hit him from his other side. Ollie rolled his eyes, while also looking slightly bemused. I giggled, quickly putting my hand across my mouth in an attempt to stifle the noise.

'Definitely my favourite. Are you sure I can't hear that giggle in a more intimate setting?' Griff made a love heart with his hands and batted his eyelashes at me. Pretty sure he waggled his eyebrows, too.

'Oh, stop,' I said and pushed his arm off of me, and hit him on the head for good measure. This felt good, like I had become a part of something. A part of a real friendship group, and honestly, it felt pretty wicked.

✦

NEARING THE END OF MY SECOND WEEK, I HAD JUST GOT comfortable in my seat next to Griff in Philosophy class when an announcement came over the school speakers.

Would Miss Crescent please make her way to Ms Hawthorn's office. I repeat, Miss Crescent for Ms Hawthorn's office immediately. Thank you.

All eyes in the class turned to me in the back row as I desperately tried to make myself invisible. Luckily for me, I didn't share this class with the worst of the bullies—but there were still some horrible, shitty people trying to make me feel worse.

'Ummm,' said Griff, making the noise a five-year-old did when another kid was in trouble. I jabbed my elbow into his rib. 'Oof, no need to hurt precious cargo, New Girl,' he said.

'Off you go then, Miss Crescent.' Ms Wells smiled at me and I packed up my table as swiftly as I could. I wondered what Ms Hawthorn wanted to talk to me about. I hadn't seen or heard of her since the assembly on the first morning, and I couldn't put my finger on what she wanted to say to me.

I made my way across campus to the main building where the administration offices were. I'd slowly become accustomed to the strange school layout, and now it didn't take me any time at all to get around.

I knocked on the door marked Ms Hawthorn and waited.

'Enter,' her voice came from through the thick wooden door.

I walked into the room and took in my surroundings. The room was quite large, with dark wood panelling and an enormous fireplace on the left-hand side. Ms Hawthorn's table was directly in front of me, with her seat facing the door and a large black ornate empty chair sitting empty across from her. It looked a lot fancier than any office I'd seen in my old school; but let's be honest, my old school wasn't for the obscenely rich. The kids (and the parents) there were lucky if they could afford to pay the bills and buy food.

'Take a seat, Miss Crescent,' she said. Her tone of voice was cold; seemed she hadn't changed her opinion of me in the two weeks I'd been a student here. She hadn't actually looked up at me since I'd entered.

I took the empty seat, and for at least a minute the two of us existed in silence, as I waited for her to finish reading the paperwork on the desk in front of her. After what felt like an eternity, she finally looked up at me and frowned.

'How are things going for you here at the Academy, Miss Crescent?'

'Err, f-fine thanks, Ms Hawthorn,' I said, rinsing my hands together under the table. A habit that would make Lady Macbeth proud.

'I take it you've settled in well to your classes and made some friends?' she asked. Her shrewd grey eyes were looking into my soul for real. There was something off about this lady, something that made me feel strange deep down.

'Yes, thank you. Clover has been a good friend. So has Griff.'

At that, her face soured like she was sucking on a lemon. It made the wrinkles around her mouth even more prominent; even more grotesque. Reminded me of that dude in that old *Dracula* horror film from the twenties.

'Yes, I've heard that Master Cooper has been paying close attention to you.' Her eyes were intense; focused on mine.

'Please remember, Miss Crescent, that we expect you to be on your best behaviour while you are a student at this establishment. I've been hearing some unsavoury things about you.'

Confused by her words, the heat of her gaze burning, I maintained eye contact with her. Knowing that if I broke it, she would think even less of me than she already seemed to.

'Yes, Ms,' I said in response, trying to sound polite. I didn't want to get on her nasty side, but I felt as though I may already be there.

'You may return to class. I'll be talking to you more, soon,' she said, in a final, ominous sort of way.

Clearly dismissed, I stood up from my seat.

Ms Hawthorn had already returned to her paperwork and clearly wanted me gone. Honestly, it made no sense to me why she'd wanted to see me in the first place. Her questions weren't overly important. Maybe she just wanted to warn me once again about my behaviour. *How odd.*

Leaving the room, I closed the door softly behind me and turned to face the corridor.

'SHIT!' I said, as I physically startled. Ollie stood outside the door on the opposite side of the hall, leaning up against the wall, a smirk planted on his face.

'Sorry, I didn't mean to scare you,' he said, looking contrite. Or at least, I thought he did. It was always hard to tell whether somebody was being true or genuinely sorry.

'That's o-okay. What are you d-doing here?'

'I heard the announcement on the tannoy. Wanted to see what the old bat wanted with you.' He gestured towards the door I'd just closed.

'Oh, well, t-thanks. I g-guess.'

'So, what did she want?' he asked, looking all sorts of handsome. He looked so good my mind was thinking of licking him, and not of the question he'd just asked.

'Errr ...' I trailed off. I'd lost all of my brain cells in the last twenty seconds. Ollie's dark hair was perfectly styled and his blue eyes were so clear, I could easily get lost in them.

'You okay?' he asked, looking like he wanted to laugh at me but was reining it in. His smile was so wide that even his teeth were showing; a rare sight from him.

'I'm f-fine.' I smiled back. Pushing my hair behind my ears, I tried to stay still and not fidget. Nerves filled me. This was the first time we'd been alone together since the library—since the kiss.

'So, are you going to tell me what that cow wanted?'

'S-she just wanted to know how I was g-getting on. F-friends and things.'

'And what exactly did you tell her?'

'A-about Clover and Griff.' I could tell this displeased him. His smile dimmed a little, and a crease formed at the edge of each eye.

'Are we not friends then, Little One?' he questioned, one side of his mouth tilting upward.

'I don't know,' I said, deciding to go with honesty.

It was probably the most honest I'd been in a while. I didn't know if I would class him as a friend or not. I'd started (slowly) to think that maybe we could be friends, but then he went and left me cold and alone in the library.

'Well, guess I'll just have to do something to change your mind.'

'L-like what?'

'L-like this,' Ollie said, mimicking my stutter. He pushed me against the wall and kissed me.

This kiss was so different to the one he'd given me in the library. This kiss was gentle. A soft brushing together of lips. His hands softly cupped my face; unlike last time when they had roamed all over me.

The kiss stopped not long after it started. It was as if we'd both come to our senses at the same time and remembered that we were in the school corridor, out in the open, outside Ms Hawthorn's office.

'W-what was that for?' I stuttered. I took a step away from him because I needed some space. It was rare that I let people into my personal bubble, and even though I wanted Ollie, I also needed to keep my head about me. I couldn't let his chiselled jaw and beautiful eyes pull me in.

'I just needed to do that,' he said, his smile once again wide and carefree. 'I'll see you later.'

He left me standing there, alone once again. But at the end of the corridor he turned, and shouted back to me, 'There's a party. Friday night in the woods. Be there.'

He knew I couldn't turn down that invitation. Not without having *The Set* come after me even harder than they already were, and believe me, they'd started coming for me pretty hard. Every class I shared with them, they had turned all the other students against me.

So far, they had attempted nothing physical. It'd all been words, or mean looks, and gestures across the dining hall or a classroom. But I knew it was only a matter of time until they escalated.

Bullies and bitches usually do.

As I headed to my next class, all I could think about was how well Clover would take Ollie's invite to the party in the woods, and if she'd even come with me.

Chapter Eleven

Friday night arrived, and we were getting ready to go out. I didn't own many party style clothes but luckily Clover had a few pieces that I could borrow; although we weren't the same size, we could get away with sharing some items.

"Are we even allowed to party in the woods?" I asked Clo after Ollie had invited me in the corridor by Hawthorn's office.

"Technically ... No. But none of the faculty ever pay any notice to what the rich kids get up to. After all, the generosity of the school benefactors pays their salaries. Benefactors who are the parents of the shitty rich kid students that go here. The only way they'd get involved is if something bad happened." Clover's eyes went out of focus for a split second and I pretended that I didn't notice. "Well, you'd think so anyway," she muttered, almost too quiet for me to hear.

"Sorry, what?" I asked, hoping that she'd clarify her mutter. But Clover didn't take the bait.

"Oh, nothing. Just me mumbling to myself as usual," she said, adding an odd 'ha' at the end, to sell it as a quirk of hers or something similar, but I'd honestly never heard her talking to herself. Of course, that wasn't to say that she didn't. I did it frequently.

So yeah, Clover had sort of—not really, but kind of—agreed to come to the party with me tonight. Mostly I reckoned she had agreed to come because she didn't trust Ollie and wanted to keep an eye on me.

The whole of the school had been buzzing about it; it had been the main conversation topic in the dining hall this last week. I'd also heard a few mentions of it while sitting in classes, too.

'Are you sure we need to go tonight? Wouldn't you rather we stay in and just eat pizza?' Clover almost pleaded with me. I understood her qualms. I worried about it all, too. But Ollie *had* asked me to attend, and I couldn't break the rule. Some girl had been suspended for the month a week ago because she'd looked at Odette wrong.

'You don't need to come with me if you're really against it, Clo,' I said, looking at her across the room. She was sitting on her bed, still in her uniform as she hadn't got dressed yet. 'But, I would love to have you there with me. You *know* I can't bail.'

'I *know* that and that is the only reason I'm coming with you,' Clover said. She pouted, jutting her bottom lip out slightly, and widened her eyes at me. It was the kind of facial expression that children would pull at their parents in order to get a later bedtime, or obtain some kind of toy.

'Don't give me that look, Clo. It's making me want to give in and give you your way. But I can't and if I'm being a little honest here, I don't want to.'

I'd tried to come to terms with the fact that a large part of me did really want to go tonight. I'd also tried to tell Clover multiple times that I wanted to go in a way that wouldn't cause conflict between us. Although I knew that Clover and I were now pretty good friends, it had still only been a couple of weeks and I didn't want to rock the boat.

Already dressed and ready to go, I waited on Clover to be ready too. Clover and I had decided that I should wear something classed as a mix between casual and sexy. We went with; high-waisted dark denim jeans, a white bardot crop top and white plimsolls. My light silver purple-ish hair styled in loose waves came down to just past my shoulders. Before coming here, I'd never made much of an effort with my appearance— except my hair. My hair was something I'd always changed. Changing my hair colour and style always made me feel better when my anxiety became overwhelming. It was something I could do for myself, too; no friends or trips outside of the house needed. Minimal cost if you got the home box dyes.

Clover dressed herself in black skinny jeans, a band shirt, and black Converse. She looked like a rocker chick, with her eyeliner super thick around her green eyes, making them stand out.

'You look hot!' I told her, raising my eyebrows up and down at her. She chucked a pillow at me.

'Stop it, I look ite. You, however, look mighty fine. The boys won't know what to do with themselves,' Clover said, grabbing both our phones. She put hers in her pocket and passed mine to me. 'By boys I meant Ollie and Griff, if you weren't sure.'

'You know Leo will totally be into how you look right now,' I replied. I wanted so badly to know more about her history with Leo, and I was sort of hoping that Clover would drink enough tonight for her tongue to loosen. Loose lips sink ships, and all that.

'I give zero shits about what Leo thinks,' she said. The bite in her tone shut me up. 'Let's go.'

I opened our door and nearly went head first into a very hard chest.

My eyes tracked upward, and I looked into Griff's eyes—I'd never noticed before, but his eyes made me think of a meadow on a summer's day. They were that truly rare colour; blue edges with a green centre. He looked debonair, or in less fancy terms, really fucking hot.

'Woah. Be careful, Sky,' Griff said. His smile was super wide, the dimples in his cheeks pressed in, his eyes shining with amusement. 'You might run into somebody who doesn't want to let you go.'

'Oh, ha, ha.' I faked laughter, smiling back at him. 'Who would that be?'

His expression changed. His eyes darkened, and I worried that I'd said the wrong thing completely.

'There are beasts lurking around every corner, New Girl. Remember that,' he said, his tone one of warning.

'O-okay,' I said, having no idea what else to say to him.

I looked around us. There was nobody around, and I assumed that was because of the party. From what I'd gathered from Clo, pretty much everybody went. Even the younger years would try and sneak out from their heavily guarded dorms to join in.

✦

THE OUTSKIRTS OF THE WOODS WERE ONLY AROUND A five-minute walk from campus, but the clearing holding the party was another fifteen minutes' walk away.

'I didn't realise the surrounding land was this big,' I said, after we'd been walking in silence for some time.

'Well, yeah. The school's on a hill too, remember? So all the land up here belongs to the Hawthorn family,' Clover replied.

'I totally forgot that Leo's family owned this place. Is he related to Ms Hawthorn?' I asked. I didn't know why I'd never made the connection before.

'Sadly, yes. His aunt,' Griff said, looking at me, and I realised it must be because Clover already knew. 'But he never acknowledges her. Best not to bring it up with him.'

'Pft, yeah, like I even talk to Leo, anyway. He's taken his side,' I said.

He had, after all, hadn't he? He may have told me that first night that I could come to him, but absolutely none of his actions afterward had backed up that claim.

'Of course he has, because he's a massive cumstain who should really just piss off,' Clover said, her eyebrows furrowing, making it clear just how much she disliked Leo.

'A massive cumstain?' I asked and laughed at her, raising my eyebrows in response when she glanced over at me. She was always so serious, but also comical, when it came to him. Even when she didn't mean to be. Like how young children acted on a playground with the people they fancied.

'You know what I mean!' Clo said, joining in the laughter though, which stopped abruptly when we came to the dimly lit clearing. Tiny lanterns placed in the trees were giving off little light, creating a seedy effect.

The music was loud, the bass thumping and vibrating in the soles of my shoes as it made its way up my legs, and there were bodies everywhere. Some stood on what looked like a makeshift dance-floor, grinding on one another. Others dotted around, standing in friendship groups; talking, playing drinking games or hooking up. It was all happening around us and I felt overwhelmed. I'd never been to a party like this before—I'd never had friends in school that would invite me to anything like this.

I spotted Ollie across the clearing, standing with Leo, but when he saw we'd arrived, he left Leo's side and came straight over to us.

'You're finally here,' he said, relieved. 'You look beautiful.' Ollie kissed my cheek in greeting and then said a quick hello to Clover and Griff. 'Fancy a drink?'

'P-please,' I said, nodding at him. I watched as he headed over to a table set up with bottles of booze covering it, all different types and strengths. I hoped that Ollie didn't get me anything too strong. I'd never been much of a drinker and was so worried that I'd end up drinking too much and embarrass myself. Clover and I had had a big dinner though, so we wouldn't be drinking on an empty stomach.

'Remember the motto, Sky.' Clover grabbed my attention from Ollie and shook my shoulder. 'Beer before liquor, never sicker.'

'Liquor before beer, in the clear,' we said together, ending the fun phrase that Clo had taught me earlier.

I took the drink Ollie offered me on his return and took a tentative sip. The taste of cranberry and vodka hit me. It wasn't overly strong, and it tasted alright, so I continued to sip at it.

'Is this your first party then, New Girl?' he asked.

'Y-yeah. Is it that obvious?' I asked back, worried I had embarrassed myself already.

'You look nervous,' he said. His hand touched my cheek and slowly trailed down my neck. The touch was sensual and full of warmth. My breath hitched. My stomach fluttered, and I felt nauseous. All I could think in that moment was I hoped I didn't look as much of a fucking lemon as I thought I did. My face must've stuck in a confused expression because Ollie looked at me and raised his brow in question.

'You okay, Sky?' he asked. His eyes raised and his lips forming slowly into a smirk, I wanted nothing more than for him to kiss me properly.

'O-of course. I'm solid,' I said. *Solid? When the fuck had I ever said that before?* Ground, swallow me whole.

'Glad to hear it,' he said, kissing my cheek. I didn't know how to react—he'd never shown me affection in public before. He sauntered to stand behind me, wrapping his arms around my shoulders, as he leant his head on top of mine. I was the perfect height for him to do it comfortably. Bewildered by his actions, I had no idea of how to react to any of this. Yeah, we'd kissed in the library (and the hallway that one time), but he had said nothing about either instance since. Was I meant to assume something here?

I felt so new to this shit. I had entered a world with multiple rules that I knew fuck all about.

✦

A few drinks into the evening, I started to feel the effects of them. To the point where I started seeing two of

Ollie. They were both hot. Even my stutter had taken a leave of absence for the night.

'Want to dance?' Ollie asked. He had snuck up behind me as I was sitting on the floor playing *Never Have I Ever*, with Griff and Clover, and rubbed my shoulders, kneading out the knots there.

I looked back and up at him. He moved his hands, so that one was now directly in front of my face, offering to help me stand. I took it, and the force of the pull had me hurtling into him at a faster speed than I'd expected.

'Woah, be careful there, Little Lady. Maybe you should slow down on the drinks,' he said, a caring look in his eyes.

'I'm okay, Big Boy,' I said. I thought that maybe I was at the point of slurring my words, but I couldn't be sure. They sounded perfectly fine to me.

Ollie laughed at me and said, 'Big Boy? I'll prove it one day.' My face heated. He had me running hot and cold all the time, so much it made me worried I'd get chilblains.

'Come dance,' he said, demanding. People filled the dance-floor, bodies thrummed to the beat, and more couples than not reenacted the opening credits from *Dirty Dancing*, or they were full on making out; no care of who could see them.

Ollie held me close, and we swayed close together.

'We can't slow dance to this,' I told him quietly. The music was upbeat, and it made me feel awkward to step side to side to it. I'd never been much of a dancer. Rhythm did *not* come naturally to me.

'We can make it whatever we want it to be,' he whispered. Fingers started touching me, fumbling with the top button of my jeans, trying to make their way inside.

'What are you doing?' I asked, shocked. I wanted him to,

but also, like, what? We were in full sight of a *lot* of people. Was this normal horny teenage behaviour?

'I know you want me to touch you. You've been giving off signals ever since we first met that you want me,' Ollie said, his hands still travelling around my hip bones, tickling me.

Lips touched mine. The fingers still reaching, trying to breach my underwear, and make their way to the place I wanted them most.

'Can't we move into the shadows?' I asked. I stopped his hand and grabbed it in mine, intertwining our fingers. I led him away from the spot we'd been in and headed further into the trees. Far enough away that we couldn't be seen, but close enough that we could still feel the bass; could still feel the thrum of energy in the air.

This time, it was me who initiated the contact between us.

I kissed him first, grabbing his face between my hands and pulling it down to my level. I felt the moment Ollie snapped. His lips pushed against mine. My hands moved down to his chest, his pecs felt hard underneath my fingertips, and his abs were even harder. He pushed me into a tree, using his strength to pin me there. He used his hands to move my thighs, causing my legs to fall apart in a wider stance. I could feel his dick pressing into my right thigh, and all I wanted to do was touch him. My hand moved towards the top of his jeans, but he stopped me by raising my hand to his mouth and biting down on it, hard.

I could feel my wetness, and every move he made, every touch, made me wetter. My jean buttons were still undone, and I didn't think he could fit his hand inside of them, but he proved me wrong straight away. His fingers were now making their way into my lace underwear, leaving a trail of heat in every place they touched. My skin on fire, the burn worth it.

Ollie plunged a finger inside of me, hard, and I gasped at the sudden invasion. There had been no buildup. No teasing.

'Your moans are so fucking sexy,' Ollie said. His mouth on my ear, and his whispers, causing goosebumps to raise along my arms.

'Don't stop,' I said.

His finger started moving in and out of me hard, building in speed, and then when I thought I could take no more, he added another finger.

'You're killing me,' he moaned. 'One day Sky, I swear, you *will* stutter because of my dick.'

I could feel an orgasm coming, climbing with each stroke of his thumb on my clit, and each time his fingers moved inside of me, I could feel it getting stronger.

It was when Ollie bit my bottom lip—his teeth sharp, causing blood to rise up and spot on my lip—and added a third finger that my climax hit me. It was like I'd been climbing until there was nowhere else to go. Light-headed and dazed, I looked into Ollie's burning gaze.

'So fucking hot,' he whispered, almost too quiet for me to hear. Probably because my pulse was loud in my ears and I couldn't hear anything else.

I sighed contentedly. A chill ran up my arms, and the cold became more obvious than it had a moment ago. It creeped back in slowly now that I was coming down from the high my body had been on. My mouth felt dry; the aftertaste of blood still coating my tongue.

Ollie stepped away from me, creating distance between us,

and raked his hand through his hair that looked slightly gold in the moonlight.

'I'll go get us another drink,' he said and walked away; back towards the clearing where the party was still raging on.

He returned after five minutes, maybe? I'd lost all track of time at that point. He had a cup in each hand. Passing me one, he said, 'Here you go, Little One.'

I took the cup and gulped down the liquid inside. The orgasm he'd given me was still moving through my body like little shock waves. I drank it all; it was the strongest drink I'd had all night, but also rather sweet tasting.

'You'll feel better soon,' he said, breathless. He hugged me close once again.

The hug felt warm and comforting. I hadn't ever been much of a hugger; I never instigated contact with people first. His arms were no longer bare. He must've had a jacket stashed out here somewhere, knowing how cold it would get. Wish I'd thought to do the same thing. An off the shoulder crop top was *not* the perfect September attire, especially when at the top of a cold, windy hill in England.

'I know. You're here after all. Nothing bad can happen to me now,' I whispered against his chest.

The last thing I remembered was Ollie's face gazing at me intently. The moonlight hitting one side of his face, almost like a mask. It made his features look sinister.

A hard glint had formed in his eyes and they looked darker than they normally did.

Then everything went black.

Chapter Twelve

I woke up, feeling the worst I'd ever felt in, probably, my entire life. I knew when people said that, it could sound like an exaggeration, but I promise you I wasn't making this up. My head felt as if a truck had hit it, or maybe like a brick had repeatedly smashed down onto my skull during the evening that I was unaware of. My throat was so dry, scratched, and it felt like the worst cold I'd ever had. I needed water and some paracetamol stat.

I opened my eyes and tried to get my bearings. I had no idea where the fuck I was. The room looked familiar—in the way dorm rooms do—so I knew I was still on school property somewhere. But with no current recollection of last night's events after a certain point, I couldn't place myself.

Beads of sweat formed on my arms, and I shook with an all body chill. My anxiety always got worse when things like this happened; things outside of my routine or the norm. *This* was one hundred percent outside of the norm. I hated surprises, or not knowing the end of a film before the start, and this entire morning felt like one massive surprise.

I could tell that I was in a boy's bedroom, but there wasn't anything too obvious on the walls and the smell wasn't too bad to give it away. It *did* smell like a boy lived here, though. The scent of tobacco and vanilla was strong in the air, and slowly, as my mind caught up to my nose, I realised where I knew that specific smell from. It had been invading my personal bubble ever since school had started; no matter that I'd tried to avoid it.

I startled when I heard a door open nearby.

Looking around quickly, I noticed that this room had an en-suite attached. This room only had one bed too—well, it was a suite more than a room. And then there in the doorway of the bathroom stood Ollie. In a towel. Looking fine as fuck.

Oh, fucking hell.

Of course, it was Ollie's room that I was in. Which meant I was currently laying in Ollie's bed. Ollie's very large king-size bed that could definitely have fit an Ollie shaped body next to my smaller one. The pillow next to me had a head shaped indent, confirming to me even more that I had slept next to Ollie. The guy who had fingered me up against a tree last night before everything went black. *Shit.*

My cheeks were aflame.

I took a quick inventory of my clothes and noticed that I was still wearing underwear but that my jeans and crop top were suspiciously missing.

Double shit.

Double fuck.

Double everything.

I decided that I would not be the one to break the silence. I tried to pretend that I was still asleep. Like I hadn't noticed where I was. Like I hadn't seen him two seconds ago standing in only a towel, with water droplets still making their way down his abs. His very fine abs.

'I know you're awake, Sky,' Ollie said, humour in his tone, hinting that he knew I was faking sleep.

'H-how do you know that?' I asked, keeping my eyes closed. I wanted to still have some form of deniability. Also, my stutter was back? I seemed to recall that at some point last night I'd been able to talk to Ollie in the same way I did Clover and Griff. Probably had to do with the fact that I'd had some liquid courage.

'Cause I've been beside you all night and your breathing was different when you were asleep,' he replied. His smile reminded me of Griff's. Cheeky and all-knowing.

'Surely, you w-were asleep too? How can you be so s-sure?' I asked.

'I didn't exactly sleep, New Girl. Had to stay awake and watch you. Be responsible. You know, make sure you didn't choke on your own vomit and all that good shit,' he said.

'What?!' I sputtered. I knew I'd had a bit to drink last night, and yeah, I couldn't remember past a certain point, but still. Surely I hadn't been *that* wasted?

'You don't remember much, do you?' he asked me, but I was pretty sure it was a rhetorical question, so I chose not to answer with words. The look of pure befuddlement I gave him must have tipped him off, though. 'Someone drugged you last night.'

He didn't sugarcoat it. Didn't slowly build up to it. Nope. Not Ollie. He just threw the words out there, with no thought to how they would sound. It was almost careless and unfeeling.

'I was WHAT?!' I raised my voice at him, my displeasure coming out in every syllable. Thinking I'd got drunk and not understanding my limits had been bad enough, but to hear that someone had drugged me, in such a casual manner, flabbergasted me—so much so, I'd thought of the word flabbergasted.

'Somebody spiked your drink. You must've accepted one that the girls had tampered with, or put yours down at some point,' he said, telling me as if it was the only explanation.

'B-but I didn't, it was in my hand at all times,' I said. I knew I didn't. It was something I had been so conscious of after reading one too many horror stories online about girls that had been date raped. 'I only took drinks from Clover, Griff or you.'

'You must have done, Sky. There's no shame in it.'

'Ollie, I swear to you I didn't,' I said, in an indignant tone, but I couldn't find it in myself to care that I could be coming across rude. I just knew that I was more cautious than that.

'Well, somehow your drink *was* messed with and I offered to bring you up here and look after you. The faculty's less likely to be monitoring these halls, especially on a weekend.'

I rolled my eyes. Then regretted it two point five seconds later as it made my head pound even more. I believed him about the faculty not monitoring these halls as closely, though. Not that Clover and I had seen them often, but every now and again we would see a caretaker or hall monitor outside our room in the corridor making sure that nothing was amiss.

I could tell that Ollie didn't believe me. That I'd disappointed him somehow in a way that didn't quite make sense to me yet. Oh, let's be fucking honest. None of this was making sense to me. All I knew was that I hadn't been careless with my drink, like Ollie was implying.

Ollie sat on the edge of the bed facing me, still wrapped in only a towel.

'I need to let Clover know where I am,' I told him.

'She knows where you are, New Girl. It took all four of us to get you back here last night,' he said, smirking.

'The f-four of you?' I asked, puzzled. Not like there were many people at this school who would help me, and we were a three without adding me.

'Yeah, me, Griff, Clover and Leo,' he said, as if it was the most obvious answer in the world.

Ah, that made a sort of sense. I felt sure they had roped Leo in to help when the others were struggling with me. I highly doubted he'd offered out of the goodness of his heart.

'Oh, right,' I said.

'There was no way I could've done it by myself. You weren't able to control your limbs, and you kept telling me how you wished that I *had* found out what your stutter sounds like with my dick inside you.'

I covered my burning face with the duvet in shame, even though I had no way of knowing whether he was even telling me the truth. You know when you could feel a blush on your face, but you had no idea how to stop it from happening? Yeah, that was happening to me right now.

'I've never mentioned it before, but you are really quite cute sometimes, Sky,' he said and chuckled. Even his chuckle sounded X-rated to me

'Are you trying to m-make me feel worse?' I asked him, after making a shrieking noise I wanted to forget I'd ever made. 'What time is it?'

'Ten. We missed breakfast but, lucky for you, I got Griff to deliver some to us before the buffet closed.'

'Don't really f-feel like eating.' I swallowed hard again, trying to get the lump out of my throat that seemed to have taken root there, and said, 'A drink would be g-great though.'

Ollie instantly got up and moved to the kitchenette area on the left-hand side of the room that I hadn't noticed on my earlier perusal of the room. Which, yeah, fair? I'd been freaked out by waking up in a strange room, after all. I'd let myself off for not noticing it.

Ollie came back with a glass of water; I took it and chugged it down in one go. He instantly took the empty glass from me and went to refill it.

He handed the glass back, and I grabbed it, and while taking small sips, I regarded him.

'Thank you. F-for looking after me, I mean—not for accusing me of being irresponsible,' I said.

Ollie's eyes warmed. I could swim in the blue of his eyes, seriously. They looked like that perfect ocean colour, the colour the sea was in places that weren't England, anyway.

'I'm not a *total* dick, Sky. I wouldn't have left you like that,' he said as he lay down beside me, on top of the cover, keeping a small distance between us. 'And we *will* find out who did this to you.'

'S-surely there's only four suspects?' I asked, irritated. It made total sense that *The Set* did this to me, right? I knew I had made no friends, but drugging somebody was a step further than mean comments during class.

'You think the O girls did this?' he asked. I'd never heard him call them that before. Come to think of it, he'd never really referred to them as anything at all. Even though they'd been the topic of conversation more than once recently. Ollie had never said more than a few words about their actions, choosing to stay silent.

'Who else would?' I asked, feeling like we were going around in circles.

Slowly, the two of us gravitated towards one another on the bed. His breath felt warm on my face, his eyes staring into mine as I told him, 'They've m-made it clear that they hate me.'

'Seems bold, even for them,' he said, dismissing me instantly, but softened the blow of his words by tucking a piece of my hair behind my ear.

'D-does it? I heard from Clover that somebody d-died last year?' I asked, curious, even though I knew I was pushing my luck with him.

'That's nothing for you to worry about,' he said, dismissing me once again. I was about to prod him more; try and get more details from him, but his face told me not to. His chiselled jaw clenched tight.

I didn't even want to examine what this meant about me, but my God, he looked even hotter when angry; I'd always found that in books and films, I was more attracted to the *bad boys*. Not that I'd actually met any before coming here.

'Whatever happened last year has nothing to do with what's happening now. I can promise you that,' he bit out.

'Yeah?' I asked, my tone unsure.

'Skylar, I swear to you, this is all because the girls are feeling threatened by you. You're beautiful, funny and every-thing they wish they could be. You've caught my eye and Griff loves you. Even Leo's got a soft spot for you.'

He was full of shit, right? That wasn't how it was at all.

Yeah, I was friendly with Griff and Ollie *seemed* to be interested in me, but that could just be because he wanted in my pants. The part about Leo was a stretch, though. The boy barely looked my way, and if he did, I assumed it was only because I was usually sitting next to Clover.

'You're s-such a liar,' I said and giggled, his words tickling me.

'Either way, those girls are bitches. Don't let them get to you, no matter what, okay? They're not worth it,' Ollie said, reaching out to trail his finger up and down my arm, causing goosebumps to rise once again.

'B-bitches with power. The other kids follow them.'

'I'll see what I can do,' he said. His ominous tone gave me pause. I thought he'd already been trying to see what he could do, but maybe the fact that someone drugged me had made him realise this was more serious than some kids taking the piss out of a girl's stutter.

The rest of the day, the two of us stayed in Ollie's room until dinner—in silence, mostly. We watched films and just lay next to one another, not touching, but comfortable in one another's company.

I didn't want to imagine how badly last night could have gone if he hadn't rescued me—hadn't looked after me. He may be a self-entitled dick, but last night, he'd been my saviour.

Okay, yeah, bit dramatic Sky.

But still, I couldn't overlook that, no matter how much I probably *should*.

Chapter Thirteen

My third week at Hawthorn Academy started the same as the others, but as the days went by, things kept getting worse and worse.

It all began when Oralie and Ophelia cornered me in the girl's toilets on Tuesday. I'd gone in there to, obviously, use the facilities, but when I'd exited the stall, the two of them were standing by the sinks waiting for me.

'Look who it is, Lee. The trashy, charity tramp,' Ophelia said. Her face was one of disgust. Her over-enhanced top lip curled upward and her eyes were narrowed into slits.

'Eurgh. What are you looking at, slut?' Oralie asked, equally livid, her face scrunched up with distaste.

'I-I'm just looking ahead?' My words coming out as a question, when really I'd wanted to sound assertive.

Even though the two of them had been making English class unbearable and were encouraging everybody to pick on me throughout the school day, I usually had either Clover,

Ollie or Griff with me. People would only say so much in front of the guys and nobody had taken anything beyond words yet, but I could feel it brewing. I knew *The Set* wouldn't stop at just slander, and I'd known that the time would come where things would escalate. Seemed today was that day.

'Nobody wants you here, skank,' Ophelia said as Oralie nodded beside her. They were standing together, a united front; one with her hands on her hips and the other with their arms crossed across their inflated chest—*Ophelia's got the fake chest, if you were wondering.*

'I'm here on scholarship. I d-didn't even choose to be here,' I said. They knew that, too. Even now, after being here a few weeks, I still wasn't sure whether I preferred it here over my old school. The only two parts that were a win for me were my friendship with Clover and the fact I didn't have to live with my mum and Andy anymore. Who, funnily enough, I hadn't heard from since I left.

'We can tell,' Oralie said, looking super smug, probably because her family could afford her tuition here. 'That you're poor, I mean.'

'You're such a little bitch. I thought at first you were putting the stutter on to get attention, but now it's clear that you're actually a scared, pathetic, pussy,' said Ophelia.

The two of them advanced towards me in tandem. I'd have been impressed if I wasn't so alarmed that they would do me actual physical harm. I couldn't recall if anybody had seen me enter the bathroom, and honestly, why would anybody take notice of that?

'Maybe we need to teach you a lesson.'

As soon as Ophelia had said those words, Oralie pounced faster than a tiger and grabbed both of my arms and held them behind my back, gripping them tightly in place. Not wanting to waste a golden opportunity, Ophelia punched me in the middle of my face, catching me on the nose, causing blood to gush out.

Shit.

That hurt. A lot.

I couldn't give them the satisfaction of letting them know just how much. Still, Ophelia kept hitting me; punching me in the face, the arm, stomach. Anywhere she could. When I fell to the floor, both of them viciously kicked me. My stomach was tender, and I knew this was going to bruise like a bitch.

The punching and kicking continued, and it felt like they were hitting me in various ways for at least ten minutes, but in reality, it was probably less than five. My vision had blurred, my anxiety peaking once again. I *was* getting beat on by two bitches, after all.

In the distance, I could hear muffled shouting. The noise slowly got closer to where we were located.

Lucky for me, the girls heard the shouts and realised that they were pushing their luck. Somebody was bound to enter the room; it was obvious to me how shocked they were that they'd gone as far as they had.

'Shit,' Ophelia said and hit Oralie in the shoulder to stop her from kicking me more. 'This isn't over charity trash.' Her spit hit my lip, yet I didn't wipe it away. I had a lot more to worry about at this point—like the intense pain in my side.

With one last kick, they left the room quickly. Leaving me sprawled out on the floor, unable to move my side in a lot of pain, and I was covered in blood from my nose.

The door didn't fully close though as somebody pushed it open, catching it with their foot before it slammed.

'What the fuck happened here, Sky?' Clover's voice reached my ears. Tears filled my eyes at the sight of her. I wanted to tell her what had happened, but the last kick winded me and I was struggling to catch my breath. 'Shit, guys! She's in here!'

Her yell caused both Ollie and Griff to storm into the room. Their fury coming off of them in waves.

'Who did this, New Girl?' Griff asked in an urgent tone.

I looked up at Griff, and the look on his face was so unlike his normal face. There was no hint of a cheeky smile now, or any dimples for that matter, and I did not want to be Ophelia or Oralie when he caught up with them.

'O-oralie ... and ... Ophelia,' I said, still trying to catch my breath, gulping in air and hoping my vision wouldn't go spotty. It irritated me how much I seemed to have blacked out in the last three weeks. It was ridiculous and if it was happening to anybody else; I'd think they *were* bullshitting for attention like the O girls had accused me of.

'Leo needs to put them on a fucking leash,' Ollie said, spit spraying from his mouth. He looked so mad; a beast, ready to rip the heads off of those responsible. Even I could admit I was slightly scared of him at that moment. I'd never seen this dark of an expression on his face before, and I was so glad that he didn't aim it at me. Ollie looked at Griff. 'Go find Leo and tell him about this,' he said, his words a command.

Griff was leaning over me, and Clover was hovering nearby, feeling out of place. When neither of them moved to follow Ollie's instructions he roared out, 'Now!'

Griff stood, leaving the room in a hurry, but not before he kissed my cheek and whispered some words in my ear that I couldn't recall even a moment afterward.

Hands helped me to sit up, and my breathing returned to normal. My nose had stopped bleeding and other than feeling a little swollen when I prodded it, I didn't think it was broken like I'd first feared.

'How are you feeling?' Clover asked—more demanded. I understood it though, I'd probably be acting the same way if she was in my position. I would hate not knowing whether they hurt her more than the eye could see.

'S-sore,' I groaned, holding my side. Lifting my shirt, I could see the bruises already forming. Swirls of pink and red blooming under my skin. The repeated kicks to my side and stomach were going to leave their mark for a while. 'I-I wasn't able to s-stop them. H-held my arms back.'

'Shh. Let's get you to our room,' Clo whispered.

'No. She'll come back to my room where I can keep an eye on her,' Ollie ordered.

'You've done enough,' Clover spat out. If a look could kill, then Ollie would be dead with the way Clover was looking at him as she told him, 'This is all your fault.'

'And how do you gather that?' he asked, in a clipped tone.

'After the party Friday, after they'd *drugged* Skylar, you knew the girls would escalate.'

'I suggest you stop right there, Clover. Just because you're Sky's best friend doesn't mean you can talk to a member of *The Sect* like this,' Ollie said, his lips forming a sneer.

Did Ollie just refer to *The Sect* and himself in the same sentence? *Odd.* I was a little preoccupied with trying to prevent Clover from clocking him one, though. The two of them had been wary of each other before today, but I never thought they'd actually come to blows. Especially over something as stupid as my safety.

'Guys, stop. I just want to g-get up off of the bathroom floor,' I pleaded to them.

Clover rushed to help me up, and I used her body to hold myself up. I felt like Quasimodo, all hunched over and standing awkwardly.

'Come on,' Clo said to me.

The hallway was clear of students when we exited, luckily. I had heard no bells while I was in there, but a new period must have started. I'd been in there a while, after all, and I'd entered between classes.

Slowly, we made our way across campus; me limping beside Clover. Ollie on the other side of me, staying close just in case I needed him. It surprised me he hadn't demanded that Clover move, but I thought maybe the two of them were trying to be civil just so I would get back to my room and rest.

After what felt like years, we finally made it back to the room Clover and I shared. Clearly, by being the one to steer me, she'd got her way and got to decide what room I went to. I just wanted to get into a bed—any bed.

'Do you want to shower?' Clo asked, and I nodded in response. I wanted to wash, but if I was being honest, I wanted to soak in the bath—I was a bath girl through and through. I'd never understood the appeal of showers. Standing up would never be relaxing to me.

'I could help with that,' Ollie said plainly. No ulterior motive hidden in his tone that I could hear. I would've been annoyed if Ollie had used a sleazy tone, but luckily for his balls, he sounded like he genuinely wanted to help me. A large part of me wanted him to help, he had the strength to hold me up, but an even larger part of me wasn't ready for that. It was next level shit.

I'd never been naked in front of a guy, and it was okay to admit to yourself that you weren't at that stage yet mentally.

'I'll do it,' Clover snapped at him. I tried to shrug at him, but the movement hurt me too much. I hoped that my face conveyed my emotions enough, though. That I wasn't mad at him, but that I wanted Clo to help me. The narrowing of his eyes told me that maybe my intention had got lost in translation.

✦

THE SHOWER HAD HELPED ME FEEL SLIGHTLY MORE human and once he'd tucked me into my bed, Ollie had left after saying that he had some errands to run. I wasn't even going to guess at what those were. Griff had arrived shortly after and hugged me so tight I thought my ribs would bruise alongside everything else.

'Honestly, New Girl, you cannot be going anywhere alone anytime soon. Those girls aren't messing around,' he said in greeting.

'Did you go speak to them?' I asked. I wanted to know if he had as much as I didn't, you know? If he had spoken to them, they might get worse knowing it was getting to Griff and Ollie.

'I hope you kicked their asses Griff, I don't care if they've got vaginas.' Clover looked so fierce that if I were *The Set*, I'd be terrified. She was not playing around.

'Classy Clo,' Griff said, his smile cheeky, but I also noticed that he deflected the question I'd asked. 'So whores, what are we going to watch tonight?'

'Whores?' I asked, sputtering. This boy was something else. My mouth moved into a lopsided smile at him.

'Is that not what the girls say? Want me to call you sisters like that beauty dude does?'

'No!' Clover and I both yelled, shaking our heads at him in amusement.

'Why do you even know about that?' I wondered, looking him up and down as he came and sat beside me on the edge of my bed.

'I enjoy watching YouTube videos at night to fall asleep. Don't judge, but I get tingles from beauty videos,' he said.

'O.M.G,' I said each letter individually, in a fake valley accent. 'Griff, I watch videos to sleep too!'

'Yes, New Girl! I knew we were kindred spirits,' he said, as we high five each other enthusiastically.

'Well, I apologise that I can't join your crew,' Clo said. She was lying on her bed, looking up at the ceiling, her tone amused at us. 'Not gonna lie, but I find that whole ASMR stuff strange.'

'What, you mean you've never experienced tingles?' I asked, shocked. I'd always wished that I'd had somebody to play with my hair or rub my head to give me tingles when I was growing up.

'I just don't get the hype,' she said, shrugging her shoulder as she did so.

'Let's pick a film, girlies,' Griff said as he got up Netflix and started flicking through the options. His watch list killed me. It had some of my favourite films on it and I smiled, wondering if Griff had them on there because he liked them or in order to have a quick "Netflix and chill" film on hand.

'To all the boys?' I asked the room, and got a resounding 'YES!' from Clover and a, 'Oh, I love a bit of Peter Kavinsky,' from Griff.

'Let's do this,' I said.

We settled in, Griff getting comfortable beside me whilst making sure that he didn't touch my side, or hurt me further. The three of us enjoyed films together, and we had a great evening. Griff even had a takeaway pizza delivered for dinner.

Having friends was such a novelty to me, but if this was what it felt like, then I never wanted this feeling to go away.

Chapter Fourteen

I 'd been at Hawthorn Academy now for six weeks, and three weeks had passed since Ophelia and Oralie beat me up in the toilets.

I'd spent the first few days in my room with the door constantly revolving; Clover, Griff and Ollie barely left me alone and one of them was always by my side—even when I didn't want them to be.

I'd returned to classes after a week—I still dawdled and my sides were still bruised, but other than that, I felt okay. I couldn't miss anymore classes without my grades suffering and Ms Hawthorn forcing me to come into her office to discuss the terms of my scholarship was not something I wanted to do right now.

Griff and I had just left Ethics and were heading towards the dining hall for lunch when we bumped into Leo, and by bumped I meant I literally walked into him. He must have been standing in my path, or maybe he'd just stepped into it, but either way, we collided with a thump.

'S-sorry,' I said, apologising for hitting him. I brushed my hands where I had bumped him, then realised what I was doing and stopped straight away, resting my hands on his chest near his heart. 'I should really w-watch where I'm going.'

'That's okay, Stutter,' he said, his mouth tilting up on one side.

Great. I'd got a cute nickname from Leo. *Stutter.*

'Must have distracted her with my manliness,' Griff said, his words catching me so off guard that I snorted loudly with laughter.

'And she snorts too. Stutter, if you ever want to ditch that tool you're currently attached to, I'm available,' Leo said, his bored tone not matching his words in the slightest. He sounded as if he didn't give a fuck whether I attached myself to Ollie, or Griff—or anybody.

'If Ollie fucks it up, which, let's be honest, could happen, then I am definitely the next in line. Right, Sky?' Griff asked, his signature grin in place.

'Sure Griff,' I said to placate him. Smiling, I pulled at his arm to get him to continue walking with me. Away from Leo's inquisitive gaze. His tone may be weary, but his eyes were anything but. He was looking for something, and I couldn't quite figure out what.

✦

A COUPLE OF DAYS AFTER GRIFF AND I HAD BUMPED INTO Leo, I bumped into him again. Sadly, this time I wasn't with Griff but with Clover. Plus, Leo was *not* alone.

We'd just left dinner, and we were making our way back to our dorm when Clo suggested we go a different way. You know, mix it up a bit.

I instantly agreed. Going our usual route typically meant we ran into Odette and the other O girls, or people who were only too happy to prove their loyalty to *The Set* and call me names. Some people even went as far as barging into me; trying to knock me into others or into walls.

According to Clover, the boys had issued a warning to the entire school when I'd been hurt. They'd made it clear that nobody could physically assault me again, and that if they did, they would have to answer to them. Whatever the boys had said, it had worked—for now.

So, that was how Clover and I found ourselves in the hallway that attached the pool house to the Hospital Wing. We avoided the pool house usually, mostly because that was where you could find Leo, and Ollie and Griff, most of the time. If they weren't with us, or in class, then they were at the pool. The three of them were on the swim team and were apparently fantastic to watch, winning the school trophies and shit. I was low-key excited to watch a meet. Mainly because I wanted to see those three in speedos. Sue me.

This part of the school was dimly lit in comparison to the rest. Griff had told me it was because these buildings were some of the oldest and they hadn't had as many light fittings installed. The school board had kept it that way too, in order to keep the original buildings authenticity.

Our conversation topic—the upcoming Parents' Day that Hawthorn threw once a year. The one where every student could invite their parents to come visit. To meet the teachers and see how their kids were doing; find out if they were engaging in any extracurricular activities. Find out exactly what they were doing with their twenty thousand a year plus education.

'I'm not asking mine to come.' Clover told me, shaking her head as if the thought of her parents coming here was too much for her to cope with.

'How come?' I asked. I knew little about her parents, actually—she'd never mentioned them.

'I don't want to subject them to it. Fuck, Sky, I don't want to subject myself to it either,' she replied.

'I get you. I've not invited Mum and Andy either. I'm already the butt of enough jokes, I don't need the two biggest jokes in my life coming here and making things ten times worse.'

The thought of them sharing air space with the likes of Ollie and Griff made me shudder. I knew they were my friends, and that they liked me for me, but still. Everybody knew already that I came here on scholarship. Inviting Mum here would only highlight just how little money I came from. Honestly, it was for the best that they never set foot on Hawthorn grounds.

'Can you hear that?' Clover asked and looked at me, making a shushing motion with her finger, even though she'd just asked me a question. I shook my head. I couldn't hear anything outside of our footsteps.

Then I heard it. What was it with us two walking into couples kissing in one of the bridge corridors leading out from the Hospital Wing?

The smooching and smacking sounds of two lips going at it got closer, and eventually we could see the couple up ahead.

Of course. It just *had* to be Leo and Odette. *Again.*

This time, at least, Clover didn't instantly run off and leave me standing alone like a creeper. She continued walking and when we got close enough for them to hear us, Clover did the whole cough while actually covering a word shtick.

'Skank,' she said, while trying to cover it with a cough. I would laugh, but the fake cough didn't cover her chosen word at all, so instead I stayed silent.

The two of them stopped what they were doing. Odette, using reflexes I didn't expect her to possess, reached out and grabbed Clover's arm.

'If you've got something to say, *Over*, I suggest you share it with the class.'

'G-get off her. You're hurting her,' I said. I didn't even think before I acted. I just grabbed Odette's hand and yanked it away from Clover as hard as I could.

It worked, but only because I'd caught Odette so off guard.

Fuck. I'd caught myself off guard.

She blatantly had something to do with Ophelia and Oralie attacking me in the toilets, and here I was not three weeks later attacking her. Even though *The Set* didn't have an actual leader, everybody knew Odette classed herself as the one in charge. Probably because she was the one hooking up with Leo, a member of *The Sect*. It also helped that the two of them were the oldest members, too.

'Get your fucking pauper hands off of me,' Odette said, shrieking and looking at Leo. Almost imploring him to save her somehow. But I could tell by the look on his face he wouldn't bite. He was enjoying this all a little *too* much, if anything. I got the impression that Odette acted submissive with Leo; even though my hands were on her, she hadn't looked at me once. 'Are you not going to say anything? Really, Leo? Again?!'

'Stop, Stutter, stop,' Leo said, obviously mocking her—and not me for once. He wanted me to stop as much as he wanted to be involved in this scenario. But that didn't stop Clover from looking over at me, betrayal plain in her features. It was clear she thought I was closer to Leo than I'd let on. The fact he'd made this *cute* nickname for me didn't help the case. I raised my eyebrows at him in warning, but he only smirked in return.

'Are you for fucking real, Leo Hawthorn?' Clover asked, disbelief in her voice. I expected a line like that to come from Odette, so I was shocked that it came from Clover.

'What's the matter, Red? Jealous of your new friend here?' Leo asked, his tone having lost the disinterest he constantly exuded. It was like he'd come to life. His eyes were sparkling with malice, the darkness simmering just under the surface, wanting to be let free. Leo calling her Red told me more than he'd probably meant to.

One day soon I would make sure Clover told me more about their history. She'd been disguising just how well they knew one another, evidently.

'I'd never be jealous of this, Bimbo Barbie. I hope you get chlamydia, or something worse. Maybe if you're lucky, your dick will drop off and save the rest of the female population. Oh, wait. They're already safe; the size of your dick won't do them any damage.'

With that, Clover walked off. Stomping down the corridor, without once turning around, away from the bomb she'd just unleashed. The bomb mostly being the part where she'd called Odette a *Bimbo Barbie*. Odette looked to be foaming at the mouth, looking very much like how I imagined a rabid dog would.

'Go on, Stutter, go after her. Better make sure Red doesn't

go find a blade and come back for more,' Leo said, dismissing me, his attention once again returning to Odette, trying to calm her down.

I walked off slowly, trying to make sense of what I'd just witnessed.

One thing I knew—Leo was playing some kind of game, and I had a feeling it could be a long one.

✳

FOR THE REST OF THE NIGHT, CLOVER WOULDN'T TALK TO me more than to tell me she was going for a shower and then putting on her headphones and getting some essays done. I found the last part highly suspicious though as Clover's classes were practical subjects with barely any writing attached, like Food Tech for example. If she wanted to block me out, then I'd let her. She wanted to stop me from asking her any probing questions.

I'd respect her wishes for now, but if I were being truthful, I was getting sick of her trying to block me out. Friendship goes both ways, or so I thought, and I'd definitely been a lot more open and forthcoming with her than she ever had with me. I'd told her things about my life before Hawthorn; my lack of friends, my relationship with my mum. I'd even told her about Andy's advances on the day I left to come here. Yet all I'd got from her was that her family fell on hard times a couple of years ago.

That was it. *In six weeks.*

I knew some people found it hard to open up, hard to talk about the deep shit, but I thought I'd made it clear that I was her friend regardless of what had happened. I wouldn't judge her, and it sucked that she thought I might.

I put my headphones in my ears and pulled up Netflix. I chose one of my favourite go to films and pressed play. I barely got through the opening credits though before my phone started blowing up.

Only Clo, Griff and Ollie had this number, which meant it had to be one of the boys. When I looked at my phone, it shocked me to see the message had come from an unknown number.

STUTTER. KEEP AN EYE ON RED FOR ME. LET ME KNOW IF **the girls bother either of you. Save this number. Use it if you ever need help.**

CONFUSED BY THE ENTIRE MESSAGE, I TRIED TO MAKE sense of it in my mind. Leo had my number and had used it to message me about Clover? But even stranger, he wanted me to save it and use it if I needed help?

I looked over at Clover and wondered whether I should bother her with this. Maybe she'd be able to shed some light on why Leo had texted me about keeping an eye on her. But knowing Clo, she'd just fob me off again, and I wasn't in the mood to disagree with her.

I quickly texted back one word.

OKAY.

. . .

THAT SHOULD BE ENOUGH FOR NOW. I SAVED HIS NUMBER under Thorn, amusing myself. After all, Clo was on there as Lady Luck and Griff was on there as Hercules—*don't ask.*

I'd debated about what to save Ollie as.

Before the party in the woods it had been *Ollie,* then after the whole drugging and rescue thing it had been *Hero,* but that didn't fit him either. After the girls had beaten me up in the toilets, and he'd been the most angry I'd ever seen him, I'd changed it to *Beast.* Mostly because I knew that deep down, lurking under the surface, he could be the worst kind of monster that existed.

Chapter Fifteen

P arents' Day was a big deal at Hawthorn Academy. It was a way for the faculty to prove to the rich parents that they were spending their hard earned cash well and that, if they felt so inclined, they could always donate more—the school would highly appreciate it. It was also the event that led into the October break; meaning that a lot of the students would return home afterward with their parents. I could sense the excitement, so palpable in the corridors it was almost overwhelming, the atmosphere almost feverish.

'Do we even need to attend if our parents aren't coming?' I asked Clover. All I really wanted to do was spend the day in our room, gorging on sweets and lusting after Ryan Gosling.

'Yep. It's a part of the required social calendar, the one on Hive that Ms Hawthorn mentioned. You got a copy on your first day, right?' Clover groaned, and said, 'Have to look like they're treating us charity cases well, after all.'

'True. So do all the parents attend?' I asked, curious as to who I might meet.

'If you're asking if Ollie and Leo's parents come, then yeah, they'll be here,' Clo said, only partially answering my question.

'What about Griff's?' I added.

'Oh, er, no,' Clover mumbled, her eyes shifting around the room. It looked like she wanted to say more, but had bitten her own tongue to stop herself. Unlike the other things she wasn't telling me, I could slightly understand this one. It wasn't hers to tell. It was Griff's, and I could respect Clover for that.

'Fair enough. I'm just glad my mum knows nothing about today.'

✦

THEY HAD TRANSFORMED THE MAIN HALL INTO A FETE OF sorts. I guessed an event like this would be better suited to outside, but the weather in England in October could be a little unpredictable, to put it mildly.

Everywhere I looked there were tables set up; each department had its own table run by the heads of each subject. Then there were tables filled with refreshments along the left-hand wall. In the centre of the room were the tables we usually ate our dinner from, all arranged with name cards for each student and their parents. *How fun.*

I was surprised to see that there weren't many tables but Clover explained to me that this was because a lot of students were related therefore they shared parents. Made sense, I guessed. Rich people *were* popping out children in hopes of business, (and/or world domination), yet didn't actually *care* about their children for any other reason.

So weird...

Clover and I arrived together, sticking to each other like glue. Not exactly like we were meeting anybody.

'I wonder whose parents they are. Must be one of the younger years,' Clo muttered beside me.

'Huh?' I asked, tuning into Clo's words as I'd been paying more attention to the band setting up on stage than the entrance to the hall.

'This couple just entered and I've never seen them before. Odd,' Clo said, shrugging.

I didn't point out to Clover that I found it odd she'd even notice this. She'd only joined last year, so how would she even know?

I turned to see the couple she was looking at and my heart melted. Fully melted, and the pieces puddled together on the floor in a big wet mess. *Shit.*

'Darling!' My mum called across the hall, and said, 'Oh, how lovely you look!'

Of course, she was trying to put on her *posh* accent, which, if anything, just made her sound even more common. Her emphasis in the middle of lovely sounded like something from a bad sitcom. Believe me, that wasn't an easy feat.

Andy, the slimy toad, stood beside her and I realised they'd attempted to dress up for the occasion. By that, I meant they'd brushed their hair and worn clothes without stains. Clothes that were obviously cheap that definitely didn't fit in with the surroundings. Mum had even put on a large red fascinator that clashed terribly with her orange v-neck top, and I was pretty sure my shame levels couldn't go any higher.

'Fuck. What are they doing here?' I asked, bewildered about what I saw in front of me.

'That's your mum?' Clover asked, sounding as exasperated as I felt.

'Yep.' I popped the p like so many heroines do. 'How did she find out about today?'

'No idea. Sure you didn't mention it to her?' Clo asked.

'Clo. I haven't spoken to her since I started at Hawthorn. I'm surprised the woman even remembers that she *has* a daughter.'

By this point in our conversation, Mum and Andy had made their way over to us, waving and grabbing everybody's attention. Luckily for me, the boys weren't here yet, but it was only a matter of time before they arrived too. There was no way to hide from them now.

'Oh, Skylar, darling, I am so happy to see you!' My mum practically shouted, making sure that all those around us could hear her. 'Look at you. You look so fancy. I didn't realise this school was so fancy either.'

'You barely listened when I told you about it, Mum,' I said, my tone flat. In one sentence, the woman who birthed me had shown just how little she paid attention to me before I left.

'I would have remembered if you told me about some-where as grandiose-ly as this. All you told us was that you'd be leaving for school and quitting your job at the shop,' she said. Of course, that was all she would remember.

I chose to ignore her use of the word "grandiose-ly". My mum always invented words and threw them into sentences constantly; an annoying habit of hers.

I wondered how they were affording to keep the roof over their heads now that I was gone and couldn't help with the bills. Knowing them, they'd probably just applied for more government benefits.

'H-how did you know to come?' I asked, looking at them in turn. I could feel my anxiety rearing its ugly head, the sweat rising to the surface of my skin, my nerves climbing, worried that Ollie and Griff were about to enter the hall with their parents and see who raised me. They knew I had a poor excuse of a mother, but knowing something and meeting it were two very different things.

'We got an invite from ya in the post.' Andy spoke up, and even just hearing his voice made me feel sick.

I hadn't really processed what he'd done to me the last time I saw him as I came straight here and events at school were more pressing and in my face. But now, seeing him, hearing him talk, made me want to scream. Or run away and not return until after they'd left the grounds. Until they were far, far away from here.

'That wasn't from me,' I said, as I looked Mum in the eye.

I felt confident that I knew who it was from, though. This had Odette and her clones written all over it. It hadn't been enough to have people bully me; it hadn't been enough to beat me up. No, they needed to humiliate me in front of the entire school, too.

'It had your name on it,' Mum said, looking at me as if she thought I'd suffered from memory loss, or maybe she thought I was lying in front of Clover. 'It said there'd be free food and drink here, so obviously we had to come.'

Don't get me wrong—I was always game for free food and drink; wasn't everybody? But that was the real reason they'd come. Mum hadn't come to see me, or even see the place her only child was living. No. The two of them had come for the free food and booze.

'Mum. Andy. This is my best friend, Clover,' I said, pointing at Clo as I did so.

'Hello darling, aren't you just a dream?' Mum asked. *Oh wow.* Mum was pulling out the works.

'Hey. Nice to meet you, Cora,' Clover said as we shared a look. A look that told me she was bullshitting through her teeth. One thing I did love was that Clover didn't suck up. Where I was from in England, you didn't call your friends' parents by their surname. Calling them by their first name and acting casual was the norm, and by Clover not calling her Mrs Hopkins, it further solidified to me that Clover and I were cut from the same cloth.

✦

An hour had passed with Clover and me making awkward small talk with Mum and Andy, showing them around the grounds and telling them about what I'd been learning. Not that they gave much of a shit, but there was still another few hours until the sit down meal happened and we needed to pass the time somehow. They'd given us a reprieve when they went to grab another drink—probably their fifth of the afternoon.

Clover turned to whisper in my ear as we re-entered the hall and said, 'I haven't seen the boys yet, have you?'

I shook my head. Not wanting to say anything more in front of Mum. She was the type of woman who loved gossip and any talk of boys would definitely pique her interest, and one thing I really didn't want her to know was about Ollie. I didn't know what was happening between us—or if *anything* was even happening between us—but I definitely didn't want her to know anything about it.

'Shit, there they are,' Clover said as she looked towards the door. It was like a scene in a film. You know that part where everybody turned to see who had arrived, like when Mr Darcy arrived at the Meryton assembly. Ollie was standing next to a stern-looking man, with grey hair and grey eyes, wearing a dark blue suit. Handsome in an older guy kind of way.

Then there was a stunning woman with her arm in Leo's, brown hair flowing to her waist, wearing a classic black dress with black court shoes. She oozed power and money. I assumed that she was his mother. Leo looked pretty dapper too, to be fair, a grey suit and white shirt highlighting the intensity of his blue eyes.

Clover gasped at the sight of him. Or at least, I think it was aimed at him.

On the other side of Leo stood his father—another stern-looking rich man who reminded me of a King surveying his Kingdom. His hair was the same colour as Leo's and you could see the family resemblance instantly. Griff stood on the end, looking carefree as usual.

Ollie and his father both looked over at me, and together they started walking in this direction. *Just wonderful.*

'Hey,' Ollie said curtly, giving me a quick head nod. 'Dad, this is Skylar Crescent. Sky, this is my father, Henry Brandon.'

'Hello girls,' Henry said, smiling, but his eyes assessed everything, surveying the entire room. My mum and Andy decided that this was the moment they'd come over and stand with us. I felt a sharp nudge in my side that definitely came from an elbow. An exaggerated cough followed.

'Ollie. Mr Brandon. This is my mum, Cora and my step-dad, Andy.'

Everybody shook hands and acted friendly enough, but I could see the level of disgust in Henry's eyes. He even wiped his hands after shaking Andy's—which yeah, fair—but it still made me feel crappy inside.

The conversation resembled a shit show from the start.

'How do you know my beautiful Skylar? Got her looks from me, didn't she?' Mum asked Ollie, surveying everybody gathered with us. Probably attempting to decipher the cumulative wealth standing in front of her.

'We're in class together,' Ollie replied, curtly. Completely ignoring the second part of Mum's sentence.

'How wonderful,' Mum said enthusiastically, 'Andy, isn't it just so super-duper that our Sky has made such handsome friends?' The emphasis on handsome nauseated me.

'Course it is, Hot Stuff,' Andy replied, leering at Mum. Could this get any worse?

He grabbed Mum's bum—in full view of everyone. Mortified, my face continued turning a deep shade of red. I literally felt as if I was overheating.

The group of us settled into an uncomfortable silence.

I clearly had somebody looking out for me as a bell rang out through the hall, letting the room know the sit down part of the evening would commence shortly.

After some awkward as fuck goodbyes, we went our separate ways to take our seats for the sit down dinner. Mum made a big song and dance about finding our seats, meandering slowly through the tables and reading each name card slowly out loud.

Obviously, there was no saviour looking out for me,

because when we found our seats, they were at the table with Ollie, his dad, Griff, Leo and his parents. *Go figure.*

A little later, I remembered that Ollie hadn't introduced his dad to Clover, but when I'd mentioned it to her, she'd just shrugged.

+

THE MEAL HAD BEEN AWKWARD AS FUCK. BARELY anybody had spoken after I'd introduced Mum and Leo had introduced his parents, Edward and Lottie. Clover sat there next to me in complete silence, only answering when Lottie had asked her a couple of questions about how her baking was coming along and how her grades were. *Weird.*

The band played throughout, and now that we'd finished the meal, Ms Hawthorn walked out onto the stage. Grumbles went out across the hall, as did a few whispers. I noticed that Leo's dad sat up taller and looked interested instantly. But then I remembered he owned this place and was related to the woman now standing in the centre ready to address everybody here.

A projector screen had also appeared behind her, which could only mean we were going to have to sit through some kind of school bullshit propaganda intended to woo the rich people, and to entice them to donate even more of their enormous fortunes. How exciting.

'Welcome to Parents' Day, where you are once again able to see how your children, and protégés, are progressing at this fine institution.' Her grey, beady eyes assessed the room, spending a fraction longer on Clover and I. Or maybe on my mum. Or maybe I was just imagining the whole thing, paranoia getting the better of me. Just because I felt disgusted by her didn't mean everybody else felt the same. 'The students of A-Level Media Studies have put together this short film for you. I hope you enjoy it.'

The lights in the hall dimmed, and the projector screen flickered to life. Images of the school were being shown to a bouncy background beat, then a voiceover started.

'Hawthorn Academy was first established in 1850 by Sir Robert Hawthorn, who hoped the future generations would have the best education that money could buy. Still today, this fine establishment does exactly what Robert set out to do.'

Exterior shots of the school played, followed by shots of students sat in classrooms, or out on the field playing team sports. 'Recently, the school has re-started the scholarship fund, in order for those less fortunate to benefit from the connections that can be made here and to obtain the best education.'

My stomach dipped as butterflies started to make a home in there. I wanted nothing more than for this section of the tape to be over quickly. I looked at Clover, who also seemed to have the same expression on her face as I did on mine. It was clear from the voice speaking that it had been recorded by Ophelia, which definitely didn't bode well.

'The scholarship students have fit in well and are a welcome addition to Hawthorn Academy. Although, they do seem to be a little too friendly with the elite business world's future leaders.'

Abruptly, the footage changed.

It became a shaky, handheld video recording, blatantly taken on a mobile phone. Whoever was recording giggled, in that way people did when they were trying to stay incognito.

Slowly, I recognised just when this footage was from—and where.

It was from the night of the party in the woods. I could see me and Ollie dancing together on the makeshift dance floor. Then I saw me, on the screen, take Ollie's hand and lead him further into the trees. I knew what came next, and I really thought I might be sick in a moment.

How dare they film that?! How dare they take a private (ish), intimate moment, and taint it. How dare they show that to all of these people?

I was livid, but also, tears were forming in my eyes, threatening to spill over at any moment. I had to sit there in silence and watch it all unfold along with everybody else.

Eventually, once the footage became clear to everybody in the hall, Ms Hawthorn rushed back to the stage and stopped the tape, the screen returning to white once again.

Whispers. The entire hall began to talk in whispers that were quickly becoming louder. I could hear parents commenting on what they'd just seen. Half of them were angry about the party. The other half were only mad that they'd been made to watch it.

Ollie's eyes met mine from across the table. He didn't look sad. He looked furious, actually, but I couldn't tell whether it was aimed at me because it happened in the first place, or if it was the fact, they'd aired it to the entire school. Not like the two of us had discussed it since. To make matters worse, his father was staring me down with a look of disdain clear on his features. I was a rabbit caught in the headlights. I didn't want to leave the hall and let them see that they'd won. Just because I hadn't seen the girls and their parents today didn't mean that they weren't in here somewhere. Biding their time. Waiting to see what I'd do. How I'd react.

My mum decided to try and break the silence at the table, and said, 'Darling, I wouldn't worry. I used to get up to a lot worse when I was at school. Like Mother, like Daughter, ay?' She even had the audacity to throw in a wink.

'Ay.' Andy winked at me too. 'Now everybody knows how much of a slut you are, Sky. Can't hide it anymore, sweetheart.' He was leering at me, and all I could picture was his face looming closer to mine, his tongue invading my mouth without permission.

Fuck this. *I'm out.*

'If you'll excuse me, I must go freshen up,' I announced. The table all nodded, and every man but Andy stood when I left. Clover quickly followed me. As soon as we made it out of the hall, Clover put her arm around me and we quickly made our way to the nearest toilets.

'Those little bitches,' Clover spat, her anger for me etched all over her face. 'I promise you Skylar, we *will* get them back. Maybe not today, but sometime this year, we will.'

I nodded. There wasn't much else for me to say. It had shocked me.

'Although ...' Clover trailed off, a cheeky prying look appearing on her face once we had some privacy. 'You didn't tell me that *that* happened with Ollie.'

I covered my face with my palm. I wasn't embarrassed as such, but I could feel a blush forming on my cheeks; bleeding outward to the rest of my face.

'I know,' I whined. 'To be honest with you, I wasn't even sure it had actually happened. I *was* drugged at some point that night, you know, and I doubted my own memories. Ollie hadn't said a word afterward about it, so I wondered if I'd just had a super feverish dream as I lay beside him in bed.'

My logic made sense, in my head at least. I hadn't wanted to assume that anything I knew of that night had happened. It was just best to keep it to myself. But apparently now that wasn't possible. Everybody knew the truth. *Great.*

Eventually, Clover and I returned to the hall where the parents were saying their goodbyes. It only occurred to me then that my mum, (or Andy), could have said anything while I'd been gone. Oh, for fuck's sake. Could I not catch a break?

I didn't look at Ollie. Or Griff or Leo. I just didn't want to know what they were thinking about me. About the whole *Ollie fingered me, pinned up against a tree* scenario we'd all just watched play out.

Ms Hawthorn came and joined the group to say her good-byes to Edward Hawthorn. Things looked tense between them. But that could be because of my amateur porn clip. The fact Ollie and I were both sixteen definitely made this even worse. For us *and* the school.

'Ms Crescent. I expect to see you in my office first thing Monday morning,' Ms Hawthorn said, her eyes narrowing at me and her lips pursed together.

'Yes, Ms,' I said in response, using my best contrite manner. Couldn't wait for that meeting. *Not.*

'It's been nice to meet you, Skylar. Clover,' Lottie Hawthorn said and gave us both kind smiles. A smile that reached her eyes and I could feel in my bones that at least one person at this table was genuine.

'Skylar. Clover.' Edward nodded at each of us and left with his wife with Leo, following closely along behind them.

'It's been a pleasure,' Henry said, his face telling me it had been the complete opposite of a pleasure, but nobody called him out on it. He and Ollie left together, and although I tried not to look at him, I could sense that Ollie looked back at me before he left the hall.

That left me, Clover, and Griff standing with my mum, Andy and Ms Hawthorn. I wondered why Griff hadn't left with the others, but it wasn't like they were his parents, so I understood why he'd stayed.

'Mum, it's been fun,' I lied, hoping she couldn't hear in my voice just how much I wanted her gone. If she knew I wanted her to leave, she'd stay longer just to spite me. She'd done it in the past, so I knew it was something she'd do. 'Glad you could make it.'

'Oh, me too, darling. I'm so glad to have found out that my daughter is just as much of a skunk as I am,' she said, slurring her words. She also meant to call me a skank, but not like I was going to correct her. The copious amounts of free booze she'd drunk today must be finally catching up with her. I hoped they could get out of here before one of them did something terrible.

'Been lovely to meet you two,' Clover said, also lying through her teeth, the pain in her eyes at her words evident to me. 'Have a safe journey home.' As an afterthought she added, 'You have a lift home, right?'

'Yer. The school sent somebody to pick us up and they're taking us back too,' Andy said. He went to hug me goodbye, but Griff grabbed me out of harm's way and put his hand out for Andy to shake instead.

'It's been real. I'll walk you to your car.'

Honestly, I could kiss him. Instead, I squeezed his shoulder, making it clear I appreciated the way he'd stepped in for me. I'd never told Griff much about my life before Hawthorn, but I think he had an inkling. Especially after today.

He'd been quiet today, actually. Taking in his surroundings and listening to the conversations going on around him, but barely joining in.

'I'll meet you two back up at your room.' Griff winked at us, sweeping his arm towards the door, and followed after my mum and Andy. Neither of them walked off in a straight line. Eurgh. All I needed now was for them to be sick before reaching the car, and my day of humiliation and shame would be complete.

Luckily for me, roughly an hour later when Griff made it back to our room, he didn't have any puke stories to share with me. I took that as a plus. According to him, they'd got in the car with no real fanfare but had promised to return when next invited.

Believe me, if I had anything to do with it, the two of them would never set foot on school grounds ever again.

Ollie never came to my room to talk to me that night. He didn't even send me a text. Nice to know he cared about me enough to wonder about me. Wondered how I was coping with what had gone down today.

Oh, wait.

He didn't.

Chapter Sixteen

The day following Parents' Day was the first swim meet of the season.

Apparently, it was a rather big deal, as swimming was a sport that Hawthorn did well at. Our team was talented and a lot of money came to the school because of it.

'New Girl, you're coming to the swim meet tomorrow, right?' Griff asked.

'Err ... I didn't know that there was a swim meet tomorrow?' I asked, confused. Pretty sure this was the first mention of it. 'Also, what the fuck even happens at one of those?'

'A lot of races,' he joked. 'You mean Ollie didn't tell you?' His eyes widened dramatically and his mouth fell open in a comedic way.

'Not being funny, Griff, but Ollie would have to talk to me in order to tell me about it.'

'Ouch. Right. I'm sure he's just busy with his dad. You know that he's staying at the Hawthorn residence on the grounds tonight along with Leo's parents. It's so they can be here for the swim meet.'

'Once again, Griff. He'd have to talk to me for me to know shit,' I said.

'Got it. Anyway, there's a swim meet and your boy is going to kill the competition.'

'By *your* boy, do you mean Ollie or you?' I asked, laughing at his use of words. For starters, Ollie was definitely not *my* boy. But if Griff was talking about himself, then I found that quite sweet in a best friend kind of way. He may have originally started to hang out with us to rile the other two boys up, but now, I genuinely believed that Griff was just as much our friend as he was theirs.

'Oh, definitely me,' he replied. His cocky grin was charming as all get-out. I wished it was Griff that I had a connection to, but all I could see him as was a brother. A bigheaded, egotistical, older brother who knew what buttons to push and when.

✳

So that conversation with Griff was how I'd found myself on Sunday afternoon, sitting in the stands of the swimming pool alongside the other students and parents in attendance. Clover begrudgingly sitting beside me, but only because Griff and I had begged her to come and keep me company. Apparently, she didn't want to witness Leo's smug grin when he won yet again. *The Sect* were the best on the team and I hated to say it, but I was excited to see just how decent they were.

Ollie had texted me this morning, the message coming through as I got ready for the day.

DON'T BE MAD. WE'LL TALK LATER. I ACTED LIKE A DICK.

ROLLING MY EYES, I'D RESPONDED WITH A QUICK **K**. After all, everybody knew what a "K" meant.

'How long does a swim meet last?' I asked Clo, having no idea what to expect.

'Too long,' she said, short. So basically, she was no help at all.

The first few rounds had been for the younger years, and it made me realise that swimming wasn't my favourite sport to watch. Not that there were many sports I enjoyed watching, but still. I was the kind of girl who would watch the Olympics, and that was about it. Maybe the odd Wimbledon, because you know, tennis could be pretty exciting to watch, and the entire country got behind it every June.

Finally, it was time for Ollie and Griff to compete. I knew that Ollie hid a hot body underneath his uniform, but seeing him like this, seeing his chest in all its glory was truly a sight to behold. A genuine work of art. He had a six-pack, so defined, that the only image going through my mind was that of him with water dripping down into every crease. Don't get me started on his legs. They were long and pure muscle. Even the tiny shorts they wore weren't enough to deter me. It ensured that my mind was now imagining Ollie's dick as he had that V. You know, the one that led to the main event. Ollie's an adonis, plain and simple, and I'd had to wipe away some drool before Clover spotted it. It did slightly piss me off that I wasn't the only person witnessing this. There were too many eyes on him, and for a split second I considered stabbing the eyes out of The Set just so they couldn't see him.

Despite my best efforts, I'd turned into a basic, petty, horny bitch.

Griff stood beside Ollie, and his body was not one to be sniffed at either. He had wide shoulders and I could also see that he was sporting a six-pack *and* an adonis belt. Even if I saw him as a brother, I could still appreciate that he worked hard on his body. All three of them did, spending a lot of their time training in the pool or in the school gym. It had paid off, that was for damn sure.

I couldn't tell you much of the race itself. I didn't know the length they swam or the stroke or anything like that. All I could tell you was that Ollie won. Every single race he'd competed in, he'd won by at least an entire second each time. The crowd cheered and hollered as he brought home yet another medal, and another trophy, for the school. Griff came second, and he seemed super chuffed with the result. His cheeky facade never faltered; his smile constantly in place. He even winked and dabbed in our direction when collecting his medal.

The last race of the day was Leo's. According to the whispers I'd heard around me, *this* was the race to watch. Ollie had been amazing, but Leo was something else entirely. A new species, almost. It also helped that Leo had an impressive body. The whole disinterested thing totally worked for him in this setting, too. He stayed calm before the race, and he flew through that water, leaving his opponents in his wake. He was spectacular and I could totally see him one day competing at the Olympics, or something major like that. Leo was just *that* good.

'Fuck me, Clo. Did you see that?' I asked, astonishment clear on my face.

'Yep,' she replied, bluntly. She looked so sour on the outside, but she couldn't fool me. I'd seen her face while he was racing. She had been as tense as everybody else here, and I could totally tell that she'd had her bum cheeks clenched just as tight as I had from start to finish. 'He's good.'

'Good?! Clover, did we just watch the same thing?' I asked, in disbelief at her indifference. I couldn't believe that she was being such a dick about it all.

After the race, Ollie and Griff went and showered off the chlorine, then came and joined us.

'Did you see how fly I was?' Griff asked the two of us, his dimples pressing in.

'Fly? Who even are you?' I laughed, shaking my head, knowing that Griff was doing his best to get a rise out of us all and be the comedian like usual.

'I was definitely better,' Ollie said, all smug, and you could tell that in that moment he really believed in his own hype. Which, yeah, he *was* good, but nowhere near as good as Leo.

'Of course you were, handsome,' Griff said, hugging him. He gave him a big kiss, lip smack and all, on his cheek. Ollie groaned and wiped it away instantly, but that action made Griff even more determined to land more kisses on Ollie. 'You were legiterally perfect.'

'What the fuck is legiterally?' Clover asked, piping up.

'You know. It's a mix of legit and literally. I made it up,' he said, his face bright.

'No way!' I gasped, acting surprised. I felt arms come

around my waist, hugging my back to a hard chest. Instantly, I smelled Ollie's vanilla and tobacco scent I loved so much. I made a note to find out what it was, because I wouldn't mind spritzing my clothes with that smell. He turned me to face him, his blue eyes looking into my soul, I swear.

Honestly, this boy gave me whiplash.

'I'm sorry, Sky,' he said, his face blank but sincere. 'I should've tried to speak to you last night.'

'Duh,' I said, not wanting to make it too easy for him.

'Oh, while I remember. I want you to come to my birthday party next Friday night,' Ollie said. It wasn't a question. It was a demand, slightly softened with a smile.

'It's your birthday next week?' I asked. *Shit.* What on earth would I get him, and why had he only just mentioned it?

'On Halloween,' he said smirking, 'Costume party in the woods.'

'W-wow. Okay,' I said, trying not to focus too hard on the woods part of the sentence. I looked at Clo. 'Guess we need to put on our thinking caps.'

She nodded, but she didn't look happy about it. I assumed she would have known it was Ollie's birthday coming up, so not mentioning it was a bit of a dick move, really. They must have celebrated last year—even if Clo hadn't been invited, she would've heard shit, right?

'Come on, babe, let's go watch a film and get some pizza in,' Ollie said. His arm came around my shoulder, pulling me to him as we walked.

Babe? That was a new word for him. Not going to mention it—obviously. I nodded in response.

'Let's go.' I smiled as the four of us headed off towards

Ollie's room. As we walked past the door to the locker room, I spotted Leo standing there, looking straight in our direction.

Dead eyes staring at us, no light in them.

✦

MONDAY MORNING, I MADE MY WAY TO MS HAWTHORN's office. Butterflies sat heavy in my stomach, and I worried what she would say to me about the whole video debacle.

Ollie and Griff had both offered to come with me, put on a united front, but I came alone. I didn't need them fighting my battles for me—well, not all of them anyway.

I knocked on the large wooden door; the sound reverberating throughout the empty hallway.

'Come in,' said Ms Hawthorn from the other side of the door.

I took in a deep lungful of air and pushed the heavy door. Or at least it felt heavier than the last time I'd been here. Maybe it was my mind that felt heavy in reality?

'Sit,' she said, curt, her face hard.

The chair cushion squished underneath my weight, the legs gave out a groan and I looked at Ms Hawthorn across the desk. I maintained eye contact for as long as I could, but her stare intimidated me.

'Miss Crescent, you are on your last warning here at the Academy.' Her eyes narrowed. 'I will not have you besmirching this fine establishment.'

'I-I-I,' I found myself saying the first thing that came to mind, but not knowing where to go with it.

'If any reports of further misconduct come my way, I must

expel you. Do you understand me?' she asked, and I nodded instantly.

'O-of course. It won't happen again, Ms Hawthorn.'

'See that it doesn't,' she said, dismissing me. Her eyes instantly back on the paperwork in front of her.

I stood and walked out slowly, trying to close the door softly behind me. I wondered if the other girls were being called in to her office today; but I highly doubted it.

If they continued to bully me, the school would expel me. Yep, sounded about right.

❋

A WEEK PASSED AND, TELLING THE TRUTH, I WAS STILL feeling a little raw about everything that had happened over the past weekend.

That my mum and Andy had been there to witness my humiliation had definitely made it one thousand times worse.

It was on Sunday night as Clover and I were sitting in our room in silence, both trying to work on our homework, that Clover turned towards me with a determined look on her face. Things had been tense between us recently. Ever since Ollie had invited us to his birthday slash Halloween party.

'Sky, do you really think it's a good idea to go to the Halloween party Friday?' Clover asked.

I rolled my eyes at her words. We'd been having this conversation on and off for what felt like forever now. I slightly got her point. I mean, the last party in the woods I'd attended I was drugged and recorded. *Not an impressive track record.*

'Honestly, I don't know. But it's Ollie's birthday, and I said I'd be there.' I smiled, thoughts of Ollie filling my mind.

Things had been great between us and I didn't want to snub his birthday party, or fuck up the tentative truce we'd come to. Also, everybody knew that Halloween parties were an excuse to dress up as a fantasy, and I had the perfect costume idea for Clover and I.

'Also, not like I can disobey. Ollie invited me and he's a member of *The Sect* so can't exactly turn it down without having more mean shit happen to me,' I added, but I think we both knew my excuses were pretty hollow at this point. The girls had backed off after Parents' Day, believe it or not, they'd got in shit with Ms Hawthorn. Not like it was hard for her to figure out Ophelia's voice on the voiceover.

The truth of the matter—I wanted to go to the Halloween party. Yeah, there was a small part of me that knew it could all come crashing down or that the girls could target me again, but it was a chance I was willing to take. The way Ollie had looked at me this week was real. I could feel it deep down inside of me.

'I get it, I really, *really* do. I've been there, you know. I was in your position once,' Clover said, staring at me intently, trying to make me see reason. I nodded at her, but I was slightly tuning her out. She meant well, but there were only so many times you could hear your best friend rail on the guy you liked without it pissing you off. 'Last year was really hard for me. I didn't have any friends, and if you think *The Set* is bad this year? They're nothing compared to last year. The two older girls last year make Ophelia and Oralie look like kittens.'

'Right, you mentioned last year vaguely before, but Clo, you've never even told me what happened. Not like they've even really targeted you this year?' I said, my voice going up at the end in question.

I had thought about it once or twice. Clover kept hinting at the events of the previous year and how bad school had been for her, but never went into much detail. Definitely not enough detail for me to form an opinion on it all. People barely acknowledged her this year, except for when she stuck up for me—and that had only been once or twice. I found it hard to believe that their shitty treatment of her would've stopped overnight. Something didn't add up.

'That's exactly it!' she exclaimed, loudly. 'I don't know why it all stopped and I have a terrible feeling about all of this, Skylar. Proper.'

'I know you do. I promise I hear you, Clo. But I can't explain it. I just feel it in my gut. I need to go to this party and I need you there by my side. You're my best friend,' I said, hoping my last sentence would sweeten the deal a little.

'I don't want to see Leo,' she rasped, her words filled with so much venom.

I rolled my eyes, hard. It was tiring constantly hearing about Leo, and how Clover wanted nothing to do with him. I could see in her eyes, though, that she wasn't giving me the full story. She'd fobbed me off with half hearted excuses, or she changed the subject to me and Ollie, or even to Griff's jokes, never letting me see the truth. I'd had my suspicions ever since Leo's mum had treated her so kindly. They totally knew one another a lot better than mere acquaintances.

'I know, Clo, and I'm not asking you to,' I said gently.

'But you are Sky. Just by wanting to be at the party with Ollie, and Griff, you're asking me to spend time with Leo because at some point you know he'll join us. He'll stand there like the dickhead he is and smirk and judge me with his fucking judgey eyes,' said Clo, who—talking of "judgey eyes,"—was giving me a very judgemental look.

I couldn't help myself.

I burst into laughter at Clover's tone and the way her face had gone as red as her hair. I could feel her anger, but it was also super clear to me that Leo got under her skin because she still had feelings for him. I said as much.

'That's where you are so wrong. I have feelings for Leo Hawthorn but you can bet your arse that the feelings I have for him are ones born of hatred,' she said, vehemently.

Struggling to contain my laughter, I tried to make my face look a little more serious. I knew that Clo meant her words, I could feel it in the air, but I also knew that she was living in denial. The sexual tension between the two of them was thick and one day they would combust. Something had to give, after all.

'Okay, okay,' I said to placate her. One thing I had learned about having a best friend was that sometimes it was just easier to agree. Easier to have them think you were with them 100% even if inside you disagreed with them. 'Course that's what it is.'

'It is, I promise,' she said, a little too indignant, but I decided not to push it any further. I could tell she was getting close to the end of her patience on the subject—and with me.

'Eurgh, fine! I'll tell you a bit more from last year. Take this and run with it, cause I don't know if I'll talk about it again.'

I nodded straight away. I'd bite my tongue from now until she stopped talking. I didn't want her to stop before she'd fully opened up.

'Basically, I've known Leo ever since I was really young. Maybe two or three. But that isn't what's important. What matters is the fact that Leo, Ollie and sometimes Griff, along-side Odette and Olivia, made my life hell last year. Every single thing I did, they would turn it bad. Turn it into something to be ashamed of. They would ruin my food, they would ruin my exam results, destroy my homework and constantly write shit about me in the toilets or on the Hive,' she said, looking into my eyes.

I stayed silent. Now that she was finally talking, I didn't want to do anything to ruin it or throw her off

She continued to talk, 'They threw rotten food at me, locked me in a dark caretaker's cupboard, spat at me in class. Literally, they did anything they could to isolate me. I had no friends and nobody to turn to, or to keep me sane and tell me that I was worth more than the treatment I was getting from them.'

I could see the tears shimmering in her eyes, threatening to fall. Talking about it had brought it all up for her again, and I felt her pain. Felt how much the experience had affected her. The girls had targeted me this year, but I had Clover and Griff to help me keep afloat. Their friendship meant that I could keep myself from dwelling on it all too much. I couldn't imagine how I would feel if I was alone this year.

'That's why I'm finding this U-turn on Ollie's part so hard to understand and come to terms with. Griff too, but, at least he apologised to me the other night, after Parents' Day. I think the girls showing that footage of you and Ollie really made him see how his actions last year affected me.'

I knew she wanted me to talk, to say something, to agree with her or accept her stance on Ollie and his actions. I wasn't sure what I could say, though. What they'd done to her was beyond shit and shouldn't have happened. But I also couldn't take in everything she said and change how I acted around Ollie, Griff and even Leo because of it.

'I'm glad Griff came to his senses. I get why you feel the way you do, Clo. I promise, I'll be sensible. But c'mon, a Halloween party sounds like exactly what we need right now,' I said, hoping to get her on board.

Clover grumbled, but I thought maybe she sort of agreed with me, even if only slightly. We even started discussing possible costume ideas.

'Fine. We'll go. But if any funny business takes place, don't say I didn't tell you so!'

'Thank you! You won't regret it,' I squealed, clapping my hands together rapidly.

Which, yeah? I could've chosen better words.

Chapter Seventeen

Friday night was finally here and, not going to lie, it terrified me. So much was riding on tonight, I could feel it. Also, my friendship with Clover had been tense ever since Monday when we'd had our mini argument about this party—well, if you could call it an argument. I had to prove that everything was fine. That nothing would go wrong and we'd be laughing tomorrow about what a splendid night we'd had and just how wrong she had been about everything. Positive thinking, and all that.

Luckily, Clover came around enough to agree to dress in a couple's costume with me. I felt giddy just thinking about it. I'd never had a friend before; never had anybody to dress up with. We'd gone for Betty Rubble and Wilma Flintstone; Clover was the perfect Wilma with her red hair and I'd donned a short black, bobbed wig for the evening that covered my silver hair entirely. It completely changed how I looked.

The only change we made to the costumes was that we

were a super *dead* Betty and Wilma so we covered the dresses, and ourselves, in fake blood. We both looked super cute but also super sexy—goal accomplished. When I caught Clo's eye across our room, I knew she was thinking the same as me. We both wondered how Leo would react to seeing her like that. She looked like the perfect girl for a caveman like Leo. Even if the two of them were trying to convince everybody that they hated one another, I just couldn't believe it. One day it was going to blow up in everybody's faces and I would happily be the one telling her "I told you so". Well, as long as she wasn't saying that after tonight. *That shit would be embarrassing.*

I also hoped that tonight would spark something between me and Ollie; something more than what had already transpired between us. The kisses and stolen moments we had shared had been life changing. Okay, a bit dramatic there, Sky. But they *had* been life affirming.

Fuck, I was making myself want to vomit.

Clover and I made our way over to the clearing in the woods around eight pm. We didn't want to get there too early and look desperate, but we also didn't want to arrive too late and have all the premium alcohol be gone. It was always a fine line; or so Clover told me.

'Sky, you still have time to bow out of this, you know. We can go back to our room and nobody will even know that we were here,' Clo said as we walked closer to the clearing.

'Why would we do that? It's Ollie's birthday, and I will not bail on that,' I said. I shook my head and rolled my eyes at the same time, which was pretty impressive actually if you asked me, but also probably made me look slightly possessed. I was a bit bored with it all, actually. I knew that she was trying to look out for me, and I totally got why after she'd told me a little of what happened to her last year. 'Plus, it was a direct order from a member of *The Sect* so not like we can disobey. I don't want to give the dicks that go here more reason to harass me.'

'And since when have we cared what the other dickheads that go here think?' Clo asked, one eyebrow raised at me.

'Well ...' I didn't want to say anything to upset her, but you know, I also wasn't gonna lie to the girl either. 'Clo, we've always cared. Even if we don't admit it out loud.'

'Bullshit!' she exclaimed, throwing her arms in the air. Catching my eye, we both burst into a fit of giggles. Leaves rustled ahead of us.

'There you two are!' Griff shouted at us from up ahead. 'I've been waiting for you to get here. Now the party can truly begin.'

He hadn't met us at our room because he'd helped set up with the other members of the ruling class. He hadn't told us what he was dressing as, because according to him, he wanted to *knock our socks off*. Whatever that meant.

Griff came towards us, dressed as Prince Harry, which made me smile super wide. Of course he was. With his hair, I should have known that he would have gone for the ex-Prince. Actually, slightly annoyed that I hadn't guessed it.

'Fuck me. You two are looking mighty fine tonight. I must say my Lady Luck that I would love to add to your pearl necklace,' he said. That cheeky grin ever present on his face. Sometimes, and I'd never admit this to him—imagine the reaction—but there were times I wished it was Griff that I liked, but even though he *was* hiding a buff body, I just didn't fancy him. At.

All. There was something so carefree about Griff, and his cheekiness always felt infectious. But I'd sold my heart to a beast, and I didn't think I'd get it back at this rate. Unless he threw it back in my face.

'Oh, ha, ha,' Clover responded, raising her eyebrows at him; almost daring him to repeat what he'd said. 'You are such a filthy bastard, Griff, I swear.'

I couldn't help my guffaw. His filthy jokes often caught me off guard, but this one tickled me more than usual.

'You wound me, kind lady,' Griff said, smirking at Clo. 'Or maybe it's the fact that my pearls aren't the ones you want. Ay?'

'Oh, piss off,' Clover said. She laughed at him, and I knew that none of what Griff's words had affected her. 'Are you taking us to the party or what?'

'Follow me, ladies. The night has just begun.'

✦

THE PARTY WAS LIVELY BY THE TIME WE MADE IT DEEP enough into the woods where the party was being held. I spotted Ollie and Leo straight away; each of them with an O girl on each arm. I quickly looked away before Ollie saw me staring. What on earth was he even doing with Ophelia on his arm?

Griff didn't leave our side to join them, though. Griff had been choosing us over them a lot recently, but I didn't want to think about what that may mean. I wanted to believe he was doing it because he liked us both, but there was another part of me that thought he could have been asked to spy on us by

Ollie, Leo—or both. Especially after what Clover had told me the other night.

Pumpkins, and fake cobwebs, and gravestones decorated the wooded area, as far as my eye could see, giving the entire place a super creepy feel. There were ghosts and witches hanging from the trees, and the alcohol table over on the right-hand side was covered in skulls and other spooky items. I wasn't sure from where I stood, but it looked as if there were fake eyeballs floating in the large punch bowl placed in the centre of the table. Lord knows what was actually in the punch bowl; probably something a lot stronger than all the alcohol I'd had in my life put together. After what had happened last time I was at a party here, I was going to make sure that I only drank from an unopened bottle. I wanted to remember this night. I didn't want to wake up with no knowledge of what went down.

I looked over at Ollie, dressed as Batman. He looked better than any Batman I'd seen before; in actual life and in the movies. The mask fit his face perfectly, really highlighting his blue eyes and his full lips. The lanterns lighting the area put everyone into shadows, making the place look sinister and spooky. I felt a chill, goosebumps prickling my entire body, although that could be due to my dress being super short and revealing.

Leo, dressed as The Joker, stood with Odette by his side, dressed as Harley Quinn. If I didn't hate her, I would totally love their couple costumes. It was really well done, and they looked great together. Something I wouldn't mention to Clover.

Shit, I thought as I spotted the large table overflowing with presents; a five tier cake beside them. *Fuck*. I hadn't got Ollie a present. I had no money, and I wasn't even sure I could get him something he didn't already own. Or even if I'd get him something he actually wanted and or liked. I also would not be one of those cliché bitches that gave their virginity as a present. I wasn't ready for that, and I hated that whole bullshit idea that virginity was a gift to give. Gross.

On the edge of the party, Ollie and Leo still stood looking over at us, ignoring the girls at their side.

'What's up with those assholes?' Clover asked, nudging Griff in the side, obviously referring to the boys.

'Who even knows girly tots. They've both been acting strange recently,' Griff said, his tone conspiring.

'Strange as in ...' I said, wondering what he meant.

'Can't explain it. Ollie barely has anything to do with Leo or the girls outside of swimming or classes now. But we're all super tight, so it makes sense that he's talking to him. It's his birthday, after all.'

'Yeah, that's fine, but why the fuck is Ophelia hanging off his arm looking like a tramp?' Clover asked, voicing exactly what was going through my mind. Ophelia, dressed as some kind of slutty nurse or something, stood next to Ollie. Practically pawing at him. Maybe she was a zombie nurse? Honestly, I didn't want to get close enough to find out for definite. I was just happy that she wasn't in a couple costume with Ollie. I'd be having some words with him if he'd done that to me.

Well, I would have had words with him in my head. We may have got closer recently, but I for sure wasn't over my anxiety around him completely. My stutter had improved though, which I counted as a minor victory. It barely happened now, unless I felt overwhelmed and/or stressed.

After what felt like ten minutes but was probably just a

few, Ollie finally untangled himself from Ophelia and came over to where the three of us stood.

'Hey beautiful. You look killer.' Ollie looked as if he wanted to eat me whole. His eyes taking me in, slowly trailing up and down, taking in every inch of me.

'I look dead. So less killer, more like I bumped into a killer,' I joked.

'Well, you're definitely the best dead girl I've had the fortune of meeting,' he said.

'Is there any good fortune in meeting a dead girl?'

'Depends on the occasion,' he bantered back. His top lip raised on one side, making it clear that he was enjoying our casual conversation. 'Right now, I'd say it's a great thing.'

He leaned down and kissed my cheek. The kiss promised more, his lips grazing my skin briefly, leaving a tingling heat in their wake.

'You scrub up well too, Clo,' Ollie said, his tone telling me he didn't mean it. Definitely a gritting of the teeth situation, but I could tell that he was trying for me, which I appreciated.

'Thanks, dickhead. S'pose you don't look too bad,' said Clo in response.

'That must have hurt, Clo,' Griff piped up.

'It really, really did. But I thought I'd try and be kind. You know, being his birthday and all,' she said, answering Griff. She turned to look at Ollie. 'Plus, my girl seems to see something in you so don't fuck it up.'

'Thanks for that.'

'She's not wrong, dude. I'll be pissed if you fuck it up, too. You've got an angel there,' Griff said, his smile beaming.

'Griff, you are such a cutie patootie,' I cooed, reaching up and scratching under his chin like you would a child. 'Remind me to give you a shoulder massage the next time we watch films together.'

'Hey!' Ollie interjected. 'Where's my shoulder massage?'

'You never give me any, plus,' I shrugged, 'Griff is my boy.'

'Oh babe, I see how it is,' Ollie said and tickled me on my side, causing me to laugh like crazy. 'I'll be getting you back sometime soon, New Girl.'

'Okay, well as lovely as this is to watch, I want to get fucked up,' Clover announced, taking Griff's hand and leading him towards the table with the large punch bowl. Ollie had stopped tickling me. He looked me in the eye and tucked a piece of the wig's hair behind my ear, away from my face.

'Do you want a drink?' he asked.

'Only if it's unopened. Don't want a repeat of last time.'

'Trust me, Sky. That won't be happening again.'

'So you know who did it?' I asked, wondering if he'd been keeping a secret from me.

'No ...' He shook his head. 'But I made it clear that if any harm came to you, I would make whoever was responsible pay.'

'Oh, okay,' I mumbled. I knew that he wasn't telling the whole truth. His eyes had started flitting around, not focusing on one spot, and then when he looked back at me he was looking at more of a spot over my shoulder than at me. 'Shall we dance?'

'Sure. Let me just go get us some drinks and then we can dance.'

I agreed and off he went to the table where Clover and Griff were still standing. Ollie shared some words with them and then made his way back to me, holding two bottles; one of beer and the other of some kind of alcopop.

Drinking when dancing, while difficult, was also fun. We were laughing and joking around with one another in a way we never had before. It was like Ollie had loosened up, I couldn't put my finger on why, but I enjoyed seeing this side of him. He seemed more like Griff; you know, carefree. A weight lifted off of him somehow, and I was so happy that I'd come here tonight. Clover's warning was a distant memory. It almost seemed stupid that I'd been so apprehensive about tonight.

As we danced, I could feel every ridge, every muscle, and I just wanted to lick him all over.

'You are hot as fuck, Sky,' he whispered in my ear, causing tingles to erupt all over my body. 'This outfit is honestly amazing.'

'It w-was my idea,' I said, quite proud of myself. I wanted to pick something that nobody else would choose. Nothing worse than being dressed the same as all the other basic bitches. Or at least that was what films and books had taught me. I'd never been to a fancy dress party, so I'd wanted my first to be the most original it could be.

'You chose well,' he said as he aimed a wolfish smile my way. 'You look amazing and I really wish that I could peel this dress off of you.'

'Maybe if you play your cards right Mister, you could,' I said, flustered. Flirting with Ollie was fun. He'd said a lot of shit to me in the past that was borderline flirty and a lot that was borderline rapey. It was rare that we had spoken like this; a back and forth with both of us as active participants.

'It really must be my birthday.'

I laughed and hugged him tight to me. This time, I instigated the kiss between us and I felt certain it was our best yet.

✦

THE ONLY DOWNSIDE TO A PARTY IN THE WOODS WAS THE complete lack of toilets. I'd tried my best to hold it in for the last couple of hours, but I'd hit that point. Hit that peak and I knew that I was about to break the seal and potentially ruin the rest of my evening. But I couldn't help myself, I needed to go.

I made my way farther into the tree line, away from the rest of the crowd, and wandered off on my own. I'd told the others where I was heading, pretty sure they'd heard me. I'd got a nod, at least from Clo.

Anyway, I found a tree that was well hidden and nobody seemed to be around. I quickly peed, then stood still for a moment. I didn't want to head straight back to the party. I was having such a good time, but I needed a minute or two alone to process it all. Rifling through my bag to find the packet of tissues I'd put there—I'd learned from the last time—my fingers brushed against a folded piece of paper.

Hm. Didn't remember putting that there. Knowing me, I could have put it in my bag forever ago. It was super rare that I cleaned my bag out, and I'd always wanted to joke about how it reminded me of Mary Poppins' bag, but I'd never had any friends to joke about it with. Huh. Must remember to use that line with Clover sometime soon.

I giggled to myself. Man, I could be funny.

Maybe I'd had more to drink than I realised. Knew I should have eaten more at dinner, too.

Anyway, the paper.

I pulled it out of my bag and read it, smiling as I did.

LITTLE ONE,

Meet me in the Pool House at Midnight.
I want to ring my birthday in with you. And
only you.

I LOOKED AT MY PHONE. THE TIME WAS A QUARTER TO midnight, and I was a good ten minutes away from the pool house, so I knew I needed to hurry to meet him on time. I wondered why he said nothing in person. There was no guarantee I'd even find the piece of paper. But then I guessed, if I hadn't found it, and hadn't disappeared to go to the toilet, he would have just taken me to the pool house himself.

I stumbled my way through the trees, heading to the pool house with one thing on my mind; to kiss Ollie at midnight, similar to a New Year's kiss, but this time it was a birthday kiss. I made it to the pool house with a minute or two to spare and quickly made my way inside.

I couldn't see him in the entrance hall, so I made my way to the pool itself. Ollie loved swimming and being beside the water, so it would make sense that he would wait for me there.

The water in the pool, the way it moved, the way the light hit it, made the room look super cool. There was no proper way to describe it, but the reflection of the water looked so pretty, so mesmerising. I stopped and stared. Taking in the tranquil feel of the water. I couldn't see Ollie anywhere, so I reckoned I'd got here before him.

Walking around the edge, I got lost in my own thoughts.

I hoped Ollie didn't expect me to sleep with him tonight.

I hoped I hadn't given him the impression that I was ready for that, even if I had joked with him earlier about peeling my dress off. *Fuck.* Had I fuelled the monster? Unleashed a beast that wanted me to the point he wouldn't listen to what I wanted?

No. Course not. *Stop being so fucking stupid, Sky.*

I was thinking maybe one day I would be ready to have sex with Ollie, cause if things continued to progress the way they currently were, I knew I'd want to sometime soon.

Lost in my mind, I jumped when I heard him enter the room. The door slammed behind him; the noise reverberating around the large room.

His footsteps echoed, the water and the large ceiling causing every sound to amplify, but I didn't turn around. It felt intimate. The tension building between us. A midnight tryst was so romantic—and super fucking sexy.

I felt his breath touching my neck. He took my wig off and brushed his fingers through my hair, his touch hard, as he pressed down slightly into my scalp. I tingled all over.

His hands rested on my back at the bottom of my spine. It felt familiar and private. Intimate.

His hands pushed forward, and I flew through the air.

I entered the pool with a loud splash.

The water rushed up around me. Entering my ears, my nose and my mouth. I thrashed around, trying to make my way back up to the surface.

A hand gripped the top of my head. Holding me down. Forcing me under.

Fuck. Water filled my mouth. I tried to get away, but there was no escape.

What in the actual fuck right now? I couldn't breathe. My vision spotted, darkening around the edges, and a sense of déjà vu hit me. It'd been eight weeks, and I'd lost count of the amount of times I'd come close to losing consciousness.

How had I ended up here?

My mind slipped away.

Maybe a little sleep would be okay.

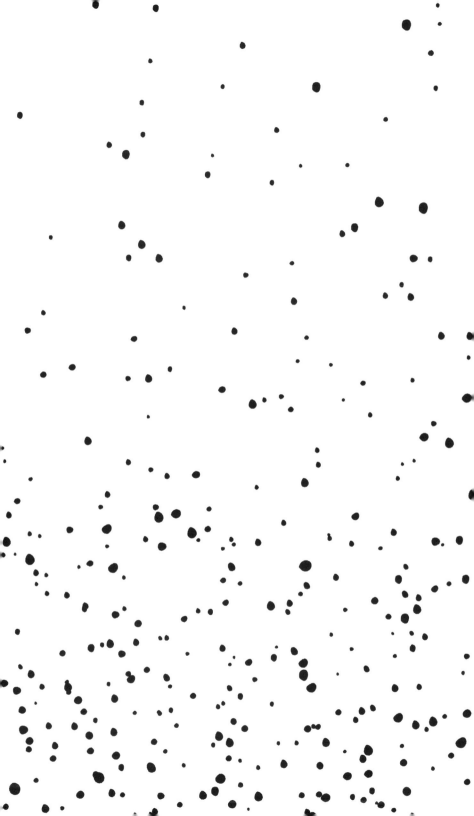

Chapter Eighteen

'Shit.'

I could hear a faint voice swearing above me. I shivered, and I felt even worse than I did after the drugging at the party in the woods. What was it with me and Hawthorn parties?

All I could think was that I did *not* want to see Clover soon. She'd undoubtedly tell me she'd been right all along about not going to the party.

'Can you hear me, baby?' A voice asked.

I was pretty certain it was Ollie's voice I could hear, but confusion filled me—he never called me baby. My ears felt clogged, as if still underwater, and I couldn't reach him from under the weight of it.

I heard music in my head. Specifically, I heard the word baby three times with an oh afterward. I giggled in my mind. What a tune. *Fucking delirious or what?*

'Baby girl, I really need you to answer me. Or just open your eyes for me.'

Eurgh, I'm trying. I screamed inside my head. I wanted so desperately to reach him. To open my eyes and see what was happening around me. Figure out why I felt so cold; so wet. I could tell that when I opened my eyes, I would be hit with a bright light. A light so bright I could almost see it through my eyelids already.

'Ollie, dude, we need to call an ambulance,' Griff said urgently. His worry hit me straight in the heart. I didn't want to cause him to worry. I doubled my efforts, trying even harder to open my eyes and reassure Big Bird that I was alright.

'I'm with Griff. Stop being such a massive dick and do the right thing,' Clover pleaded, causing a sharp pain through my heart. The two of them had grown to mean so much to me in such a brief space of time. If nothing else came from this scholarship, I would still be so glad I took my place here because of them. Shit, oxygen clearly was leaving my brain. I was starting to get sappy.

I needed to knock that off, fast.

Wake. The. Fuck. Up.

I tuned back into the conversation happening around me.

'Call an ambulance and everybody will know our shit,' Ollie growled.

'Maybe he's right,' Leo said. For once, he didn't sound bored. Although, he didn't exactly sound worried either. For once he sounded slightly interested.

'Not you too, Leo,' Ollie snarled, but then his tone once again softened. 'Baby, it's me, please open your eyes.'

Almost as if a switch turned on in my brain—or, you know, the fact that I needed to take a deep breath—I sat bolt upright.

Coughing and spluttering up water, I tried to take in deep lungfuls of air. I was right; the light was far too bright.

I was beside the pool, surrounded by Ollie, Leo, Griff and Clover. Clover's make up was streaking down her face, the black mascara marks showing her despair. Griff had his arm around her shoulders, looking sombre.

Leo looked like hell. I'd never seen him show many expressions outside of boredom; not for a long period of time, anyway. His hair was wild, as if he'd been running his fingers through it and pulling it in every direction in despair. It tugged at my heart. Maybe he cared a little more about me than he let on.

Ollie was the last of them I focused on.

If I thought Leo looked like hell, then Ollie looked like he'd been living there for the last year. He'd taken off his mask, his face pale and sickly looking. As if the worry had seeped into his pores. He moved as if he was going to hug me, but I darted back out of his reach. Somebody had tried to drown me, and Ollie had been the person who had wanted to meet me here.

I had to be cautious. I had to put myself first.

'Get away from her.' Clover bit out. Her face had transformed from that of somebody upset to that of somebody who was burning up with anger as she said, 'You did this to her.'

'What?!' he shouted so loud that I flinched.

'You! I can't figure out how Oliver, but I know you're the reason for this.'

'Wow. How did you reach that conclusion?' he asked Clo, his tone filled with derision.

'Don't talk to her like that,' Griff said, sticking up for Clo. 'Lay off her.'

'Lay off her?! Dude, she's implying that I had something to do with this!'

'Sky must feel similar because she just moved away from you, bro,' Leo said. He moved closer to me, 'I'll take you to the Hospital Wing.'

I went into his arms and let him pull me to my feet. He did say to contact him if I ever needed help. This time, he was already present.

'Don't walk away, Sky. Or at least let me take you,' Ollie said, almost begging me. His eyes didn't match his tone as they flashed with anger.

'N-no, I'll g-go with Leo,' I said, my stutter back—more from the shiver I hadn't got rid of yet.

'And how are you going to explain this?' Ollie asked, facing Leo.

'I'm a Hawthorn, I don't exactly need to explain this,' said Leo, in his most haughty tone.

'Oh, using Daddy's name once again. That's rich,' Ollie spat.

'Let them go,' Griff said, still holding Clo, as he looked at Ollie, trying to make him back down. 'Go on bro, go make sure she's okay.'

Leo and I ambled away, leaving the other three standing beside the edge of the pool. I could hear Ollie and Griff growling at one another, with Clover every now and again piping up, but I couldn't hear exactly what it was they were saying. It definitely sounded like Ollie was protesting his innocence, though.

✦

THE HOSPITAL WING LOOKED NO DIFFERENT TO WHEN I was here last and I let Leo do all the talking with the head nurse. She looked rather worried at having a soaking wet dead Betty Rubble and The Joker in the room with her; maybe she was one of the faculty members who wasn't aware of the Halloween party currently raging in the woods. *Doubtful.*

She checked me over, and I lay down on the bed she'd assigned me. The nurse wanted me to stay overnight to monitor me, which made total sense really. I got comfortable as I prepared to be here until morning and tried not to think too hard about the whole near drowning thing.

'Thanks, Leo. For everything,' I mumbled and smiled tentatively at him. 'You didn't have to bring me here.'

'Yeah Sky, I did,' he said, looking at me. He said nothing more than that and got comfy in the seat next to my bed in silence. He slumped down, not intending to move soon. I was trying to understand his motivation for all this, but I couldn't figure it out for the life of me. Other than the odd occasion I'd bumped into him in empty hallways, I had spent little time with Leo. Especially not one-on-one like this. Instantly, I felt like a child, too scared to talk, not knowing what to say.

An hour passed. We both must have fallen into a very light sleep as a commotion somewhere else in the wing startled us both awake. I could hear shouting and items being thrown around. Great. Ollie, Griff, and Clover must finally be here.

'Skylar ... Skylar!' Ollie called. My name getting louder the closer he got to us, and when he flew through the curtain that surrounded my bed, he looked frantic, like he'd been trying to get away from Griff and Clover for a lot longer than he'd wanted to be.

'Skylar, I promise I didn't do this to you,' he said, going straight to reach for my hand.

'Calm down, bro,' Leo said. He stood, raising his hands at Ollie to keep him back and away from me, preventing him from touching me. 'The nurse said to stay calm and not distress Sky too much.'

'Since when have you known what's best for Sky, Leo?' Ollie asked. His tone filled with suspicion, like Leo and I were hiding something from him. 'You two don't even talk to each other.'

'Just leave it, Ollie. Say what you've come here to say and then leave so Skylar can rest.' Leo's words were definite and his tone brooked no argument.

'Skylar, believe me. I wouldn't do that to you,' Ollie said. His eyes bored into mine, causing the complete opposite effect of the calm he was trying to instil. 'What were you even doing at the pool?'

'Y-you asked me to meet you there,' I said. My stammer had returned in full force. 'You left me a note in my b-bag.'

'No, baby, I didn't. You must have left your bag somewhere and somebody played a mean trick on you,' he said, attempting to placate me.

I didn't take it off once; I thought, but didn't voice it out loud. I shook my head at him instead. *A mean trick? Bit of an understatement.*

'Then they must have slipped it into your bag when you weren't paying attention,' he tried again to give a plausible solution.

'It's a bum bag dude. There's no way somebody could have slipped shit in there without her noticing or at least feeling it,' Leo said, sounding bored again, but this time he wasn't directing it at me. He aimed his tone at Ollie, calling him out on his attempts to get out of everything.

'I swear to you, Oliver, that I would have n-noticed,' I said, feeling small.

'What did the note say, baby?' he asked.

'To m-meet you at midnight, to ring in your b-birthday.' I smiled faintly at him. 'Happy birthday, Ollie.'

He smiled in return and took a couple of deep breaths in order to calm himself down some more. I reckoned seeing me in the Hospital Wing, alive and safe, had made him feel slightly better.

That was when Clover and Griff burst through the curtain.

'Eurgh, that nurse woman is such a job's worth,' Griff grumbled. 'Wouldn't let us through as you two douche canoes are already here. Tried to tell her that Sky here would prefer us two, but she wasn't listening to a word of it.'

'I'm happy you're here,' I said as Leo allowed them to get close enough to me to hug me. I felt overwhelmed at the amount of love surrounding me. 'I w-was just telling Ollie and Leo about the note I got.'

'What note?' Clover asked, her eyebrows furrowed, and she looked just as perplexed as everybody else.

'Y-yeah. To meet Ollie at the pool at midnight.'

'Okay ...' Clo said, tapering off. She regained her train of thought almost instantly and asked, 'But why didn't you tell any of us you were going there?'

'I found the note when I was going to the toilet. It seemed pointless to walk back to you, when I could head straight to the school and not walk back on myself.' I shrugged, it had made total sense to me a couple of hours ago.

With hindsight, it wasn't the best decision I'd ever made, but I'd made it.

Couldn't change it now.

'Makes sense ...' Clo said, gazing off into the distance.

'How did you know I was there?' I asked. I'd been wondering about that ever since Ollie had been so adamant it wasn't him, because if he didn't send the note, then the pool wouldn't be the first place to look for me.

'We didn't. We were searching the trees for you for a while, but then Leo came over to us and told us to look at the school. The pool house was the closest building from where we exited the trees,' said Clo, her eyes narrowing when she mentioned Leo's involvement. I understood what she meant. The pool house was closest when I'd exited the trees, too.

'Which is pretty suspicious, Leo,' Ollie said in an accusing tone. He turned his gaze to Leo, obviously doubting even his best friend in that moment.

'Dude, I'd heard the girls talking about it. They'd spotted Sky walking off alone and were hoping she'd come to harm,' Leo said, shrugging. I couldn't put my finger on why, but I believed Leo. He sounded sincere to my ears.

'So proof that they had something to do with it,' snapped Clo.

'Not really Clover, but nice try,' Leo said, the words clipped. It was strange to hear Clover's name being said so formally. So stiff. I could feel Leo's hate emanating off of him in waves.

'Got any better ideas, twat?' she asked. Her eyes glinted with challenge.

'No. But I know it wasn't the girls. They wouldn't have the strength,' Leo sneered back.

'Funny that. They definitely had the strength when they were beating on Skylar in the bathrooms a few weeks ago,' Clo said, her voice rising with every word she uttered.

The room went silent. Everybody nodded, seeming to agree that the girl's motives seemed shady. Even if they weren't solely responsible, I felt sure they knew more than they were letting on. But something deep inside of me knew that it hadn't been one of them in the pool room tonight. I could tell from the footsteps, from the height of the person that stood behind me, that it was a guy. The scent, the strength; there was no way a girl had done this.

'Do you still have the note, Sky?' Griff asked, reaching for my hand and squeezing it tight. I squeezed his back. His warmth filled me, travelling up my arm and into my body.

'It's in my bag. Or at least it should be,' I told them. My bag had gone into the water when I did, so I wasn't sure how much the contents had suffered.

Clover grabbed my bag and had a good root through it, finding the note. It wasn't completely untouched by water, but it was still legible. The four of them passed it around, each of them inspecting it thoroughly, trying to figure out where it had come from and who had written it.

The nurse came along, obviously realising that none of the people that had come back here had returned.

'Miss Crescent needs her rest, so you need to be leaving now,' she said, her manner brisk and no nonsense.

Instantly, Ollie and Leo disputed who was going to stay with me. I stayed quiet because honestly; I wasn't getting in the middle of those two. I also didn't actually know right now which one I *wanted* to have here. It would make sense for me to want Ollie nearby, but there was still a tiny part of me that was cautious of him.

I also shouldn't feel safe with Leo. He'd done nothing wrong, but he hadn't stood by me throughout the bullying and harassment either. He sat with the girls and was usually attached to Odette by at least one body part.

Clover and Griff accepted that they were being kicked out and leaned down to give me an awkward hug simultaneously; the most awkward group hug I'd ever been a part of. Actually —the only group hug I'd ever been a part of.

'See you tomorrow, Sky,' Clo said.

'We'll be here bright and early, New Girl,' said Griff.

With a smile, they left together, meaning I was left with Leo and Ollie.

They both stayed, neither of them accepting defeat. The silence between the three of us was so fucking loud. But nobody broke it.

Eventually, I fell asleep to the sounds of their breathing. Just as I was about to drift off, I heard four words. Quiet, hanging there in the darkness.

'I'm so sorry, Sky.'

But I wasn't sure which one of them said it.

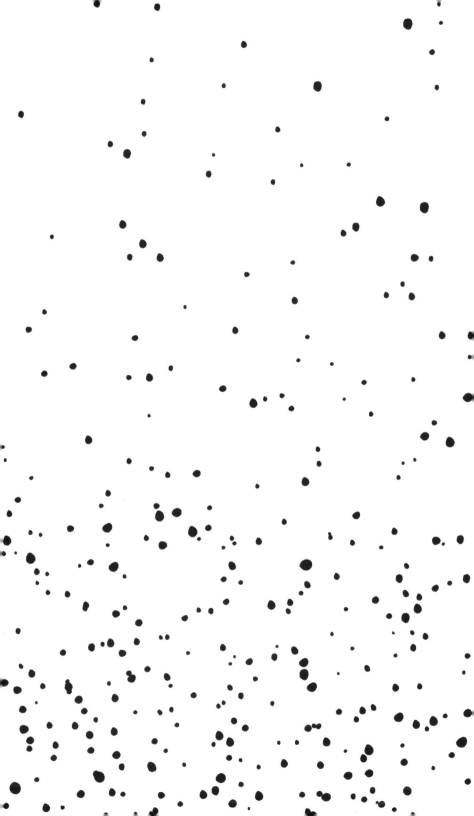

Chapter Nineteen

I spent one night in the hospital and then returned to my dorm room the next morning, bright and early, just like Griff had said it would be.

Both Ollie and Leo were quiet in the morning, and Leo left without saying another word to me. He did, however, text me not long after leaving my side.

I MEAN IT, STUTTER. CALL ME IF YOU NEED ME.

I WAS CURIOUS ABOUT LEO'S MOTIVES. HE ALWAYS ACTED so secretive and he clearly didn't want anybody to know that we were in contact privately. I could understand why he wanted to avoid conflict with Ollie and Clover, but I got the impression that they weren't the only reason he wanted to keep our friendship of sorts on the down low.

Ollie once again told me of his innocence, that he hadn't given me the note, and that he would get to the bottom of who did. I knew he meant well, but I was too tired to get into it all with him. He walked me back to my room, both of us silent, and only when we arrived back did he talk. I stepped into my dorm, using my body to cover the entrance so he couldn't slip around me.

'New Girl, I promise you I didn't do this,' he said. Oddly, I didn't hate it when he called me New Girl anymore. At first, it had been a slur of sorts, but now he and Griff used it affectionately.

I tilted my head, my look one of questioning.

'Ollie, please can we do this later?' I asked, my eyes finding his. 'I'm so tired and I just want to be in my own bed.'

'Can I come over later tonight?' he asked, pushing his luck. He meant well, though. Or at least I thought he did.

Clover scoffed at his question, telling me without words that she wouldn't stay quiet if he came to our room later on. Honestly, I couldn't be arsed to have them two going into it again, especially when my head felt the way it did; like an axe was attempting to split in two any moment.

'How about I come over to you tomorrow if I'm feeling better?' I asked, tentative, not wanting to wake the beast I'd seen a glimpse of a couple of times.

I thought it was a pretty solid compromise to be fair. It also meant we could talk properly with no distractions—and no Clover talking louder than me, or worse, talking for me.

'Okay,' he conceded, reluctantly. He leaned down, his lips brushing against the top of my head. A quick moment of pressure, fleeting, and gone just as fast.

'I'll text you. I promise,' I said, closing my dorm door in his face.

I turned around to find Clover standing directly in front of me, blocking my path to my bed. The bed I'd been desperately dreaming of all night. I gritted my teeth as I prepared myself for whatever she felt the compulsion to say next.

'You can't trust him, Skylar,' she blurted out. The seriousness in her tone wasn't lost on me.

'Why n-not?' I asked, intrigued to hear what reason she'd give.

'Because he sprinted off ahead!' she said, the words bursting out of her. I could tell she'd been holding this in all night. 'We arrived after he did, by at least five minutes.'

'Oh,' I said, unsure of what else to say. I understood where Clo was coming from—and sure, I didn't realise they hadn't all arrived together, but still. This was Ollie. Dark and mysterious, Ollie. He wasn't always a dick though, and I'd shared some deeper moments with him, I knew I had. As an afterthought, I asked, 'How long does it take to fall unconscious through drowning?'

'Like I bloody know,' Clo replied, her phone appearing in her hand in an instant. I knew what that meant. Google. Clo loved to google search everything. For example, we'd be watching a film, and I'd innocently ask what other projects an actor had starred in, and she'd have a list of their entire filmography in less than one minute flat.

'So?' I asked, growing impatient.

'A-ha!' she exclaimed, her eyes shining in triumph. 'Two minutes. It takes two minutes to become unconscious. I *knew* the fucker had the time and the opportunity.'

I rolled my eyes at her theatrics. To me, she sounded like a bad detective from a police drama in the noughties. You know, the ones they showed on reruns past midnight.

'Right ... but do you really believe he could'a done it?' I asked, stressing the word "really". Because I *really* didn't know for definite. Whoever it was had printed the note, meaning no handwriting could give it away. Plus, they had put it into my bag and although I was certain nobody had access to it, I supposed they could have without my noticing.

'Yeah, Sky, I really do,' she mumbled. Fucking fantastic.

I wanted to find a reason to trust Ollie, but it didn't look good. I didn't want to believe he could have tried to kill me. It was too extreme. I'd keep searching for a way to prove his innocence.

Blow me.

✦

I found myself outside Ollie's door the next day, trying to build up enough courage to knock and alert him to my presence.

I'd been standing there for at least five minutes, and the people that shared this hall were giving me funny looks as they went to and from their rooms.

Sundays were the day that people could relax and visit with friends without repercussions from the staff. Griff had told me that the only reason he and Ollie could visit with us on weeknights was because they were a part of *The Sect*, and therefore above the average school rules. It had its perks, for sure. The pizza delivery being the main one in my eyes. Man, I loved pizza. I'd never understood how people didn't just want to eat it every, single, day. I would if I could. Easily. Happily.

But whatever. No more procrastinating, distracting thoughts. Time to lift my hand to the black door in front of me.

I'd never noticed the ominous and foreboding nature of Ollie's door before. Showed how observant I'd been—not.

I needed to sum up the courage to hear Ollie out. To listen, and not just assume the worst because all the pieces looked bad. *Really bad.* I didn't feel scared of being alone with him, exactly, but I felt a sense of dread rising in my gut. When Ollie lost his temper, he frightened me. Only a little. But enough to create a seed of doubt.

Finally, after what was definitely too long of a time, I knocked on the door in the pattern Clover and I used. If it annoyed him, then tough shit.

I heard him moving around inside of his room straight away, and I barely waited ten seconds before the door opened wide and he pulled me close to him in a tight hug.

'Sky, I was so worried last night,' he said, squeezing me even tighter to him. His heart pounded in his chest underneath my ear. All around us, I could feel his fear as if it were a tangible thing. 'Please don't do that to me again.'

'I can assure you I don't intend to,' I said, my voice muffled by his taut pecs. I chuckled, as if any of it had been my choice in the first place. Oh yes, Ollie, I just loved nearly drowning. *Real highlight of my night.* 'I've had enough happen to me this year to last a lifetime.'

He let me out of his warm embrace, but grabbed my hand instantly and pulled me further into his room, kicking the door closed. Then, on a second thought, he went back and locked it.

I raised my eyebrow at his action, giving him what I hoped to be a stern look. Not sure it translated too well though, as he was looking at me in the way I imagined the wolf looked at Little Red Riding Hood. Like he couldn't wait to eat her whole. I asked, 'Expecting something?'

'Nope,' he said, a smile on his face, 'Just thought you'd like some privacy. Knowing that dickhead Griff, he'd happily burst in here to check on you. The fact that it would irritate me would be a bonus for him.'

Okay, I'd give him that one. Griff would totally try and do something like that, but I knew he was keeping Clo company while I was here. Leo also knew I'd come here because I'd text him to tell him so. He hadn't responded, but the two blue ticks had appeared, so I knew he'd seen my message.

'So ...' I looked around. Should I sit on the bed? Or was that too presumptuous?

Hang on, no. I didn't want him to assume that I'd forgiven him and we could just skip straight back to where we were before this shit happened. Eurgh, where even were we before this shit happened? Ollie acted so hot and cold towards me. A gentleman and a prince one minute; a dark, brooding beast the next.

I chose to sit on his gaming chair instead. It gave me enough distance from him and I could breathe without his scent completely overwhelming my senses. Just being in his room was hard enough. Once I was comfy, and he'd seated himself on the edge of his bed facing me, I said, 'Talk.'

'Right. Where shall I start?' he asked.

'I've heard the beginning is a good place. You know, usually,' I smarted, losing my stutter and my worries. I meant business and if I sputtered my way through this conversation, he wouldn't take me seriously.

'Oh, ha, ha, Sky. I meant more what do you wanna know?'

'You wanted to talk to me, remember?' I said, acting a bit bitchier than I'd intended to. I put hard emphasis on the word "remember".

'I wanted to prove to you it wasn't me,' he said. The way he looked at me, so contrite, definitely made me want to just believe him. I couldn't put my faith in a contrite look, though. 'Promise, I didn't give you that note. I had no fucking idea where you'd gone and it worried me that somebody hurt you.'

'Somebody did hurt me,' I said.

'I know and I'm sorry.'

'Why apologise if you had nothing to do with it?' I asked, confused. What did he have to apologise for?

'I'm sorry that I didn't stick by your side the whole time,' he clarified.

I could tell he meant it. That he really felt pissed at himself for not being with me the entire night. He then said, 'If I had, this would never have happened.'

'You know, Ollie, when you say shit like that, it makes me think that you had something to do with it,' I said, knowing how it sounded. But to me, by saying it wouldn't have happened if he had stayed with me, I started to think maybe it happened because he had the chance to tell somebody I was alone. I'd lost it, hadn't I?

'Right,' he huffed out. 'So you've let Clover get inside your fucking head.'

'What?' I asked, shocked by his tone. His face flushed and his eyes glinted with cruelty. I'd made him so angry, so quickly. I shivered, apprehension filling me. 'W-what does that even mean?'

'You heard me, Skylar. Clover has been turning you

against me, twisting shit like she always does,' he said, eyes narrowing in disgust.

'No, Oliver, she hasn't. Am I not allowed to form my own opinions?'

'Of course,' he said, brushing away my words as if that wasn't the real problem here. As if he hadn't meant it in the way I'd heard it. 'It's just suspicious timing. Even you can see that, surely.'

'Can see what?' I asked, bewildered. I didn't understand how Clover talking to me would be suspicious timing.

'You know,' he said, imploringly. 'You've been attacked, and now Clover's turning you against me. How well do you know her, really?'

'Seriously?' I asked, shocked at his implication. 'Well, for starters, Clover has said nothing. Second, I'd like to think I know her pretty well, thank you very much.' I was on a roll. I took a deep breath, and continued, 'How well do I know *you*, really?'

'Explain. Now.' His tone was demanding, leaving no room for misinterpretation.

'I just don't know where I stand with you. Like. Not at all.'

'Where would you like to stand?' he asked, his tone lighter. Amused.

'W-what?'

'What do you want, Sky?'

I ran my fingers through my hair, and I looked everywhere in the room but at him. I took in my surroundings to take my focus off of him. His room was surprisingly bare. Not that this was the first time I was noticing it, but it was the first time I'd really thought about it. Ollie was somebody I couldn't figure out, and as much as I felt attraction to him and wanted to be with him, I also wanted to run far, far away from him.

Something was screaming at me to get out of the situation I had found myself in.

Should I be bold? Tell him what I wanted, for real this time, and hope he wanted the same thing?

Fuck it. I was going to take a leaf out of a confident person's book and go for it. I wanted so badly to believe him, to give this thing growing between us a try, that I threw caution to the wind.

'I want you,' I said plainly.

At first, I wasn't sure he heard me as I had spoken so quietly. I'd mumbled for sure. 'I want you,' I repeated, louder this time.

Ollie's eyes widened. I'd shocked him. For probably the first and last time. Clearly he'd never expected me to be so open and honest with him. To just come out and say what I wanted, damn the consequences.

'Shit, Sky. That isn't what I thought you were going to say,' he said, looking flustered. A blush had formed on his pale cheeks.

I shrugged, not sure what else to say. I'd got out what I wanted to and even though I hadn't completely accepted that he had nothing to do with what had happened to me, I also wouldn't ruin my potential happiness over it.

'So ...' Ollie said and stood up from the bed, slowly making his way towards me. I sat frozen. Unable to move, trapped by his gaze. 'How about we make this official?'

'W-what do you mean?' I asked, stuttering.

'How do you feel about being my girlfriend?' he asked. He

stood in front of me and I looked up at him, falling into his blue gaze. I felt like his prey.

'S-sorry what?' I asked, sure I'd heard him wrong.

'Be my girlfriend,' he said.

This time, it wasn't a question.

✦

CHRISTMAS BREAK CAME AROUND SUPER FAST AFTER that, or at least it felt like it did.

So much had already happened since I joined Hawthorn Academy, and I'd only been there three months. I couldn't believe it was that short of a period. It felt like I'd been there for years.

Clover believed *The Set* were responsible for both my drugging and drowning, but Griff and Ollie were adamant that they knew the girls had nothing to do with it.

Apparently, the rulers of the school had their own set of rules that us mere plebeians had no knowledge of, and the girls wouldn't have been able to make such enormous steps without two of the boys agreeing. They'd stressed the two when telling me about it and clarified that Leo didn't have that kind of power alone.

I'd never mentioned Leo giving me his number to any of them. Well, thrusting his number on me by texting me first. It felt like something I should keep a secret. Something for only me to know, and because I knew this, I didn't think that Leo would set the girls on me. No matter how many times Clover tried to convince me otherwise.

Christmas Day itself was Griff's birthday, which I reckoned had some bearing on the fact that he thought he was God's gift to the world.

Honestly, I was pretty sure he'd even said to me recently that he thought of himself as the second coming of Christ. I'd rolled my eyes at him and laughed.

The four of us were spending the holidays at Griff's parents' estate as they weren't there and the entire mansion would sit empty otherwise. If I thought about it, Griff had never mentioned his parents, so maybe it wasn't that unusual that they weren't here to spend Christmas, or his birthday, with him. They hadn't attended Parents' Day either, and nobody had questioned it.

To be fair, if my mum had the opportunity to leave me alone for my birthday then she most definitely would. What I did know was that Griff was an only child and that without Leo and Ollie, his childhood would have been extremely lonely. It made me realise that Griff's cheeky, cheery personality probably had something to do with his upbringing. He obviously used humour as a coping mechanism for something darker.

Clover had agreed to come when she had thought that Leo wouldn't be there, but apparently he'd changed his plans when he'd heard she was going. At least, that was what Ollie had told me in private. When she found out, she was so pissed at Griff for not telling her earlier.

My relationship with Ollie had grown so fast, and it still felt super surreal to me that I could call that gorgeous specimen of a human my boyfriend. After he'd demanded I be his girlfriend, I'd stayed quiet. But then he'd bent down, put his hands on my shoulders, and kissed me, hard. Let's just say that had swayed me. Then he'd spent the rest of the evening trying to make it up to me with my favourite pizza. He even let me watch one of my favourite comfort films, *Bride and Prejudice*. Every time I watched it, it made me feel young again. I knew the entire film off by heart. Ollie hadn't even got mad when I'd quoted every word the entire way through—and sang every song, too.

Clover was still trying to make me at least question him about the drugging and the drowning; but I wouldn't bite anymore. He was the one who had been there for me after both instances; who had looked after me and ensured that I was okay. He'd never given me any actual sign that it could have involved him. Okay, he'd acted majorly shady and had been hot and cold with me ever since I'd met him, but Clo was trying to imply that was because his ocean blue eyes and his wide smile blinded me. Which? Yeah, they definitely did. But that wasn't why I trusted him. Not completely. His actions after the fact just didn't add up to him being the person responsible. The way Clover told it though, I should believe that Ollie held me under the water one minute and then gave me mouth to mouth in the next. *Insert eye roll here.*

We'd arrived at Griff's estate a few days ago and I still couldn't believe I was spending Christmas in such an elegant, yet slightly intimidating, house. Mansion. Whatever you wanted to call it—it was huge.

Christmas Eve Eve came, and we were all sitting together in the cinema room and a conversation had started about what film to put on next. The room had a huge projector screen at the front and then there were sofas and reclining forest green chairs dotted around the rest of the room. Clover, Leo, and Griff were sitting on the corner sofa. Ollie's arms were wrapped around me as we sat together on one of the loveseats.

They were warm around my waist, anchoring me to my surroundings. My anxiety around him had definitely improved since we'd become a couple. It was rare for me to stutter in front of them anymore too, which was a major improvement.

'I want to watch *Polar Express*,' Clover announced to everybody in the room.

'No. That film is for Christmas Eve itself. How about *The Nightmare Before Christmas*?' Leo asked, his tone bored per usual, but the fact he'd spoken at all gave away the fact that he was about to get some entertainment.

'That's a Halloween movie!' Clover's voice was rising.

'It isn't,' Leo drawled. 'Fine. Let's watch *Die Hard*.'

'That is *definitely* not a Christmas movie!' Clover said, her cheeks flushing a deep shade of red, her face slowly matching her hair.

It had been like this between them ever since we arrived. Clover and Leo had been at each other's throats the entire time and hadn't been able to agree on anything. Not on snacks, or when was best to give presents, or on what to watch. Basically, anything that *could* divide opinion, they disagreed on. I could tell that it was getting under Clover's skin, but I could sense Leo was getting a major kick out of it.

'It definitely is a Christmas film. The entire film revolves around an office Christmas party. Right?' Leo asked the room, gesturing at Griff to back him up.

'Sorry dude, you're on your own for this one.' Griff shrugged his shoulders 'I'm all for *Santa Clause 2*.'

'I'm with Griff on this one,' Ollie said, piping up.

I looked behind me and saw Ollie smiling down at me. He knew that it was one of my favourites.

'*Polar Express* and *Muppets Christmas Carol* are on tomorrow's agenda. They're definitely Christmas Eve films,' Ollie said, his tone ensuring there would be no argument.

I'd told him this yesterday, so I was glad that he'd been listening to me. It made me feel warm and cosy, knowing he hadn't just ignored my ramblings. I *loved* those films, and they were easily my top three. There was just something about the Muppets that made me smile, no matter how down I felt.

It was nice to feel heard with Ollie. The past Christmases I'd spent with my mum had been pretty dire and we'd never spent time doing what *I'd* wanted to do. It was always her films; you know, the awful kind that the Christmas Movie Channel shows? They were her jam. The ones that were obviously made straight for TV and should never have seen the light of day.

'Sounds like we all agree,' Leo said. Clover looked belligerently at him and he said, 'well, all of us that matter, anyway.'

I rolled my eyes at their pettiness. I slipped my phone out of my pocket, trying to hide the screen from Ollie's watching gaze. I blind texted Leo.

WILL YOU KNOCK IT OFF?

I WAS SO SICK OF THIS SHIT BETWEEN THEM. I'D BEEN hoping that spending time together at the estate in such a small group would improve the frostiness between them. Nope, it had just made it one thousand times worse. Go figure.

. . .

WHO SAID I'M THE ONE THAT NEEDS TO KNOCK SHIT OFF, Stutter?

LEO COULD GET UNDER MY SKIN TOO, DON'T GET ME wrong, so I understood how Clover was feeling. But I also found Leo's boredom and overall dick-ish behaviour kind of charming—and being fully honest—really fucking hot.

✦

CHRISTMAS MORNING WAS EVERYTHING I'D DREAMT IT would be and more.

I'd told the guys I'd never had a great Christmas experience, and they were all determined to make sure that this year would be the best one I'd ever had. There were so many presents under the biggest tree I'd ever seen, and we had cheesy music playing the entire morning. Well, most of them were cheesy. Now and then a classic would slip through the cracks. Griff sung *Good King Wenceslas* at the top of his lungs, extremely loud—and extremely off-key.

Actually, it was all a little overwhelming. I'd opened a fuck ton of cool gifts, like multiple designer handbags and a brand new phone, which seemed excessive. My current phone was relatively new, secondhand sure, but I'd got it from the school so I was surprised to see the boys had got me the newest make.

Even Leo had gone all out and got me a diamond necklace with matching earrings. He had also handed me a tiny gift box, impeccably wrapped in white paper covered in red berries. Inside, there was a tiny glass bottle with an even smaller rolled up scroll inside. A card sat next to the bottle.

Merry Christmas ...

'IT'S A TINY TELEGRAM IN A BOTTLE,' HE WHISPERED TO me as I examined it. Ollie had left the room to go do something or other, and Clover and Griff were paying more attention to each other than to us two.

'I love it,' I gushed, 'I love tiny things.'

We both laughed at my words, as he said, 'Not in all things, Stutter, I'm sure.'

I smiled and said, 'No, not in all things. Thank you, Leo.'

'The note inside is real, but don't open it yet. I'll let you know when.'

Inside, my stomach bubbled with nerves—not knowing what he wrote on the note would be torture for me. I quickly put it back in the box it came in and placed it inside a bag I'd received.

Ollie re-entered the room and dropped down beside me. Pulling me to him once again, placing a kiss on my forehead. Warmth filled me at his gesture. I also felt dirty, as if I was keeping a secret from him.

Feeling overwhelmed, I excused myself from around the tree and went to the kitchen. I needed a moment to myself to just process what was happening here. In the past, I was lucky if my mum had even been home on Christmas, let alone if she gifted me a present.

Griff flew in and saw me standing there, almost hyperventilating. He put his arms around me in a massive bear hug, and said, 'It's all gravy, Sky.'

'Yeah ... I've said happy birthday, right?' I asked him. I couldn't remember if I'd said it or not. Damn, having your birthday on Christmas day couldn't be fun. The days about a dead dude, or presents and shit, and you're lucky if people even remember you.

'Yeah, you're good,' he said. Releasing me, Griff opened the cupboard and pulled out mugs to make everybody a drink, an alcoholic one, even though we were all under age and it wasn't even three in the afternoon at that point, but hey, Christmas usually led to rule breaking.

'You don't need to make those for everyone. Let me help,' I told him, wanting to feel useful, and wanting to take my mind off of the amount of gifts I'd received.

We made the drinks together, peppermint schnapps hot chocolates, and joined everybody again to watch Christmas day TV together and eventually watch the Queen's speech cause who didn't love that?

It was the best day, and by far the best Christmas of my life.

I finally felt like I belonged; like I was a part of a group that mattered, that cared.

Chapter Twenty

New Year's Eve was upon us, which meant that the New Year's Gala was here and I knew that I wasn't ready for it. Not one bit.

Ever since Ollie had invited me, I'd been anxious about it and I'd even tried to get out of it a couple of times.

Ollie had been trying to make me feel better about it all week—he'd even sent me and Clover shopping for our dresses before Christmas, and I knew that he was looking forward to it. Ollie had arranged for us to be chauffeur driven to the nearest expensive boutique and have our dresses designed and created bespoke especially for us; he'd obviously had to pay extra for it to be ready on time, too.

I knew that he wanted me to enjoy this evening and, mainly; he wanted to show me off as his piece of arm candy to his father—and to all of his father's associates. I still hadn't decided how I *truly* felt about it. You see, part of me was thrilled that he thought that I could be considered arm candy, and then the other part of me found it insulting that I was amounting to nothing more than my looks. Then again, I had never had much confidence in myself, or my looks, so I was back to being thrilled all over again. It had become a vicious cycle.

I was getting ready with Clover and the boys were going to come pick us up sometime around seven.

The Gala itself was being held in the main hall of the school. I'd asked Ollie the other day why it wasn't being held outside of the school at a fancy manor or some place like that, but he had just said something about the school always supporting the charity the Gala was for. Or something to that effect, anyway. I clearly hadn't listened closely enough as I found myself getting lost in his eyes more often than not. Yes, I was completely aware how disgustingly lovey dovey that sounded. *Shoot me.*

Our final fittings had been a couple of days ago, and I was excited for Ollie to see me in this dress for the first time. If I did say so myself, I looked good in it. Really fucking good.

The light blue of the dress suited my pale skin tone perfectly, and it also went with my silver-purple hair—not many clothes did. I felt like a mix between a fairy tale princess and an elven queen in a fantasy novel. The second I'd seen myself in it, I'd fallen in love. It reminded me of Cinderella's classic dress for the ball. It was an A-line gown with off the shoulder half sleeves. Blue flowers trailed from the bust down to the waist. I felt like a real life princess while wearing it.

I'd never had much self-confidence growing up. Part of me constantly worried that the reason I didn't have friends was because I was unattractive; almost like I was too ugly to be seen with.

Being with Ollie had changed how I saw myself.

I didn't look in a mirror now and question what I saw. I didn't worry that I was too fat, or too curvy, for people to love me. Even if this thing between us didn't last, I'd always be thankful to him for making me feel cherished in a way I'd never experienced before.

I was also hoping this dress would lead to Ollie wanting to rip it off me later tonight after ringing in the New Year together and we were alone. The timing felt right, and I knew that I wanted to lose my virginity to him. We'd been close enough once or twice after sharing a room over Christmas break, but we'd never gone through with it. I hadn't been ready. It was an enormous step and something you couldn't take back after. I had nothing against those girls who just wanted it gone, and I couldn't say that I was saving it for the person I'd be with forever—I wasn't even saving it per se. I just knew that I wanted it to be with somebody that cared. Somebody that meant something to me, and somebody *I* meant something to back.

Clover entered the room from the bathroom and stopped dead.

'Fuck me, Sky. You look beautiful.'

'I look beautiful? Pur-lease.' I rolled my eyes at her compliment and said, 'You look stunning, Clover, really, honestly, truly beautiful.' She was wearing a long satin jade green gown with a v-neck and spaghetti straps. The slit went up to her mid-thigh, and now and then you'd get a flash of leg. It looked amazing with her hair colour too. She had debated wearing red to try and break the stigma, but she hadn't found a dress that she liked enough.

Our eyes shimmered with unshed tears at the sight of each

other looking so good, but we quickly laughed and stopped ourselves, not wanting to ruin the makeup we'd spent the better part of two hours on. I didn't want to have to touch it up before we'd even got there.

'Ollie is going to cream his pants when he sees you.'

'Ew, Clo, did you have to lower the tone with the word *cream*?' I fake gagged, but really that word genuinely made me want to gag. There was nothing sexy about that term—like at all. Sadly, I'd read one too many books that had used a term like *pearly cream* and nearly put the book down and not continued.

'Fine. Seriously though, Ollie is going to want to rip that dress off of you when he gets here.'

'Well, I won't let him before the Gala ...' I trailed off, a hint of a smile playing on my lips.

Clover looked at me, shocked at my insinuation.

'Woah, Sky. You think you're ready for that?' she asked, one of her eyebrows raised in disbelief.

'Yeah, I do. It just feels right, ya know?'

She nodded in response, skepticism rife in her features.

'Did you just know?' I asked her abruptly. Clo had told me she'd lost her virginity, but hadn't gone into too much detail about it.

'Mhm,' she said, a thoughtful expression on her face, almost as if she was envisioning the day she'd said yes to her first. 'But I would take it back now if I could.'

'Thanks for the vote of confidence,' I said, sarcasm clear in my tone. We smiled at each other, and I chose not to pry too much—yet. 'Even if this isn't the right thing in the long run Clo, I know that it's the right thing for me *now* and that's all I can go on.'

'True, and for your sake, my beautiful bestie, I hope you're right about him,' she said, stopping her sentence when we heard a knock on the door. Clover yelled, 'Come in.'

We were getting ready in Ollie's suite, as our room had little space and our bathroom was nowhere near as luxurious as his, meaning they could enter without us letting them in.

After Clover's yell, they entered, and the surrounding air turned to ice, leaving me slightly lightheaded.

Griff was the first to see us, his eyebrows raising when he took us in fully.

'Wow, you girls clean up nicely!' He hugged me briefly and then moved to hug Clover. It was at that moment that Leo entered the room and saw the two of them hugging. For the briefest of moments, Leo looked lost. He covered it up straight away though, and when Ollie entered the room, I lost interest in what the others were doing. All I could see was Him.

Ollie looked the hottest I'd ever seen him look, which trust me, was tough to do. I mean, even in our school uniform, I was into it. Into him. Of course I liked his personality, but his looks definitely helped, especially on those occasions where he'd acted like I had a disease. He wore a black tuxedo jacket with black skinny fit suit trousers and honestly; I was in love. I wiped the corner of my mouth with my hand, just in case some drool had escaped the confines of my mouth. That would be awkward as fuck.

'This dress is fucking amazing. I want to rip it off of you and taste what's hiding underneath. Do we even need to go to this thing?' Ollie asked. His eyes were heated, staring into mine. I could feel the flame and I honestly just wanted to burn with it.

'You're the one who said we have to go to this thing, so we're definitely going,' I told him, scolding him slightly.

'Fine. But tonight you're mine,' he said, his words filled with delicious promise.

I shivered. Goosebumps popped up all over my arms. The night held even more potential now than it had a few moments ago—and you wouldn't find me complaining.

✳

The Gala was filled with older people dressed in their finest suits and expensive gowns, and I felt completely out of my depth here. I hadn't grown up in this world. The fanciest event I'd attended was a wedding reception in a barn a few years ago. And believe me, there had been nothing fancy about it at all.

I spotted Ollie's dad, Henry, straight away, standing over by Lottie and Edward Hawthorn. They all looked exactly how I'd always imagined rich, powerful people to look, dripping in diamonds and designer suits. We made our way over to them in our group, and the greetings and handshakes started up instantly.

'Skylar, you look enchanting this evening,' Lottie told me, who looked amazing herself. You would never know to look at her right now that she was as old as she was. Standing next to Leo, she looked like she could be his sister, which was actually slightly creepy if you thought about it too hard. 'Clover darling, you look amazing too.' She leant down and kissed her cheek. Clover gave her a tentative smile in return.

'Hey, Mum. Dad,' Leo said and gave his mum a kiss and hugged her tight. Edward nodded at Leo and looked happy enough to see him—even if he did have a slight grimace on his face.

Edward and Ollie had a much frostier response to one another. They barely made eye contact, and sort of nodded towards each other. After seeing the two of them together on Parents' Day, I'd known there were a few issues between them, but I hadn't expected the iciness currently emanating off of them.

'Oliver. Skylar,' he greeted us, smiling at me, his mouth wide with teeth showing.

Henry Brandon was an imposing man, standing tall at over six foot and in a black suit that looked more expensive than my entire wardrobe—my new one. He was intimidating, and I clearly wasn't the only person who thought that, because everybody else in attendance seemed to be giving this group of people a wide berth. 'Glad that you could join us this evening.'

I saw Ollie roll his eyes in my peripheral. Without putting much thought into the action, I reached out and took his hand in mine, intertwining our fingers. I saw his lips twitch, forming a small smile that lasted for all of a second. But I saw it and it made me feel good inside, like I'd done something right.

'Evening, Dad. How was your Christmas?' Ollie asked tersely.

'Fine thanks, Son. Spent it at the townhouse. You know how it just hasn't been the same for me since your mum died,' Henry said, looking away from us, trying to school his features back into those of somebody indifferent. I could tell he missed his wife. 'I hope you all behaved yourself on the estate.'

'We did.' Ollie was being curt, not giving his dad much of anything to work with.

I piped up instead, 'We had a lovely time, thank you.'

Within seconds, my hand was icy once again. I'd obviously said or done the wrong thing, as Ollie had not only removed his hand from mine, but he had also taken a visible step away from me. No matter how many times I felt like I was getting somewhere with him, growing closer and understanding his inner workings, I was proved wrong. Clearly, I was an idiot who should've known better.

'After the dinner, I must introduce you two to some of my colleagues. I've told them how a young, beautiful girl has swept my Oliver off of his feet. They said they'd believe it when they saw it,' he chortled, as if he'd just told a rather funny joke and not some well-worn remark.

'We look forward to it,' Ollie spoke through gritted teeth and it was pretty obvious to everybody in this circle that he wasn't telling the truth. 'If you'll excuse me.'

Ollie turned away from our conversation and walked away briskly without another word, leaving me standing there with Henry, Leo and his parents. Clover and Griff had slipped away when the conversation had started, and I wished I'd gone with them.

'He'll be back soon,' Henry said to me, clearly amused at his son's antics.

Minutes passed in silence. I wanted so badly to be rescued, I didn't even care by who.

'Come with me, Stutter,' Leo said, grabbing my stiff hand in his much larger one.

In an instant, he swept me through the hall, passing people I either recognised as students from school or parents I must have glimpsed during Parents' Day. Out the main doors we went, and into the next corridor.

Ollie stood alone a little further up the hallway, facing the wall. His hand clenching beside him in anger. He turned to face us; a twisted smile playing on his face.

Stalking towards us, I cowered a little into Leo's side.

'Come here,' Ollie commanded, and like a silly, submissive heroine, I went towards him willingly.

He hugged me against him, his scent filling me with joy, the heat of our bodies causing my nipples to harden. He whispered in my ear, 'Let's go, Little One.'

Ollie took me with him, further down the hall. Nobody was around in this area of the school. It was deserted and, shielded by the dark, we continued until we were in front of a wooden door .

He pushed me into the caretaker's cupboard, using more force than necessary, then turned me to face him. He looked livid. His anger palpable, coming off of him in waves and entering the small space around us. The closet was tiny; barely enough room for a few shelves and a mop and bucket.

'What. The. Fuck. Do you think you're doing, Skylar?' he asked, in an aggressive manner. With every word, some spittle left his mouth, and I watched it fall in the small space between us.

It was at times like this that my anxiety climbed and I really started to question the choices I'd made that had led me here.

'I-I-I,' I said, stuttering again, trying to voice the thoughts that were scrambling around in my head. Common sense was battling it out with an apology. I didn't get time to say any more though as Ollie violently captured my lips with his, the kiss hard, no ounce of love and affection in the action. This was pure need. Pure emotion driving his actions; an emotion that was *definitely* not love.

'Don't say anything around my dad,' he bit out. His harsh words entered my ear, his breath causing chills to run down my body. 'Stay quiet and look pretty.'

At that, my anger came rushing forward, and I tried to take control of the kiss. Locked in a fight of teeth and tongue, both of us tried to gain the upper hand. I could feel his hardness pressing into me, making me want him even more. Recently, all I could think about was having sex with him, and I'd already decided that I wanted to make it happen tonight.

He pushed my dress down, uncovering me, and took a nipple into his mouth, taking turns biting and sucking while I moaned. His hands trailed down my body, but the full skirt of the dress made it impossible for him to get anywhere further. He groaned, part in frustration and the other in need. His trousers didn't present the same problem, so my hand could wrap itself around his dick with no problem. He thrust into my hand, the two of us completely caught up in the moment, forgetting we were in a caretaker's cupboard.

Our senses returned to us when we were interrupted by a loud, hard knock on the door.

'Dinner's about to begin, get out of there.' Leo's gruff voice made its way through the door. That he thought to tell us about dinner surprised me, but I put the thought to the back of my mind quickly. Ollie gave one last sharp pinch on my nipple, teasing me, before he helped me pull my dress back into place.

'Later,' he promised. His whispered word sounded like a threat.

It made me shiver—in excitement, not fear.

✳

THE DINNER WAS AWKWARD AND STILTED BETWEEN ALL parties sitting at our table. The group consisted of Ollie and I, Griff and Clover, Leo and then his parents and Henry. Every now and again, a question would be asked and answered, then the table would return, once more, to silence. I could feel Henry looking in our direction, but then when I'd look at him he'd look away or start up a conversation with Lottie beside him as if he'd never been gazing my way.

After the torture of dinner had finally ended, the announcer encouraged everybody to congregate in front of the stage to watch the swing band play. Clover took my hand, leading me to the dance floor, as the band had just started playing one of our favourite Frank Sinatra songs. It was nice to just let loose and dance and sing along with her; to pretend like we weren't out of our element here, surrounded by people who made more in a month than our families did in an entire year— or five.

A slow song came on, and I felt a body come up behind me.

'May I have this dance?' A deep voice asked.

Henry stood behind me, and I assumed that it was me he wanted to dance with. Clover motioned with her hands that she was going to get a drink and got out of the area in rapid time.

'O-of course,' I replied.

Our hands came together, and we moved into the traditional slow dance position. Not much of a dancer, I hoped that Henry was well versed and able to help me through this. I didn't want to humiliate myself; or Ollie.

'Skylar, I've been wanting to talk to you alone,' Henry said.

I spotted Ollie over at the side of the dance floor by the bar, with Leo and Griff, all three of them looking at us. Ollie looked wary, Leo looked bored, and Griff was smiling at me—his eyes were the only part of him that gave away how he was truly feeling. His eyes showed just how apprehensive he was.

'H-how come?' I asked, my nerves causing me to laugh. People like Henry Brandon could smell fear and nervousness. They didn't get where they were without having that sense ingrained in them.

'It's rare that Oliver leaves you alone, and there are some things I wanted to ask without him around,' he said. His eyes glistened, a lopsided grin taking over the bottom half of his face.

I nodded, still none the wiser to why he wanted to talk to me alone. Surely there was nothing he needed to say to me without Ollie around?

'Now's your ch-chance,' I joked. Joking around didn't help the nerves. If anything, it just made the nausea moving around in my stomach worse. Although I wasn't sure that Henry could tell that I was trying to be carefree in my response. It felt as if my entire body was responding to him negatively.

'After meeting your delightful mother, I felt rather intrigued to learn more about your father. Oliver tells me you haven't mentioned him.'

Bewilderment filled me. Why would Henry want to know about my dad? There was nothing I could tell him, as I knew *nothing* about him.

'I-I-I,' I said. Not quite sure what to tell him, I decided to go with the truth. 'I d-don't know who he is, Sir.'

Henry's eyebrows knitted, his eyes narrowed. I expected

him to comment more about my dad but all he said in response was, 'No need to call me *Sir*, dear. Call me Henry.'

'Henry,' I whispered, feeling caught in a trap; a web I didn't know how to untangle myself from. 'I'm s-sorry I don't know more.'

'No need to apologise. Forgive me for intruding.'

His hands moved lower, slowly, heading from my waist to my hips. All of it felt wrong. He was making me uncomfortable the way Andy had, and all I wanted to do in that moment was take a brush to my skin and scrub—hard.

'It's f-fine,' I told him. I pulled myself away from his touch, trying to keep my disgust off of my expression. 'I must go find Ollie. Thank you for the d-dance.' Looking around the room, I could see many people, but none of them were Ollie or Griff. Hell, even seeing Leo would be a blessing.

'It was my pleasure entirely. I'll see you soon, Skylar,' he said. His tone ominous; his words a threat.

I located Ollie as he re-entered the hall with Leo, so I headed towards the two of them. Moments from reaching them, a body fell into my side, knocking me slightly off balance. I quickly righted myself, turning to see who had bumped into me.

'Watch where you're going, bitch,' Odette said. Her tone scathing. 'I nearly spilled my drink because of you.'

'S-sorry,' I apologised quietly. It killed me inside to apologise to her, but I really wanted to just make it to Ollie and Leo. I knew if I didn't say sorry, I could be stuck with them for far longer than I would like to be. 'I didn't see you there.'

'What Ollie sees in you I'll never know,' she said as her eyes flashed with envy; her entire face hardened.

'Well ...' Olivia said, about to add her two senses to the

conversation, but Odette quickly elbowed her to get her to shut up. She grunted in pain, but knew her place and didn't say anymore.

'You are nothing but trash. You've never belonged here at Hawthorn, but don't worry. Everybody will see that for themselves soon,' Odette warned.

With that, the two of them dispersed, leaving me alone once more. Odette's parting words weren't overly encouraging, but with Henry's threat still ringing in my ears, I focused on that more. After all, the girls had already tried to get me kicked out of Hawthorn. Fuck, they'd also potentially orchestrated my drugging and near drowning, too.

Making it back to Ollie's side, he checked me all over, checking to see if I was all in one piece. His eyes simmered with heat as he took me in, checking me out in other ways simultaneously. All night I'd been taking him in, mostly because I couldn't believe that somebody as gorgeous as him was *my* boyfriend. Fingers crossed he saw tonight ending the way I did.

In bed. Naked. Wrapped up in one another.

'Shit. It's already five to midnight. I've got to go,' Leo announced.

I jumped at the sound of his voice. I'd been so preoccupied with looking at Ollie, and him looking at me, that I'd totally forgotten that Leo was still standing with us.

'Where's he off to?' I asked Ollie, confused by Leo's urgency, but Ollie just shrugged in return.

Arms encapsulated me, pulling me up against a hard body in a warm embrace. Heat filled me. What a way to start a new year.

The countdown began, and I turned to face Ollie. Looking

into the depths of his blue eyes, I saw a few different emotions flicker in his gaze, but none of them stayed for long. A mixture of caring, lust and anger all played out on his face in quick succession; warring to be the dominant emotion. He settled on a serene look; or as serene as I'd ever seen him look, anyway.

'Happy New Year,' he whispered, when the countdown hit zero.

'Happy New Year,' I said in return.

Our midnight kiss was like the one I'd dreamt about receiving ever since I was young. I'd had nobody to share one with before, having spent a lot of my New Year's alone while Mum and Andy were at the local pub. We kissed passionately, and happiness overtook me. This must be what it felt like to feel wanted.

I'd wanted that forever; that feeling of being desired.

The New Year had so much promise and I couldn't wait to see what it had in store for me.

Chapter Twenty-One

The moment the door of his suite closed behind us, a chill ran down my spine. I'd been anticipating this moment for quite some time, and it was finally here. Ollie grabbed my waist from behind, his lips trailed kisses up and down my neck.

The room was lit by moonlight, adding to the magical atmosphere; now and then the light would catch Ollie's eyes, the spark in them beckoning me forward. His hands roamed while I put mine around his neck, pulling his mouth closer for more kisses. Feverish kisses, desperate kisses. I could feel how wet I was, the lace of my underwear becoming uncomfortable.

'Get naked and lay on the bed,' Ollie demanded, pushing me onto the bed with a little too much force and I stumbled, nearly tripping on the skirt of the gown.

'H-help me?' I asked, hoping my nerves would calm the fuck down soon.

Ollie came up behind me and slowly unzipped the back of

my dress. It fell and pooled around my feet, leaving me standing there in my matching light blue lace underwear set.

I turned to face him and stepped out of the material at my feet.

With the way Ollie was looking at me, I thought I'd combust from all the sexual energy surrounding us.

My hands shaking, I removed my bra and slowly slid my bottoms down, watching his eyes as they tracked my every movement.

Ollie removed his suit, the anticipation climbing with every piece of clothing he removed. Nerves filled me, my stomach a sea of thrashing waves. We'd never been this far before, never been this bare to one another.

After what felt like forever, he stood before me naked.

His dick was big. Really big. Even though I'd touched it before tonight, I'd never seen it up close. I'd never seen any up close.

I knew every teenage virgin seemed to say it, in every film and book, but I really didn't know how he was going to fit.

Now we were both naked, and there was no going back. I wanted this with him. I wanted to feel him so far inside of me we became one person. One soul.

Ollie's hand wandered down my body, until I felt a long digit enter me, followed soon after by a second and then a third. My wetness easing his movement and I honestly couldn't think of a time I'd been this wet before.

'Are you sure about this, Sky?' he whispered, his words skating across my skin.

I nodded, and sighed in pleasure, his thumb lazily circling my clit.

'P-please.' My voice came out as a whimper. My eyes were

at half mast, and I shivered just looking at Ollie's full lips. He kissed me hard, removing his fingers to

Laying on my back, Ollie spread my legs and rested himself on top of me. I could feel him rubbing the head of his cock up and down my entrance and fuck, if he didn't put his dick where we both wanted it soon, I was going to take over.

Without warning, Ollie took one hard thrust and fully seated himself inside of me.

I winced. Shit. The initial sting hurt. Books had lied with the whole: *it didn't hurt as I was too lost in the pleasure* bullshit. My eyes watered, but it wasn't long before the pain eased and I felt full.

He stayed still until I kissed his neck, and as soon as I bit him, all bets were off.

He started thrusting slowly at first, but then something broke in him and he began to thrust in earnest, creating sensations that I didn't even know I could feel.

'F-fuck,' I moaned.

His breath was hot in my ear, one hand on my nipple pinching me hard, the other grasping my wrist and keeping it pinned above my head. No way for me to move it.

My free hand was in his hair, pulling sections every time he hit that spot inside of me that was elusive to most. Fuck.

I'd never felt this close to somebody before and there were tears in my eyes, both from emotion and the passion between us. It was overwhelming.

'Fuck,' Ollie hissed out through his teeth. Just the sound of his moan caused the sensation of butterflies in my stomach.

I could feel my orgasm coming. My clit was throbbing and I could feel the pressure climbing. It wasn't a foreign feeling—I was a virgin, yes, but I knew what I liked. Everybody should.

'Touch me,' I said desperately at Ollie. I needed him to rub my clit. Now.

He understood instantly, and the second he rubbed his thumb over the spot, I came.

I moaned, 'Ollie!'

My moan seemed to push Ollie over the edge, as after a few more deep strokes, I felt him spill inside of me.

Shit.

We didn't use a condom.

Thank fuck for this school's weird rule about health check ups and contraception.

Ollie got up and went to his en-suite and returned with a wet towel he then used to clean me. It was strange, but that act felt more intimate to me than the whole *losing my virginity thing* that just happened.

After a moment, Ollie moved to lie beside me, and we were silent for a while. The events of the evening catching up with us both.

'How are you feeling?' he asked, his voice thick.

'I'm good. That was—fuck, Ollie—that was. Wow,' I sputtered out. I was finding words hard. I felt incoherent. Like my entire body, and brain was mush, and I'd never be able to form complete sentences again. I wondered if every girl felt like this when they first discovered sex. I made a mental note to ask Clover.

'Told you I wanted to find out how your stutter sounded with my dick deep inside of you. Trust me, baby, it did not disappoint.'

I could only describe the sound that left me next as an embarrassed chuckle. I had sex with Ollie. Like, what?! Yeah, it had been on the agenda for some time now, and I'd known pretty much from day one that I wanted to have sex with him. But wanting something and having it become reality were two very different things; and they came with two very different emotions.

I fell asleep in Ollie's arms as the little spoon, and I felt safe. Protected. Fuck, it felt good.

✳

I WOKE THE NEXT MORNING WITH A START. ON OPENING my eyes, it took me a second to adjust and remember that I was in Ollie's room, in Ollie's bed, and that he was laying next to me. Still sound asleep, he looked so peaceful. His eyebrows relaxed and I could honestly say I'd never seen such a serene look on his face. When awake, his mind was constantly working a mile a minute, and he never seemed to switch off and just sit and relax. It made him seem more human in this moment. Like an actual person, with actual emotions—almost.

I got up and went to the toilet. I contemplated brushing my hair and sorting out my face, but I decided not to. Ollie had seen me at my worst, meaning there was no need to hide who I really was now. Actually, I'd never understood that whole concept. If brushing your hair first thing in the morning made a difference to a relationship, you needed to reevaluate.

I got back into bed and heard Ollie mumble, 'Morning', then he pulled me back up against his chest and I got comfortable again. I didn't know the time, but the New Year already felt promising enough, even if it had barely begun. We must have fallen back asleep though as the next time I opened my eyes, the light coming through the windows made me think it was late afternoon.

Back at home, I didn't have blinds on my windows because my mum had refused to pay for them. Apparently, she and Andy would rather spend the money on something more important. I'd never found out what was more important, but there you go. Anyway, because of this, I had got pretty good at being able to decipher what time it was just by how the world was looking as it came through the windows. Not a helpful skill at all, but a relatively cool one—ish.

'Afternoon,' Ollie mumbled this time, before kissing up and down my neck, covering every patch of skin available. 'How are you feeling?'

'I'm good,' I told him. Feeling like I needed to emphasise my words, I wriggled against him. I could feel his dick pressing into my lower back and I smiled. '*Really* good actually,' I said and turned around to face him. He pulled back, so I had some space to turn in.

He was about to say something more when we heard a piercing scream from out in the hall. At first, neither of us moved. But clearly other people who did live in this wing of the school did, as the commotion outside got louder.

'Skylar,' Griff shouted through the door. I found it a little odd as this was Ollie's room. Why wouldn't he be calling for him?

Quickly, I threw on one of Ollie's tops and a pair of his trackie bottoms that I rolled up so they didn't just instantly fall down. I shuffled my way to the door and opened it to see a frantic Griff, his hair looking as if he'd been pulling at it, staring at me with worry in his eyes.

'What's up?' I asked. I looked past him and could see a group of students surrounding a door a little way down the hallway. 'What's going on down there?'

'Come with me,' he said urgently. Ollie came up behind me then, now dressed, and Griff added, 'You too.'

We followed Griff out of the room and entered what must be Leo's room next door. I'd never been in here before, but it looked similar to both Ollie's and Griff's. Leo stood in the middle of the room; he must have been waiting for us to arrive.

'What's going on, dickheads?' Ollie asked, looking at them both questioningly. Sceptical of their motivations.

'Olivia's dead,' Griff said, panicked. He looked sick, like he was one breath away from losing the contents of his stomach entirely. It took me a moment to picture Olivia in my mind. Oh, right, the fourth member of *The Set*. To be fair, I'd almost forgotten she even existed. It was rare that I had much to do with her; it always seemed to be Odette, Ophelia or Oralie that gave me a hard time.

'What? How?' Ollie barked out, making me jump beside him.

'Stabbed. She told the girls at the Gala last night that she was going back to some guy's house but wouldn't tell them who. Just that they'd be shocked if they knew the truth,' Griff replied.

'How do we know if she wasn't even on the grounds?' Ollie asked, sounding bored now he'd heard more.

'That's just it, they did find her on the grounds. Her body was lying on the steps of the pool house. They found her first thing, but you know what gossips are like, it spread round the school pretty fast.'

Leo was yet to say anything, instead he stood still, contemplating everything that was being said. Taking it all in.

'So, why have you got us out of bed?' Ollie asked, pissed. I could tell that he didn't think this was a valid enough reason for us to get up. 'You could have told us at dinner.'

'Maybe, Dickhead, because she was holding a lock of Skylar's hair in her hands and a piece of her blue dress from last night,' Leo said as he locked his gaze on mine.

'S-sorry, w-what?' I sputtered, confused as fuck that this was happening. Why would she be holding my hair or some of my dress? How did she even get a hold of those things?

'Yep,' Griff answered me, then looked at Ollie. 'So, that's why we came and got you, Wanker.'

'W-who found her?' I asked. I had to know. Not that it was okay for whoever found her, but it would be worse in my mind if it had been a pupil in one of the younger years.

'Ms Hawthorn,' Leo responded in a dull tone.

Wonderful. The woman already acted like she couldn't stand me. Now that I guessed I'd become a suspect, she would hate me even more. Fuck, *would I be considered a suspect?*

I asked as much, and the responses from the guys in the room with me weren't positive ones. I understood. A corpse showing up holding your hair—distinctively coloured hair at that—definitely did not help your cause.

'So, what shall we do about it?' Ollie looked pissed still. Whether he was aiming it at me or them, I didn't know. Either way, it wasn't any of our faults that this was happening. He had to know that.

'No clue, man. That's why we wanted you two here, so we could all talk it out.' Griff looked exasperatedly at Ollie, and I totally got why. He was acting like a total dick right now. I knew he had different plans of how he'd expected this morning to go—so did I, if I was being honest—but it wasn't like we could help it now. You'd think he'd be a little more caring that Olivia was dead. He'd known her for years, after all.

'Doesn't sound like there's much to talk about. Olivia's dead and Sky's being implicated,' he deadpanned.

'God, you are such a frustrating dick, you know that?' Griff asked, his face slowly turning the shade of a tomato; I'd never seen him this angry before. 'Who would do this to Sky?'

'W-what do you mean? Shouldn't we be asking who would do this to Olivia?' I asked, confused about the point Griff was trying to make.

'Not being funny, New Girl, but literally anybody could have done this to Olivia,' Griff said. 'No. Somebody planted your hair and dress on purpose and we need to figure out who.' He gave a questioning look to both Leo and Ollie, one that I didn't fully understand.

Great.

More secrets.

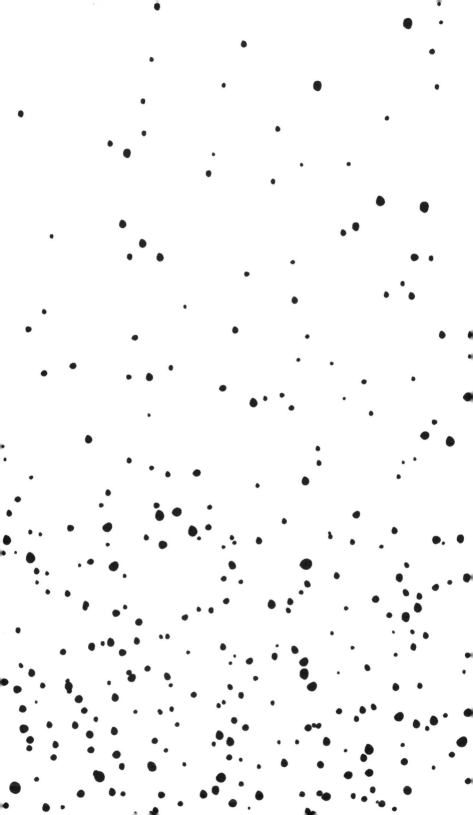

Chapter Twenty-Two

School started back up a week after the Gala, and things with Ollie were amazing. Ever since that night, we were inseparable. He'd somehow bribed the dorm monitors into letting him have me stay in his suite every night, and there was no way I was going to turn that down.

You know how when you read about heroines in books losing their virginity? They always said some crap about how different they felt or how much sex they wanted to have now the barrier had gone? *I was now one of those basic heroines.* All I could think about was him—spending time with him, both in the biblical sense and just watching films together and enjoying one another's company. My thoughts were even boring me, but I couldn't help it. I was truly happy for the first time.

After Olivia's body had been found, investigators invaded the school and questioned everybody. They summoned every single student individually to Ms Hawthorn's office, and we all had to relay our whereabouts from that evening. Even those who hadn't even attended the Gala were being questioned.

I had no clue what strings Ollie pulled, but they allowed him to sit beside me throughout the interview—seeing as we'd spent the evening together anyway, I supposed it made sense to question us at the same time. Ollie was honest and explained that neither of us had any idea how Olivia had been found holding my hair.

Ollie was adamant that somebody had framed me.

The detectives told us to remain available for future enquiries. All I thought when he said that was, *Sure dude, like we have anywhere else to go except for school.*

'So, my dick is obviously the biggest,' Griff said at the exact moment I tuned into the conversation going on around me. I sputtered, causing my drink to spray out of my mouth. Griff raised an eyebrow at me, the smirk on his face giving away the fact that he was trying to shock.

'Oh, give over Griff. Like I'm even going to say anything to boost your ego, or that dickheads for that matter.' Clover nudged her head towards Leo and Odette, who were sitting at a table across the room with the other members of *The Set*.

'I'm just saying, my little Lady Luck, that if you *wanted* to look, you'd be happy with what you'd find. More than happy, actually. Fucking ecstatic. Maybe even shed a tear.'

Clover hit him, hard, on the arm, but I could see that she was trying to hold her laughter in. I did laugh. There was just something so lovable about that stupid boy; even if I knew he was hiding something. Most people were. Especially the ones who used humour as a way to hide from those around them; those closest to them.

'Shut up, prick.' Ollie looked amused, but there was a

slight underlying look of distaste in his expression. I couldn't figure out whether it was aimed at Griff or Clo, though. Recently, Ollie had been talking to me about Clover—how he was worried about her. Worried that her words would cause me to question him or his actions sometime in the near future.

I'd laughed when he'd first said that to me. I told him that unless he gave me a reason to feel that way, then we'd be golden. I may be quiet, and maybe I didn't always stand up for myself the way that I should, but I could think for myself. Regardless of how Clover may feel towards him, that wouldn't sway my feelings for him. I kept telling him that Clo had barely said much since Halloween, anyway. Once we'd made our relationship official, she'd kept her mouth shut about it all.

'You kill me, Griff,' I said, chuckling. 'Please can we move off the subject of dick size?'

'Miss Skylar, are you sure you don't wanna join in?' he asked, his grin ever present. I shook my head in response, going back to eating my gourmet meal.

'Join in with what? Not like I can make any comparison notes for you,' I added.

'True, true. But you could just lie and make me feel good, you know, as my best friend,' he said. Having these people to call friends made me ecstatic, but at times like this, I wondered why I kept them around. *Oh, who was I kidding?* I tried my hardest not to do anything that would cause them to stop being my friend. I couldn't go back to being a friendless loser. Being here had made me fully understand just how empty and miserable my life had been before.

'Pretty sure I'm her best friend, Dickweed. Eat your food and shut up,' Clover told him, effectively putting an end to that conversation.

✦

Odette and Leo became an official couple a few days later and, of course, shit hit the fan. I'd been given a reprieve from *The Set* for a bit and no harm had come to me since Halloween and the whole being held under water sitch. But now it was a new year. Apparently, I was fair game again. It made little sense, though. Why were things getting worse now that somebody who supposedly looked out for me was dating my bully? I'd thought it would have gone the other way and maybe ended entirely. Clearly that had been wishful thinking.

At the Academy, the bathroom toilets had graffitied walls. Apparently, they had always had graffitied walls, and no matter how often the school tried to paint over them, they would always just reappear the next day. It was a constant battle between the caretaker and the students. Right now, my name was on every toilet stall wall. Every time they painted the messages over, they came back worse and more aggressive. The school had given up now and was letting them accumulate. The comments were things like:

Skylar Crescent should just kill herself.

S.C doesn't deserve O.B.

You have to be a low level of scum to call your daughter Skylar.

Making matters worse, there were arrows coming off of the original comments, with more comments underneath. I wanted to be disgusted at how many girls had stooped to this level, but really; I wasn't. It didn't surprise me at all.

Eurgh, she's a skank.

Wish Ophelia had hit her harder.

Whoever attempted to drown her should have done a better job.

Even I could admit that some were funny and so obviously false.

S.C has gonorrhoea.

S.C is a walking STD.

And my personal favourite:

Sky fingers herself with an electric toothbrush.

Original *and* classy. The best kind of slur.

The messages weren't just all over the bathrooms. Nope. They were all over the Hive too. On every message board and feed. Literally every single place that students had the chance to slag me off, they were doing it. These words were repeated in whispers in every corridor, every class, and even at mealtimes. I thought my sort of friendship with Leo meant that things would get better, seeing as he was dating the ring leader, but he hadn't stopped jack shit from happening to me. My hair was pulled, my clothes covered in paint from paint balloons they had thrown at me, and the essays I had sent off electronically were being altered. They came back from the teacher with a poor grade, the wording completely different to what I'd written and sent in.

I tried my best to not let any of it affect me. Tried to keep my head held high and staying above it all. Tried to tell myself they were all just jealous or spiteful—or both. Majority of the girls had grumbled that I'd used a witch's spell to get both Ollie and Griff under my thumb. How pathetic. Like I'd just been sitting in my room with Clover saying spells over a cauldron like some *Macbeth* shit. Petty girls really will say and believe anything to help themselves buy into their own delusions.

Clover had been acting funky ever since Leo and Odette

had officially got together. By funky I meant that she wouldn't be anywhere near them, barely spent any time with us anymore and basically became a hermit that stayed in our room. It was odd, and I didn't know what to do to make it better. Not like I could ask Ollie for help as he and Clover barely tolerated each other at the best of times.

"I don't want to sound like a bitch Sky, but I really don't know what you see in Ollie."

"I mean ... you definitely do sound like a bitch, Clo." We were sitting in our room one night after dinner where Clo was trying to make me see 'sense' as she called it.

"I just want you to be careful."

"And I will be. But please, can you shut up about it? It's getting pretty boring."

So yeah, Clover and I *were* struggling a bit. All friends go through this though, right? You were allowed to disagree with people in life, even the people closest to you. It sucked, though. I was lucky to have Ollie because at least it meant that I had somebody to spend time with, even if he was the reason Clover didn't want to spend much time with me.

I just wasn't sure what to do to make things go back to how they were before. Not like I'd split up with Ollie to appease Clover. But I also didn't want to lose a friendship because of a guy. Hoes before bros and all that.

'Want to watch a film tonight?' Clo asked as the two of us were walking back from dinner and hooked her arm with mine.

'Err, I was going to hang out with Ollie tonight.' I cringed, worried that she was going to start an argument or switch from a playful mood into one made of pure bitchiness.

'Oh. Right.' Her tone had soured. So much so I could taste it.

'But I can cancel,' I said, feeling guilty, and got out of my phone straight away to cancel on Ollie. Yeah, he'd probably be a little pissed at me and blame it on Clo, but I hadn't spent time with Clover, just us two in a while and I could tell she was missing me. I missed her too, and things had been so weird between us. Hopefully, if we spent the evening chilling out, things might go back to being a little more normal.

'Only if you're sure?' she asked. She looked happier though, like she really wanted me to cancel but wouldn't voice it out loud.

'Course I'm sure. You're my girl,' I told her. When I saw the smile beaming on her face, I knew I'd made the correct decision. 'Let's go watch *Mean Girls* and quote every line.'

'Sounds good to me.' She pulled me closer to her side, and I knew that eventually we'd be okay.

+

'Do you think that's how American schools actually are?' Clo asked me out of nowhere.

'What do you mean?'

'Like, all cliquey and bitchy?'

'Clo, it's like that here,' I said, laughing at her. But now that she'd mentioned it, I thought a little deeper. I had always wondered about American schools, whether they were depicted correctly. I added, '*The Set* is our version of The Plastics.'

'True, true. Although I've always wondered where the appeal is, ya know? Like, why do so many people want to be Regina George?' Clo asked, her face one of confusion. Her brows had furrowed and her eyes were blank.

'I have no idea. Only thing I can think of is the fact that people are attracted to power more than the person. If a person wields power, they're instantly more appealing.'

'Like Ollie and Leo are sexier because of the power they hold?' she asked.

'Yep. Exactly that,' I replied without much thought. It took me a moment to realise that not only had she brought up Leo's name, but she'd also called him sexy. What the fuck was happening here? 'Clo, are you feeling alright?'

'I think so ...' Her voice went higher at the end, so it came out sounding more like a question than a statement.

'You just used the name Leo and the word sexier in the same sentence.'

'I mean, I may hate him, but damn, he's fine,' Clo said, chuckling.

'Yeah, he totally is,' I agreed. We both laughed, and I could feel the iciness between us slowly melting away. It felt like it had back at the beginning of term, when we'd just met and the guys hadn't got between us yet. 'They're both sexy and they know it too.'

'They definitely know it. I think that's one of the many reasons I detest Leo so much. He flaunts his looks to anybody with eyes, I swear. He's a rich bastard too, and that usually has all the girls fighting for his attention. Look at Odette.'

'Odette's not exactly full of brains though is she,' I said. I couldn't be certain as she was in the year above and I didn't share any classes with her, but from the conversations I *had* overhead, the girl wasn't the brightest. Couldn't always be helped though, sometimes people struggled at school and that was okay. But I could tell Odette didn't care. She believed that she'd bag a Hawthorn and never have to work again—something I'd *legiterally* heard her say. *Oh, for fuck's sake.* I'd started to think like Griff.

I hoped that Leo would see sense soon when it came to Odette. Seeing as he was looking out for me, part of me wanted to look out for him in return. 'It irritates me how she's all over him at all times.'

'Why does it bother you?' Clover looked at me, her eyes narrowing in suspicion. I still hadn't told her that Leo and I were in contact outside of group activities. It was almost as if I'd kept the secret too long and now, if revealed, it would look bad. She'd think I'd been hiding it from her—which was exactly the case, but still.

'It doesn't. Just don't want to see him used by her,' I said. I thought I'd got away with sounding like somebody who had no active interest; more of a third-party opinion type of response.

'Believe me, I think he's the one doing the using.' Clo pretended to gag and stuck her finger into her open mouth. I laughed, loving her exaggerated actions.

'Eww!' I squealed, 'I've walked across those two too often now. Gross.'

Clover went quiet, probably imagining the image I'd just put into her head. Clo had been with me on a couple of those occasions too, so had also witnessed some of it firsthand.

'Thanks for the visuals, Sky,' she said. I felt a pain in my shoulder and caught sight of Clover's fist as it moved back from the punch it had just delivered. I grunted.

'Bitch,' I muttered. Clover just grinned at me like a maniac, teeth and all.

'Whore,' she replied, with her smile still firmly in place. I rolled my eyes, and we went back to watching the movie, quoting all the best parts. It was nice spending time with her like this.

No boys.

No distractions.

Just us two spending time together and relaxing. Pigging out eating our favourite sweets. The perfect evening between best friends. Hopefully, it would stay this way between us for a while; I hated feeling judged by her all the time. Judged for my choice in boyfriends. Judged because I wasn't making the choice she wanted me to. I always thought that girl friendships were filled with hyping one another up and supporting each other's decisions, but I guess I'd got it wrong.

In all fairness, I shouldn't have got all of my real world beliefs from films and fiction. *My bad.*

Chapter Twenty-Three

O n a Tuesday morning, History was the first class of the day and it excited me to sit with Ollie and learn more about the Tudors. He had swim practise before school so I was waiting for him at my locker, lost in my own thoughts, when a wet sensation spread from my head downward. Liquid covered my head. Freezing liquid. All I could think was that I hoped it wasn't pee, but that would surely be warm, not ice cold. The smell gave it away as some kind of ice slush drink that smelled super sweet and was quite obviously super sticky.

For fuck's sake. This was my last clean uniform. The others were all in for cleaning and Clover wore a different size to me in uniform, so it wasn't even like I could go up to our room and steal hers. I didn't even know where the staff did the uniform cleaning, so not like I could venture there and see if mine was clean already—or if they had any spare.

'Shit, Sky,' Griff said, appearing in an instant. Whoever

had put the drink over my head had long since disappeared. I hadn't even got a glimpse of who it had been, but who was I kidding, it could literally have been any student at this school —of any age. 'Listen up!' Griff called out to the hallway and every student in our vicinity stopped and turned to look at him.

'If I see anybody picking on Skylar, or throwing shit at her, or tripping her up, then you *will* face the consequences. *The Set* may have told you that this shit is okay, but as a member of *The Sect* I will make your lives here hell. Now, go to class!'

Everybody scattered as quickly as possible, bumping into one another in their hurry to get away from Griff's wrath. I'd never seen him look this mad. I expected it of Ollie, and even Leo to an extent, but not happy-go-lucky, cheeky, Griff.

'Are you okay?' he asked, finally taking my appearance in from head to toe.

'Yeah, I'm okay,' I said and gave a tentative smile, 'but I smell like a blue raspberry.'

'Haven't you always wondered what a blue raspberry is? Like, what? How? They're not even real,' he said. His lip quirked up at the side, a laugh fighting to leave him, but he seemed determined to keep a straight face.

I laughed at Griff's obvious attempt to cheer me up. Although he was telling the truth, who decided what a blue raspberry was or what it tasted or smelled like?

At that moment, Ophelia and Oralie walked up to us. The smug look on both of their faces told me that even if they weren't the ones who'd poured the drink on my head, they definitely had okayed it. They were visibly thrilled about it.

'Did you have anything to do with this?' Griff harshly whispered to the two of them, trying not to draw any more attention to the four of us. Bless him for trying. But we'd been the centre of attention before the girls had even come along. The girls entering the scene had just made us more interesting to the onlookers.

'Who, us?' asked Ophelia, using that look that all pretty girls thought would get them off the hook. She moved her head to survey the entire corridor and everybody watching. If anything, her voice was louder than normal; she wanted people to hear this.

'Yes, you two. Who else would have planned this?' Griff asked, anger clear in his voice.

'Pretty sure, Griff, there are many people here who would do this to the New Girl. We don't tolerate trash around here. Hawthorn Academy has always been for the elite,' said Ophelia.

Sadly, I knew there was a lot of truth in Ophelia's words. There were a large amount of students here who wanted to get on *The Set*'s good side by terrorising me.

'I'll be talking to Leo about this,' Griff threatened them, but I wasn't sure at this point what difference it would make.

I would've liked to think that Leo had my back a bit. Even if he wasn't able to come right out and say that we were friends. Which still made no actual sense to me. I'd been meaning to ask him, to find out why he acted like he cared about me via text but was also happy to sleep with the ringleader of my bullies. It didn't add up, and it wasn't like I could discuss it with anybody else. Nobody knew that Leo and I were in contact with each other.

'Leo's on our side. He can't stand this piece of shit either,' Oralie piped up, shaking her head at Griff, showing how stupid she thought he was.

Now, I was even more confused than I normally was, and fuck, I hated feeling confused. It was one of my biggest pet hates in life. Anything that made me feel stupid was something I typically avoided.

'Come on, New Girl, let's go get you another uniform,' Griff said over his shoulder as he walked away from the scene. I followed Griff quickly, getting away from the girls. Plus, Griff knew everything about this place. Literally, Griff seemed to know every secret and every staff member. When I'd mentioned it to him though, he'd said, 'It always makes sense to know as much as you can about a place like this.'

Which I guess made sense, even if it was a little cryptic. Griff's been a student here ever since he was eleven, and I could totally imagine the three boys learning all they could about this place. Leo's dad owned the place, so maybe he knew more than he'd even told Griff. You didn't rule the school without knowing everything about everyone. They even had dirt on the girls, but they hadn't utilised it yet—or so they'd told me. I couldn't see why they had reason to lie. They were waiting for them to do something really dark, which basically meant that they needed to succeed in killing me, because they'd already drugged and nearly drowned me and the boys had done fuck all. I didn't want to doubt them, or be that annoying girl who asked too many questions, but something didn't add up around here.

Actually, something fucking reeked.

Something besides me and the blue raspberry slush I wore.

＊

After dinner, for the first time in a while, I was alone with Clover back in our dorm room. I still hadn't told her about what had happened between Ollie and me after the Gala, and it was playing on my mind. No matter how much Clo disliked Ollie, I still wanted to share this with her. Best friends didn't always need to like, or agree with, each other's decisions, but they needed to be supportive and understanding, regardless.

'Clo ...' The moment I said her name, and she looked at me, I wanted to pussy out. What if she judged me too hard? I would hate that so much. My only other option was to talk to Griff about it, and no matter how great he was, I didn't want to talk about this with him. I wondered if Ollie had already told him...

My mind had wandered again when Clo harshly called my name to grab my attention. 'Earth to Skylar!'

'Huh?'

'You said my name, then stared off into the distance. You okay?' she asked. I could tell she was worried about my mental state because she'd moved over and sat down next to me on my bed. She knew I wasn't a huge hugger but risked my wrath anyway by entering my personal bubble, wrapping her arm around my shoulder.

'Right, I did do that,' I mumbled. I took a deep breath, preparing myself to tell her.

The moment she felt me take in the deep breath, something must click in her mind. I looked at her as her face soured, almost crumbling into itself, and the look of disgust hit me hard in the gut.

'Please, please,' said Clo, shaking her head. She took in a

deep breath to match mine. 'Seriously Sky, please don't tell me you fucked that arsehole?'

'I can safely say I didn't fuck any arsehole.' I go with humour—and deflection. *Sue me*. It was also a little funny.

'Fuck off, you absolute comedienne.' I could tell she wanted to stay stern, but her face cracked a little. 'You know what I bloody well meant.'

'C'mon. I am kinda funny.' I nudged her with my elbow, on purpose digging into her rib a little more than necessary. I was feeling aggressive towards her, so an elbow dig seemed perfectly adequate.

'Yeah, funny looking for sure,' she said. This time, I nudged her harder. 'Ow!'

'Stop being a bitch,' I told her.

'Stop trying to tell me shit I don't want to hear then.'

I swore everybody in the entire school could hear the gigantic sigh I made at that moment.

'Do not sigh at me. I'm trying to look out for you, but girl, you are not making this easy for me,' she reprimanded me.

'Should I? You've not made getting to know you easy for me.'

'Touché,' she said.

We both started laughing at that, laying down on our backs and getting comfortable. 'I know I sound like a massive dick ninety-nine percent of the time Sky, but I promise I am looking out for you. I know what they're capable of.'

'I get that but just try to be a *little* happier for me,' I whined.

'I'll try,' she huffed. 'So, spit it out then.'

'Fine.' I took another deep breath. 'I slept with Ollie.'

'Beside him or ...' I could tell by the naughty glint in Clo's eye that she was trying to make me say the words out loud.

'Grrr. Fine,' I said. I covered my face with my hands, thinking that would make it easier to say the next part. 'I had sex with Ollie after the Gala.'

'I knew it!' she exclaimed, almost poking me in the eye with her finger. 'I knew you were acting differently. I mean it was a toss up between that or, you know, the whole Olivia being found dead thing.'

'Wow, Clo, didn't know you were so sensitive.'

'Piss off. I know you know what I mean,' she said. It was something we said a lot to one another. To the point that in texts with one another we'd shortened it to IKYKWIM, and both saved it as a shortcut on our keyboards.

'I get you. But yeah, Olivia definitely threw me for a loop. What do you mean I've been acting differently?' I asked.

'Honestly, I can't explain it. It felt like you were avoiding me, so subconsciously maybe you were without meaning to. Or realising it.'

'I guess I could've been without knowing it,' I said, reluctant to agree to her words that easily.

'Anyway, I want all the juicy deets,' she said.

'Do you actually?' I asked, skeptical.

'Of course. I may not like the boy, but you're my best friend. Course I wanna know everything!' Getting comfortable, she crossed her legs and leaned forward a little,

'Well, I'm not sure what to say, actually.' I was at a loss, and I felt a tad bit embarrassed just talking openly about it with her. It had been hard enough to spit out I was no longer a virgin. 'It was good.'

'Just good?!' Clo looked at me with one raised eyebrow and looked sorry for me.

I laughed at her reaction. It reminded me of a cartoon, or a caricature; so over the top and exaggerated. 'More than good,' I said, 'Finding words is hard.'

We both laughed in earnest then. 'That sentence was, honestly, shocking! You're meant to be the English student out of us.'

'Meant to be? I *am* the English student out of us,' I said. I picked up the closest pillow and threw it at her, but she dodged it. 'I don't know Clo. It was really, really good. Like, orgasm on the first try, good.'

'Woah. Now that *is* good!' She actually looked impressed for a moment. Then remembered it was Ollie we were talking about and caught herself. 'I'm surprised he knew how.'

'Oh, ha, ha. Hilarious.'

'You know I am. Seriously though. No regrets?'

'No regrets.' I shook my head emphatically. 'At. All.'

'I'm glad then,' she said and leaned over to hug me briefly, and I was happy that she hadn't made me feel shitty about my decision. 'Happy for you, girl.'

'Thanks,' I said, unsure she meant it fully, but I was happy that she'd said it, even if it was pretend. 'The timing felt right.'

'As long as you're okay with it, then shit, it doesn't matter what anybody else thinks. I've got your back.'

For the rest of the evening, the two of us spent our time gossiping about students, teachers and celebrities. The whole time, though, I wished I'd felt comfortable asking her for more in-depth sex knowledge. It wasn't like Clo wouldn't tell me shit and be honest with me; it was more me not wanting to rub in my relationship with Ollie more than necessary. I knew she wasn't jealous of *him*. Actually, most of the time I thought she was plotting his demise. However, I knew she *was* jealous of Odette, no matter how many times she'd said otherwise. When she thought nobody was looking, she'd glance in Leo and Odette's direction, trying to watch them unnoticed. Leo would turn to look back at her, but he'd always find her looking at anything but them. Being an outsider, I could see it all happening. Even if the two of them thought it was secretive.

I'd given up asking at this point. She clearly wouldn't tell me anything, and I wasn't in that place with Leo where I could ask him deeply personal shit.

Oh, well. If they wanted to keep shit to themselves, then I wasn't getting involved.

Chapter Twenty-Four

Valentine's Day.

The first one in my life where I'd actually had a boyfriend. Somebody to spend the day with—well, actually the weekend with. I was beyond excited. I tried to keep my full excitement to myself though, as I knew Clover was feeling a little sore on the subject. Especially now that Leo and Odette were official. Whenever I brought it up, all I'd got from Clo was, "Leave it Sky. I don't care who *it* fucks. I hope his dick falls off." So I'd said nothing more to her about it recently.

But before I could truly celebrate with Ollie, I had to get through the school day. Putting on my uniform before heading to breakfast, I made an extra effort with my hair and makeup. More than usual, anyway. I'd never been so happy to attend an upper school that had a uniform. I had anxiety just thinking of the anxiety I would have if I had to pick out my outfit every single morning. I struggled enough as it was picking out weekend clothes.

Clover hadn't got out of bed yet; she hadn't even stirred. Come to think of it, her *many* alarms hadn't gone off. I left it as late as I could before trying to wake her.

'Clo,' I called across the room, but when that seemed to make no difference I approached her bed and leant down to her. I softly shook her shoulder.

'Fuck!' she startled and sat bolt upright—hitting my nose with her head in the process.

'Ow!' I exclaimed as I tried to stop my vision from seeing multiple Clover's. My nose was gushing blood in an instant, and I ran to the kitchenette area to grab some tissue. Of all the days, I did *not* need Ollie to come get me for breakfast and find me looking like the victim of a crime.

'I am so, so sorry Sky! Shit! I know how much you've been looking forward to today,' she apologised, breathless.

'It's okay, really. It's not like you meant to do it.' I tried to smile, but it was hard to do while holding the tissue against my nose. I only had the one clean school shirt—definitely starting to become an issue of mine—as it was Friday, and these days I had half the amount I'd started the year with after Ophelia had decided to destroy my things.

Obviously at that exact moment there came a hard knock on our door. A hard knock followed by three quick raps; the code that Griff had made up and Ollie had adopted. I rolled my eyes, knowing that we would have to explain the shit that had just transpired. I knew that Ollie sometimes only put up with Clover's presence because of my friendship with her, and I seriously didn't want to give him any more reason to dislike her.

I opened the door to find Ollie leaning up against the frame, holding a massive share size bag of crisps and an even larger bag of chocolates. On seeing me, he smiled, but his face faltered when he actually took in the state I was in.

'What the fuck happened, Sky?' he asked as he launched himself into the room, slamming the door behind him. I knew he'd closed the door so that nobody in the corridor could look in, but it made me feel wary. I shook off that feeling. Of course, I shouldn't have to worry about Ollie. He'd been nothing but a great boyfriend ever since Halloween and my near death experience. Some nights I woke up in a cold sweat. Seeing the water surround me, feeling it cover my skin. Feeling the pressure of the hand forcing my head down. But as soon as I called him and heard his voice, I felt better. Then there were the nights where he was beside me when they happened. He'd wrap me in his arms and hold me tight; making me feel the most loved I'd ever felt in my entire life. I couldn't believe that I'd never felt this kind of care before. I'd always known shit with my mum was bad, but this had confirmed it.

Arms surrounded me again, pulling me into a hug I didn't want to end. My mind was moving a mile a minute, so I hadn't realised that Ollie and Clover had continued talking. Actually, they were raising their voices.

'I didn't mean to do it, *Ollie*. Sky was leaning over me to wake me up and she scared the shit out of me. It was a knee jerk reaction. Nothing more to it,' Clover said to Ollie.

I could tell by the look on Clo's face, and the shade of red it was turning, that this wasn't the first time she'd said this. I knew I needed to get involved and stick up for Clover. It really had been an accident.

'Oh, so this has nothing to do with the fact that today is

Valentine's Day and that you didn't set your alarms because you were hoping to skip this day entirely? Nothing to do with last year or Leo? Hm?' Ollie's chest was vibrating as he spoke. I tried to loosen the hug so I could look at Clover, but he just tightened his grip on me. His fingertips digging in. I winced, sure he was leaving marks on my skin.

'You think you know everything, don't you? Eurgh, people like you make me fucking sick,' she spat, livid.

'You just want Sky all to yourself. You know that you have no fucking chance of making any other friends in your pathetic little life, so you want to latch on to my girlfriend. I won't let you take her down with you.'

'Take her down with *me*?! God, you're actually delusional. Tell me you're hearing this shit, Skylar?' Clover asked me, spinning to look me in the eye.

I broke free from Ollie's hold and looked at Clover. Her green eyes filled with unshed tears and I knew that the dam could burst at any moment; she would hate herself if it happened in front of Ollie.

'Babe, I'll meet you outside in two minutes, okay?' I said to Ollie, hoping that he wouldn't get mad at me. I didn't want him to think that I was choosing Clover over him, but I also needed to let him know that she was my best friend and I wasn't gonna get pissed at her for a nose that wasn't even bleeding anymore. It wasn't like she'd broken it or even caused me to need a change of clothes. Accidents happen. Ollie should know this better than anyone.

'Fine,' he spat, 'but you better not take too long, Sky. I won't be waiting out there like a dick forever.'

I sighed.

'I'll be two minutes, tops,' I said, standing on my tiptoes to kiss his cheek to placate him. He nodded, and after sending another filthy look Clover's way, he put down the food he was still holding and left the room, letting the door slam behind him. The force of the door slamming closed caused a shock wave of sound to emanate throughout the room.

Clover faced me, a look of pity on her face.

'Do you get it now, Sky? Can you see even slightly where I'm coming from?' she asked, her voice small but her words sure.

'I mean ...' I trailed off. I could see Clover's point of view, but I also did slightly get where Ollie was coming from. Clo had a lot of internal anger for Leo and, by proxy, Ollie. 'I get you. Can you also slightly see where he's coming from though?'

'Sorry, did you just ask me if I believe that I'm trying to take you down with me?!' Her anger was palpable. It tasted all burnt and bitter. 'Honestly, Sky, you're pissing me off. Why are you so determined to fuck up our friendship and choose his side?'

'There aren't any sides here, Clo. I just want my best friend and my boyfriend to get along. So please, do me a small favour and just be civil for now. It's Valentine's Day. Please,' I pleaded. I knew I was asking a lot of her. I also knew it would piss me off if she asked the same of me, but I didn't know what else to do. I'd never had a best friend or a boyfriend, and of course I just wanted both of them to get along.

'I'll try for now but I swear to you Skylar, if I find out he's playing you in any way, shape or form, I will do everything I can to make you see the truth.'

I nodded. I didn't think he was hiding shit from me, but I could tell Clo really thought he was.

'Go. Enjoy your weekend,' she said and hugged me, then made a shooing motion. I left the room quickly, knowing that Ollie was still waiting on the other side of the door. I reckoned he was probably five seconds away from busting the door in with impatience.

After this weekend, I was going to sit down and weigh up just what Clover had been telling me. I wanted to believe that I trusted my own judgement, but honestly, I was so out of my league here.

✦

I met Ollie outside my room and went to breakfast with him, and from then onward, the day had flown past.

Everybody had left me alone today. It was a pleasant surprise; I'd totally expected some kind of Valentine's Day prank. I thought maybe it had something to do with *The Sect* issuing some kind of warning on the Hive to leave me alone. I hadn't actually read it as I didn't want to read the hateful comments I knew would accompany it, but Clover had told me the gist of it last night. It was the first time that there'd been a *Sect* sanctioned pause. After all, all three needed to approve it in order for it to become true. Meaning Leo had finally stood up for me.

I felt bad all day about what had happened between Ollie and Clover that morning but, if I was being honest with myself, it had been brewing for some time; always lurking underneath the surface. No matter how many times he'd tried to prove himself as worthy; she'd found a reason why he must be false, or tried to at least, and it bored me.

The hotel Ollie was taking me to later that night was one

I'd never have gone to before starting here and meeting him. Man, even the cheapest rooms there were far out of my price range. Not that I ever went into London often, and when I did I wasn't staying overnight in a hotel.

The day moved fast and the next thing I knew; we were in London eating at a fancy restaurant I'd never heard of, before going to see my favourite musical, *Hamilton*—and not from the cheap seats either. I nearly pinched myself multiple times, wondering how this had become my life. I didn't know what I'd done in a past life, but clearly something was starting to go right for me. We had a full packed schedule for the weekend before returning to school, and it all felt so surreal. We'd checked into the hotel under Leo's name though, something to do with the age you had to be to book a room here, or some such shit. Although I was pretty certain that if they'd thrown enough money around, that wouldn't have mattered at all. One thing I'd learned from these guys, and those at the Academy, was that if you had enough money to waste, people would do literally anything for you.

I reckoned Ollie actually enjoyed the secretive nature of the arrangement—and really, so did I. It felt sordid; in the very best way.

'Quick question. Why do fancy restaurants have so many pieces of cutlery?' I asked him, staring down at the large plate of food in front of me. I knew that it wasn't a very original question, but seriously, a fork's a fork, right? Like, who really needed that much cutlery for one meal?

'Pretty sure it's another way to make the little people feel little.' Ollie smirked, not realising that he'd lumped me in with the "little people" he was mocking.

'Right ...' I mumbled, not completing my sentence. I smiled

halfheartedly, taking in the surrounding scenery. I was glad that I'd been dining in the dining room at Hawthorn for the last few months, otherwise I'd have been even more star-struck with how this place looked. Although this place was more sleek and modern—no dark, ornate, wooden panels in sight.

Ollie's cutlery clattered as it landed on his plate. Lips pursed and eyebrows narrowed, I could tell that something had irritated him. Specifically, that *I* had irritated him.

'What's the matter?' he asked, his eyes hard; the spark that had been there a moment ago fading, about to disappear entirely. 'Tell me.'

'N-nothing,' I said, using the universal code girls used to signify that they were not okay but wanted you to try harder to get a real response.

'I'm not doing this shit, Sky. Tell me. Now.' He slammed his hand down onto the table, causing me to jump and the plates and glasses to clink. His rage had come out of nowhere. Was I being overly sensitive?

'I just didn't like being considered a *little* person. It's different for you. You grew up with money.' I shook my head at him, not wanting to get into this here. We'd been having such a great time together. It was our first time out of school with nobody else there. Christmas had been good, and we'd spent some time alone, but the others were always down the hall, or at least somewhere close by in the house. 'I didn't have a lot growing up. At all. Fuck, before I got the scholarship here, I worked my butt off trying to keep food on the table.'

'Not like you had to do that, Skylar,' he drawled, his cavalier attitude pissing me off. Dismissing what I had said without even fully processing it. 'Cora could have got a job.'

Now I really did laugh. So loud that other people sat at the tables nearby turned their heads to look in our direction. I hated that he was talking about my mum as if he knew her better than I did. As if she would have gone and got a job if I'd simply told her to. *Yeah, right...*

'Cora does nothing she doesn't have to. Trust me on that.'

'Andy should have found work, then. Been the man of the house,' he said, choosing to ignore my tone and continuing to pursue this line of conversation.

'Sorry, but did you meet the same people that I know? Can you even hear yourself right now?' I asked, disbelieving. I'd stopped eating too but, unlike Ollie, I'd put my cutlery down gently. Everything I was hearing out of his mouth right now was honest bullshit. Pure and utter bullshit.

'You could have refused to work. Forced their hands.'

'What and not eat?' I rolled my eyes at his ignorance, 'K.'

I couldn't right now. If I continued talking to him, I'd get mad, and it'd ruin our weekend before it had even begun. I picked up my cutlery and continued eating, ignoring him. The two of us now sat in an awkward silence.

Ten of the most uncomfortable minutes of my life passed. Then finally, Ollie looked up from his empty plate.

'Sorry,' he mumbled, so quiet that I only just caught it. I was going to make him sweat a little, though. No way was I just taking his piss poor sorry at face value.

'Can you hear somebody talking?' I asked the empty space, acting childish but fully aware of it. 'Or was it the wind?'

'Oh, ha, ha, you twat,' he said. He was smiling at me though, so I knew he didn't actually mean it. 'I'm sorry, okay? What I said was out of order.' He had a sheepish look on his face, and I knew that he was replaying his words in his head and hearing them from my perspective. Or at least that was what I assumed he was doing in his head. I mean, that was what he should have been doing.

'I'm going to accept your apology, I mean, it mostly sounded sincere,' I joked, smiling at him close mouthed while twisting my hair around my finger. I was going for coy—or something like that. I attempted to flirt too, but I wasn't sure I'd done an outstanding job of it. Ollie's expression was one of bemusement, as if he wasn't sure whether I was flirting and trying to be sexy, or whether I was just constipated.

I stopped my attempt, and then promptly burst into laughter. Fuck me, was there anybody more awkward on their first Valentine's Day date than me? I knew that we'd been dating for a while now, but this felt serious. Real.

We went back to sitting in silence; this time, a comfortable one. The silence you could enjoy with somebody you shared a bond with.

For dessert, I chose a simple basic bitch option of raspberry sorbet. I'd never really been that into sweet food, though. Chocolate and cake weren't my thing. When I'd first told Clover she'd looked at me as if I had three heads; she was incredulous and ever since had forced me to try everything she baked in class in order to convert me. Turned out, there wasn't too much left for me to try and nothing so far had made me fall in love. At one point, she was so offended I thought it'd come in between our friendship. Even more than my relationship with Ollie had already come between us.

Ollie clearly had no qualms with eating what they called *a proper dessert*. He'd got this real fancy look pie tart thing—at least I *thought* it was a tart. Either way, he seemed to enjoy it.

Good for him.

＋

THE CAR PULLED UP AT THE FRONT OF OUR RATHER POSH hotel and I waited for Ollie to get out first and open my door for me. Every time he did something chivalrous like this, I swooned inside. He could be a dick, a proper Beast, but then he'd melt me by acting like a real Prince.

The show we'd seen tonight had been spectacular—I would definitely have the songs on repeat for the foreseeable future. It was the first time I'd seen a show in the West End that close to the stage, and I'd loved every moment. The fact I'd had Ollie to share it with had made it all the better.

On entering the dark suite, I instantly gravitated towards the large floor to ceiling glass windows that looked out onto the London skyline. I loved London at night. Ever since I was young, I'd loved the story of Peter Pan. The boy who never grew up; an adventure filled with pirates and mermaids and fairies. Who the fuck didn't dream of that? I used to fall asleep wondering what it would be like to fly high above London; to look down and see tiny cars the size of ants, people barely a speck, if visible at all. Looking down on it all, rising above the little people—rising above the position life had handed you.

Ollie came up behind me, wrapping his arms around my waist. I transferred my weight back into him, using him as my support.

'It looks beautiful like this,' I whispered. The darkness surrounding us in contrast to the brightness of the world outside. I'd never been a city girl. Never wanted to live or work in the city. But damn, I would consider changing my mind if I could look out at this every night. This view was everything to the dreamer inside of me. To the girl who lived with her nose stuck in a book, the Belle of her own story.

'My view's beautiful,' Ollie whispered in my left ear, leaning down to brush his mouth against my ear. His breath caused shivers to cover me from head to toe with goosebumps.

Heat rushed through me and my stomach filled with jitters at his words.

Was it a line? Of course.

Did it work? *Of fucking course.*

'Have you ever thought of what it would be like to fly over a view like this?' I asked, my words the only noise in the large room.

'What, like on a plane?' Ollie asked, confusion mingling with his sultry voice. 'I know what that's like.'

'I guess,' I replied quietly, feeling stupid for asking the question. Of course he'd seen the city like this from a plane; he'd lived a much different life than the one I'd known. 'I've never been on one.'

'Never been on a plane?' he asked, surprised.

'Nope. Mum wasn't big on taking trips when I was growing up. Not ones that would cost a fortune outside of the country, anyway. If you couldn't drive there within five hours, then we didn't go.'

When I was younger, I'd always been so jealous of the girls at school who would come back after the holidays with a tan and braided hair. It seemed so exotic to seven-year-old me. My mum drove us to Calais once, but only because she could get cheaper cigarettes on the French border than she could at home. We were in France for a grand total of six hours, tops.

'Maybe one day I'll get to take you on one,' Ollie murmured, and when I turned in his arms to look at his face, I caught him deep in thought. His light blue eyes glazed over, like he wasn't in the room with me, but was instead somewhere else entirely. I'd noticed he did this often, and at first, it had worried me, wondering where his mind went. But now I let it happen without comment.

He'd come back to me.

He always did.

'Let's go to bed,' Ollie whispered, his eyes glistening with an emotion I couldn't place as he took my small hand in his larger one. We moved towards the largest bed I'd ever seen, the sheets a luxurious cotton that beckoned me in.

Gently, Ollie let go of my hand. He removed his clothes, one item at a time, as I sat on the edge of the bed staring at him. No matter how many times I saw this view, I couldn't help looking at him like it was the first time. His broad shoulders, his taut stomach; every single part of him turned me on. Every time I looked at him, I forgot we were the same age.

Excited for his touch, I lay down in anticipation, my dress raising up and resting on my thighs. Before I could get comfortable, Ollie gripped my hand once again and pulled me back to sitting. Naked, he was standing directly in front of me and my eyes rested on his dick. I licked my lips. I grazed my bottom lip with my teeth and smiled.

I took his hard length in my hand, barely able to wrap it around fully, as it twitched in my grasp. Licking the tip, I tasted his salty pre-cum, instantly wanting more. He moaned, his eyes filled with want when he looked down at me. I opened my mouth, and he slid his cock inside. Heat filled me, I felt hesitant at first, no idea how to do this right.

'Fuck,' he said, his voice thick, causing the hairs on my

body to stand on end. His praise filled me with warmth, a low buzzing feeling sitting low in my stomach.

I let go completely, his praise spurring me on, as I stretched my mouth wider, drawing him in and to the back of my throat. I sucked my way up and down his length in a slow, rhythmic motion.

He reached for me, his fingers feathering up my arms until they stopped at my neck. The brush of his thumb on my bottom lip caused a chill to trickle down to my toes. I closed my eyes; the sensation overwhelming.

'Open your eyes,' Ollie demanded.

I opened them instantly, not wanting him to get angry at me. His eyes locked on to mine, his dark indigo eyes boring into my soul. My heart beat in an unnatural pattern; getting faster with every inhale. My entire body was growing hotter from his stare. I needed him—now.

As if he could hear my thoughts, he slid from my mouth with a light popping sound, knocking my confidence, but then he pushed me down onto the bed, holding me there with his strength. His eyes intense, in a way I'd never seen before, his body moulding to mine.

'I need my cum inside you,' he whispered, his tone rasping. He kissed me slow and deep and added, 'But not here.'

Ollie kissed me again, bruising, as his hand reached between us and under my skirt.

My back arched involuntarily off of the mattress, as his large hand palmed me through my underwear.

'I need to feel you here,' he murmured, giving one last long kiss to my neck as his knuckles ran along my slit. 'So fucking wet.'

I writhed under his touch, whispering, 'P-please,' even though I didn't know what I was asking for.

Without hesitating, Ollie lifted himself off of my body, grasped my legs to align himself and then slowly moved my underwear to the side to allow himself the access he needed.

One slow movement, and he filled me to the hilt. Our bodies trembled with desire; his forehead coming to rest on mine. The action tender—almost too tender.

He stayed there, quiet, for the longest time. The two of us silent, no words between us, our connection saying all that was necessary. The darkness of the room created an intimate vibe; nobody could see us here.

The intimacy overwhelmed me; the silence deafening. I broke it with a whisper, 'I need more.' I pulled his lips to mine, and I sucked on his bottom lip. A tease of teeth making little bites.

He pushed up on his arms to take me in, to look me in the eye, and I saw apprehension laying underneath the surface of his. I swallowed, my nerves threatening to stop this beautiful moment.

With his lips slightly parted, his hand trailed down the centre of my chest. His smile tugged on the corner of his lips as he bunched up the material of my dress, as if he needed it gone. Needed to see me bare to him; see where the two of us joined as one. No barrier between us.

Ollie took his time, lazily thrusting into me until we were both breathless and fixated on only each other, racing for the release we both chased.

'Shit.' The muscles in his broad chest seemed to coil tight, his chin dropping as his hand grasped my hips, pulling me to him with urgency. They held me in place, tight, desperate, as if scared I'd fly away from his grasp.

A tortured growl vibrated from his throat.

'Come with me,' he demanded.

The pad of his thumb found my clit, teasing it in slow, pressured circles and sending me into a frenzy as my body fought for release.

'Oh my God,' I panted, almost at the peak.

My walls suffocated him, clenching and unclenching, as my body tumbled over the edge, over the precipice and into the best kind of ecstasy; and he came willingly with me.

Our gaze locked. Ollie's blue stare filled with a hunger, yet also one of wonder.

I smiled softly at him, the only words on the tip of my tongue ones I wouldn't voice out loud.

I think I'm falling for you.

Chapter Twenty-Five

Monday morning came, and I was still on a major high from my trip to London with Ollie. We'd had such a wonderful time, and I knew I'd said that I was going to sit down and weigh up Clover's worries, but after the wonderful time we'd had together, nothing negative was going to compute in my brain. My brain was basically now mush. It was a heart-shaped pile of squidgy matter, and I was a sucker for letting it happen. Since day one Clover had warned me against the boys and here I was in a relationship with one of them. We were happy though, and that mattered to me.

Spending time together this weekend without the distraction of school, and other people, was exactly what we'd needed. Every day, I felt a little more in love with him. I couldn't stop it at this point even if I tried—and believe me, I'd tried. Not like I was going to tell him, I didn't want to scare him off. Nobody liked the clingy girl who gushed her feelings too fast. Plus, it would mortify me if he didn't feel the same way.

Rooting through my school bag, I wondered if I'd put my History textbook back after the last lesson had ended. I located it and once I did; I felt a note sticking out of the top of it. It was a simple, handwritten note in Ollie's distinctive scrawl:

Meet me outside after third period.

He must have put the note there earlier this morning when I wasn't looking. Or maybe it was from ages ago and I'd only just found it? For a moment, I wondered whether or not this would be similar to Halloween. But that note had been typed to disguise the sender, and I sat next to Ollie most days in History and knew his lettering.

Either way, I'd go stand outside after third just to make sure. I could always text him to find out for definite.

Heading into English, a spring in my step, I smiled.

How exciting this relationship stuff could be.

✳

The moment my third lesson ended, I rushed outside straight away, barely stopping to take a breath. I wanted to give myself enough time to spot Ollie before lunch. If the note wasn't from today, then I'd know within ten minutes.

'Skylar.' My name sounded like dirt coming out of Odette's mouth. Ever since Olivia had been found with a lock of my hair, I'd worried the girls would escalate.

'I'm w-waiting for Ollie,' I said. Maybe if they knew he was coming soon, they'd bugger off and leave me alone.

'Oh,' Ophelia said, confused. 'I thought I saw him by the tree line a moment ago.'

Right, like I was going to fall for that one. They probably just wanted to get me alone over by the trees. Barely any teachers would be over there at this time of day, making it a prime spot.

'Thanks. I'll w-wait for him here,' I said as I got out my phone, realising that I should text Ollie and have him clarify whether that note was from today. I could also text Leo if shit got out of hand too. I tapped out a quick message while the girls stood and stared at me, their hatred shining on their faces.

HEY BABY, DID YOU PUT THAT NOTE IN MY HISTORY BOOK today?

IT WASN'T LONG UNTIL I GOT A REPLY FROM HIM.

YEAH, I'LL BE THERE SOON. JUST SETTING UP.

I WONDERED WHAT HE MEANT BY SETTING UP. IT BEING lunch time, maybe he'd sorted some kind of picnic out. That'd be quite cute—sexy, too. I'd always wanted somebody to care about me and make me cute sandwiches and shit.

'H-he'll be here in a moment,' I said, stuttering for the first time in a while. Not sure why I felt the need to fill them in, but oh well. And yeah, I wanted to rub it in a little. Okay. A lot.

After all, Ollie had picked *me*. Not one of them, with their over-bleached hair and their obviously enhanced features.

It also frustrated me. I'd been doing so well recently at not stuttering, and then *The Set* came along and fucked it up for me. My anxiety still lived underneath the surface, lurking in the dark, but I had found it easier to breathe recently.

'Eurgh, I thought you'd got rid of that fucking horrible stutter,' said Oralie, fake shivering. 'You could have been one of us, New Girl, if you weren't a poor fucking freak.'

I made a big deal of rolling my eyes. Even their insults weren't hitting the mark the way they usually did. Maybe it was my newfound confidence guiding me.

'If you'll excuse me,' I sassed, walking away from them with a sway of the hips, leaving them standing with their mouths wide open. I think they were just as shocked as I was. I'd walked away from them, for maybe the first time, and, damn, did it feel good!

Meet me by the treeline.

Maybe Ophelia had been telling the truth after all. Stranger things had been known to happen.

'Hey, beautiful.' Ollie came up behind me and scared the ever loving shit out of me. I jumped as he grabbed my waist to steady me. 'Fancy a picnic?'

I smiled, turning around so I could see his face. His eyes were the lightest of blues today, like a really clear ocean, or maybe more like a sky on a really cloudless day. A super rare sight.

'I'd love one. Please tell me you have cheese sandwiches?' I asked, almost whining at him to give me good news.

'Course I do, they're your favourite,' he said, simply, like there hadn't been another option for him. My heart thumped an extra beat, my stomach fluttering.

'Let's be honest, Ollie, they should be *everybody's* favourite. Honestly, there are monsters out there who don't even like cheese, that's some serious effed up shit.'

'But, babe, there's people who like cheese and then there's you.'

Taking my hand, Ollie walked me a little way into the woods to where he'd arranged a picnic blanket and a basket. The blanket was one of those quintessential red check picnic blankets that I swore you saw in every film and TV show. How cute.

'Oh, ha, ha. Hilarious,' I said sarcastically. I grinned like a mad person, loving the fact that I felt like I could be myself around him these days. 'I like cheese. Is that a crime?'

'No. But it should be a crime *just* how much you love it,' he joked.

'I can't help if I'm a turophile,' I told him. I'd learned the word for a cheese lover recently, and I thought it sounded like something else entirely. 'Actually, I found an article the other day about a guy who puts cheese on top of his milk cereal AND on his ice cream.' The look of disgust on Ollie's face was a picture. I wasn't even joking either—and, of course, the guy was British.

'The day you put cheese on ice cream babe is the day I leave you.'

'That's totally fair,' I said with a laugh, accepting his statement as fact.

I got comfortable on the blanket while Ollie sorted out the food and drinks. I couldn't decide what he was hoping to get out of this, but he was winning some definite brownie points, for sure.

The food tasted delicious. Alongside cheese sandwiches, Ollie had made the kitchen prepare some of my favourite snacks. At times like this, I fully realised that he must *actually* listen to me. Or notice what foods I loved. I'd never had this level of attention on me and my habits before.

'Thank you,' I said. I leaned over to him and gave him a quick kiss on the lips. It was brief, but filled with my gratitude. If I hadn't been sure that I was falling before, I knew for definite now. The boy had hit me in the heart.

'No problem. I have another surprise for you.'

'You do?' I asked, my lips forming a smile.

'Yep. I'm just gonna go grab it. Don't move from this spot,' he commanded. He stood and left our secluded area at a fast pace. He was out of my eyeline in no time.

I laughed at his retreating back. Where would I even go?

Ten minutes passed, and I worried that he wasn't coming back. Which would be odd, but maybe a teacher had caught him and sent him to his lesson? There were a multitude of possibilities, after all.

A rustle of leaves behind me made me pause. I hadn't seen anybody else since we entered the woods, and I didn't think it was Ollie as the sound was coming from a totally different direction to the one he'd sprinted off in.

Wonderful.

A dull pain shot through my skull.

What.

The.

Fuck.

I tried to catch my bearings before the next blow came, but they were too quick. This time, pain rippled across my shoulder, making its way down my entire right arm.

I glimpsed over-bleached blonde hair in my peripheral. Of course, it was a member of *The Set* hurting me. Or maybe all three of them. They must have watched me enter the woods when I met Ollie. Purposefully staying close by in case a situation like this one presented itself.

Where the fuck had Ollie got to?

'Let's teach this little bitch a lesson,' I heard Odette say, and then giggling followed.

'Yeah, New Girl,' Ophelia spat. 'This is for Olivia.'

The kicks and punches continued and my vision faded; the pain vibrating through my entire body. Man, it hurt like a motherfucker.

Even after the blows ended, all I could feel was pain everywhere.

'Sky? Sky? Are you okay?' Griff's voice called out to me. Footsteps got closer and although I couldn't see him, I knew it was him. I couldn't mistake that voice. When I tried to call out to him, no noise came out of me except for a harsh rasping breath.

His footsteps came closer, then I heard a, 'Shit, Sky' which meant that he'd found me.

I wanted to cry in happiness that he'd found me and that I didn't need to crawl through the woods in my current state.

Although, that wouldn't have happened if Ollie had come back.

Fuck. *None* of it would have happened if Ollie had come back.

The real question was, why didn't he?

✦

ONCE AGAIN, I FOUND MYSELF IN THE HOSPITAL WING. At this point, I may as well put my name above a bed and make it permanently mine. Griff sat in the chair beside my bed, cheeks flushed with emotion. After he'd found me, he hadn't left my side. He really could be super sweet and caring—the perfect gentleman.

'This is getting fucking ridiculous. I'll be having words with Ollie and Leo later,' he grumbled. He got out his phone and started furiously typing. 'Can't you and Clover beat them up at some point?'

'Erm ...'

Don't get me wrong, I'd thought about it. The repercussions didn't seem worth it though, as we could lose our scholarships. Plus, Clover was in her last year here and had plans to go to a great university. I couldn't ruin that for her.

'Not really,' I said, my tone sure.

'Well, it's not like Ollie and I can. We can make them outcasts, yeah, but can't physically harm them,' he said. The look on his face told me that fact pissed him off. I also didn't believe they could make them true outcasts, either.

'I want to. Believe me, I would love to see Ophelia with a broken nose because I punched her so hard. But I just feel like I'm above that, right?'

'Yes!' Griff said enthusiastically. 'You are above them, New Girl, completely.'

'Thanks Griff,' I said, smiling at him. He always knew the perfect thing to say that would make me feel better.

'Sky.' Griff's voice got quieter, and he stopped me from grabbing my phone off the counter to text Ollie. 'I need to talk to you.'

'Okay ...' I got more comfortable in the bed and asked, 'What about?'

'About my parents,' he whispered, sheepish. Worried, too. 'So, I don't know what you know about them?'

'Err, honestly, not much. Nobody will tell me anything.'

'Right.' The chair cushion groaned as he fidgeted. 'So, my mum's name was Eliza Hawthorn and my dad was Damien Cooper. They died when I was five in a car crash. I was in the car too, but I don't remember any of it.'

I was completely thrown. I hadn't expected him to tell me that. I'd spent Christmas at his parents' estate and nobody had ever mentioned that they weren't alive. Parents' Day too, it was just sort of said that they couldn't be there. Now I felt like a right bitch—I'd grumbled to Griff so many times about my mum and Andy.

'After it happened, I went and lived with Leo. His dad, Edward, is my uncle, cause he's my mum's older brother. The other option was to live with my mum's twin, Millie. Ollie's mum.'

Slightly struggling to keep up, I nodded my head, trying to wrap my head around it all. I knew that the three boys were close, but I didn't realise that they were all related; that they were all cousins and had a Hawthorn link.

'So you're related to Ms Hawthorn too?' I asked. Who even knew why that was the first question that came to my mind. Maybe it was because I didn't want to say anything else too deep.

'Yep, she's my aunt too, but having a different surname

means Ollie and I can keep more of a low pro. I forget that you haven't known us all since birth. Most of the kids here have parents that are in the same circle as us.'

'Wow.' It felt like it wasn't enough, like I needed to say a lot more than that, but I just didn't have the words right now. How had I known them all this long and not known any of this? I knew the boys had been keeping secrets from me, Clover too, but I'd put them to the back of my mind, mostly.

'Yeah, wow,' he chuckled. He looked lighter, if that was even possible. Like finally getting this off of his chest and letting me in had made him feel better. 'You okay?'

'Not gonna lie Griff, I didn't even know what your surname was until just now, but honestly, I'm good,' I chuckled too. 'Seriously though, are you okay?'

'I'm good, New Girl.' The playful smile returned to his face. We were both silent for a moment, then he piped up again, 'I really think my mum would have loved you.'

'You reckon?'

'Yeah,' Griff shrugged, 'she was beautiful. Her smile could light up a room.' His eyes were glossed over and I knew his mind had travelled elsewhere. 'You remind me of her.'

'I do?' I asked, surprised.

'Mum was strong. Let nothing phase her. Just like you.'

'I don't think that's entirely true,' I mumbled. 'I definitely let shit phase me.'

'Maybe on the inside New Girl, but it rarely shows on the outside.'

'Why are you always so nice to me? Even on day one, you weren't horrible to me.'

'Honestly, I'm not sure why I wasn't. They'd instructed me

to give you a hard time. New girl in the school, on scholarship, nobody was sure whether you could hack it here.'

'Have I proved that I can hack it now?'

'Girl, you proved you could hack it after that first party in the woods.'

'That feels so long ago. But here I am, still finding myself in here.' I gestured around, the rest of the Hospital Wing empty.

Griff reached out and took my hand in his, squeezing it tight. The gesture made me feel loved, and as if the two of us shared a secret of sorts. Like I'd made a friend that liked me for me. Not because he wanted in my pants. Not because he had some misguided sense that he needed to protect me. It felt good.

'I'm glad. Not that you're in the Hospital Wing again, obviously. But the fact that you're here. At Hawthorn still. I worry that one day, you won't want to be friends anymore.' His eyes were more green than blue today, and they stared straight into mine. He leaned closer to me and squeezed my hand again. 'Promise me that no matter what else happens this year, we'll still be friends at the end of it?' I could feel his nerves as he asked. Not sure if the nerves were because he was worried about my answer or just the fact that he'd voiced an insecurity like that out loud. Usually, he came across so carefree. I slightly wondered why he felt the need to ask. And yeah, it was suspicious as fuck.

'I promise,' I answered instantly, no qualms about making him this promise, even though I felt unsure of his reasoning. I opened my arms wide for a hug and Griff instantly leaned into them. It was one of those tight hugs, where you could hear your ribs groaning in revolt. Believe me, mine were screaming.

I spotted Ollie over Griff's shoulder and I lifted my lips into an unsure smile, slowly leaning out of the hug I'd just started. Griff noticed that my attention was elsewhere and glanced behind him.

'Hey dude,' Griff said through gritted teeth, anger rippling off of him. 'Wondered when you'd get here to be with your girl.'

'I would have got here faster but apparently *my girl* and my best friend were too busy getting cosy to let me know where they were.'

Huh? Griff had been writing furious texts the whole time we'd been here, and I'd assumed they'd been to Ollie—but clearly not.

'S-sorry. I thought you knew where we were.' My voice raised at the end, so it came out more like a question. I really thought he knew we were here. Surely he must have known that the girls had got to me again?

'No. I did not,' he growled. His eyes, like his words, were hard and I could see the anger there; the anger directed at me. Like any of this was my fault. I wanted to say, *Oh yeah Ollie, sorry I didn't tell you where I was while three girls were ganging up on me.* I rolled my eyes. 'Got something to say, sweetheart?' he drawled.

'Oh, I don't know, dickhead. Maybe you should ask her if she's okay?' Griff stood, puffing up his chest, taking a step closer into Ollie's space.

I was pissed. He hadn't even asked if I was okay. He'd glanced briefly at the bruises forming on my face when he'd first entered, but other than that, he hadn't even tried to come closer and touch me.

'Stop it. Both of you,' I shouted loud enough that the two of them stopped sizing one another up and turned to look at me. 'Maybe you should go.'

My eyes were staring intently into Ollie's. As much as I wanted him here to comfort me, it didn't seem like he'd be doing that soon and honestly, *fuck that*. I deserved to have somebody by my side who wanted to be there and cared that I was hurting. Griff had been nothing but nice since he'd found me, and Ollie's presence was ruining the camaraderie we'd established.

'You seriously want me to leave and have this fuckwad stay here?' Ollie asked me, one eyebrow raised.

'Y-yes.' I held firm, our eyes boring into one another. 'Go.'

'Fuck this,' Ollie growled.

The curtain around my bed fluttered as he stormed out, the door of the wing slamming not long afterward.

I sighed.

I had wanted him to fight me on it. To grovel, ask to stay. Fuck, even just ask me how I was. But he hadn't. He hadn't fought at all, and it was the worst he'd made me feel in the entire time I'd known him.

Chapter Twenty-Six

Ollie had been acting strange for the last couple of weeks and, not gonna lie, it pissed me off. Ever since I'd left the Hospital Wing for the gazillionth time, things had been strained between us. I didn't understand why he wouldn't just talk to me about it. I'd happily listen to him, no matter what had been playing on his mind. But instead of confiding in me, he'd just spent less time with me. Which sucked. Our relationship had been going fantastic, and I didn't want to lose sight of that because he was acting like a super douchebag right now.

Monday morning came with an entire school mandatory assembly. I had seen little of Ms Hawthorn recently, and no part of me felt upset by that. Every now and again I'd see her in the hallway up ahead, but when that happened either Griff or Ollie would purposefully lead us in a different direction. Pretty sure they were avoiding her more than I was. They were related to her, after all. From what I'd witnessed, though, she didn't show them any preferential treatment because of it. I'd never seen her even smile at one of them.

'Ready to get this shit show on the road?' Clover asked me as we left breakfast, Griff and Ollie trailed along behind us. They were in deep discussion about something swim related—honestly, I tried to keep up with them, but I had no clue about any of it.

'Any idea what it could be about?' I asked.

'Probably announcing the annual charity fundraiser. Takes place at the end of the Easter term every year,' Clo answered, matter of fact.

'Who decides what the fundraiser is?'

'*The Set.* But everybody in the upper two years has to take part in some capacity. Last year it was a silent auction ball that I could hide away during, while working in the cloakroom.'

'Fingers crossed for us that we're able to hide away this year,' I said. We locked our arms together, only breaking apart when we reached the hall.

Ollie dropped into the seat next to me on one side and Griff the other. I'd grown quite fond of being in the middle of an Ollie and Griff sandwich. The jealous stares started the moment we sat down—girls of every age giving me the evil eye. *Petty much.*

As usual, the hall was full of chatter until Ms Hawthorn appeared on the stage and then all talking ceased. Just like that. Her mere presence had this effect on everybody and more than once, I'd wondered how she had the school so under her control. Nobody wanted to get on her bad side.

'Quiet now,' Ms Hawthorn said once she'd reached centre

stage. Even though you could have heard a pin drop in the auditorium and her words were unnecessary. She always had hit me as somebody who took a thrill out of being in control. 'I have gathered you all here today to discuss the end of term charity effort this year.'

Not for the first time, I wondered if Ollie knew what it was going to be. Surely if it was decided by *The Set*, the boys would have some clue of what it was. However, when I'd asked, he'd changed the subject.

'This year, boys and girls, we shall put on a Charity Fashion Show for the same charity the school always supports.'

The room erupted into noise all at once. Instantly, groaning came from the older years, and the younger years cheered and laughed as if this was one of the best outcomes.

I looked behind me to catch Clover's eye. I found her sitting a couple of rows behind me with Leo and Odette next to her. She looked back at me; her face livid, her brows furrowed in anger and the straight line of her mouth told me just how pissed off she was at the situation.

'Settle down, children. Settle down.' Ms Hawthorn spoke softly, but her words cut through the noise instantly. 'The students of the upper years will be organising and modelling in the show. Odette Aston has the list of assigned roles. The Hive will have a copy of the list too, so make sure you are aware of what we expect of you.' Her gaze found mine, sat between the boys, and I swore her facial expression became even more severe. Like her grey eyes were looking into my soul, or maybe attempting to poke around in my grey matter somehow.

'That will be all for today. In rows, you are to depart the

auditorium quietly and in single file. Make haste to your first period.'

With that last sentence, Ms Hawthorn took a step away from the microphone and stayed there. As each row slowly left the hall, I saw her assessing everybody. I had a feeling that nothing happened at *her* school without her knowing about it. Meaning she knew about my multiple attacks and hadn't once called me into her office about any of them. Not sure why it was only hitting me as odd now; but fuck me, that was odd. She'd called me in about the video after Parents' Day, but really, that had been a tactic to pacify the parents who had witnessed it.

I found myself lost in thought, leaving the room in silence with Griff and Ollie beside me, and it was only when we entered the hallway again and Griff spoke that I came out of my trance.

'Reckon they'll ask me to model underwear?' he joked. He wagged his eyebrows comically, 'Everybody needs to see this package, right?'

Ollie and I chuckled at him. Honestly, this boy. I could never decide whether he was 100% playing around or if a part of him did slightly believe his own hype. He flirted with everybody—and I mean everybody. I'd never seen him with anybody outside of our group, either. Even at the parties we'd been to, he'd stuck by mine and Clover's sides throughout.

His words settled into my brain, trickling in at a slow pace. I sputtered, 'S-sorry, they could ask us to model underwear?!' I could hear the incredulity in my tone, my shock radiating through me in stages. We were sixteen, for fuck's sake. Well, aged from sixteen to eighteen, but only people with an early birthday in year thirteen were actually eighteen. Respectable institution, my arse. They constantly sold that vision to the people shedding out the big bucks, but clearly, they were full of shit.

'Potentially. I mean, Odette and her cronies set this up, remember? They'd love to show off their figures in front of a large crowd,' Griff said, turning to face me.

'How large of a crowd?' I asked. The cogs started to turn in Griff's head, as he tried to come up with a suitable answer that would placate me.

'A couple of hundred, I guess? It depends. Last year's silent auction ball had a large audience—you know how much rich people love flaunting their wealth. They were all fighting to outdo one another. The year before though was boring and barely any parents attended.'

'What was it?' I asked, curious.

'Honestly, it was so shit I can't even remember. But I will say, the elite love to appear benevolent. Even if they couldn't give any fucks in actuality,' he said, shrugging.

'Right ...' My sentence hung in the air, and I felt none the wiser about any of it.

Clover came and joined us, having finally fought her way out of the hall and through the masses of younger years, all congregating together to discuss the news.

'Girl, you are not gonna like this.' Clover fidgeted, rubbing her hands on her thighs, clearly agitated.

Well, shit. That sounded foreboding.

'Stop with the dramatics. Some of us have places to be,' Ollie said, assessing her. His eyes narrowed—the way you'd look at shit on your shoe.

The two of them still weren't on the best of terms, and to be honest, I was over it. If they wanted to act like bloody children, then I wouldn't stop them.

'Go on, Lady Luck, don't keep us in suspense,' Griff joked, playing with Clo's hair. Wrapping a strand around his fingers and twirling.

'Right. So, I got waylaid by dickface and ogre number one as they just wouldn't leave the row and they weren't letting me pass. Anyway, Odette had her list of roles, ready to bark at anyone who wanted to listen. I found out what's "expected of us".'

I giggled at her choice of words. Dickface and ogre number one, what a great way of describing at least one of those people. No matter what had happened, I still couldn't marry my opinion of Leo with Clo's one of him.

'And ...?' I tried my best to not roll my eyes at her, but she was dragging this out a little longer than she needed to. The suspense clearly gave her a thrill.

'And we've been assigned to model in the show!' she said. She ended her sentence with a big flourish, both arms raised above her head before flopping down; all heavy and full of purpose.

'W-we what?' I screeched, causing everybody near us in the hallway to turn and look in our direction. I always seemed to draw the attention; and not always in a good way. 'We have to m-model? Model what?'

I started hyperventilating, feeling the onset of a mini panic attack—obviously it was at that moment that Odette and Leo finally left the hall and became witnesses to my meltdown. *The Set* had done this shit to me on purpose. The smug look on Odette's face told me as much.

'Whatever the co-ordinators decide you'll look best in,' Odette said as she gave me a snotty look from head to toe. 'But let's be honest, New Girl, I highly doubt they'll find anything that will look good on your boxy frame.'

Yep. I resembled a box because I wasn't stick thin with ribs showing. Nice one, Odette.

I didn't say that though. No. I said, 'Oh.'

Nice one, Sky.

'Let's go,' Leo said as he pulled Odette away from us, walking her down the corridor, his grip firm on her arm as they went. When our group started up their conversation again, I looked down the corridor to see Leo looking back at me. He winked, his lips raised into a smirk, before disappearing into a classroom.

'... you won't even help us. Typical. Don't you think he should, Sky?' Clover asked me.

I looked back at the group to see Clover staring at me, Griff looking over my shoulder to where Leo had just been, his features forming a quizzical look, and Ollie looking rather proud of himself.

'Huh?' I asked, confused what Clo wanted me to have an answer to. I'd clearly missed something when I'd been looking at Leo.

'Ollie should intervene with *The Set* and put us on cloak-room duty.'

'Err ...'

Did I think that? I knew that was what Clover wanted me to think—to agree with her wholeheartedly and hope that we could get out of this shit pile we'd somehow landed in. But I wasn't so sure. The tradition *was* for the girls to organise the charity effort, and I wasn't going to make myself even more hated by trying to mess with tradition.

Rich people took that shit seriously.

Fuck, my mum took tradition seriously, and she lived in a house paid for by benefits—benefits I felt pretty certain they'd swindled, or outright lied, to obtain.

'Oh, for fuck's sake, Skylar. You really are turning into a pathetic, desperate whore of a cunt, you realise that?' Clover said, derision filling her face. Her features twisted, her whole face contorting in a grotesque manner.

She stomped away and all I could do was stand there in shock; frozen in place like an ice statue.

She'd never spoken to me that way before. Never called me names or made me feel small. If I was in a cartoon, my jaw would have dropped to the floor like an anvil, exaggerated and comedic.

But this was real life. And no part of what just happened was comedic.

So, I did what any respectable girl would do in my situation. I cried.

Ollie and Griff both stood still, uncomfortable and unsure of the best action to take. A split moment later, Griff hurried away to catch up with Clover and Ollie came and hugged me tight to his hard, warm body.

I instantly felt a little better.

'She had no right to say that to you,' Ollie whispered in my ear, as he moved us into an alcove so we were away from the foot traffic surrounding us. 'And I don't think that you are pathetic or desperate and you are definitely not a whore. Or a cunt.' His eyes hardened on the last word, filled with anger at Clover.

He lifted my chin up, tilting my face so he could see me fully, and I gave him a small, tentative smile. Even though he sort of had to say that, being my boyfriend and all, it still made me happy that he did.

Was I slightly pissed at Griff for ditching me to go after Clo? Yes.

According to her, they'd bullied her last year, and she was here on scholarship too, so it wasn't like she'd been friends with them before I came here.

Okay, so maybe I was more than slightly pissed off. I thought Griff, and I were closer now. Obviously, I'd been blind to the truth.

'Try to forget about her babe. She's just jealous and bitter and not worth it,' he told me in a calming tone.

Ollie's hands started rubbing up and down my arms in a soothing, circular motion. It grounded me and although the tears didn't stop; they slowed down. I nodded, mostly to make him feel as if I agreed. I didn't know if I did, though.

'Do you want me to talk to Odette? Cause I will if *you* want me to. Clover, of all people, will not force me into it. She was trying to save her own arse and not yours like she claimed.'

I thought about my decision for a minute or two. The two of us were still standing in the alcove; the rest of the hall quiet as pupils had moved to their first class of the day.

'Babe, we're going to be late for class,' I told him, but not making any effort to move from his hug. I took a deep, calming breath and said, 'I don't want you to talk to Odette.'

He hugged me tighter, squeezing me to the point that I felt my lungs cry in protest.

'You sure?' he asked as he swept a strand of hair from in

front of my face and tucked it behind my ear. Every time he did that, I melted a little more inside.

'Yeah. We don't need to antagonise them more and I can model in the fashion show. How hard can it be?'

Famous last words?

Duh.

Chapter Twenty-Seven

It felt strange to not be on talking terms with Clover. Our room was silent whenever we were both there, and no matter how hard Griff had tried to resolve the issues between us, nothing he'd tried so far had worked.

In my eyes, Clover needed to apologise for what she'd said. It was uncalled for and even if she believed it to be true; I was still fucking insulted she'd put the words out into the universe. She could have continued to think it and I'd have been none the wiser.

'C'mon Sky, you two need to talk,' Griff implored me as we listened to Mr Somes drone on about Bentham and Utilitarianism. Okay, I wasn't listening at all. I was in my head thinking about everything and nothing at the same time. My mind stuck in that place where I weighed up my feelings about my friendships and relationships—but also about what pizza toppings I preferred. 'Clo wants to talk to you, I know she does.'

'Not gonna lie to you, Griff, but I'd rather hear that from

her. Not once has she tried to talk to me, and we share a fucking room. She's had enough opportunities in the last week.'

I doubted Griff had intended to piss me off, but trust me, he'd succeeded.

The fact she was trying to use Griff as a go between was such a shitty thing to do. It wasn't fair for him to be in the middle, but also, part of me felt like he'd taken her side, anyway. Yeah, he was talking to me while in class, but outside of class he spent every minute with her.

Shit, they weren't even sitting with Ollie and me at dinner or anything.

'She's worried. She knows she fucked up, New Girl. You've just got to give her the chance to say sorry,' Griff said, sounding worried himself.

'I didn't know she needed me to come to her for an apology,' I snapped, irritated that he couldn't see where I was coming from. 'If she's as sorry as you say, then she could have told me already.'

'I've told her that, but she's worried you hate her.'

'Of course I don't hate her. But I do feel like she's been thinking shit about me behind my back for a while. She meant what she said at the time she said it. She called me a cunt, Griff.'

'Yeah, at first I reckon she meant it. But I know she doesn't *actually* think that of you.'

'Oh, has she told you that then during one of your super secret couple's nights?'

Griff blushed, a sheepish expression on his face, as he faltered in his response.

'It's not like that.' His meadow eyes felt as if they were pene-
trating my soul, reaching deep inside of me, trying to make things
right between us. 'She doesn't feel comfortable around Ollie
right now. She's worried he's going to retaliate on your behalf.'

'Eurgh, I am sick of her always trying to paint Ollie as the
bad guy. He's done nothing to her all year. She believes you've
turned over a new fucking leaf, so why can't he have too?' I
raised my voice, causing the other students in the class to turn
and look at us. The teacher shook his head at us, but continued
chatting about ethics. Even if he didn't really talk about it,
Griff *was* a part of *The Sect* and that gave him sway, even if he
never abused that power.

'I did actually say sorry to her,' he mumbled. Maybe he
thought being quiet would make me less mad at the fact that
he was obviously criticising Ollie; and probably Leo, too. 'Look
Sky, I don't want to fall out with you too, but just know that
Clover's coming from a good place. A true place. Ollie hasn't
always acted this way ...' Griff trailed off, not saying any more,
which made me even more curious to get to the bottom of what
he meant.

'In what sense?' I asked, hoping he'd give me a little more
to go on. But he didn't. He merely said, 'Just be careful, babycakes. You don't have the full picture.'

'Give me the full picture then,' I demanded, frustrated that
he was being so cryptic with me.

He shrugged, and said, 'I would, but it's really not my
place babydoll.' Honestly, his words and attitude disgusted me.
"Babycakes"? "Babydoll"? *Seriously?*

'You can be a right wanker. You know that?'

'True, but I'm a wanker with your best interests at heart.

Remember that,' he said, his whole demeanour condescending.

I continued to ignore him for the rest of the lesson, as I hoped my silence would lead to him revealing something to me.

He didn't.

So when the bell rang, I left the classroom as fast as I could, ignoring him calling my name behind me.

✦

BEFORE THE SHIT STORM THAT WAS PHILOSOPHY AND Ethics, I had felt that ever since Griff had opened up to me, we'd grown even closer. I felt like I understood him so much more now, and I also now understood why he covered a lot of his genuine emotions with humour. Yes, he'd annoyed me, but ultimately I knew we'd make up. He was one of my favourite people in this shit hole.

One person who wasn't that happy about how close I'd become with Griff was Ollie. Well, *"wasn't that happy"* was an enormous understatement.

He was pissed. Really pissed.

'If you'd stop spending time with Griff, then maybe we could actually spend some time together?' he grumbled.

'We do spend time together?' I asked, confused why he was confronting me about this—again.

'Yeah, we do, but rarely just the two of us.'

'I don't think you're being fair,' I told him. I could slightly understand his point, but I'd never had an issue with it before. 'It's not like Clover or Griff crash our time alone often.'

'What did Griff talk to you about?' he asked, accusation thick in his voice.

'When?'

'In the Hospital Wing. After the woods.'

'Nothing. Well, nothing of importance to you, anyway. He was telling me about his parents, mostly.'

'Sure you're not lying?' He looked so paranoid, and I didn't know why. Something had agitated him, 'Are you keeping shit from me?'

I laughed out loud, literally, in his face. We were sitting next to one another at a table in the library as we shared this free period, both of us trying to work on our English home-work. Or at least I was. Ollie had been giving me sex eyes, and I knew he wanted to resolve this tension between us. He didn't seem to understand though that he'd caused this tension in the first place. I was matching his energy; not the other way around.

'Why would I lie to you?! There's literally nothing to lie about ...' Although that wasn't exactly true. I was keeping some of it from him, only because I didn't want to share too much. It was for Griff to talk about, not me. It wasn't my business to talk about *his* business.

'I'm sorry. Just seems like you'd rather spend time with him recently,' he said, pouting a little, his bottom lip jutting out and looking totally biteable.

'That's not it at all. I want to spend time with both of you and I *do* spend time with both of you.'

'Well, I want to spend time with you alone,' he said. I couldn't be certain, but I thought I glimpsed Ollie's eyes roll in my peripheral.

'Okay? All you have to do is ask or, you know, communicate with me. If I'd known you were feeling insecure, I would have spoken to Clover and Griff about it.' I shrugged.

Not having had a boyfriend before, this was all new to me and so stupid. I said nothing about Ollie still spending time with Leo, and I *never* mentioned the fact that he'd spend time with Odette and Ophelia because of Leo. Those girls were the reason for everything that had happened to me this year, or so we assumed, yet he acted okay with them when I wasn't around. Come to think of it, that was worse and even more disrespectful towards me than my friendship with Griff ever could be towards him.

Also, it wasn't like Clover was fighting to spend time with me recently.

'I'm not insecure,' he spat out, his anger growing, and for the first time, I felt a little scared of him. His eyes became so dark, his mouth forming into a sneer. 'I shouldn't have to beg my girlfriend to spend time with me. You should want to without being asked, Sky.'

Okay, so I could understand his point of view. But—and it was a big but—it didn't mean he was right. It just meant that I could see where he was coming from. I guess I'd just assumed that he was as happy to hang out as a four as I was. I knew I'd been trying to keep everybody happy; now I was being pulled in two different directions as a result.

'Of course I want to,' I mumbled. I rolled my eyes, probably for the millionth time during this conversation. 'How about tonight we hang out in your room? Just us two.'

I waggled my eyebrows, hoping to make him laugh. Who was I kidding? Ollie rarely laughed out loud. I hoped he'd give me at least a slight smile, though. Fuck, I'd settle for a lip twitch at this rate.

His face didn't move, which made me feel even more stupid. But he did then respond with a curt, 'Sure.'

Not overly convincing, but I'd take it. I needed him to be okay with me. I didn't want yet another person I cared about to decide that I wasn't worth knowing.

✦

OLLIE'S ROOM, EVER SINCE NEW YEAR'S EVE, BECAME A place I took comfort in. Maybe it was because of the whole "losing my V-card thing" but part of it was the fact that I felt closer to Ollie here. Like I could see inside of a tiny portion of his brain.

The room was neat and minimalistic. Barely any furniture occupied the room, other than the bed and the sofa. No photos or posters adorned the walls. No personality at all. Really though, when I thought about it, the room showed his personality perfectly.

We were snuggled together under the duvet in Ollie's massive bed; the credits having just started on one of my favourite action films. Ollie let me pick the film. He was clearly trying his best to get on my good side.

'Griff told me that Clover wants to apologise,' I blurted out, without thinking about the words themselves. It'd been playing on my mind ever since Griff spoke to me in Ethics, and now I couldn't think of much else. Ollie groaned the second it left my mouth, moving away from me in the bed slightly.

'Course she does,' he said sardonically. 'What she did was out of order.'

'Right. But should I forgive her?' I asked, unsure whether I even wanted to hear his opinion but needing to know, anyway.

'Depends on what she says really, doesn't it?'

'Guess so,' I said, reluctant to agree with him.

I reached out to him, hoping to pull him tighter to me again, but he resisted. I could tell I'd annoyed him, but I wasn't sure why. Either he didn't want me to forgive Clover or he was just aggravated that I'd brought it up on our couples' night.

'Look, you clearly want to accept her apology. I can tell that she's been at the front of your mind ever since she said what she said.' Ollie sat up, the cover falling down to his waist, and I got slightly distracted by how good he looked in his white school shirt. 'Just go running back to her.'

I followed suit and sat up too. I asked, 'What's that supposed to mean?'

'It means, little Sky, that you obviously don't give a shit that she was a total cunt to you. You're going to go give her a rim job the second she says sorry. No need to lie and act otherwise.'

'I'm not going to go *"give her a rim job"* as you've so delicately put it,' I spat, pissed that he'd even said that. Having a best friend and wanting them to be happy didn't mean that you were licking their arse. 'But I am going to hear her out. Everyone can say shit they regret in the heat of the moment. I'm sure you've done it.'

'Course, but she called you a pathetic, desperate whore of a cunt. Not exactly something that springs to mind without having thought a little about it first.'

'Rub it in why don't you,' I said with a wince, the words hurting just as much now as they had the first time someone had hurled them at me.

'I'm just saying. Have some respect for yourself.'

'What did you just say?'

My blood boiled in my veins as I fought the urge to hit him. Who did he think he was, telling me I should have respect for myself? What a fucking wanker.

I climbed over him and got up out of the bed. Fuck staying here with him in this kind of mood. What on earth was happening around here?

'There's no need for you to leave.' Ollie looked at me and I could see the anger on his face, his lip twitching in irritation. 'You're going to let her ruin shit between us? Again?'

'Right now, Ollie, you're the one ruining shit between us. I'm gonna go before one of us says something they regret.'

I made my way to the door, opened it with a force I didn't know I possessed, and slammed it behind me. So blinded by my anger, I didn't spot Clover standing in front of me until the very last second. I halted, centimetres away from a full-blown collision.

'Hey,' she mumbled, looking embarrassed I'd caught her standing outside of Ollie's door. 'Can we talk?'

'Sure,' I replied, irritation still in my tone, wanting to get this talk over with. My emotions were all over the place currently, and I wasn't sure if I trusted my own instincts right now. 'Let's go back to our room?'

I was headed that way anyway, and I didn't want to have this conversation with her out in the open. Also, I didn't want Ollie to come out of his room and find the two of us standing there together. That would not go down well.

We made our way across campus in silence. Neither of us wanted to break the moment; the truce we'd come to while walking.

In no time, thank fuck, we were back at our room. Clover entered first, and I went in behind her. It filled me with anxiety. I knew she wanted to apologise, but I also worried that she was planning to give me some "home truths" or some other type of advice that I did not want to hear right now.

'So ...' I said as I perched down on the edge of my bed. Across the room, Clover did the same on her bed. Our room was so small we were still close enough to see each other clearly.

'So ...' Clo said in response and I giggled. This was silly. We were best friends, which meant we were above this shit. We should never have let it get to the point where we weren't even on speaking terms. 'I am so sorry, Sky. I should never have said what I did, and for the record, I don't think you're a whore. Or desperate and pathetic either. I was mad, and I let my anger come out aimed at you.'

I noticed how she'd left off a major word from her apology, but honestly, I could move past it.

Clover giggled too, as we both realised telepathically at the same time just how stupid we'd both been.

'Can you forgive me?' she asked, wiping a tear from underneath her eye, looking at me imploringly. 'I've been a right twat.'

I laughed, agreeing with her.

'Guess I could find it in my desperate and pathetic heart to forgive you.'

She laughed at me, and I could tell that we were going to be fine. We were like a pot that had boiled over and had now simmered back down again; the temperature no longer heated and back to almost normal.

'Promise you forgive me?' Clo pleaded, her eyes watery once again.

'Honestly, Clo, there's not much really for me to forgive.

You said something you regret and you've said sorry. Let's just move on and act like it never happened.'

'You're the best! Now, tell me why you stormed out of Ollie's room,' she said, crossing her legs on the edge of her bed to get comfortable. I rolled my eyes and said, 'Well ...'

And I spent the rest of the evening doing just that. The two of us discussed why boys were such dickheads sometimes and how they didn't even know it.

It definitely made me feel better.

Having a best friend could be pretty cool.

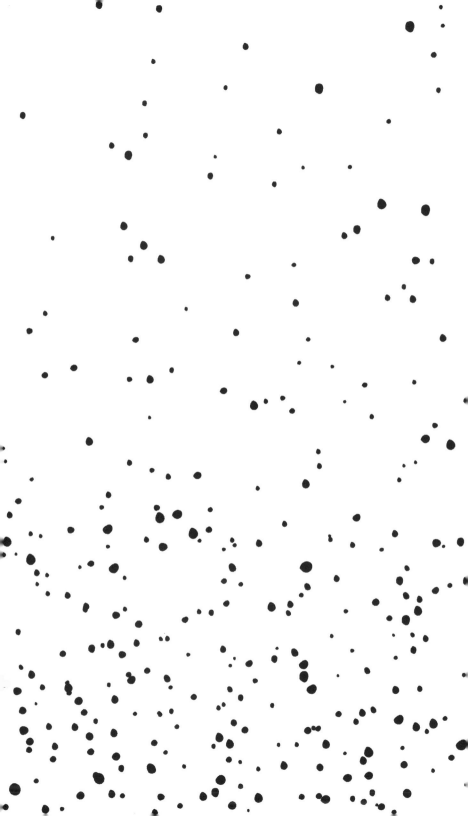

Chapter Twenty-Eight

O llie and I still hadn't made up a week later. At first, my anger had blinded me and I hadn't wanted to speak to him at all. He'd text a couple of times, but I'd ignored them, too mad to want to talk to him. Now, I was just a little sad about it. Every couple had their first fight, and I supposed this was ours.

History class had become a bit awkward, and Ollie had even moved from the desk next to mine at the back and had gone and sat up front next to some girl who looked way too happy about it.

As soon as he'd done that, it solidified to me he was being petty and that we should have some space away from each other. Everything had gone super quick after we'd first slept together on New Year's and taking a step back was probably for the best in the long run. Even if it made my heart physically hurt.

My phone buzzed in my blazer pocket and I removed it

and looked when Clover wasn't looking in my direction. She'd taken a rather dim view of Ollie's actions and was getting annoyed that he was still texting me.

CHECKING IN. YOU OKAY, STUTTER?

LEO REACHED OUT TO ME AT LEAST ONCE A WEEK, EVER since the events of Halloween night, and it made me see him in a new light. It was super nice of him and totally went against his whole bored vibe. Rarely did we speak in person; he spent all of his time with Odette and *The Set* were still attempting to make my life miserable. Recently, I'd found rotting food in my schoolbag and they'd attempted to trip me up in the corridor multiple times. Luckily, I always found my balance at the last moment and hadn't gone down face first—yet. The day was coming where I would though, I could sense it.

'So, do you think we'll be able to get out of the fashion show?' Clover asked once we sat down for breakfast. 'I mean. Ms Hawthorn's not actually going to penalise us, is she?'

'Honestly, I doubt we can get out of it. I totally reckon she would punish us,' I replied. The woman had looked like she meant business when she'd announced it during assembly, and the fact it was for charity and to make the school look good meant that we probably had to join in. 'The woman is a bit of a dictator.'

'True. The Hawthorn's have always been sketchy motherfuckers.'

'What do you have against the Hawthorns?' I asked, for probably the millionth time.

'Hm?' Clover feigned ignorance, like she couldn't hear me or didn't understand the question. She ate her food, making her mouth so full that she didn't have to respond straight away.

'You know what I mean. You always use every opportunity you can to slate them, but I don't really understand why. Lottie always seems so happy to see you.'

'Guess so. I don't want to talk about it, but one day I will.'

'Is that a promise?' I asked, sceptical as all get out.

'Nope. Just maybe.' We both chuckled, but mine was fake as fuck. It irritated me, or should I say, she was irritating me. I felt like I gave a lot in this friendship and Clo never reciprocated.

'So, what happened?'

'Okay, so don't be mad at me, but I may have lied about what happened at last year's Charity event.'

'Okay ...' I had absolutely no idea where this was going.

'I didn't really work in the cloakroom,' she said. The revelation slightly irritated me, but I kept calm. My face clearly didn't give me away, as she continued with, 'I was one of the girls on stage who announced the winners of the silent auction part of the evening.'

'So what happened?' I asked.

'Well, it was fucking horrible, and they pulled a *Carrie* on me.'

I'd just taken a sip of my coffee, and spat it out onto the table in front of me. 'Sorry, what did you just say?' Maybe I'd misheard her.

'They pulled a *Carrie*. When I announced the winner of the weekend getaway to New York, they poured red paint all over my head and they ruined the expensive designer dress I was wearing.'

'You've never mentioned it,' I replied, petulant.

'Course I haven't. It was fucking embarrassing.'

'You could have told me, though. They've done some pretty shitty things to me this year. Would've been nice to know that you understood,' I said, confused. Like how had she not mentioned any of this to me in all this time?

'I know. I know you'd understand, too,' she said. Her spoon stopped halfway to her mouth. 'I was just ashamed.'

'What's there to be ashamed of?' I asked, baffled at why she'd feel that way around me. We were best friends, and that meant never feeling ashamed around one another.

'I wanted to come across as somebody who had their shit together. You were the one person here who knew nothing of the past. I kind of wanted it to stay that way.'

'Huh?'

'Being new here, you knew nothing, and all I wanted was to be your friend.'

'We are friends, Clo,' I stressed.

'Yeah, now we are, but I didn't know that to begin with.'

'Okay ... In future you can talk to me about it. If you ever want to.'

'Thanks.'

Clover and I didn't speak for the rest of breakfast, and I couldn't say it was a comfortable silence. Both lost in our own thoughts, thinking of what we'd said. I felt slightly pissed at her, to be honest. She'd had so many chances to tell me exactly what had happened last year and that she related to how I was feeling. It just made me question our entire friendship and whether it was as solid as I'd believed it to be. Eurgh. Questioning shit sucks.

✳

ARE YOU FREE? CAN WE TALK?

THE TEXT FROM OLLIE CAME THROUGH AT THE END OF last period, and I wanted to reply straight away, but also at the same time I wanted him to sit and stew for a little longer. It *had* been an entire week, though, and I wasn't mad anymore. Mostly I'd wanted him to realise how silly he was being about my friendship with Griff. He was also pissed that I'd forgiven Clo so easily, but then a new text came through and I melted a little.

COME TO MY ROOM?

OKAY. I'D LET THE BOY SUFFER ENOUGH. AFTER GIVING IT a moment's thought, I messaged back that I'd meet him at his room after I'd been to my own and dropped my stuff off and got changed out of my uniform. Wearing a stiff blazer and tight skirt all day wasn't the comfiest after a six-hour school day.

I changed into a baggy top and some leggings. I wouldn't dress up for Ollie, especially not right now when he needed to grovel big time.

'Where are you off to?' Clover asked, arriving back to our

room covered in flour, when she saw I'd already changed out of my uniform.

'Going to Ollie's room,' I told her, pulling my jumper over my head so my words came out muffled.

'Oh,' she said. I turned to face her, and she looked confused, like she couldn't understand why I'd be going there. 'You gonna forgive him then?'

'I mean, it depends on what he says, but I'm no longer mad at him if that's what you're asking.'

'Honestly, I don't know what I'm asking.'

'Right ...' I forced a smile, 'I'm going out, now. I'll see you later tonight.'

'I won't wait up,' she said, resigned.

I closed the door on her strained facial expression and tried to put the tension between us to the back of my mind. Something was brewing between us, and I knew that eventually we'd come to blows. Knowing that and accepting it were two completely different things.

✳

OLLIE LIVED IN A DIFFERENT BUILDING BLOCK TO US, SO I made my way across campus to his as quickly as possible. Walking alone around here always gave me the heebies. You never knew who could be hiding around the corners. Or in plain view.

I knocked, and the door opened instantly, warmth surrounding me. Vanilla and tobacco had recently become my favourite scent. It surrounded me everywhere now, and my brain automatically linked it to Ollie.

Ollie stood on the other side of the door, looking nervous.

'Hey,' he mumbled and moved aside to let me in.

'Hey.'

I went and sat on the two-seater sofa he had in his suite and he came and sat beside me. I crossed my legs underneath me and turned to face him. For the first time since knowing him, I could see genuine worry in his features. He studied me, scrutinising my face, so I made my lips form a small smile so he'd know I wasn't here to fight again.

'Thanks for coming,' he said. I felt the warmth of his hand on my knee, and as he talked, it moved in a familiar circular motion, creating a swirling pattern. 'I'm sorry for being a dick.'

My face must give away my shock because as soon as he saw it he said, 'No need to look so shocked babe.'

'I-I'm surprised you came straight out and said it, that's all.'

'You are, huh?'

'Yeah, I dunno. Thought you might try to talk circles around me or something,' I said, shrugging. Not like he hadn't done it before.

'Why would I do that?'

'You can be a little forceful,' I told him tentatively.

'Oh yeah?' he said in a calm tone, but his nostrils flared, like he was making an extra effort to come across as composed. 'Forceful how?'

'You sort of railroad me a lot.' I shrugged again, finding it hard to think of exact examples when his eyes were boring into mine the way his were at that moment. 'I can't pinpoint an example right now.'

'Well, I'm sorry for that too, I guess,' he bit out. Slowly, his hand moved from my knee to take my hand in his. 'I don't want to be like my dad.'

'Huh?' I asked. Not sure how we'd found ourselves on the topic of Henry, but I'd roll with it.

'My dad has always railroaded everybody around him. He did it to Millie when I was younger, and he does it to me now. Or at least he tries to.'

'Millie?' I asked. Ollie surveyed my face, scrutinising me.

'My mother.'

It surprised me to hear him mention his mum. In all the time I'd known him, he'd never actively talked about her.

'Oh.' The shock must show on my face as he was still looking at me questioningly. 'Want to talk about her?'

'What about her?'

'Well, you've never mentioned her ...' I was tiptoeing around him, worried that I'd say something to piss him off and close himself off before we'd even begun. 'What was she like?'

'Obviously she was beautiful. Rich. Full of grace and poise.' He nodded, as if all of this was a given and hadn't really needed voicing out loud. 'She and her twin Eliza were the youngest of the four Hawthorn children and were very close.'

'Eliza was Griff's mum?' I asked, recalling what Griff had told me in the Hospital Wing.

'Yeah. The two of them were thick as thieves, always keeping secrets from everybody else. It drove their husbands insane, and then when Eliza died, my mum couldn't cope. She went completely off the rails and everybody worried about her.' I lost Ollie to his thoughts, and I could see the torment in his eyes. 'I remember little as I was only five, but I've heard a lot from the staff and my dad.'

I stayed silent, not wanting to interrupt his flow with an inane interjection. He didn't need me to speak. He moved our position, so he had his arms around me; I was sitting in between his legs, no longer able to see his face. His voice vibrated through his chest into my back.

'I remember though how my dad would treat her. He couldn't understand her grief. Wanted her to keep up the impression of a *stiff upper lip*. Henry made her feel small, and I've never wanted to make somebody else feel that way.'

I nodded, knowing that he could feel the movement. Having met Henry Brandon, I could fully believe what he was saying. The man had seemed no nonsense to me—and creepy as fuck.

'When I was ten—five years after Eliza died—Mum decided that she couldn't survive anymore. Didn't want to live on a realm without her twin.' Ollie sniffed behind me, and I assumed that he was trying to hold back his tears. I knew Ollie, though. He would never cry in front of me; fuck, I doubt he'd cry in front of anybody. 'She committed suicide. Took a lethal cocktail of pills and alcohol and went to be with her dear Eliza. Left me with *him* without much more than a goodbye.'

I wasn't sure what to say. I knew that his mum had died, but I didn't know the circumstances had been so sad. Not like this was an everyday topic. Unsure what to say next, I paused. I personally hated it when somebody said that they were sorry for your loss. It always seemed so disingenuous to me. Not like they'd known them.

So I said what I'd want to hear.

'I bet she's so proud of you, Ollie. I can already tell that you're ten times the man that Henry is and fuck, she knows it too.'

'You think so?' he asked, his voice low, and I wondered if anybody had ever told him that before.

'I do. None of it is your fault, remember that.'

'Right ...' he trailed off, distracted.

I could tell by his tone that he didn't believe me, but I'd known that he wouldn't. I sensed that there was a lot more here than what he was showing me on the surface.

I could be patient, show him that I wouldn't be going anywhere, no matter what he thought about himself. Or how much he believed he was like his father.

Chapter Twenty-Nine

Mother's Day had always been a Sunday that I didn't really care for. Not like I wanted to spend an entire day celebrating my mum and my nan had died when I was younger. I knew nothing about the guy who helped make me, so I had no clue whether he had a Mum alive out there somewhere.

Hawthorn opened up the school grounds on Mother's Day and invited them to come here. They set up an Afternoon Tea type shabang; the highlight of a proper British afternoon. Meaning Mum would receive an invitation to come here and, after the last time, I knew she was going to come. Free food and booze? Sign her up. She wouldn't turn down that kind of free shit. Especially if the school sent a car like last time.

'Clo, is your mum coming today?' I asked, fiddling with the tiny buttons on my floral tea dress as I tried to fasten them.

'God, I hope not,' she responded so fast, I knew she meant it. She'd still never really opened up about her parents, and I knew she hadn't seen them since the beginning of the school year. They were in contact over Christmas via text, but that was the only time. Still one more occasion than my mum had texted me though—so ya know.

'Would it be so bad?' I asked.

'Definitely. Lottie Hawthorn's going to be here,' said Clover, as if that explained everything.

'Again, is that a bad thing?' I asked, not really getting it. Leo's mum would be here, so what?

'Yeah,' she muttered. Clo didn't elaborate and I just couldn't be fucked trying to get more out of her. Was this normal for female friendships? I wish I knew. Not even like I could ask Griff, because I doubt he'd be able to help much—even if he did love to act like one of the girls.

'Okay ... Cool.' I stopped talking to her and continued getting ready. The boys got me some great clothes for Christmas, so my wardrobe had improved so much since I'd first started here. No more stained, holey items that were obviously cheap or secondhand. I knew beyond doubt that Mum would comment on it, probably out of jealousy. She'd always wished that she could afford designer clothing and the newest trends. I didn't even want to think about just what she'd be wearing today. If I knew her as well as I thought I did, there would be animal print on her outfit somewhere. *Great. Can't wait.*

✦

MUM WAFTED INTO THE SCHOOL IN A CLOUD OF KNOCK-off perfume and hairspray. Honestly, I thought she was auditioning for the West End production with the way her blonde hair coiffed into a rather large bouffant. You couldn't make it up. Of course it was *my* mum looking like she belonged in some bad soap opera from the nineties.

'Oh darrrr-ling, don't you look bee-u-tiful,' she said the moment she saw me. Seriously, the woman had no low volume setting. Her voice carried and the entire hall heard her greeting. Shame filled me. 'Your outfit is divine!'

'Thanks, Mum. Happy Mother's Day,' I said, keeping my voice down, not wanting to draw any more attention towards us. Fuck, people already called me charity case and constantly reminded me that I was here on scholarship. Then Mum came along and made it even more obvious that we were *not* in the same league as the other pupils here.

I was also right about her outfit. Mum was wearing a short denim miniskirt, cheap fake UGG boots and a tight vest top which, you guessed it, was zebra print. But not just a black and white zebra print, nope, it was black and silver glitter zebra print. I shuddered just looking at it. Blatantly a market stall purchase. Or from one of those shops that sold every item in one size at one price.

'So, what kind of spread they put on today? I made sure not to eat breakfast, you know, to make the most of being here,' she told me, in a conspiratorial manner.

Sometimes you just had to roll your eyes. Especially on those occasions where you were about to either laugh or cry. Really, I should be glad she hadn't shown up drunk. Small mercies and all that.

'Where's that ginger friend of yours?' she asked, her face focused on mine intently.

Ground. Swallow me.

'If you mean Clover, she's back at our room.'

'Shame, I really like her,' said Mum, nodding, clearly

remembering the last time she was here. 'She was nice. Glad you've made friends, sweetie. It surprised Andy and me. We didn't think you'd make *any* friends. What with you being so boring and all.'

'Gee Mum, thanks for that,' I said, thick with sarcasm, but I could tell by the look on her face it didn't register the way it should've.

'No problem, darling.' She patted me on the shoulder, nodding her head at me.

'Afternoon.' A deep voice joined us and before I could turn around, Ollie slung his arm around my shoulder and squeezed. I hadn't asked him what he planned to do today, but I thought maybe he'd be spending it with Griff. After all, neither of them were getting a visit today and as much as I grumbled about my mum, at least she could be here. 'Nice to see you again, Cora.'

'Oh, hello, Oliver,' Mum said. I swore she actually tittered at him. 'You are just as handsome as I remember. Still putting up with my moody daughter, I see.'

'Actually, we're in an official relationship now,' he said and smiled at Mum, and as far as I could tell, he wasn't judging her too hard—yet. 'Skylar isn't too moody with me either.'

'Aren't you a lucky one then? I'll let you in on a little secret.' She leaned closer to him, almost putting her lips into his ear. 'Sky's always been difficult. Ever since she was a little girl. Used to write all kinds of things in her diary.'

If I thought shit was embarrassing before, it had nothing on this moment. Her loud arrival and god-awful outfit had clearly been the tip of the iceberg. She'd always had a thing for the Titanic, after all.

'Well thanks, Mum, for that.'

'Oliver should know just who he's dating.' She shrugged,

looking around the room, people watching most likely. I loved to watch people too, but my mum was judging everyone. Laughable really, seeing as they were all definitely judging her more. Fuck, I was judging her, and we were related.

'I think he knows,' I said. Ollie and I smiled at one another, a stiff smile on his face, his upper lip almost a straight line.

'I'll let you and your mum enjoy the day and I'll see you later, baby.' Ollie gave me a brief kiss on the cheek and I couldn't decide whether I was glad he wouldn't see the shit show that was my mum or if I was mad that he wasn't saving me from being alone with her.

'I'll see you later. I'll text you when Mum goes,' I said to him.

He nodded, gave my mum a kiss on the cheek too and then left the two of us alone. The blush on Mum's face from the kiss almost made me laugh. She looked beside herself with joy; who knew if it was because I had a nice boyfriend or that a handsome young boy had kissed her. I decided to not even ask.

'I honestly don't know how you pulled that one, Sky.' Mum looked confused, as if she really didn't see what Ollie could see in me. Whoever said Mums were a confidence booster had obviously never met mine. 'He's gorgeous, and you're so drab and plain.'

'Loving this time together, Mum. Let's go get a drink.'

'You know me, Skylar. No need to tell me twice!' she replied, chortling to herself.

There was a bar set up in the main hall again, and the dark-haired bartender visibly winced when he saw us heading in his direction. Nice to see that Cora had made a lasting impression.

'Two gin and lemonades,' Mum said. Using her knuckles,

she rapped on the bar, as if that worked in place of a *"please"*. It didn't. Also, she was ordering both drinks for herself. Guess she was going to spend the day double parked.

'Diet Coke please,' I said, beaming at the barman, trying to make my "please" cover both of our orders.

'Sure thing,' he replied smoothly, no longer wincing. The pitying look on this guy's face was almost enough to make me wish the ground would devour me whole and spit out my bones. I already didn't want to be here with Mum today, but if she got drunk, the day would only get worse.

'Once you've got your drinks, we'll go outside? Think they've set up some stalls out there,' I gestured out the large windows, to where we could see people hovering.

'Ooooh, I would love to see what stalls a fancy-smancy school like this deems acceptable for a day like this.' Mum got out her mobile and began to pay more attention to that than to me, probably messaging Andy. When I'd lived at home, I'd found her behaviour irritating, but now, I was kind of glad that her focus was off of me for a while. 'What time is this Afternoon Tea, then?'

'In a couple of hours, so we've got time,' I said, the unfortunately implied but not uttered.

'So we can have a few more drinks here first. We're in no rush,' she said, her gaze fixed elsewhere, looking at the stained glass window.

'The weather's good right now though, Mum. Never know when rain could strike, we're on top of the hill, remember?' Plus, I didn't want her to have more time to drink.

'A little rain won't hurt us. Well, it might hurt my hair a little,' she guffawed. Loud. Even the people far away from us looked over with disgusted looks on their botoxed faces. Being honest, it surprised me that any of the Mums here could show emotion at all. 'I spent quite some time back combing this beauty.'

Mum started smoothing her hair with her hands, looking too proud of herself. I swore the woman saw something different in the mirror than what everybody else saw.

Hang on. Was I being a snob all because I now stood wearing a dress more expensive than my mum's rent?

I thought about it for less than a second.

Nope, that had nothing to do with it. Guess I'd always looked down on her, for some reason or another. Even when I was standing next to her wearing secondhand clothes, I still looked down on her.

'It looks great, Mum,' I said, soothingly. Sometimes it was easier to placate somebody, rather than tell them the truth. 'Top looks good too.' I nearly choked on my lie.

'Do you like it? Leslie got it for me at the market the other weekend,' she said, twirling around with her arms wide, so I could appreciate it from every angle.

Nailed it.

'It's definitely something.'

✦

THREE HOURS LATER AND MUM WAS THREE SHEETS TO the wind. I'd known that this was going to happen, but I'd hoped that it wouldn't, anyway. We'd made it outside to look at the stalls, thankfully, and the sun was really shining, which was rare for a Sunday in March.

'Skylar, darling, is that you?' Lottie Hawthorn seemingly appeared from nowhere and swept me into a big hug. Her

Chanel perfume entered my nostrils, warm and deep, and exactly how I'd always imagined an older, rich lady would smell. 'You look wonderful!'

'Thank you, Lottie. You remember my mum, Cora?' I asked, sweeping my arm to indicate the woman stood next to me. Not that she'd needed it. Mum stood out like a sore thumb.

'Yes ...' With a grimace she nodded daintily at Mum. 'How have you two been? Leo mentioned that you had a great Christmas together.' Lottie swept her arm and motioned Leo over, who had been standing a little distance away.

Coming over to stand beside her, his blonde hair glistened extra bright in the sunlight as it shined through the clouds. His blue eyes sparkled at me, like we shared a secret. Which I supposed we do. He still texted me from time to time checking in, and I'd started to think of him as a friend.

'I'm good, thank you. Leo's telling the truth, Christmas was wonderful,' I replied to Lottie. I smiled at Leo, surprised that he'd even mentioned it to his mum. Or that they'd even approached us right now, especially after seeing my mum wobbling while standing still. A skill. 'How have you been?'

'I've been well, thank you. So happy I could come here today and see my baby boy.' She rubbed underneath Leo's chin and he blushed, a light pink colour entering his cheeks. He looked embarrassed at the affection his mum was showing him. 'Just hoping I don't run into Winifred,' Lottie added in a conspiratorial tone. Seemed Mums both rich and poor loved to share confidences.

Mum and I both looked at each other in confusion. Who the fuck was Winifred? Leo must notice our befuddled faces, though as he clarified, 'Ms Hawthorn.'

'Ohhhhhh.' Mum and I both said at the same time. I'd

honestly never wondered *what* Ms Hawthorn's first name was. Forgot, she'd even have one, to be honest.

'How comes?' Mum asked, slurring the end of the sentence, making a shh sort of noise.

'Oh, Winifred thinks that we should talk just because she happens to be my sister-in-law. I've tried to make it clear over the years that just because we're related by law doesn't mean that we're friends,' she said, adding a light laugh at the end, to soften the harshness of her words.

'Mum ...' Leo said to her in a curt tone. 'You're just like-able. Course she wants to be your friend,' he added, clearly saving himself, because Lottie smiled warmly at him in return.

'Thanks, sweetheart. Would you two like to join us for Afternoon Tea?' Lottie asked, the smile still embedded on her face.

Honestly, I wasn't sure whether we should agree. I thought that, if anything, Leo and Lottie would sit with Odette and her mother but when I'd thought about it, I realised I hadn't seen either of them.

'We would love to, wouldn't we Sky?' Mum answered before I'd even fully formulated my thoughts, fully empha-sising the word *love*.

'Of course,' I said through gritted teeth, not wanting to sound ungrateful but dreading it all, nonetheless.

✦

THINGS WERE GOING OKAY.

Well, as okay as they could with Mum ordering Irish coffees instead of going for the traditional English Breakfast tea. The catering staff had filled the platter in the centre of the table with mini sandwich triangles and mini cakes. I'd put a couple on my plate, not wanting to look greedy. Mum didn't have that worry. She'd instantly piled her plate high, to the point where at least two-thirds of the platter sat on her plate alone.

'So, Skylar, what does your father do?' Lottie asked, attempting to restart the conversation.

'Mum, Skylar's dad isn't around,' Leo said in a hushed tone, trying to prevent embarrassment for both me and his mum.

'Oh, I'm so sorry Skylar, I didn't realise.' Lottie looked flustered, her cheeks the same shade of pink as Leo's had been earlier. I wanted to make it better, but had no idea how to.

'Don't apologise to her, love. Sky is better off without her father around,' Mum said, after a beat. This was probably the most my mum had ever said on the subject of my *father*. She barely mentioned him to me, even when super drunk, and I'd never been able to get much out of anybody who may know more. Her words slowly became more slurred and incoherent. 'You see, Jacob Cooper was a total dick. But damn, he was a hot one.'

'C-cooper?' I stuttered. I only knew one Cooper, and that was Griff. How odd that my surname could have been the same as his. Instead, I'd got stuck with Crescent. Sixteen years old and *this* was the first time I'd ever heard the name of my sperm donor.

'Jacob Cooper?' Lottie and Leo asked simultaneously. Lottie's face was a mixture of confusion and shock. Leo's face was a mix of somebody trying to feign boredom, and somebody acting hard to seem as if the news had shocked them. But I could tell it didn't shock him at all. His jaw tightened, the muscles in his cheeks flexing. Like he'd known already.

'I said that, didn't I?' Mum asked, laughing at their expressions. 'You know him?'

'Yeah. Or at least I used to know somebody by that name.' Lottie looked like she didn't want to say much more than that. 'Way back when.'

'What a coinky-dink. Well, I've not heard anything from him since Sky was born. He split not long after he found out about her,' Mum said, hitching her thumb in my direction. This was what she'd always told me when I'd asked growing up, so at least that hadn't been a lie.

'Maybe it's for the best Cora that you haven't heard from him,' Lottie said, her tone darker than I'd ever heard it. Her words sounded ominous. The closed off look on Lottie's face also made me think there was a whole lot more to the story.

'Oh, I know Lottie darling, I definitely have found the best in Andy. He's my knight in shining armour,' said Mum, winking at Lottie as she did so. Almost as if the two of them were best friends and in one another's confidence.

And yep. My mum classed the man who kissed me without consent as her knight in shining armour. *Wonderful.*

'He sounds charming,' Leo piped up, trying to take the heat off of the subject of my dad. 'He seemed like a great guy when you were both here for Parents' Day.' Honestly, if I didn't know Leo, I would have believed his act to be genuine. His eyes widened with interest and a smile played around his mouth. The boy could charm anybody. But was he the charmer, or the snake? The thought hit me, and I moved away from it. There were more important things to focus on. Who knew what would come out of Mum's mouth next.

'Skylar. Why are you with Ollie when you know this perfect specimen?'

Jesus. Could my mum go a day without saying things super cringeworthy? Just one day. Was that too much to ask?

'Mum,' I snapped.

'Ollie's pretty great too, Cora,' Leo said, coming to my rescue by listing a couple of Ollie's great attributes. He finished by saying, 'He really cares about Sky.'

'That's good, of course. But you would also be great for her,' said Mum, the slurring slipping into every other word and I knew I needed to get Mum out of here now.

'Come on, Mum. Andy's probably wanting you to come home soon,' I said, wrapping an arm around her shoulder. I was actually surprised that she'd been here as long as she had been without mentioning going home to him. It was super rare that the two of them spent time apart—especially this much time apart.

'True darling. It's been so nice to see you two. Lottie, we must do this again.'

I chuckled in my head, slightly confused why my mum was treating this like Lottie herself had invited her here, but oh well. I nodded along, sure if I agreed with her then she'd leave quicker. Here's to hoping, anyway.

'I'm sure our paths will cross again.' Lottie smiled, no teeth this time, and nodded at my mum. 'Come on Leo, let's give these two some space to say goodbye. Can't wait to see you soon, Skylar.'

'Right. Good to see you, Cora. I'll text you Sky,' Leo said, nodding his head at me in a secret message of sorts that I didn't understand.

I raised an eyebrow at Leo.

We all waved at one another and they left the table. I watched them go, wishing that I could talk to Lottie or Leo some more about Jacob Cooper. The thought of my dad had never overly fascinated me—I'd never wanted to learn anything about him, for that matter. Clearly he ran in classier circles than my mum once and now that I had a name, I could admit I was slightly more interested.

I walked Mum outside, and we waited for the car to pull up. I felt more than happy to stand and wait in silence, but apparently she had other ideas.

'Sky, Jacob Cooper is a wanker. You should be glad that I never told you more about him.'

'How did you meet him?' I asked, curious, wondering how much she'd say.

'I was staying at a hotel that had a Gala that evening. Bumped into this penguin suit wearing man who had gorgeous blue eyes and black shiny hair.'

'Sounds romantic.'

'It was something,' Mum grumbled under her breath.

The car pulled up and Mum went to get inside. She gave me a brief hug, something she always did, but I never hugged her back. Not because it was Mum, but because I didn't like to hug *anybody*.

'See you soon, Mum.'

Hoping that it wouldn't be too soon.

Hey, I'm done with Mum. Where shall I meet you?

. . .

I texted Ollie the moment I saw the car meandering down the hill. I was hoping Ollie just wanted to have a chill night in with some pizza or something. I really wasn't feeling up to talking loads or doing much. While staring at my phone, a text came through from Leo that made me smile wider than I had all day.

Thanks for today, Stutter. I enjoyed it. We'll talk about Jacob Cooper soon.

I hoped he'd stick to his word and tell me more about him soon. I was certain that the news of my father hadn't surprised him one bit.

Meaning Leo probably knew a lot more than I'd given him credit for.

Fuck.

Chapter Thirty

With a week until the Fashion Show, every time I thought about it, I worried that I would embarrass myself completely. The library had recently become a refuge of sorts, and I'd spent the majority of my free periods there. Mostly because it was easier—and away from the other students.

'Sky, I need to talk to you.' Clover came flying towards the table I was occupying, avoiding a trolley of books at the last moment. 'Urgently.'

'Okay ...?' Puzzled, I put down my pen and stopped what I was doing.

'In private,' she whispered. I looked around, confused why Clo had specified privacy when we were the only two people in this part of the library.

'Can you not talk to me about it here?' I asked with a groan, not wanting to move.

'No. Let's go,' Clover said as she packed up all of my things in a hurry, putting them into my bag for me; not giving me a chance to stop her.

Within moments, we were leaving the library, and I found myself speed walking behind her back to our dorm room.

Rushing inside, Clover almost threw me down onto my bed and took the space beside me. I turned to face her, crossed my legs and got comfortable. This should be good.

'Sky, there's no simple way for me to say this.'

I rolled my eyes at the dramatics.

'Just tell me. It's obviously important enough to take me away from studying—and from people.'

'Look. I overheard the girls talking and I really think you need to hear what they were saying.'

'Go on.'

'They were talking about what Ollie has planned.'

'Right ...?' I felt as though I wasn't fully understanding her point. Yeah, it'd be odd for Ollie to be talking to the O girls about his plans, but he might have done if Leo was there too.

'Sky. It's bad shit. Like, he's the reason for everything that's happened to you this year, bad shit.' She made eye contact with me, I could feel her imploring me to believe her. To believe that what she'd been telling me about Ollie all along was true. She'd made her feelings clear about him all year, after all.

'Not trying to be a dick here, but what does that even mean?' I tried to stay calm. Tried to keep my tone casual. Tried not to let my anger show.

'It means that everything that has happened to you this year at the hand of *The Set* or the other students was at Ollie's say so. He's been pulling the strings this whole time.' She grabbed my hand and gave it a tight squeeze.

'A little far-fetched, don't you think?' I asked, laughing, but the look on Clo's face told me she wasn't joking around. She truly believed it all. 'How do you know the girls didn't just say it for your benefit?'

'Sky, they didn't know I could hear them. They thought they were alone.'

'Where were you?' I knew I sounded suspicious but, fuck. I was.

'In the food classroom cupboard getting more supplies. They came in and only checked to see if the classroom was clear, not the cupboard.' Her words were coming out super fast. Soon I'd need subtitles to keep up. 'Odette was telling Ophelia and Oralie how Ollie had come to her during second period to tell her the plan for the Fashion Show.'

'And pray tell, what exactly is the plan for the Fashion Show?' Using my best posh British accent, I attempted to make a joke out of the situation.

Clover did *not* appreciate it.

'This isn't a fucking joke, Skylar. I'm trying to save you from being *Carrie*'d too. Not exactly like you can exact your revenge with telekinesis, is it?'

She had a point. They *had* blindsided me on Parents' Day, and we never figured out who took the footage they'd shown. How could Clo explain that one as Ollie? I asked her as much.

'One of the girls or Leo must have filmed it for him.' She nodded at me, like this made total sense in her head. 'I was with Griff that whole night so that rules him out at least.'

I should fucking hope that I could rule Griff out. He really had become one of my closest friends—ever. I didn't want to believe that he could have done that to me.

'But we've always known that it was one of the girls. What

I mean is, *why* would Ollie orchestrate that? Why would he want that kind of footage made public?'

'If his end goal is to hurt you, then I'm sure he wouldn't care.'

'Clo. What they showed that day was child pornography! Do you really think he'd risk that just to hurt me?'

Her response was so quiet I almost didn't hear her. It was only because I was looking so closely at her face I saw her lips move and say, 'I do.'

Wonderful.

'What reason does he even have to hurt me?'

'The girls kept mentioning something about your family and how you deserve this.'

'My f-family?' I stuttered, unsure what my family would have to do with anybody that attends this school. My family had never been rich. At all. Then it hit me like lightning. 'Reckon this has something to do with my dad?'

'Thought you didn't know who he was,' Clo snapped.

'Well, I don't, really. Mum told me his name on Mother's Day and both Lottie and Leo seemed to recognise the name.'

'You didn't tell me,' Clover accused, as if I'd on purpose hidden this from her rather than having forgotten about it. 'When were you with Lottie and Leo?'

Shit. Now I remembered why I'd forgotten to tell her. I hadn't wanted to explain spending time with the Hawthorn's. Clover always tried to avoid them whenever we were in the same place.

'Oh, didn't I mention it?' I asked, hoping she'd take the bait, but all she did was look blankly at me. Staring through my bullshit. 'They joined us for Afternoon Tea.'

'You definitely didn't mention it. Since when were you and

Leo close enough to spend time together, with your mum's there too?' Clo's incredulous tone irritated me.

'My bad, thought I did.' I shrugged it off. God, I am such a liar. 'Well, Lottie's always been nice to me, and she wanted to join us. Leo didn't exactly get a say.'

This was definitely *not* the moment to tell Clo about my sort of friendship with Leo. I saw her nod in response; it made sense to her that Lottie would do something like that without caring about her son's opinion.

'So, your dad?' Clover gazed at me, trying to suss out why I'd failed to mention such big news. 'Who is he?'

'Somebody named Jacob Cooper. You heard of him?'

Clover shook her head and said, 'I don't think so. It *sounds* familiar though.'

'Right? I thought that too, but then I realised it's probably just because Griff's surname is Cooper too.'

'Yeah, that's probably it.' She didn't look convinced. 'I don't know though Sky, I feel like this year is going to be worse than what happened to me last year.'

Part of me hoped I'd sidetracked her so much that she wouldn't go back to talking about Ollie and the girls.

'I really wish you'd listen to me. *The Set* plans to reveal the truth about everything at the Fashion Show, whatever that means.'

Great. I spoke too soon. I knew Clover, and she would not be dropping this soon. Trust me to get a best friend, and a boyfriend, and have them both hate one another. Of course. It would be too easy for them to just get along.

'Well, did you hear anything specific?'

'How much more fucking specific did you want them to get?!'

'I don't know. Just seems odd to me they didn't mention any actual part of the plan. Like they wanted you to overhear them.' I shrugged, because to me, this seemed like the perfect way to cause me to act paranoid. If they'd known Clo was listening, they could have said shit on purpose, knowing she'd run straight to me and repeat what she had heard. They did talk about it in the cooking classroom, the one place where Clo was always known to be.

'Or they didn't say any part of the plan because they were being cautious, not wanting anybody to learn of their plans.'

Okay, so Clo had a point too. Either scenario could be the correct one, and there was no way to know for sure. I'd ask Ollie, in a subtle way, and try to feel him out.

'Just be on your guard, yeah?' Clo asked, raising an eyebrow at me. Her green eyes were shining with worry for me, and I hated that we were still on such awkward footing with each other even after I'd forgiven her. I nodded, and she added, 'You sure you don't want to ask Ollie to see if you can swap roles with somebody else? If their plan revolves around you being on stage, then you can at least make it a little harder for them by working backstage, or something.'

'I'm sure. If I do, they'll know I'm running scared and I don't want to give those bitches the satisfaction. We're modelling in the show, Clo. Deal with it.'

'Fine. But I don't have to like it.'

Fuck, I didn't like it either, but I meant what I said. I wouldn't bow down in fear; not to *The Set*. Not to anybody.

✦

I WAS SO EXCITED FOR CLOVER'S SEVENTEENTH BIRTHDAY and for her to see the present I'd arranged for her. It was hard to get her something with no access to money. Ollie had offered to let me use his card, but I didn't want him to think I was with him because he was rich. I'd heard the way the girls in this school spoke about the boys as if they were their meal ticket to a better life. I wasn't going to be one of those girls, especially as I didn't come from wealth. I'd look like even more of a gold digger than the one they'd all already accused me of being.

It had pained me to do, but I'd messaged my mum asking her to send me my nan's recipe book. When my nan was alive, she'd loved to bake and had always enlisted me to help her. I'd never really fallen in love with it the way she'd hoped, but she had passed down her recipes to me when she died. I obviously wasn't going to give Clo the original copies as they were in Nan's handwriting and the only thing of hers I owned. But I was going to give her a scrapbook with them in.

I'd also included pictures of us from this year; the Gala, Christmas and some random fun selfies we'd taken while trying out silly filters. I really hoped she'd like it as I'd been working on it in Ollie's room in secret and it had taken me quite a few hours to put together. It had taken so long because I had made sure, multiple times, I'd copied every recipe and ingredient exactly how my nan had written it. Clo was family to me now, and I wanted to pass on my family's food to her.

We were spending her birthday with just the four of us. Griff had ordered Clo's favourite food, and we were going to watch her favourite films. It was a Thursday night, so our options were pretty limited and we'd all agreed that a gathering in the woods was not the way to go.

After classes had ended, I'd rushed back up to our room trying to get there before her. I wanted to put up some banners and balloons and decorate a bit. I'd never had the chance to do this for somebody before, and I was so excited to see her reaction. Bitch better appreciate all the effort I'd put into making the day a great one for her.

✳

THE EVENING WENT PERFECTLY; CLOVER HAD LOVED HER present, and I was so glad I'd thought of it.

"Sky, this must have taken you forever! Thank you so much. I'll cherish this shit, I swear."

It was the best kind of evening. Ollie and Clo hadn't made up, but they did make sure to keep the sniping to a minimum— which made for a nice change.

The guys left around ten, and the moment they did; I jumped into action.

'Right, I'm going for a shower.'

'Ite babes. Try not to use too much hot water!'

'You're the birthday girl so you can totally shower first if you want,' I told her, feeling generous today. I hated showers really, so I always needed to psyche myself up for them.

'It's cool, just don't take too long.'

I took ten minutes tops, but when I re-entered our room, Clover was looking at me with a narrowed gaze. Her mouth pursed together into a point.

'Something you want to tell me?' she asked, venom in her voice.

'S-sorry what?' I asked, confused, having only been gone a

short while. I had no idea what could have upset her in such a short timeframe.

'You left your phone out here,' Clo said, her voice so quiet I had to strain to hear her.

'Right ...?'

I usually did when I showered. With a bathroom the size of a toothpick, I worried I'd get it wet and damage it beyond repair. I'd never had a nice phone before and didn't want to fuck it up; it had been a Christmas present from Ollie after all.

'You got a message from somebody named Thorn. Sound familiar?' She held my phone out to me.

I froze by my bed, towel still wrapped around me, and wondered what she was going to say next. She could have guessed that it was Leo who had texted me, but there was no way for her to know for sure, right?

'Oh, thanks,' I said as I took my phone from her outreached arm. When I looked down, though, I saw that it was unlocked and someone had opened the message thread. Had Clo been going through my texts?

'Been spying on me for Leo, have you?' she asked, her tone scathing, and I wasn't sure how to respond. I *hadn't* been spying on her for Leo, but I'd answered questions he had about her. She'd never given me a good enough reason not to, and he'd never given me a good enough reason not to, either.

'It's not like that,' I told her.

'You sure? Cause that's exactly what it looks like.'

'Positive. He just checks in every now and again,' I said, not feeling comfortable enough to tell her anymore than that. I wasn't exactly in the mood to be kind to her; she'd gone through my phone and broken my privacy. Knowing her, she'd argue it was because she cared about me.

'And you're so stupid Sky that you don't even see how shady that is.'

God, I was getting bored with her calling me stupid—or whatever name she'd decided on that day.

'Shady how? It's the complete opposite of shady.'

'Oh, continue telling yourself that. The boys are up to something and if you don't want to believe me, then that's on you.' Clover shook her head at me, a sad look on her face. 'You know what, there's nothing I can do to help you anymore. You're intent on ignoring me and I honestly can't be fucked with it.'

'With it? Or me?' I asked, knowing what she really meant.

'Any of it, Sky. I'm done. I hope they do fuck with you at the Fashion Show. You'd deserve it,' she spat spitefully.

With that, she stomped into the bathroom, leaving me standing there in my towel, wet and cold. This time, I knew there wasn't a simple way for us to come back from this. She'd pushed me too far. This was different to her snapping at me about being a whore. This time she'd severed my trust and snooped her nose into places her nose definitely didn't belong.

For fuck's sake. Once again, the boys had come between us, causing a chasm that felt too wide for either of us to breach.

Though, I never thought it would be Leo who caused our rift.

Chapter Thirty-One

The night of the Fashion Show arrived, and you could cut the tension with a blunt knife.

Everybody had been on edge, but not for the same reasons. Clover, although barely talking to me, was still adamant that shit was going down tonight. Even though she'd said only a few sentences to me, they'd all been to do with Ollie and what she'd overheard Odette, Oralie, and Ophelia whispering about. I wasn't sure at this point who would be more surprised if shit didn't go down; her or me. Griff had also acted distant with me since Clo's birthday, choosing once again to side with her. I couldn't find it in me to argue; but the entire situation made me sad.

Ollie acted on edge more often than not, mostly due to the fact that he was worried that I actually believed Clover. I'd told him so many times I trusted him and that if what Clover overheard had any truth to it, then he should let me know now.

Not sometime later down the line when I'd found out the truth, but he was adamant that wasn't going to happen.

'Clover's just jealous and bitter, babe,' he said every time I brought it up—well, some kind of variation of that phrase, but that was basically the main gist. The thing was, I could see his point. She had been acting like somebody slightly jealous, but I also needed to weigh up our friendship. We were best friends. Would she lie? And if she would, what would she gain?

Somehow, Ollie had got out of modelling in the show. He and Oralie were working the music and backgrounds—or something like that, anyway. I wasn't overly sure, but I knew that I wished I was working alongside him. Instead, I would model six different looks, with five people who weren't my biggest fans; Griff, Clo, Ophelia, Leo, and Odette. It was a crazy world that I was inhabiting when Leo was the one I felt closest to right now. Showed how quickly things could turn to shit.

An hour until show time and I was in the makeshift dressing room they had given me; really, one of the French classrooms had been given a slight makeover. Ollie and I were looking at what they expected me to wear, confused expressions stamped on our features.

'You're gonna look great babe,' he said, giving my arm a quick squeeze to reassure me.

'Thanks for trying to spark my confidence, baby, but I really don't feel like I will. Odette was in charge of who wore what, so I've definitely been given the worst looks out of the six of us. Honestly, the sleepwear makes me look like I'm ready for sleeping. On the streets.'

Odette had not been playing around when she had chosen my clothes. Even Clover looked a million pounds in her six outfits; then there was me, wearing clothes from a high street brand while they were all wearing couture. I'd stayed quiet about it though, because really, it could be a LOT worse. If this was a part of the "messing with me" that Clo spoke about, then I could deal. Bad clothes wouldn't be the end of the world.

'Maybe so, but I know you're going to be the hottest one on that stage.' He kissed my cheek softly, and then promptly went back to looking at his phone. 'I would.'

A cheeky smile overtook his face, and it made me feel warm inside. We hadn't said it to one another yet or anything like that, but I definitely felt as if I was falling for him. I hoped he felt the same way, but I hadn't been brave enough to voice it, just in case he didn't. How fucking embarrassing would that be?

'Well, maybe not after you've seen me in the sportswear outfit,' I joked, but part of me did actually think he'd see me in a different way after he saw the camel toe the leggings gave me. 'What time do you need to head backstage?'

'Guess I should head there now.' He stood, gave me a long kiss on the lips and gathered his things together. 'Good luck. You'll do great.'

'Th-thanks. Now get out of here before we get distracted.' That kiss had made me want more, made me want his lips to press firmly into mine while his hands roamed south—but now was *not* the time for that to happen.

'I wouldn't mind watching you change into the first outfit,' he said, raising his eyebrows up and down at me in a way that definitely didn't do it for me. I laughed and shoved his shoulder in a playful push.

'Get out of here. You'll meet me here as soon as the show is over, yeah?'

'Of course,' he said, then gave me one last lingering kiss before leaving me there alone.

There were six rounds; swimwear, sleepwear, office wear, sportswear, and formal wear. The one I was most looking forward to was formal wear. A, because my dress was beautiful. It was the one piece of clothing that didn't look cheap. I think they'd been donated, so Odette hadn't been able to sabotage me. And B, it would mean that the show was over and I'd survived.

I changed into the swimwear and felt sad that I didn't have Clover by my side right now. We could have laughed about all of this together. Honestly, the message from Leo hadn't even been that exciting. All he'd done was ask how Red's birthday had been and if we were both okay.

I felt lonely, though. Especially without Ollie around. It was a feeling I'd got used to before coming here, but this year I'd stopped feeling alone altogether. I hated that I was back in that space mentally; my old frame of mind.

✱

NOBODY HAD EVER MENTIONED TO ME JUST HOW NERVE-wracking modelling clothes could be. Not that I knew anybody who would have been able to tell me, but still, every time I went out on stage I was close to bricking it. It took everything in me to not trip and fall flat in front of the crowd.

Everywhere I looked while on stage, all I saw were eyes staring back at me. There had to be at least five hundred people here, a mix of students and parents, all watching us closely.

I'd never felt so scrutinised. This must be how a bug under a microscope felt.

I'd made it through the first five parts of the show with no major mishaps. I'd stayed upright, worn all the clothes the way Odette had told me to, and I hadn't vomited or passed out, so I was counting the night as a win. I'd been the third in the lineup for every look, so at least I wasn't last. My final dress of the show was the most intricate, and it took me some time to get into it and style my hair. Odette had mentioned it was the most expensive one, but honestly, she could be bullshitting me for all I knew.

It was a beautiful, yellow satin two piece. The top was in the bardot style and was flattering for my cleavage as it had a sweetheart neckline, and because the sleeves were off the shoulders (my signature), I didn't look as wide as I normally did. The skirt was a flattering A-line skirt with pockets, reaching the floor, and I felt like a princess. It reminded me of a modern-day version of Belle's ball gown.

Somehow, I put my hair up in a low, loose chignon, and the look was perfect. I wished Ollie was here to see me now, but I knew he'd get a kick out of taking it off of me once the show was done.

One of the other students working the show popped their head into the classroom and said, 'Skylar, you're up.'

'Let's get this shit over with,' I said to myself as I followed the guy to the stage. Just one more turn of the catwalk and I was free.

The moment I walked up to the steps, the air felt different. I couldn't put my finger on what had changed in the brief time it took me to change, but something clearly had.

I looked up to find Odette coming down the steps from the

catwalk, and instantly I knew shit was off. The plan had been for Odette to finish the show; to be the last one down the catwalk.

'Don't trip, New Girl,' she whispered in my ear as she passed, her arm brushing up against mine.

Music pumped through the speakers, and I heard my cue. I had no time to change course before a hand on my lower back pushed me up the steps towards the stage.

I tried to keep my head facing forward; tried not to look at all the heads in the crowd, all the eyes glued to me.

I got to the end of the catwalk, and that was when shit changed.

The music cut out abruptly, leaving me standing there not knowing what to do next.

A voiceover played, Odette's nasally voice filling the auditorium.

Fuck. Maybe I should have listened to Clover.

I turned to the back of the stage, as a video started to play on the wall.

'Hello everyone,' the voice said, addressing the room. 'I hope you've been enjoying our Fashion Show this evening and plan to give money to our charity.'

I went to walk back towards the steps, but the voice stopped me.

'Stay right there, Skylar. I think you'll find this next part interesting.'

That didn't sound good.

'I'm here to tell you tonight about *our* favourite charity case—Ms Skylar Crescent. Skylar is a scholarship student here at Hawthorn Academy and has had quite the eventful year. I'm sure you all remember Parents' Day.' I saw some heads nodding in the distance, the bright lights stopping me from seeing too much. 'Let's have a look at some of her other high-lights, shall we?'

The video began to show a reel of everything that had happened to me this year. Me getting covered in blue rasp-berry slush in the corridor; me being tripped up and pushed around. Rotting food falling from my locker, how I'd looked after being found beaten in the toilets and in the woods.

They had recorded literally every single thing that had happened to me this year and were playing it for everybody to see. And all I could do was stand there and watch it unfold.

'As you can see, Skylar has had a hard time this year. Even her best friends have turned against her.'

The scene changed to footage clearly taken from inside mine and Clover's bedroom. What the fuck? How long had there been a camera in there? My mind instantly went to thinking about what else that camera could have seen, but then the screen once again stole my focus.

The footage playing was of Clover and Griff sitting next to one another on Clo's bed. The date stamped the video as the day she'd called me a whore. This must have been after Griff had followed her.

Their heads got closer, the two of them sat as close as they could be. Then, watching through a dream-like haze, I saw the moment the Griff and Clover on the screen kissed.

Betrayal trickled down my body, starting at my head and reaching my fingertips and toes. An ice queen forming, frozen to the spot.

At no point had either of them told me about this. They'd carried on like nothing much had happened in the time we weren't on talking terms.

I looked around, and I caught Leo's eye. He was standing by the screen, his expression blank, and I could tell that he was unimpressed. But was he unimpressed for me, or for the kiss?

'Forgive me. Let me formally introduce the poor, sad, pathetic case of a human still standing at the end of the stage. Everybody, this here is the daughter of Jacob Cooper who I believe those amongst this circle knew well.'

Instantaneously, the crowd gasped.

A secret had been outed, and I had no idea why this was such shocking news. I knew that Lottie and Leo had recognised the name, but Leo never had got round to talking to me about it. I'd forgotten to ask him after what had happened with Clover; it had completely slipped my mind.

The images still flickered on the screen, footage still rolling of every kiss Ollie and I had shared this year. All the times they'd picked on or harassed me.

The night I'd lost my virginity played next, and although grainy and difficult to decipher, I knew exactly what was being shown on the screen. How dare they? How fucking dare they take that away from me, too?

The only footage that wasn't shown was from the night I'd nearly drowned. I guessed if they had shown that then we'd know exactly who had tried to drown me, and I knew the girls didn't want that to become public knowledge. Or maybe they genuinely didn't know?

I shivered, the hairs on my arms standing on end. I needed to leave. I couldn't stand here any longer listening to this shit.

'Poor breeding.' Odette's voice filled the room again, and I knew that if I could, I would make her suffer. I'd been a doormat for too long. I had to stand up for myself.

I rushed to the back of the stage, to where the screen was

showing footage of my mum and Andy from Parents' Day. Of the two of them necking back drinks and acting like the pissheads, everybody had already guessed they were.

Shame filled me.

Everybody here knew everything now.

Even something that I didn't know.

Why did it even fucking matter who my dad was?

Catching Griff's sad and confused look as I climbed down from the stage, I wondered what he was thinking. I could tell that he wanted to say something to me, but really, what could he say that would make this all okay? I felt humiliated once again. Was everything a lie?

I should have seen this shit coming. Should have listened to Clover when she'd told me that the girls had something planned. But then I remembered how Clo had been lying to me for weeks, too.

I wanted to cry, but I didn't want them to see me crumble. I didn't want to give them the satisfaction of breaking in front of them all. They were all as bad as each other.

So I did the next best thing.

I ran.

Chapter Thirty-Two

I ran from the auditorium as fast as I could. I wanted to put as much space between me and those people as I could. I felt cheap—dirty; like the charity case they'd constantly told me I was. I kept tripping on the dress I was wearing, the length too long for a quick getaway. Fuck me, no wonder Cinderella lost her shitting glass slipper during her escape.

I could hear heavy footsteps behind me, getting closer. For every two steps I took, I swore they were only taking one, which meant they were going to reach me soon. I could not let that happen.

✦

I LEFT THE MAIN BUILDING AND RAN TO THE POOL HOUSE. I definitely would not have headed there if I wasn't in fight-or-flight mode. Not after some unknown person had attempted to drown me there after the Halloween party. That we still didn't know who had done it was a problem, but not one that I wanted to focus on right now. I needed to be alone.

After entering the pool building, I ran up the stairs and made my way to the connecting corridor that led to the Hospital Wing. I stopped. I heard voices coming from that direction; angry ones that were getting louder. I pivoted on the spot and made my way back down the stairs.

On entering the pool room itself, I came face to face with Ollie.

He was standing at the other end of the pool, staring at me silently. His face hard in anger in a way I'd only seen once or twice.

'H-h-hey. I'm sorry I ran away. I just c-couldn't stay there,' I stuttered my way through my sentence, feeling embarrassed that I was finding it hard to talk to him. Which was ridiculous? This was Ollie. The guy I'd lost my virginity to and had had all of those meaningful moments and conversations with. Although, when I looked up, it didn't feel as if the same Ollie stood in front of me at all. All I wanted was to run to him, fall into his arms, but I stopped myself.

'You deserved what they did.' His tone was ice cold. His words weren't making any sense to me. 'You've deserved all of it.'

'S-s-sorry?' I couldn't believe this was happening. Where was the Ollie who I'd woken up next to this very morning? The one that had made Easter break plans with me and kissed me like he would never get enough of me?

'Sky, did you really believe any of this year was real?' he scoffed. 'Every single thing that *The Set* has done to you has been on my command. I asked them to do whatever they could to turn the entire student body against you.'

'But I d-don't u-understand ...' I trailed off. None of this added up. I was so sure that Clover must have misheard everything, that she had just heard the girls' conversation out of context.

I felt so stupid. I had fallen out with my best friend over Ollie and now it turned out that I should have believed her all along. I'd acted like every idiotic heroine I hated.

'That's because you're too stupid to understand anything, Skylar. The fact that you couldn't see the truth right in front of your eyes tells me as much.' Ollie seemed to enjoy this. I could tell by the smirk on his face. 'The amount of times we've all been laughing at you behind your back and you never even knew.'

Don't cry. I repeated this mantra in my head, knowing that if he saw my tears that something would snap between us. Something I wasn't sure we could ever come back from. Maybe I was stupid like he said because none of this made sense. Had I really just been that blind to the truth?

Clover had tried to warn me. Even Griff had made some cryptic comments recently that I hadn't looked into enough. Things had been going so well with Ollie that I hadn't wanted to rock the boat. Make a nuisance of myself. The only one who had said fuck all was Leo.

I knew that things had taken a turn for the worse when I looked into Ollie's eyes and could see the true depth of His hate.

His eyes, normally a startling bright blue, were now a dark indigo filled with anger and loathing. I could see the exact moment that the mist descended.

I shivered.

I wasn't sure what else to do, and I didn't know where I could run to; a place where He wouldn't find me.

Trapped. The worst part was the fact that I'd been blind to my situation and had walked willingly to my fate. I was the reason I was here; there was nobody else to blame. For this I hated myself, maybe even more than I hated Him in that moment.

I couldn't help but ask, 'W-why are you doing this?'

I had to know. I was certain something must have happened in the last few hours to have caused this change. No part of me could accept that this had been coming for longer ... the alternative was just too much to think about.

'You don't belong here, Sky.' He smirked at me. 'You never did.'

I crumbled. I could feel the tears pricking my eyes, and I was trying my hardest to stop them from falling. The second I let a tear fall, I knew that this would all become real. That He really was looking at me like I was worthless. A look I hadn't seen on His face in the last six months.

I should have known better. I should never have fallen for the Beast, and I most definitely should never have thought of myself as the Beauty.

✦

I FLEW OUT OF THE ROOM. I COULDN'T STAND TO SEE THAT look in Ollie's eyes a moment longer. The one that made me feel an inch tall. That made me feel like the charity scholarship case. Since September he'd been adamant that he didn't see me that way. More fool me.

I ran around the corner and made my way quickly up the staircase, heading towards the corridor to the Hospital Wing. Fuck the voices I'd heard. I made my way along the corridor and turned a corner to head further into the building. It was then that I saw a shadowy, tall figure standing ahead of me in the dark hallway. None of the lights were on in this part of the school. Everybody was over in the auditorium dealing with the fall out from the fashion show. After all, today had been the last day of term and nobody was expected to be needing this building for another two weeks. I paused. I needed a moment to try to quiet my breathing—to make myself invisible.

That was when I saw it.

The body laying on the floor at the feet of the figure. I couldn't make out who it was from here, but it definitely looked like a girl; the dress similar to the one that Odette had worn as she'd brushed passed me.

I tiptoed closer.

The figure still hadn't seen me, too focused on the limp body at their feet. A body that wasn't moving, or making any sound. They were still. My mind tried not to connect what a still body meant.

The closer I got, the I just knew that it *was* Odette. The dress she had been so smug about earlier torn and covered in dirt. Her face trapped in a scared expression, her mouth slightly open and her eyes wide—stuck forevermore. Blood covered her stomach, a knife handle visible in the centre. Bile rose up my throat as I tried to get my breathing under control.

I tried to take a step back. I somehow caught my footing on the bottom of my skirt, and I gasped at the twist of my ankle. I tried to keep my balance so I wouldn't find myself sprawled at the stranger's feet.

It was the gasp that did it. The figure turned.

I glimpsed their face, their hair, their eyes—I couldn't breathe.

None of this made sense.

It was as if my mind couldn't compute what my eyes were seeing. My vision blurred around the edges and I fought the black out I knew was coming; the black spots in my vision already forming. My breathing shallowed, my heart beating so slow, yet so loud, I thought that they could hear it as loud as I could.

The figure approached. I tried to turn, but my legs had turned to jelly. I couldn't move, no matter how much I wanted to. The moonlight coming through the windows caught the glint of a knife. A knife that was heading very close to me. A knife getting closer with each step of the figure.

Then pain.

Nothing but pain.

Then nothing at all.

Epilogue

I smiled as I watched her walk away. Well, more like she
ran away.

Everything had gone perfectly. My plan couldn't
have gone better. I'd achieved what I had set out to do.

To ruin her.

To make her feel worthless.

I knew I'd touched a nerve, and I felt pure happiness shoot
through me at the thought of her leaving this place and crumbling. I'd wanted to wait until the end of the school year, but
things had snowballed of late. The situation started to run
away from me and I knew I had to act.

Who knew girls could be such bitches when given free
rein?

I didn't feel any guilt, but I knew when to say when. If I'd
let it continue, she would have ended up dead. And I didn't
want that—not yet, anyway.

I hoped she would never return to Hawthorn Academy.

She didn't deserve to be here. With Easter coming up, we had time away from this cursed place and I was hoping she'd make the right decision. The *only* decision. To leave.

If she showed her face around here again, I would make her regret it. It would make this first half of the year feel like a holiday.

After all, things could always get worse.

Coming May 2021

Disease
Hawthorn Academy Series: Book Two

The Hawthorn tree.
You can eat the berries. Taste the juice.
But the seeds are the deadliest part.
And I was going to become the seed.
I was going to be the cyanide that destroyed Ollie and
everything he valued.
The Set—what was left of them anyway—and Leo were going
to pay for what they did to me. For the shit they put me
through.
They *drowned* me.
Drugged me.
Humiliated me.
But I was not going to let them take my dignity.

ACKNOWLEDGMENTS

Writing and publishing a book has been one of the most time consuming and stressful things I have ever done. Without these people, I honestly would have fallen off the ledge so thank you!

To my editor, Kieran. This book would not have been possible without you. The story really developed under your eye, and I'm so grateful for your time and effort.

To my Alpha, Jess, who is brutally honest at all times, even when I may not be in the mood for it. You're the best, and probably super emotional reading this... if you notice its changed.

To Fiona, thank you for being the best book bestie there is. I'm so glad we talk everyday and honestly, your love for this story definitely kept me going!

To Taylor, thank you for being there, I love you.

To my Betas, thank you for helping me tweak Skylar's story to what is here now. I am in debt to you.

To the Fourway, I love you. I'm so happy that the four of us are walking this journey together, y'all rock! (hehe)

To Billie, without you, I'd have lost my sanity. Your inspirational, and forceful, voice notes always help me keep my head screwed on straight.

To Elss, thank you so much for your enthusiasm and love. I really hope this lived up to your expectations! Continue to change your own story, as I know you'll ace it.

To Court, my little chuckle bean. Thank you for always hyping me up even when I've been the biggest Debbie Downer.

To my ARC readers, thank you for taking the chance on a new author and for helping to hype me up on socials! I truly appreciate it, and can't wait to find out what you think of Disease.

To my fiancée, Megan, cheers for putting up with me when all I did was complain when I was filled with self doubt (that is still very much here).

To Fluff, for believing but never seeing.

To my Mum, who didn't get the dedication and made her displeasure clear. Thank you.

And to the rest of my family, ta.

Last but not least;

To you, the reader, thank you for taking a chance on a new author and I hope you will stick around and read Disease, because let me tell you, Skylar's story is far from over.

ABOUT THE AUTHOR

Katie Lowrie is a twenty seven year old Brit who loves to read and write; basic, right?

A list in no particular order of her greatest loves:
- Henry VIII and the Tudor era
- Her baby cat, Cress
- Musicals
- Disney
- Cheese
- And sometimes her fiancée, Megan

Disorder is Katie's first book—but definitely not her last.

She loves to stalk people online (in a good way) and understands if you do too.

instagram.com/katielowrieauthor

goodreads.com/katielowrieauthor

facebook.com/katielowrieauthor

bookbub.com/authors/katie-lowrie

HAWTHORN ACADEMY SERIES

Disorder -

February 2021

Disease -

May 2021

Book Three -

August 2021

Book Four -

November 2021

Want more Disorder?

Head to:

www.katielowrieauthor.com

Printed in Great Britain
by Amazon

57671441R00248